I0669403

Essence
A Nico Scarlatti Novel

By
Christopher Merlino

©2017 by Christopher Merlino

ISBN: 978-1-947292-01-7

All rights reserved. No part of this publication may be reproduced, transmitted, or distributed in any form or by any means without written permission from the publisher.

Any Scripture references or quotations taken from the New American Standard Bible.

This book is a work of fiction. Names, characters, places, and incidents are either products of the author's imagination or used fictitiously. Any similarity to actual people, organizations, and/or events is purely coincidental.

Cover Image by Christopher Merlino

Published by Christopher Merlino

Edited by Sydnee Thompson

www.christophermerlino.net

This book is available in both print and eBook formats.
Printed   in   the   United   States   of   America

For Duane

Acknowledgements

For my first effort in the supernatural/fantasy genre, I was mostly on my own, as none of my usual crew are into this kind of story. However, as we worked through the manuscript, I noticed the characters begin to grow on all of us. As the story took shape, it was interesting, and, I must say, amusing, to see the sudden interest in a supernatural story. So, I would first like to thank my team, as a whole, for sticking with it even though the genre was different and the storyline a bit darker than my usual work.

To my wife, Charm, probably the only one who was excited for a supernatural project, you inspire me to push through, even when writing becomes burdensome. This story quickly became your favorite of my novels, and that alone makes me want to continue the saga. Thank you for your never-ending support and longsuffering with my late nights and long days at the computer. You are a treasure and I love that we get to share this together.

To my best friend, Duane, you continue to encourage me, and push me to be better with every story I write. Of all people, I was stunned at your reaction to this story, and love to hear how fascinated you are with the characters and the world in which they exist. Your enthusiasm makes it easy to stay engaged with every story I begin.

For this story, I enlisted the help of an outside editor. It was the first time I had ever worked with an editor who did more than check for grammar and spelling mistakes. Sydnee Thompson, thank you for your efforts and your input. Your contributions were a godsend and I look forward to working with you on future projects.

Finally, I would like to thank those of you who took the time, and spent your money, to read this work. I hope you enjoyed reading it as much as I enjoyed writing it.

Prologue

"This is crap."

Nicholas Scarlatti punched the steering wheel as he drove his midnight-blue Honda Civic through a raging downpour. It was not the best vehicle for lousy weather. His wipers couldn't keep up with the pounding rain, and things would get a whole lot worse over the next twenty-four hours as Hurricane Jessica approached the mainland. He was not excited about battening down an entire stone-yard by himself. Nonetheless, it was his job to get it done.

"Yeah!" Nicholas shouted to no one. "Let's just work all day Saturday and not button things up before we go! It's not like a hurricane is coming or anything! Check the weather once in a while, jaggass!"

He pounded the steering wheel again to emphasize his point. When he turned onto Industrial Drive, his anger boiled even further. Patches of asphalt peeked through here and there, but the road was more than three quarters covered in water, which meant the yard would be a lake.

"Friggin wonderful," he grumbled. He navigated the flooded street at a snail's pace. The last thing he needed was to stall in the middle of a hurricane.

Nicholas pulled into the flooded yard and hit the remote for the oversized garage door, opening the twenty-foot high door

1

just enough so he could drive his little Civic into the shop. Fortunately, the shop was built on the highest point on the property, and the grade sloped away from the building on all sides, so the shop was dry inside...for now. At the rate the water poured from the heavens, the shop would flood in an hour or two. Not that it mattered. The floor of a stone fabrication shop was almost always covered in water.

With a deep sigh, Nicholas dragged himself from behind the wheel and strode to his locker. He pulled on his waterproof boots—standard issue in a stone shop—and threw on some rain gear. He grabbed the ropes and headed for the open garage door. When he stepped outside, the winds grabbed him in an instant. He leaned into the wind and trudged through ankle-deep water, muttering the whole way about his slacker coworkers and boss. He was grateful, for the hard-packed gravel though. At least he wouldn't have to struggle through thick mud.

With a hurricane due to make landfall within the next twenty-four hours, Nicholas had to admit it was necessary to rope the slabs of stone sooner rather than later. The yard consisted of one-hundred a-frames; each held as many as ten slabs of granite per side. The total retail value of the Scarlatti Stoneworks inventory was a little over three hundred-thousand dollars, and high winds were the enemy. As heavy as a slab of three-centimeter granite was, a gust of wind could easily topple one over. It had happened before with far lighter winds than the hurricane-force gusts Nicholas had to deal with now.

He began at the back of the yard and worked his way to the front, making trips back inside, as needed, to retrieve more rope. Each rope was pre-cut to the correct length and knotted. All he had to do was toss the rope around the tops of the slabs, and tighten it about a foot or two from the top where the slabs almost met. It was a simple job, when a hurricane wasn't bearing down. Of course, when the owner was a big goof, easily distracted by pretty girls, it wasn't surprising when these things didn't get done. It was particularly annoying when the owner happened to be his older brother.

"What a jerk-off," Nicholas muttered, tightening up the last rope.

The water was midway up his shins as he sloshed through the yard. After five steps, Nicholas stopped in his tracks and blinked in disbelief. Through the pouring rain, he saw the figure of a man sprawled face down on the ground in front of the shop entrance.

"What the hell?" he said. He blinked through the downpour, which decided, at that moment, to triple in intensity. Rain came down in torrents.

Nicholas grunted against the swirling wind. He couldn't see ten feet in front of him. The increased intensity of the rain, coupled with a sudden increase in wind velocity forced Nicholas to lower his head as he plowed through the rising floodwater. He could swear he felt a current try to grip his ankles. Nicholas approached the place where he saw the man on the ground. He stopped and stared when he found no trace of a person. Wind and rain swirled all around him as he stared in confusion. Out of the corner of his eye, he caught movement inside the shop.

"Hey!"

He hustled to the entrance. Once inside, he scanned from side to side as he moved through the shop. He saw no one, but a trail of water indicated he wasn't out of his mind. Nicholas took a deep breath. The musty scent of granite dust filled his nostrils as his heart thudded in his chest. Part of him wanted to jump in his car and get out of there, but what if the intruder was hurt?

"I know you're in here!" Nicholas shouted. "If you're hurt, I'll help you! If you're looking to steal something, good luck. There's no money and nothing valuable you can carry!"

He heard a grunt from around the corner. It was more of a moan, and as Nicholas followed the sound, and the water trail around the corner, he heard labored breathing combined with more grunts of pain. He peered around a large, beige compressor tank. A man slouched in the corner with his shoulder against the wall. He had the whitest hair Nicholas had ever seen. It was pulled into a disheveled ponytail and fell to the middle of the man's back. Even his eyebrows, well-trimmed mustache, and goatee were white as snow. What struck Nicholas even more was the man's attire. He wore a cream-colored tunic with medieval style trousers of the same color. Both were splattered in what had to be blood A tattered brown cloak draped over his shoulders.

Nicholas felt as though he had walked onto the set of a *Star Wars* movie and found a Jedi Master. For a brief second, he let his eyes roam over the hunched figure. He swore, if he saw anything resembling a lightsaber, he was outta there. It would have been funny, except for the condition of the man. His face was contorted in pain. He was pale as a ghost, clutching his side. Blood seeped through his fingers and pooled on the concrete floor beneath him.

Nicholas gasped. "Holy crap! Are you okay?"

One look into the man's black eyes was all the answer he needed. "Right." He shook his head. "Stupid question." His mind raced and his heart tripled its already elevated pace. "Hang tight. I have a first aid kit in the other room."

He ran to retrieve the medical box. When he returned, he dropped to his knees in front of the man, who looked like he was about to pass out. Nicholas pulled out a package of gauze pads and some tape. He opened a bottle of hydrogen peroxide.

"All right," he said. "With that much blood, I think you need stitches. Let's get you bandaged up as best we can and I'll drive you to the hospital."

The man grabbed Nicholas' arm and peered into his eyes. Nicholas didn't have much experience staring into other people's eyes, but he was instantly transfixed. It was like staring into space. The depth of the piercing black was hypnotic, and what seemed like millions of tiny flecks of silver stood out like stars and galaxies, stretching into eternity.

The man shook his head and coughed. Groaning in pain, he mustered the strength to say, "No hospital…no doctor."

Nicholas looked down at the man's other hand, still clutching his wounded side. Even with the pressure and the blood-soaked tunic over the wound, blood seeped between his fingers. Nicholas shook his head and raised his eyebrows in a skeptical grimmace.

"Dude, I don't think you can just let that go. That's bleeding...a *lot*."

The man ignored his words, drawing a deep breath. His face transformed from pain-stricken despair to authoritative calm. "Listen to me. I am going to ask you a question. And your answer will determine the course of the rest of your life."

"What question?" Nicholas asked. "How about you ask me on the way to the hospital?"

"Shhh!" The man waved a dismissive hand. "We have no time. The thing that did this to me...he will be here soon. I am using every last chakra I have to keep myself alive long enough to pass my legacy on."

"Legacy? Chakra?" Nicholas scrunched his face. "What are you talking about...and who did this to you? He's coming here? How do you know?"

The man's breathing shallowed and he took a moment to regain control.

"I know because he can sense my use of chakra. He is tracking me. We have minutes, if we are lucky, and you waste time asking stupid questions, boy!"

Nicholas shook his head in bewilderment. "Are you a hindu or something? Why do you keep talking about chakras?"

The man sighed. "Forget that. What would you say if I offered you power beyond anything you have ever imagined?"

Nicholas wanted to laugh in his face. If the man wasn't deadly serious and quite possibly uttering his last words, he probably would have, but the man's face betrayed zero humor. Nicholas ran a hand through his damp, brown hair and realized, vaguely, he was in desperate need of a haircut. He shook the thought off.

"I-I don't know what you're talking about, sir."

"My name is Mattaeus," the man said. He grimaced as he shifted his weight. "Unfortunately, I do not have time to explain properly. All I have is what is inside me. Either I pass it on to you, or it dies with me."

"And this..." Nicholas shrugged, "...*whatever* it is that's inside you, will make me powerful?"

The man nodded. "My powers will certainly make you powerful, but the one who is coming for me…if we can get what is inside *him* into you, and what is inside *me* into you, I suspect you will be so powerful even the gods would fear you."

"The *gods*?" Nicholas replied. His eyebrow shot up and he grinned despite the gravity of the situation. "You mean like Zeus?"

Mattaeus shrugged. "Among others."

"This is crazy," Nicholas muttered. The guy was either certifiable or…did blood-loss cause delusions? "Let's just get you to the hospital."

Nicholas moved to help him up, but Mattaeus slapped his hands away.

"It sounds crazy; I know that." The urgency in his voice pulled at Nicholas' gut. "But that is because you only know the world you *see*. You have no idea…"

Mattaeus tilted his head and scrunched his forehead. His eyes grew more alert. He looked at Nicholas with renewed urgency. "You must decide. If you want what I offer, we need to prepare. If not, you need to leave right now and forget you ever met me."

Nicholas scowled. "What the—"

"Now!" Mattaeus commanded. "Decide *right now!*" His eyes softened, and his voice dropped to a whisper. "Or leave."

Something in his tone caused Nicholas to believe. He had no idea why he suddenly trusted a bloody mess of a man who sputtered lunacy, but he did. Something about Mattaeus drew him in. Nicholas' gut refused to let him abandon the dying man. He surrendered.

"What do I do?"

Mattaeus nodded. "Understand, my son, this will be dangerous, but the reward is well worth the risk."

"Okaaay?"

Doubt clouded Nicholas' mind. He wasn't the risk-taking sort. He wasn't much of a ladies' man, and he was awkward socially. His brother, Dominick, was the fun one. Nicholas spent most of his free time on his computer, building websites and writing programs. Sure, he was almost unbeatable in World of

Warcraft, but he wasn't sure those skills would translate well into real life.

"Help me to my feet." Mattaeus said, holding his right arm up. His left hand continued to press the wound on his right side.

Nicholas pulled Mattaeus to his feet and held him steady as the man regained his footing. Nicholas worried the guy would topple to the ground at any moment. Mattaeus shifted and slid his free hand into his cloak.

"First," Mattaeus said. "You must take this."

As Nicholas stood in stunned amazement, Mattaeus pulled a gleaming sword from within the folds of his robe. He held it up for Nicholas to see. It was breathtaking, but for its simplicity. It was not ornate and contained no gems. The slender, curved blade was about three feet long and seemed to glow. There wasn't a smudge or scratch on it. It was so sharp, Nicholas couldn't make out the edge.

Mattaeus bowed his head and spoke some words in a language Nicholas didn't recognize and held it out in both hands. Speechless, Nicholas accepted the incredible weapon. It was far lighter than he expected. He moved it from side to side in gentle arcs. It was almost weightless, but the moment he accepted the weapon, he felt a tremendous sense of power surge through his body.

"You will get used to the feel of it," Mattaeus assured him.

"It's so light," Nicholas mused. "What's it made from?"

"Illidium," Mattaeus replied. When Nicholas frowned, he held up a hand. "It does not exist in this world."

Before Nicholas could respond, he continued. "We don't have much time. You need to do exactly as I say…"

ᚦ A ⅋ ψ ς

Nicholas crouched behind an a-frame of marble slabs. They stored marble indoors because it was susceptible to discoloration from the sun. All the lights were off, and Mattaeus leaned against the wall ten feet away, barely able to stand. Nicholas couldn't believe what he was about to do, but Mattaeus had been adamant. Whatever was coming for Mattaeus was close and Nicholas had no time to think. They had a plan and Nicholas needed to execute his part. World of Warcraft had nothing on this moment. Nicholas squeezed the grip of his new blade and took several deep breaths.

The atmosphere in the shop darkened. A shiver crept up his spine and Nicholas felt every hair on his body stand on end. Someone else was in the room. Nicholas peered around the marble slabs. A figure stood with his back to him. It was as if it materialized out of thin air. Nicholas clamped his mouth shut to stifle a gasp. The figure moved to stand before Mattaeus. Nicholas was finally able to make out the silhouette of a person. Other than his face and hands, the figure might as well have been a shadow.

The black-clad figure moved again and Nicholas saw dark hair pulled back in a tight, thick braid reaching past the man's waist. He turned his head enough for Nicholas to get a look at his eyes. There was no mistaking the fact that those two glittering, black eyes were the scariest things Nicholas had ever witnessed. It was like seeing into a hate-drenched soul. He was glad the guy hadn't caught sight of him, hiding in the shadows. His body shook with such violence, Nicholas had to squeeze his eyes shut and lean hard against the marble to calm himself.

"Well, well, well." The dark figure's laugh chilled Nicholas' blood even more than his jet-black eyes. "The mage falters. Mattaeus, you ran off like a coward, Mattaeus."

"It would appear," Mattaeus replied, "that my time has come."

"That it has, old man. You know, I am almost sorry to see you meet your demise." He closed the distance and leaned over to stare into Mattaeus' eyes. "Even though you sought to rob me of the pleasure of watching your eyes close forever, I enjoyed our rivalry. You were indeed a worthy adversary."

"As were you, Sansata," Mattaeus croaked. "As were you."

"So…" Sansata said. "Shall we finish our final battle?"

Mattaeus straightened up and Sansata leapt back, stretching a hand out to the side. A sword appeared, just as otherworldly as the one Nicholas held, but different in appearance. It was jet black, like a shadow. It just looked evil, and Nicholas felt his bones turn to jelly.

Sansata assumed a fighting position. "Draw your weapon, *mage*, and prepare to die."

"Alas." Mattaeus shrugged, grimacing in pain, his hand still clutching his side. "I cannot."

Sansata relaxed his posture and stood up straight. "You refuse to fight?"

"You have already won," Mattaeus said, lifting his hand to reveal his bloody wound.

Sansata's sword disappeared. He flipped Mattaeus' cloak open and stared at the dying man. Mattaeus met his gaze. In the darkness, Nicholas saw them only as silhouettes. They were two shadows facing off. The one called Sansata folded his arms across his chest.

"Where is it?"

Mattaeus shrugged.

Sansata let out a menacing growl. "I will make your final moments far more excruciating than they ought to be."

He spread his hands slightly and Nicholas couldn't believe his eyes as he watched violet crackles of electricity appear in his palms. It was like the man held tiny bolts of lightning between his fingers. *What the hell was that!* It was all Nicholas could do not to gasp in disbelief. He felt his head swim and beads of sweat broke out on his forehead. He shouldn't be seeing this.

"The sword," Sansata demanded again.

"It is gone," Mattaeus whispered.

That was Nicholas' cue. He steadied his breath. His body tensed for action, an action he wasn't entirely convinced he had it in him to take.

"Gone?" Sansata demanded. "Gone where? Is that why you ran? To hide the sword?"

Mattaeus sighed and met Sansata's gaze with a grim smile. "I could never allow you to possess such a powerful weapon."

Nicholas felt the rage ooze out of Sansata. It was pure evil and Nicholas hesitated. Did he really want to mess with a guy like Sansata? Was he even a guy? Was he even human?

"You will tell me where it is."

Sansata spoke in a measured, ominous tone. Mattaeus was unaffected, but Nicholas froze in place, convinced Sansata wasn't bluffing. Mattaeus stared at Sansata without a word, without a hint of fear, without any expression at all.

"Very well," Sansata nodded in resignation, his palms glowing as blue and purple bolts danced over the tips of his fingers.

It was now or never. Nicholas crept into position, grasping the sword in both hands. When Sansata raised his hands to direct the purple energy at Mattaeus, Nicholas gritted his teeth and lunged. He squeezed his eyes shut as the point of the blade slid into Sansata's back, punching between his ribs with no resistance. Sansata stood rigid as Nicholas buried the blade up to the hilt. The crackling energy disappeared from his fingers. Sansata's breath came in gasps and his body shook as he looked down at his belly. Nicholas wondered what he was thinking. What would go through a person's mind? Sansata's body went limp and began to tremble in Nicholas' arms. Nicholas lowered him to the floor.

"Do *not* remove the blade!" Mattaeus' voice broke through Nicholas' thoughts. "It is the only thing keeping him alive."

"*Alive?*" Nicholas shrieked. He stared at Mattaeus with bulging eyes. "For god's sake, why?"

"Just for a moment." Mattaeus sank to the floor and gasped in pain. He took several long breaths before returning his gaze to meet Nicholas.' "Listen to me. You must act fast, and do exactly as I say. Set him on his side. You're going to pull the blade out and, very quickly, set your face right in front of his and as close as you can get, staring into his eyes."

"What?" Nicholas exclaimed. "What in hell for?"

"Just do it!" Mattaeus shouted. "Quickly!"

Nicholas shook his head but followed instructions. He laid Sansata on his side. Sansata quivered, but didn't resist. Nicholas positioned himself in front and reached around to the handle of the blade. He took a deep breath and pulled the blade hard. It slid out with ease and Sansata's body convulsed, making it difficult for Nicholas to hold him steady.

"Argghh!"

"Quickly, Nicholas!" Mattaeus urged. "Stare into his eyes! Get as close as you can!"

Nicholas stared straight down into the furious eyes below him. He saw pure blackness as the life left Sansata. Without warning, he felt his own body begin to quiver. He vaguely heard Mattaeus muttering something in the background. The breath left him and Nicholas felt a painful chill for several seconds before he collapsed on his back. His breathing was rapid and shallow. The room spun worse than any hangover he'd ever experienced.

"Now," Mattaeus said. "Bring the sword over here. Quickly, Nicholas! There is no time."

Responding to Mattaeus by instinct, completely on autopilot, Nicholas dragged himself and the sword over to the dying man.

"Do not be afraid, young Nicholas." Mattaeus nodded with a reassuring smile. "I envy you. You are about to become something this world has never seen before."

For Nicholas, it was out-of-body. He could see and hear everything, but didn't feel like a participant. In any case, he was unprepared for Mataeus' next words.

"Now…plunge the blade into my heart."

Reality whooshed back and Nicholas snapped his head up. "What?"

"You *must* do this."

"You're crazy," Nicholas said, pulling his arm away. "This is all crazy!"

Mattaeus closed his eyes. "Listen carefully, boy. What you took in is pure evil. With nothing to balance that force, it will consume you. I am dead already, my son. Allow me to provide for your survival."

Tears filled Nicholas' eyes. He'd known the man for less than an hour but felt like he was losing a family member. He didn't have it in him to kill a friend, even if the friend wanted him to do it. On the other hand, an hour ago he never would have believed he had it in him to kill *anyone*, so who knew what he was truly capable of?

Mattaeus lifted the blade and held it to his chest. "You must do this; do it before the life leaves me. Plunge it in, then pull it out. Stare into my eyes just like before. You must do it *now*."

Nicholas shook his head as the tears poured forth.

"Don't forget to take his dark sword," Mattaeus said weakly. "It is bound to you now. Take *both* swords and keep them safe." He nodded urgently. "Now do it!"

Nicholas leaned over to drag Sansata's sword to his side. He looked at Mattaeus and shook his head. "I can't. I just can't do it. I can't kill you."

"You can and you will," Mattaeus insisted. "DO IIIIITTTTTT!"

The power and authority in his voice broke through the shell Nicholas' mind had erected. Without a second thought, he plunged the gleaming illidium into Mattaeus' chest, burying it up to the hilt. He pulled it out and stared into the eyes of the dying man as Mattaeus gripped his shoulders and gasped. The old man muttered the same incoherent words as earlier before he breathed his final breath. Nicholas fell back on the cool concrete floor. Like before, he felt the convulsions, the lost breath, the cold, and then everything went black.

Chapter 1

His senses screamed.

Nicholas squinted as morning light streamed through the windows. His head pounded with every heartbeat, and lightning pulsed across every nerve. His skin tingled as if he were sunburned from head to toe. A high-pitched ringing flooded his ears. Even his nose felt irritated and dry. Every inhalation was like snorting fire. On top of all that, he felt like he was going to puke...and soon.

With an anguished groan, he managed to turn his head. The digital alarm clock on his nightstand was dark. *Figures.* He closed his eyes for a moment before summoning the strength to reach for his cell phone. He looked at the screen as he pushed the Home button. Nothing happened. He pushed it again. Nothing. The battery was dead. *Awesome.* Finally, he picked up a remote and tapped the power button as he pointed it at his TV. Once again, nothing happened. He groaned as he let his head fall back to the pillow.

"Power's out...great."

He remembered the hurricane. The world was flooded, last he remembered. He listened for the sound of a storm but heard nothing. He frowned as his dulled brain made the connection between bright, morning sunshine and no pounding rain.

"I slept through a hurricane?"

The events of the previous day filled his mind and his entire body began to shake. Visions of cold, black eyes brought with them a sense of dread. In his mind's eye, Nicholas watched the life drain from Sansata's body. He recalled, in vivid detail, the light of life leaving Mattaeus' eyes just moments later. That was all he remembered, other than the cold.

After several panicked moments, Nicholas chuckled, sort of. All the symptoms, the headache, the nausea, the fever...everything added up.

Shaking his head, he muttered, "Hangover. Really?"

He tried to sit up without vomiting all over his bed. Nicholas couldn't recall drinking the night before. He hadn't had anything before going to the shop to rope off the slabs. He couldn't remember anything afterwards. He must have gotten pretty blitzed. But what about Mattaeus? What about Sansata? Did he really just pass out and dream it all? He'd never been *that* wasted.

It was almost a relief to realize he hadn't, in fact, killed two men, that he hadn't, in fact, witnessed things that should be...and *are*...impossible. On the other hand, he was mildly disappointed he would not be getting all the amazing powers Mattaeus had promised him. Seemed like a rip-off.

"Just a friggin dream."

He placed his feet on the floor, took a breath to steady himself, and pushed off the bed.

"It wasn't a dream, Nicholas."

Nicholas froze at the voice, and then every muscle in his body seemed to react at once. He tripped, flailing backward onto the bed. He scrambled to his knees with his arms outstretched in defense. His head swiveled in frantic arcs until his eyes settled on a dark-haired man perched on his rickety dresser, across from the bed. Nicholas wondered how that piece of junk was holding the weight of a full-grown man, but he had more pressing issues. There was a stranger in his bedroom. How drunk had he gotten? The man's dark, blue eyes followed Nicholas with detached curiosity. For an uninvited guest, he seemed oddly relaxed.

"Who the..." Nicholas sputtered. "Who the hell are y...?"

"My name," the man said, "is Zha'riel."

"Zha...what? Why are you in my room?"

The man frowned. "Because that is where *you* are."

Nicholas shook his head. "W-what do you want?"

"You are changing." Zha'riel's face remained expressionless. "Can you not feel it?"

Nicholas pinched the bridge of his nose. Bile rose in his throat. He didn't have time to talk. This was about to happen. He swallowed hard and took a deep breath through his nose.

"I don't know what you're talking about, but you need to leave. I have a wicked hangover and I'm going to puke soon. I don't have time for this."

Zha'riel stared back at Nicholas with the same detached curiosity. "You did not have anything to drink, Nicholas."

Nicholas' head snapped up. He'd had it drooping between his knees, trying to quell the nausea. Now he was suddenly more alert.

"How do you know my name?"

Zha'riel shrugged and picked up a magazine from the dresser beside him. He held it up, pointed to Nicholas' name on the address sticker, and waved it back and forth with raised eyebrows. It was the most animated his face had been so far. Nicholas shook his head and tried to calm his stomach.

"Wait a minute," Nicholas replied, his mind finally catching up. "Are you telling me all that stuff was *real*?"

"Precisely."

"Oh, my God," Nicholas groaned. That meant... "So, I really did it then?" His eyes pleaded with Zha'riel. "I killed two people?"

Zha'riel pursed his lips in consideration. He finally nodded. "In a manner of speaking...yes."

Nicholas groaned. He wrapped his arms around himself as a chill washed over him. It all felt wrong. Looking down at where his hands gripped their opposite arms, his eyes widened in disbelief.

"What the...?"

He scrambled off the bed, tearing his sweat-soaked t-shirt off. He stood in front of the door and looked at himself in the long mirror. His eyes widened in disbelief.

"What in the world?"

He ran his hands through his hair, peered at his own eyes, felt his chest, stomach, shoulders, and arms. He was staring at a familiar stranger. The guy in the mirror could have stepped right off the set of a Hollywood movie. He turned to Zha'riel but had no clue what he should say. Zha'riel's face remained impassive.

"Are you displeased?"

Nicholas looked back at his reflection. How could he complain? His fair skin and lanky build had given way to a tanned, muscular physique. Usually awkward socially, especially around females, he suddenly felt like he could just stroll along the beach, take his shirt off, and let the ladies flock to him. Puffing out his chest a little and flexing his biceps and triceps, he grinned, despite his nausea.

"I look like a pro athlete...or a soldier, or someone you'd see in a movie."

He ran his fingers through his hair again. Normally a boring brown, it was shades darker, almost black, and his eyes, formerly a dark hazel, had morphed into a lush shade of violet. Was that even possible? He couldn't pretend he was unhappy, but he still felt deathly ill. His symptoms, which had disappeared momentarily in his adrenaline rush a moment before, returned with a vengeance. He was unsteady.

"You are changing, Nicholas," Zha'riel said again. "You must rest."

"You said that before," Nicholas said, feeling claustrophobic. "I'm going outside. I need some air."

"You cannot go outside," Zha'riel said. "It is not safe in your condition."

Nicholas chuckled. "Is that right?"

As he stepped toward the door, Zha'riel, his face still expressionless, lifted his left hand. Nicholas felt weightlessness take over. The next thing he knew, he slammed face down on the bed.

"Ooomph!" He rolled onto his back and sat up, looking at Zha'riel in stunned disbelief. "What the…! What did you just do to me?"

Zha'riel closed his eyes. He might have been frustrated, but Nicholas couldn't tell. Maybe he was tired. When he opened them again, he stared hard at Nicholas.

"Shall we dispense with the foolishness, Nicholas? You wandered into a dangerous world, one for which you are woefully unprepared. You have within you essences which took their masters decades, even centuries to learn. Those powers are not sitting still, waiting for you to access them. They are dynamic…organic…they live and breathe. If you do not take control of them, they will consume you, and tear apart your fragile mind."

Nicholas stared in rapt attention. The authority in Zha'riel's voice surpassed even Mattaeus' from the night before. Nicholas' mind focused on one truth—there was something in the room with him that he could not explain. The night before, he'd operated on pure adrenaline, drawing from Mattaeus' energy, following the orders of a man who knew how to command others. Now, Nicholas was all alone, able to think things through, and let them sink in.

"Oh, my friggin god," Nicholas breathed as his mind digested the facts.

Zha'riel frowned. "I would think you would want God on your side right now."

ƀ A ž ψ ς

Abdiel was in no hurry; that much was certain. It was a classic case where the messenger was not long for the world. None of it was his fault, but he was certain to reap the punishment when he delivered the news. He would be lucky if he was simply banished to Purgatory. As horrific as that thought was, it had to be better than the alternative.

Why did he have to go off on his own?

They had won. When Abdiel had last glanced in his direction, Sansata delivered what looked to be a fatal strike against the old mage. He'd watched as Mattaeus sank to his knees, but the old man fought for life. He'd managed to gather his chakra and escape. Then, though the death blow had been dealt, and though it was dangerous to chase an adversary alone through the ether, Sansata followed.

By the time Abdiel and his team could disengage from the fight and track Sansata down, all that remained was his death aura, right alongside Mattaeus.' The prince was gone, lured by the wily old mage into a trap. It was the final act of Mattaeus' long life. They would have to continue their battles on the other side.

Killed by a dying old man, Abdiel thought, shaking his head with a grimace. It didn't seem right.

He came to the entrance of the throne room and was confronted by three demon guards. Their coal-black eyes challenged Abdiel without expression. He stood tall before them and met their gaze with a glare of his own.

"I have news for Prince Azazel."

His tone was clear and firm. A general in the dark army, Abdiel was used to instant obedience, but the throne room guards were not his usual constituency. Though they were lowly demon guards, they were not impressed with his rank. One of the guards stepped forward.

"You may tell me the news, General, and I will pass it along to the prince."

Abdiel shook his head. "This news must be presented in person and immediately."

The guard stood firm. An indecisive frown crossed his face. Abdiel knew it was his job to keep the riff-raff out of the throne room; the door guards had to judge what was worth disturbing their master. The consequences for sending in the wrong visitor could be severe, but the consequences for *not* sending in an important visitor were far worse. Ultimately, the centurion waved a hand to the underlings behind him.

"Open the doors for the general."

As the doors closed silently behind him, Abdiel felt the change in temperature and atmosphere. It was cool...just a little bit too cool. Humans always assumed Hell was a superheated place, filled with fire, lava, and sulfur. That Hell was coming, the entire underworld knew that, but it was not the Hell they currently belonged to. It was more than a little curious that the Lord of Darkness would name his dwelling place after the coming judgment of God, but what could one expect from the angel that launched a rebellion to take the throne from the God who created him? Lucifer had a warped sense of irony.

Unfortunately for Abdiel, he wasn't there to see Hell's Emperor. He was there for Azazel, Lucifer's most loyal and trusted advisor. It was hard to imagine a more terrifying being than Lucifer himself, but Azazel was such a being. Lucifer was at least somewhat rational. He could be reasoned with. The same could not be said for Azazel. One of the most powerful archangels in existence, and Lucifer's closest friend, Azazel had survived more than a millennium in Heaven's most fearsome prison, under constant angelic torture. Heaven's angels could break anyone.

Abdiel shuddered at the thought before snapping back to the present. Under normal circumstances this would be a bittersweet moment. His prince was dead, but it meant Abdiel would be in line to take his place...except Azazel was going to kill him in a few moments, so it would be a short command, and not one that he would have relished had he lived. That kind of proximity to pure madness was far too frightening to be desired. Abdiel was good at what he did. A degree or two of separation ensured he wouldn't have to make these suicide trips to the throne room.

Abdiel took a moment to let his eyes adjust to the flickering light. When it came to his personal space, Lucifer never took advantage of human technology, preferring to maintain an eerie décor, lighting his throne room with torches. The center of the room, before the massive iron throne, was lit by an equally massive chandelier, rimmed with fire. Somehow, all the fire didn't serve to bring the temperature up a single degree.

Abdiel approached the three figures seated around a thick, ancient, wooden table off to the side of the room, away from the room's centerpiece, an enormous iron throne. The Viceroys, Asteroth and the infamous Beelzebub, were in attendance. While the Viceroys were certainly worthy of Abdiel's fear and respect, it was the third person at the table that caused him to tremble as he stepped across the floor. He saw the tell-tale silver flash followed by the white glow of Azazel's eyes. The presence of such evil chilled Abdiel. It was an unusual feeling considering he was just as much a creature of the underworld and just as much a fallen angel, as Azazel, but the power coursing through Azazel's essence was surpassed only by his maniacal temper and creativity in meting out pain and suffering.

Ordinarily, Abdiel would put his chances of returning alive and well from a visit to the throne room at one hundred percent. He was a loyal and faithful servant with a track record for excellence, but today, he had to face Azazel with terrifyingly bad news and figured surviving the next hour was no better than an even money proposition…and that was probably too optimistic by half.

Azazel sat between the two viceroys. They were in intense conversation as Abdiel approached, crossing over a thick, ancient rug, depicting Lucifer's ongoing war against Heaven. The flickering torch-light Abdiel knew better than to interrupt, so he maintained a respectful distance and waited until he was acknowledged. It didn't take long. Azazel sensed his fear; at least, that was how it felt to Abdiel. When those glowing white eyes flashed silver and centered on him, it was like his every thought was laid bare for all to see. He couldn't feel his legs. Was he trembling?

"General!"

The sharply spoken words snapped Abdiel from his terrifying daydreams and caused him to stand at rigid attention. He met the eyes of Viceroy Asteroth, commander of Hell's army, who stared with the eyes of an ancient warrior who had seen everything there was to see. Abdiel tried his best to focus on those eyes and not the glowing white eyes that scorched his very essence.

"Y-yes, sir!" Abdiel struggled to maintain some modicum of dignity in what he assumed would be his final moments.

"Yooou…have something for us?" the viceroy said, raising his eyebrows.

"Yes, sir." Abdiel took a deep breath. "I bring news for the Prince."

Though the title of Prince was just a step above Abdiel's own rank of general, Azazel's title was more accurately a reference to his relationship with Lucifer; it was not a rank. He was Lucifer's right hand and handled Lucifer's most dangerous and messy work. It wasn't that Lucifer demanded it of him; Azazel just liked it. He *wanted* to be out there, inflicting pain and anguish.

Now, his terrible glowing-white eyes focused on Abdiel's. "For me?" Even his voice was terrifying. He spoke in a soft monotone. It was almost a whisper but it carried with it such power and authority, Abdiel heard it loud and clear.

"Y-yes, Sir." Abdiel knelt in terrified humility and just got it over with. "I'm afraid it concerns the Prince's son, and the news is not good."

"Tell me."

If it was possible, Azazel's voice got even softer while still conveying awesome terror. Abdiel was paralyzed with fear.

"I-I-I'm afraid the Prince's son was killed in action."

Chapter 2

"All right," Nicholas said. He pulled two bottles of water from the fridge and handed one to Zha'riel. The power was still out, so they weren't all that cold. "Could you please just start from the beginning?"

Zha'riel shook his head and frowned as he scrutinized the bottle. "You bottle water. How convenient."

It sounded a lot like sarcasm, but Nicholas couldn't be sure based on Zha'riel's expressionless expression.

Zha'riel sighed. "It is amazing where you humans direct your resources."

Nicholas almost choked on his first sip. "*Us* humans? What does that make *you*?"

"That is a question for a later time." Zha'riel spun the bottle in the palm of his hand. "You asked that I start at the beginning."

Nicholas sat on his ratty old blue couch and wrapped himself in a blanket while his uninvited guest sat in a crappy brown recliner which no longer reclined; well, it probably would, but the handle fell off a couple years before. It was eighty-plus degrees inside since the mid-summer hurricane took out the power. The nausea had passed, but Nicholas felt feverish, hot one moment and freezing the next. He eyed Zha'riel. Other than tossing Nicholas onto the bed with a flick if his hand, there was no indication he meant any harm. Nicholas was exhausted and in pain, but he needed answers.

"Go on."

"Mattaeus," Zha'riel continued, still spinning the bottle in his hand. "The man you met, was a powerful mage."

Nicholas blinked at him and furrowed his brow. The World of Warcraft reference had to be a joke.

Zha'riel tilted his head. "Mage is a general term for one who masters the forces of nature."

Nicholas stared at him for a moment. He wasn't about to bring up WoW; he'd learned that lesson long ago when his brother ridiculed him for a week after Nicholas made the mistake of trying to explain the game. "You probably think that makes sense." He shook his head. "It doesn't."

Zha'riel breathed in. "Consider the natural world. Wind; Fire; Earth; Water. These forces are powerful and need no prompting from those who populate the Earth to exist. Humans have learned to harness these forces to some extent. It would be more accurate to say they have relearned that, but we will leave that distinction for another time. Anyway, you have the ability to use these forces to your advantage, and there are some who have mastered those ancient arts. They can call upon these forces to do their bidding. Those people are called Magi."

"So, they're kinda like witches?"

"No. Witches are quite different." Zha'riel shook his head. "It can be confusing. For now, you just need to come to terms with reality—these beings exist, the powers they possess are real, and *you* are now a part of *their* world, as well as your own."

Nicholas sighed. "You're saying magic exists...like...for *real*?"

"What you call magic," Zha'riel pointed out, "is nothing more than a being accessing and using chakra, the energy that binds all life."

Something clicked in Nicholas' mind. He tilted his head to one side. "Mattaeus said something about that. He said Sansata tracked him because he was using chakras to stay alive."

Zha'riel nodded. "All living creatures draw chakra from the ether for their survival. Some, like Mattaeus, understand how to manipulate chakra. Mattaeus held on as long as he could, but no one can push back death forever."

"That's sad." Nicholas shook his head.

"It is war."

"War?" Nicholas frowned. "Between who?"

Zha'riel's face contorted into an almost comical frown. "Between *who*?" he repeated. "Why, between good and evil."

Nicholas chuckled. "Good and evil, huh?"

Zha'riel closed his eyes and gritted his teeth. "Nicholas, get serious, or you will die before you have a chance to live. Sansata was important."

Nicholas' heart sank. He didn't want to know what that meant. He was certain his imagination wasn't doing the situation justice. He had felt the cold energy surrounding Sansata. He'd heard death in his voice. He'd seen it in his eyes, right up until the life faded away. Sansata was sure to have friends or family seeking revenge. Perhaps that explained Zha'riel's presence.

He looked at Zha'riel. "Am I in danger right now?"

Zha'riel nodded. "You have been in danger from the moment Mattaeus orbed into your life."

Nicholas sucked in a long, deep breath. "Do I want to know what "orbed" means?"

Zha'riel shrugged. "It is simply how some beings travel. It is like teleporting, to put in words you might understand. There are many variations, each one used by different species."

"Like Star Trek." Nicholas chuckled "Beam me up, Scotty!"

"Nicholas." Zha'riel tilted his head. "You will find that much of your art contains within it the realities of the universe. Though you seldom know it, what you create, and then dismiss as fantasy, often is a manifestation of reality—like a vision, or more accurately, a subconscious understanding."

Nicholas shook his head and sighed. Aside from being drained, nauseated, freezing one minute and on fire the next, and having a pounding migraine, he was frightened and confused. He couldn't understand half of what Zha'riel said. He stood and took three steps toward the living room window before almost collapsing from fatigue. He held up a hand to keep Zha'riel from aiding him. He took a few deep breaths and crossed the room until he could lean with his hands on either side of the window. The light streaming in caused him to wince. He leaned against the wall and slid to the ground in a seated position. Zha'riel handed him his water bottle.

"What does any of this have to do with me?" Nicholas finally asked, sipping from the bottle.

"Nothing." Zha'riel sniffed as he paced the room in front of Nicholas. "Until you met Mattaeus and breathed in his essence, along with the essence of a prince of darkness."

Nicholas spit out his water. "A p-prince of darkness? Tell me that *sounds* a lot worse than it really is."

Zha'riel shrugged in an offhand manner. "It is actually far *worse* than it sounds."

Nicholas closed his eyes. "You know, you're not the most encouraging person I've ever met."

"No," Zha'riel agreed. "I am not."

Nicholas stared at him for a moment. "Well, is there any *good* news?"

Zha'riel contemplated for a moment. It was as if he was trying to decide whether to tell Nicholas the truth. He finally nodded.

"There is. You *could* be turning into one of the most powerful creatures this world has ever seen."

Nicholas stared. "Uhhhh…really?" He tried not to laugh. "Because right now I feel like I might die any second."

Zha'riel shook his head. "You are most certainly *not* dying, Nicholas. You are changing."

"What exactly am I changing into?" Nicholas asked. "Maybe I don't want to change."

"It is irreversible," Zha'riel replied. His tone was firm; his eyes bored into Nicholas as he flipped the unopened water bottle in his hand. "It is your deepest vision of yourself." Zha'riel put the water bottle on an end table. "What would you be, if you could be whatever you wanted?"

Nicholas took a deep breath. "So, these muscles, my hair color, my eyes…they're all what I really wished I looked like?"

Zha'riel nodded. "In a sense, but it goes even deeper. Your entire physical and mental make-up is changing. You are becoming your ideal inside and out."

"How do you know all this?"

Zha'riel thought for a moment. "Because I have seen your entire world, from the beginning—the beginning of time."

"Okay," Nicholas said slowly as he narrowed his eyes. "So, what does that make you?"

Zha'riel smiled. "It makes me a being of light."

Nicholas stared blankly at him. Zha'riel raised his eyebrows.

"A messenger of God."

Nicholas scrunched his forehead. Zha'riel stared at him in disbelief and sighed.

"I am an angel of the Lord, Nicholas."

That broke Nicholas out of his stupor. "Really? An angel?" He shook his head and his eyes sparkled. "This gets better and better." He burst out laughing .and his stomach responded with a violent cramp, doubling Nicholas over.

"Nicholas," Zha'riel said. "Now that you know what I am, you should take what I say very seriously."

"Okay, fine," Nicholas said with a hand raised in surrender. The other clutched his belly. "So, you're an angel and I am turning into...something."

Zha'riel continued. "In addition to your human essence, you have taken in the essences of two supernatural beings...two very *powerful* supernatural beings."

Nicholas' heart raced. "I guess that's the bad news?"

Zha'riel shrugged. "You may enjoy the new physical and mental benefits, but you are ill-prepared for the powers you possess."

"What kind of powers?" Nicholas asked.

Zha'riel rattled off a list of the most common powers Nicholas was likely to "inherit." They ranged from awesome to unbelievably awesome as far as Nicholas could tell. The ability to travel anywhere, anytime in an instant, control over the elements of nature, a body almost impervious to the creations of mankind, were just a few broad strokes the angel sketched for him. Nicholas began to imagine the kind of life he might lead.

"You need to understand one thing," Zha'riel said, as if he was reading Nicholas' mind. "These powers, in and of themselves are neutral, not evil. How you choose to use them is what makes them...and you...good or evil. Selfish gain is a typical motivation, but selfishness is evil, even if it does not seem so. It leads you down a dangerous path."

"Anger. Fear. Aggression," Nicholas said in his best Yoda voice. "That dark side are they. Once you start down the dark path..."

Zha'riel's eyes flashed a dazzling blue before returning to their natural state. Nicholas felt his heart strain with the increase in pace. Zha'riel stared him down.

"You have been warned."

And he was gone. Nicholas couldn't believe his eyes. One moment Zha'riel was there, the next he wasn't. There was no smoke and no flash of light. He didn't fade away or break up into tiny particles. He was just gone.

Nicholas collapsed into bed, hoping the worst was over. He should have asked whether anyone had ever died transitioning. *That* would have been an interesting piece of information.

$$ Ɓ A ž Ψ Ϛ $$

"I-I-I'm afraid the Prince's son was killed in action."

The words hung in the air for what felt like centuries to Abdiel. He heard gasps from the two viceroys flanking Azazel. Abdiel kept his head bowed; he had no desire to see it coming. He could hear Azazel's breaths. For a moment, he thought he smelled ozone. That was bad. He felt the icy burn of Azazel's gaze. There was a weight to Azazel's stare, like he could push with it.

Azazel finally spoke in a low, menacing monotone. "On your feet, General."

Abdiel snapped to attention. Azazel stood and walked around the table, dragging his fingertips along the ancient surface the whole way. He was dressed in jet-black robes with silver accents adorning the sleeves near the cuffs. Like his deceased son, Azazel wore his hair pulled straight back, in a heavy braid. His appearance was as severe as his reputation.

Abdiel kept his eyes forward. Out of his periphery, he saw terrified looks on the faces of both viceroys. Azazel perched himself on the edge of the table, never taking his eyes off Abdiel's. It was an unexpected, and casual act, made all the more horrifying for the circumstances.

"Well," Azazel said his voice almost gentle, yet still fear-inducing. "There must be some kind of a story."

Abdiel reluctantly told Azazel everything. Sansata, using one of the ten cohorts under Abdiel's command, had executed a brilliant trap. Six hundred demon soldiers were lying in wait when Mattaeus appeared to stop what he had been led to believe was a plot to uncover a powerful artifact. No sooner had he appeared then the cohort of demons attacked, forcing him into a long and violent battle. Mattaeus succeeded in calling in reinforcements, which prolonged the battle, but it was clear that the demons would ultimately win. Mattaeus sounded the retreat, but Sansata had already crept into a flanking position and dealt a fatal blow.

Mattaeus should have died quickly, but he clung to life and managed to escape into the ether. Sansata, blinded by hatred of his long-time adversary, took off after him. Abdiel, locked in mortal combat with multiple adversaries of his own, was unable to follow. When he finally dispatched his opponents and gave chase, he was too late. He found Sansata's body in the ether, absent his essence.

Abdiel fell silent and awaited Azazel's reaction, fully expecting it to be loud, violent, painful, and final. Azazel didn't lose his cool; that was almost worse. Abdiel couldn't tell what was going on in the prince's mind, but the awesome white glow of Azazel's eyes was enough to render him petrified.

"So," Azazel finally spoke. "You allowed your prince to venture, unaccompanied, into the ether to chase down the most dangerous mage in existence? Is that essentially what you are telling me?"

Abdiel shook his head. "I tried to stop hi—"

"No!" Azazel slammed his hand down on the table. His eyes flashed silver and then returned to their normal white glow His voice dropped back to his trademark ominous monotone. "Generals do not *try*. Generals succeed. Do you agree, *General*?"

"Y-yes, Sir." Abdiel wasn't about to argue. Death could come in many forms and he wasn't interested in seeing how creative Azazel could be.

"So," the archangel continued. "We agree. You allowed your prince, my *son*, to chase down a dangerous foe without due support."

Abdiel began to reply, but Azazel held up a hand. "Silence, General, or I will remove your tongue."

Abdiel clenched his jaw. Azazel left his perch on the table and approached Abdiel, scrutinizing his face. The proximity caused sweat to break out on Abdiel's forehead. Even his hands felt clammy. Azazel shook his head in disgust.

"Coward," he spat. "You are nothing but a sniveling coward, unworthy of your position in this great army."

Abdiel remained silent, his head bowed in humility, and hoping for the best, which at that point would be a quick and painless execution. Azazel paced in front of him, oozing rage, but maintaining absolute calm. Perhaps he was tired of his reputation as an out-of-control lunatic. Perhaps, Abdiel thought hopefully, he wanted to be recognized as professional and thoughtful. It was almost too much to hope for.

Azazel must have caught a whiff of Abdiel's hopes because he peered into the general's eyes. From a distance the glowing white of Azazel's gaze was awesome and intimidating. Abdiel had been petrified at twenty feet, but inches away from his face, Abdiel was paralyzed with dread.

"Tell me," Azazel without emotion. "How long do you think it would take me to tear you into a million pieces?"

"I-I-I d-d-d-don't kn-know." Abdiel barely managed to choke the words out.

"*I* do," Azazel said matter-of-factly. "I know *exactly* how long it would take."

Abdiel could feel the electrical force crackling at Azazel's finger tips. He heard the sizzle and once again smelled the release of ozone. He even glimpsed the violet hue as it cast a shadow over Azazel's face. He braced himself for pain.

This is it, he thought. *This is the end.*

He was right. Azazel's right hand tore into Abdiel's abdomen and angled straight upward to his heart until the maniacal archangel grasped it in his fingers. Abdiel's first screams were the product of fear and shock, but when the pain hit his screams intensified tenfold. When Azazel surged massive jolts of energy through his fingers, Abdiel's cries became bloodcurdling. Azazel lifted him off the ground with one arm and sent so much energy through his fingers, Abdiel was engulfed in the tangled web of a violet-hued electrical storm.

As the energy pulsed through him, Abdiel was powerless to move. He was held with his arms and legs splayed out slightly. The power surging through his body was killing him, but at an excruciating slow pace. It felt like his body was melting off its bones, but it never actually melted away. It was just the constant feeling of burning alive without the relief of death. Azazel was a true master.

After several moments of blind agony, Abdiel was hurled through the air across the room. He slammed against the onyx wall and crumpled to the ground. Smoke rose from all over his body. Remnants of electric pulses continued to crackle all around him. His clothes were burnt to tatters. He didn't try to move; he couldn't. All he was able to do was lie there, groaning, hoping Azazel would mercifully kill him instead of subjecting him to another round of torturous shocks.

"To fail your prince is unacceptable, Abdiel," Azazel said, his voice not unlike that of a teacher instructing his student. "But you have also failed *me.* You gave my son over to that *stargazer.*"

Abdiel groaned in agony. His mind couldn't keep pace with Azazel's words.

"And now." Azazel's voice softened. "You *will* die." He leaned in close to Abdiel. "But not quickly, *General.* Not quickly."

He strode back to the table. "Get up," he commanded as he retook his place between the awestruck viceroys. "Now!" He raised his voice for the first time as Abdiel, unable to control his limbs, failed to stand.

Abdiel managed to bring his legs underneath his body and plant his feet enough to force himself up the wall. He stood with all his weight against it. No sooner had he reached his full height than the violet electricity shot from Azazel's hands, surrounding Abdiel and lifting him off his feet in a blinding storm of agony. His screams reached epic proportions as Azazel expertly sucked the life out of him, a morsel at a time.

"ENOUGH!"

The voice carried such absolute authority, Azazel instantly released Abdiel and let him fall to the ground in a crumpled, smoking heap. Electricity once again crackled around him for several seconds. All eyes turned to the new arrival as the viceroys threw themselves from their seats to the floor, face down and prostrate before their king. Azazel didn't react like the viceroys. He stood formally to greet his friend and master.

"My Lord," Azazel said as their hands clasped and they pulled one another in closer. The ritualistic greeting looked like a wristlock but was far more familial. "You're back early."

"Yes, old friend. As soon as I heard about Sansata." Lucifer's crystal eyes took in the scene. With a glance he dismissed the viceroys, who didn't need to be told twice. They couldn't get away from Azazel fast enough. Lucifer turned back to his friend. "I see you have been keeping yourself busy."

Azazel glanced off-handedly at Abdiel's crumpled form. "This is the one responsible for Sansata's death."

Lucifer's eyes squinted. "This is one of *our* generals. I was led to believe Sansata died at the hands of Mattaeus."

"It was his job to protect his prince." Azazel folded his arms across his chest and leaned on the table. "He failed."

31

Lucifer gave him a thoughtful nod. "Perhaps." He took a breath. "I assume you haven't heard about the condition of Sansata's remains then?"

Azazel frowned. "The condition?"

Lucifer pursed his lips.

"I want you to remain calm," he warned.

Azazel clenched his fists and his jaw tightened. Lucifer shrugged and leaned against the large wooden table, tracing the ancient carvings with his finger. He tapped the center of an intricate pentagram with his middle finger before continuing.

"His essence was stolen." Lucifer said it so easily, it almost slipped past Azazel. Almost.

"It was...*stolen*?" Azazel exploded. "By who? The mage?"

Lucifer shook his head. "Not the mage."

Azazel frowned. "Then who?" He glanced back at Abdiel. "You don't think…"

Lucifer shook his head again. "Of course not. Even if he was stupid enough to try something like that, he wouldn't come back here."

Azazel shrugged and nodded at the same time. He really didn't care to discuss it. He wanted action, revenge. He wanted blood, and at the moment, Abdiel was the only outlet for his rage. Before he spoke, Lucifer continued.

"The mage was also without his essence."

Azazel's glowing white eyes flicked to Lucifer's. That was interesting.

"You think the old fool actually managed it?"

Lucifer shrugged. "Perhaps. He was crazy enough to try."

Azazel took a breath. "Do you think it's even possible?"

"I think it's more than possible," Lucifer nodded. "It's just not easy. The timing must be perfect, and look at the risk Mattaeus ran."

"Risk?"

Lucifer nodded. "Yes, of course. He gave up his own powers. That means the recipient must have been weaker than he was. Sansata's powers are the dominant powers. He will tend toward evil."

Azazel pursed his lips. "But who could Mattaeus have contacted with so little notice?"

"No one," Lucifer pointed out.

Azazel frowned. "Then how…?"

"If Mattaeus could have called someone," Lucifer pointed out. "He would have called for an angel friend to heal him. Instead, he allowed himself to die…or rather, to be killed before Sansata's wound could run its course. That means someone else finished Mattaeus off, someone less powerful and easily manipulated."

"So?" Azazel shrugged. "What does all that mean?"

Lucifer raised his eyebrows. "It means we're looking for a human."

Chapter 3

Nicholas awoke to the buzzing of his cell phone. It was his brother, Dom, probably wondering whether he was ever going to return to work. It was a fair question. How long can a guy be out sick? Nicholas wasn't yet in the mood to deal with his brother. He was busy feeling no pain for the first time in his life. At first, he attributed it to normal relief he'd expect after the week of suffering he'd just endured, but he realized it went far deeper. It was as though his new body was showing him how much pain he had previously lived with. Maybe everyone existed in varying degrees of pain, and lived with it because it was all they knew.

After a shower, Nicholas wiped the steam-covered mirror and admired his new physique. He stepped closer and peered into his own amethyst eyes. It wasn't possible. He'd never heard of someone with purple eyes, yet no amount of blinking changed their hue. He felt an odd sensation as he gazed deeper. There was a depth to their color and the same silver-specked galaxy of stars he had seen in Sansata's eyes. It was hypnotic. Nicholas wondered if women would like them, or did just exchange dull and awkward for freakish and…well, awkward. He would find out soon enough, but he had more important things to worry about. He was ravenous. Food first, then girls. He grabbed the door knob and pulled…

...and the next thing he knew, Nicholas opened his eyes in his kitchen, in front of his refrigerator, pulling *that* door open!

"W-w-whaaat?" he stammered, letting the door go and taking several steps back. He whipped his head from side-to-side but saw no one. "What the heck was that?"

He headed back to his room, closing his eyes and shaking his head...

...and then, he was there!

"Holy crap!" he exclaimed, remembering his conversation with Zha'riel. "This is crazy!"

Did he just...*orb?* He sat down on the edge of his bed. It just wasn't possible. Despite everything he'd seen and heard, Nicholas's mind hadn't even begun to wrap itself around his new reality. Nicholas had breathed in two essences, according to the...angel. That apparently meant he had their powers and abilities within him. He was still a little skeptical about Zha'riel, but Nicholas remembered how Mattaeus and later, Sansata, had appeared out of thin air. If Nicholas now possessed their essences, and their powers, it stood to reason he would be able to travel the same way they did.

He spent several minutes trying to get a handle on his newfound power. Within a few tries, he could transport himself from one room to another almost every time. He could feel his mind control the process. For such a small action, Nicholas sensed tremendous power supporting it. He also began to understand what it took to control his thoughts and *not* orb; *that* ought to save him some embarrassment.

He hadn't eaten anything heavier than chicken broth for days. He made himself a heaping plate of scrambled eggs, and added half a pound of almost-burnt bacon. While he ate, Nicholas wondered about the other powers inside him, and how he might access them. He'd only glimpsed what was possible. Sansata exuded power. What would it take for Nicholas, who had never even been in a fistfight, to match Sansata's presence? The thought triggered a yearning from deep within. Nicholas felt a thread of cold rage begin to wind itself throughout his core. For a brief moment, his hands shook and he saw a flash of bright silver. He tamped down the inexplicable anger, and breathed through his nose, long and steady, until he felt calm.

He spent some time trying to summon lightning from his fingers to no avail. If it was an online video game, he'd have it mastered in an hour, but it wasn't. Frustrated and confused, Nicholas decided he needed a diversion. It was time to take his new, well-muscled body out for a spin. After careful consideration, he decided the beach was the best place for a trial run. After all, that's where the ladies would be. He loaded up a cooler, got into his car, and ran to the store for a beach chair and a couple of large beach towels. It was a worthwhile investment; he might be spending a lot of time on the beach.

Once he situated himself on the 50th Street beach in Sea Isle City, Nicholas stripped his t-shirt off and stretched, cracking his neck from side-to-side as the sun beat down on his skin. He took a few deep breaths and inhaled the salt air. Each breath brought memories of his childhood, much of which had been spent on New Jersey beaches. The sounds of children squealing with delight mingled with the thunderous crash of waves. Every now and then, a whistle pierced through it all as a lifeguard stood up and waved some wayward swimmers back to safety.

Fortunately, his body transformation included an olive complexion, so he didn't look like a ghost standing amidst a well-tanned college crowd, down for the summer. Nicholas watched as some guys tossed a football around while others played a beach game Nicholas hadn't seen before and didn't think he'd particularly enjoy. The girls either stood around and watched or lay out on towels, soaking up the sunshine. There were smooth, tan legs, belly-button rings, and skimpy bathing suit tops as far as the eye could see. Nicholas pulled his sunglasses down over his eyes and tried not to stare.

Within a half-hour, Nicholas felt a tingle at the base of his skull. Reclining in his chair, he casually shifted his eyes from side-to-side behind his sunglasses and spotted a group of girls watching him, then another, and another. All of a sudden, his world was populated by bikini-clad college girls of every size and stripe. He briefly wondered if he was dreaming or if, perhaps, he had actually died and landed in Heaven.

He played it cool. It took an excruciating hour for one of the girls to gather the courage to talk to him. After that, he wasn't left alone for more than a few minutes at a time. He wound up swimming with several girls and was invited to parties every night of the week. He had a cell phone full of new phone numbers by the end of the day, and walked off the beach with a decision to make as to how to spend his evening.

He drove home, planning to take a shower, grab some take-out for dinner, and figure out which girl he would call first. When he pulled to a stop at a red light, the bank across the street caught his eye. A dark chill ran down his spine and he squinted his eyes at the unpleasant memories. The short story was that Nicholas got smacked with seven insufficient funds charges in one day because he deposited his paycheck at twelve-thirty-two instead of twelve-sixteen, when the checks he'd written began streaming in. It was the second time in six months and the bank manager refused to refund the charges again. Nicholas, after two months of futile complaints and letter writing, closed his account and went elsewhere.

He pulled into the WaWa across from the bank and stared. Thoughts of revenge and righteous indignation consumed his mind. Perhaps the time had come for a little payback. For once in his life, Nicholas felt as though he was in a position of strength. He had an idea. Since he could orb in and out of rooms, would it be possible to orb into a bank vault, at night, grab the money and escape undetected? Why not? If he did trip an alarm, he could just orb out when the police showed up. If he wore gloves and disguised himself, how could anyone identify him? The question was, should he go for it?

Why not? After all, that bank screwed their customers. He couldn't be the only one. Banks have all the power, and they wield it like despot dictators. That bank still had a couple hundred of Nicholas' dollars. It wasn't like he was rich. He worked his tail off every day for his money, and the richest people in the world, who really didn't need his two hundred dollars, still found it necessary to stick it to him. Why not hit them back now that *he* had the power? Why not take a little back from the bank that screwed their poorest customers? Maybe it was time for them to taste how it feels to have someone reach in and take what was theirs.

As those thoughts roamed free in his mind, Nicholas felt a tremendous release of...something...and it was euphoric. It was also dark, almost frightening, and nothing he could ever recall feeling. There was a part of him that knew he should push the feelings aside. Who reveled in dark notions? Psychopaths, that's who. He knew he was on the verge of crossing a line but somehow, it felt good. Right and wrong was out the window.

After driving home, Nicholas dug up an old, black duffel bag with no logo. He dressed himself, head-to-toe, in black and tossed his wallet, along with any other identifying items, on his dresser. To complete his look, he pulled on a pair of latex gloves and wore a winter ski mask over his head and face. He added a pair of sunglasses to hide his violet eyes from any cameras.

He opened his laptop and went online, pulling several addresses off the bank website. While he waited for nightfall, he called one of the numbers he'd gotten earlier and told the girl on the other end—Gina—he'd meet her at a local bar around ten. She told him she'd be there with her group and she couldn't wait to see him.

With his alibi set, Nicholas took a breath and closed his eyes. Why was he doing this? He wasn't raised to return a bad deed with a bad deed. In his heart, Nicholas knew he ought to stop what he was doing and go have fun with the ladies he'd met on the beach, but his urge to exact revenge on the abusive bank won out. He took a moment to compose his thoughts before directing his mental focus.

He orbed right into the vault of his former bank. It was dark, but for the emergency lighting. His eyes adjusted within seconds. He listened but heard no alarm. He moved through the small room and located as much cash as he could. He expected all the cash to be locked away, but it was out in the open. The vault door was the only defense against theft. He loaded every dollar he could find into the duffel. It was far less than he'd expected, but it was free money, so who cared? Plus, it was far more than they had stolen from him, but he figured he deserved some punitive damages, like when a plaintiff gets a hundred bucks for winning the lawsuit and then another million-and-a-half for pain and suffering.

Without wasting a breath, Nicholas orbed into the next location, and the next, and the next, finding similar setups, which made things easy. Two hours, twenty locations later, plus three trips back home to dump out the duffel, and Nicholas was back in his living room, stacking towers of hundreds, fifties, twenties, tens, fives, and ones. He totaled just under one point one million in cash. Not bad for two hours' work!

Nicholas stashed the loot in his closet, taking a fist full of twenties for his wallet. He got in his car and drove to the bar to meet his alibi/date. He felt bad about using her, but she had no idea and he wasn't likely to need an alibi since he was unidentifiable in his disguise. It was the perfect crime, and one he intended to replicate soon.

Her name was Jenna, and she was several appletinis in when Nicholas showed up at Kix McNutley's, one of Sea Isle's hottest nightclubs. On the beach, Jenna's strawberry hair had been pulled into a tight bun. Now, it was a mass of curls, made messy from an hour of wild dancing to the pulsing club music. She squealed when Nicholas found her, and broke away from her three friends to run into his arms. He steadied her, and she giggled, pulling him with both hands. They bypassed her friends, who grinned as Jenna, wearing a short, tight, red dress, dragged him to the dance floor.

Dancing was not an activity Nicholas was interested in or good at. He spent the next half-hour trying not to look too stupid. Why hadn't Mattaeus gifted him with supernatural dance moves? It didn't matter; Jenna wasn't interested in his moves. Her hands were everywhere at once. When she pushed her back against him and gyrated her hips, Nicholas almost went into cardiac arrest, but he figured there were worse ways to die.

He enjoyed an evening of drinking and partying with Jenna's group of seriously drunk college ladies, which was kind of like living the dream. Nicholas wasn't used to the kind of attention these girls paid him. They fawned, finding reasons to touch him, first on the arms and hands, then more provocatively as the liquor flowed. Strangely, Nicholas drank as much as the girls, yet he felt no adverse effects. He wondered if the supernatural were supernaturally tolerant of alcohol.

Jenna tried to get him to go home with her, but his mind was elsewhere. All he could think about was how he could score even bigger than at the banks. His mind went to all the entities that screwed people out of money. Casinos were the first ones on the list, but he knew getting in and out of those vaults would be a bit trickier. Casinos were twenty-four-seven. They never closed, and cameras were always on and always monitored. He'd have to think about that before going in half-cocked.

By the time he loaded the girls into a cab at the end of the night, Nicholas was ready for more action. He went home, opened his laptop, and found more locations of the same bank as before. This time, he sought out locations in a different region. He found another twenty banks scattered across the Midwest, chuckling as he considered the implications of so many robberies of the same bank in every state across the country. Tomorrow's news ought to be amusing.

He "worked" for another six hours, ultimately stealing over ten million dollars in cash. He hit exactly one hundred banks in every state in the nation including Hawaii and Alaska. He even hit one in Puerto Rico, four in Canada, and another in Mexico City. He was a one-man North American crime spree. He organized, counted, and stashed the money in his closet. As he stared at the stacks of cash, his stomach twisted and his throat tightened. He sat down on the edge of his bed and put his head in his hands.

"What did I do?"

Without warning, a flash of silver lit up his eyes and his resolve returned with a vengeance. It wasn't about the money. It was about the principle. What's done was done. It was time to move on. He would deposit some of the money into his bank account over time. The rest he would put into an offshore account. Since he wasn't restricted by planes and security, Nicholas did a little research and found the banking laws in Samoa, of all places, would work to his advantage. After a couple hours on the phone with a financial consultant, he secured a meeting for the following morning.

When he orbed into Apia, the capital city of Samoa, Nicholas found himself alone in the rest room of a busy eatery, across the street from the bank. He brought two, wheeled cases containing a total of seven million dollars in cash. He crossed the street and pushed through the glass doors at the front entrance of the bank. To the credit of the bank employees, not one eye blinked at the sight of an American entering their branch with two suitcases trailing behind. Nicholas checked in with security and was ushered into an interior office.

Moments later, a well-dressed, refined man entered the room. His jet-black hair was cut close and glistened in the light. In a random thought, Nicholas wondered what kind of product the guy used to achieve that shine.

"Hello," the newcomer said, extending his hand. Monogrammed gold cufflinks gleamed as a light blue sleeve slid out from under dark-blue pinstriped Armani. "Welcome to our humble financial establishment. My name is Enele Siulai. We spoke on the phone yesterday."

"Yes," Nicholas replied as he shook Enele's hand. "Good to put a face to the name."

Enele smiled and nodded. "I believe I have everything prepared, just as you requested."

He turned to a sleek computer on the desk and brought up a check list. He rattled off the requests Nicholas had made. With each one, he brought up the options available. Ultimately, Nicholas just wanted it to look like he was a consultant of some kind and that the money he brought in would be given a clean history so it would appear he'd earned it over time. Within a couple of hours, everything was finalized, and Nicholas walked out of the bank with a debit card, a checkbook and everything he would need to access his money from anywhere in the world. Anyone searching for answers would find that Nicholas Scarlatti earned the money over the course of a year. He would declare some of it on his taxes when the time came, and pay the tax debt, just like any other law-abiding citizen. If the questions got too uncomfortable, Samoan law ensured complete privacy.

With his finances secure, Nicholas returned home and prepared for a trip to the nearest Maserati dealership. It was time to upgrade from his ten-year-old Civic. A quick orb to a private location, a cab-ride to the dealership, a few signatures, and one big check later, and Nicholas was cruising south down the Garden State Parkway in a brand-new, fully-loaded, electric-blue Quattroporte convertible. With perfect weather, he drove with the top down, opened up the throttle, and let the vehicle do what it was made to do.

$$ \hbar \; \text{А} \; \check{\text{З}} \; \psi \; \text{G} $$

"Tell me about him."

Rafael was an imposing figure. Tall in stature with the build of a mighty warrior, the archangel's presence dominated the moment he entered a room. Zha'riel, even after eons of service under Rafael, was never completely at ease in his presence. Rafael had a special ability to put other off balance. He also knew humans better than any of Heaven's agents. Dressed in the attire of a wealthy human businessman, Rafael hid his angelic identity well, and walked among the humans, always studying, always learning.

He stood at the window wall of a Manhattan penthouse. His gaze swept the city as Zha'riel stood behind him. The penthouse was decorated in a classic contemporary style, with lots of white and gold, and soft, curved lines. The main room was a wide-open oval. The vaulted ceiling was supported by round columns. Rafael furnished the place in a style common to the rich and powerful. What set it apart was the art. Rafael's collection included paintings, sculptures, and relics from places and times long-since lost to the world.

Zha'riel was summoned to discuss Nicholas Scarlatti. He was baffled at how one young human aroused such interest. He was unique in that he had taken in the essences of good and evil supernatural beings, but so what? He was a foolish, impulsive, selfish child who wasn't very long for his life, in Zha'riel's opinion. But Rafael was interested, and that was all that mattered.

"He is going to get himself killed," Zha'riel replied, trying, and failing, to mask his disdain for the young upstart.

Rafael's forehead wrinkled in a strangely human expression. His long years in the natural world and proximity to the human race caused him to take on some of the nuances of their humanity.

"That would be unfortunate," he finally replied. "He is important."

"But why?" Zha'riel asked. "Just because he took in good and evil?"

Rafael tilted his head. "Not just good and evil, but the essences of a fallen angel and a powerful mage. Trained properly, he could shift the balance of power."

"Not this kid." Zha'riel shook his head. "He is far too self-absorbed. He uses what powers he *can* control to enrich himself. He is not the kind to…*get involved*. Plus, he is insular. Perhaps this will change as he gains confidence and learns how to harness his powers, but I suspect he will use it all for his own gratification. He already slides down that path."

"Then you must return to him and guide him," Rafael commanded. He turned from the window to face Zha'riel. "Ensure he does not fall prey to fleshly temptations. Ensure he chooses good. He will be a powerful asset. Imagine, Zha'riel…one who could walk among them with impunity. He could implode the underworld from the inside."

"I doubt that," Zha'riel said. "He is not worth our time."

"He is," Rafael countered. "Because there is no one like him anywhere in creation."

Zha'riel rubbed his temples and shook his head again. He could do the whole act-like-a-human thing too. "If he is so special, why do we not simply create more like him? Why not capture demons and fallen angels and…" Zha'riel closed his eyes; he wished he would have thought before speaking.

"And what?" Rafael challenged.

It was simple. Angels could not deliberately sacrifice an innocent. Doing so would cause them to fall from grace. They could lose their angelic status and end up in any number of diminished capacities. The worst-case scenario was to be cast out and disavowed. Lucifer and his minions were the first, and greatest, example of that fate. Though the powers involved were beyond anything the natural world could understand, there were still rules, and some rules could not be broken for any reason without dire consequences.

"So," Rafael continued. "Do you understand why it is important that we do not allow young Nicholas to fall into the hands of the Dark Army…or any other evil enterprise?"

Zha'riel nodded, already able to see where the conversation as headed. He should have known.

Rafael smiled. "Our goal must be to guide him onto the path of righteousness. Your task is to ensure that Nicholas Scarlatti finds the good within him, and cling to it. He must not be lost to evil."

Zha'riel nodded. He could scarcely imagine a more tedious and mind-numbing assignment, but it appeared he was stuck with the insolent human for the foreseeable future. On the plus side, there could be a fair amount of action involved. If Scarlatti was truly a powerful being, it was just a matter of time before the Dark Army came for him. As much as Zha'riel wanted to get excited about his mission, it was still a garbage assignment.

Chapter 4

Nicholas spoke Dom's name and the Bluetooth did the rest as he peeled away from the curb in his new, Maserati convertible. He knew where Dom was, and he also knew Dom wouldn't answer the phone, but Nicholas tried anyway. Sure enough, there was no answer. Nicholas leaned back in the softest leather he had ever felt and decided it was time to go see his brother. He felt bad enough about quitting; the least he could do was break the news in person.

Dom wasn't going to be happy, but Nicholas wasn't about to spend eight or more hours a day tied to a job. His newly acquired powers would be wasted fabricating and installing granite counter-tops. He would much rather spend those hours bringing in *real* money, or relaxing on the beach with the sand between his toes. Plus, he really needed to hone his skills. Zha'riel, in addition to being a royal stick-in-the-mud, seemed convinced danger was looming.

Zha'riel was clear Sansata was not just some low-level demon, whatever that meant. He was a prince in Lucifer's dark army. More importantly, he was the son of a powerful and maniacal fallen angel named Azazel. Zha'riel was cryptic about the details of this Azazel character and that was more unnerving than anything else. What was the cryptic angel hiding?

Though Nicholas had been sparing in his use of his powers, following the bank heists, if it was true that the use of magic could be traced, he should expect a confrontation at some point. That should have made him fearful, if anything, but it didn't. Whenever the thought crept into his mind, Nicholas felt the same cold, dark tug, deep in his core. As unfamiliar as the feeling was, Nicholas took a strange comfort in it, and began to welcome the idea of a violent confrontation. As always, he was uncertain what to do with such foreign thoughts.

As he pulled into a parking space in front of Ripped Fitness, Nicholas grinned in anticipation. Dom was going to flip out when he saw how cut up and muscled Nicholas was. Nicholas concocted a reasonably believable story as to how it happened under Dom's nose. Nicholas usually wore baggy clothing and never hung out with Dom and his friends, so it wouldn't be like Dom saw one thing a week ago and something different today.

The moment he entered the gym, he felt uncomfortable. The color scheme was loud, red walls with black splatter. Obnoxious posters promising fast results adorned every wall, along with advertisements for protein shake mixes and weightlifting supplements. The clink of free weights mixed with the drone of treadmills. Nicholas hated it all, especially the smell. He didn't understand why it was so hard to get the sickening odor of sweat out of the walls. How did no one notice?

As he approached the front desk, he saw something—or rather, some*one*—Dom and the guys had been talking about for months. He'd never met the girl, never seen so much as a picture of her, but she fit the guys' descriptions to a tee. Her name was Stephanie, and the moment they made eye contact, he swore he was looking at an angel, which was a bold thought to float across his mind considering recent events. Her eyes shimmered blue, while golden locks fell midway down her back in perfect layers, leaving some strands a little shorter to frame her face. Her smile was bright and cheerful. Nicholas couldn't breathe.

For the briefest of seconds all the confidence he'd gained on the beach throughout the week faded away. His mind regressed into its former state of shyness and self-doubt, but that only lasted a second or two. The new Nicholas surged back to the forefront. His confidence returned…at least, outwardly it did. Inside he was a wreck, but he managed to bottle it up and flash the gorgeous girl in front of him the same smile that had melted the ladies on the beach all week.

It worked, or seemed to. Stephanie's eyes widened as her face flushed just a bit, and she bit her bottom lip. She looked down, but it was only a second or so before her eyes returned to meet his. She blushed again, and Nicholas couldn't believe it. She probably had guys chasing her all over town. According to Dom, Stephanie recently broke up with a cheating boyfriend and had been sad and depressed for weeks. Dom, and every other guy in the gym, hadn't wasted any time going after her…quite unsuccessfully as far as Nicholas had heard.

She was the first to speak.

"Hi. Can I help you?"

It was such an innocent, simple question, yet the responses filling Nicholas' mind were anything but. He fought the urge to spout something disgusting. Why did his mind go right to the worst possible approach? He decided against the alpha male nonsense and instead opted for cute and sweet. It suited his personality and had to be better than what she usually got in a gym full of big oafs, like his brother, who thought grunting and snarling was sexy.

Nicholas smiled and leaned on the counter. "I'm just here to see my brother real quick. Dominic Scarlatti?"

Stephanie's expression fell. She nodded and jerked her head over her shoulder. "He's back there," she said, "with the other meatheads."

Nicholas chuckled. Gorgeous eyes. Gorgeous hair. Perfect body. And doesn't think much of Dom and the other "meatheads." This girl was pretty cool.

"Meatheads, huh?" he replied, keeping his smile turned up.

She cringed. "Sorry about that. He's really a nice enough guy. It just gets old hearing the same line day after day from guys at the gym."

Nicholas nodded as the points in Stephanie's favor ticked upward in his mind. "I get it." He shrugged in an offhand manner. "I think he's a horse's ass myself, so I'd say 'meathead' is generous."

Stephanie burst out laughing and put her hand over her mouth. "You're funny."

Nicholas frowned. "I was going for cute."

She bit her lip again and slowly let it slide between her teeth. She shrugged as her face turned a shade redder. "You're cute too," she finally said softly.

Score! Bingo! Home Run! All those things!

Nicholas contained his excitement and raised his eyebrows with a sly grin. "You think I'm cute, huh?"

She rolled her eyes. "Oh, here we go…"

Nicholas spread his hands out. "Hey, I was just standing here, minding my own business, when you said I was cute."

Stephanie's eyes widened and she turned even redder. "You were *not* just minding your own business. You were standing there with that pretty smile and those eyes."

"What about my eyes?" Nicholas grinned, his face a picture of youthful innocence.

She rolled her eyes, grabbed the handle of the hand truck she had been loading, and wheeled it into a storage room in the back. "Nothing. Just forget it."

Nicholas followed her with his grin still in place. "Just say it."

"Just say what?" Stephanie shot back.

"Just say you think my eyes are pretty."

"I'm not saying that."

"Why not?" Nicholas asked as he grabbed the top box and put it on the shelf. "You don't like purple?"

Stephanie giggled. "I didn't say that."

"So, you *do* think they're pretty."

"Ugh!" Her shoulders slumped a little in defeat.

Nicholas took her hand gently and turned her to face him. The feel of her soft hand in his made his heart leap. He opened his eyes wide. "Take a good look."

Her eyes met his and he saw, and felt, her tremble slightly. Or was that him? It was a powerful moment for Nicholas. He'd never had such an effect on a girl before, and it felt amazing. The coldness welled up inside him and he had to push hard to force it back down. Whatever it was, it was getting worse with every passing moment. He would lose control of it at some point, but at this moment, all Nicholas wanted was a few minutes peace to talk to a girl who took his breath away.

"So?" he said lightly, pulling her a little closer. Their faces were inches apart. It would be so easy to close that distance and kiss her soft, pink lips. He could barely keep from staring at them as it was. "What do you think now?"

She let out a breath and ran the tip of her tongue over her lips "They're beautiful."

Her eyes flicked to Nicholas' lips. He could tell she expected him to do something, but he resisted the urge. Instead, he stood up straight, threw the remaining boxes onto the shelf, and pushed the hand truck into a corner. He stood in front of the still shaken Stephanie, and studied her. He shook his head.

"What?" she said, regaining her wits.

"What am I gonna do with you?" Nicholas asked, still shaking his head.

For the briefest of seconds, her mouth started to curl up into a smile and he knew a dirty thought had passed through her brain. He was elated. "You totally wanted me to kiss you just now."

"What? I did *not!*" she said, letting out a soft giggle and shoving him. "I have to get back out there."

She turned to head back out to the gym floor. Nicholas took her hand again and pulled her back to him. She didn't resist. He gently walked her back until she was against the door. He was sure she expected him to *really* kiss her this time, but instead of doing the obvious, he leaned in close to her ear.

"I totally want to kiss you," he whispered. "But I'm not going to. I don't want our first kiss to be in the back room of a gym."

Her breathing shallowed again and he felt her tremble against him. Nicholas pulled back slightly and put his forehead against hers. She bit her lip again and looked into his eyes.

"Let me take you out tonight."

There it was…the moment of truth. He had never in his life even *dreamed* of being so forthright and confident with a girl, certainly not one who looked like Stephanie. For whatever reason, though, his new look, the reaction of the girls on the beach, even Stephanie's reaction just moments before, all combined to give Nicholas a serious confidence boost. Dom told him Stephanie was ungettable. Now, Nicholas had that same ungettable girl pressed up against the wall with her forehead against his. She bit her lip, but couldn't keep from smiling.

"I'd lov—"

"Whoa! What's going on here, Steph?"

Nicholas recognized the booming voice in an instant. He didn't have to turn around to know it was his older brother, Dominick. Dom couldn't recognize him from behind, especially with the darker hair, muscular build, and beach clothes. Nicholas was more of a jeans and t-shirt guy. When Stephanie slid away from him, Nicholas caught her embarrassed expression, but she played it off easily enough.

"Oh," she said, strutting to the front counter and sitting on a stool behind the register. "I was just talking to your brother."

Dominick whirled around as Nicholas turned to face him. His eyes widened as he took Nicholas in. His mouth dropped open, but no words formed on his lips. He just stared and squinted his eyes. Nicholas didn't say a word to help him work through his confusion. The guys with him, Matt and Jordan, both coworkers of Nicholas' at the granite shop, also stood, staring in wide-eyed disbelief. It amused Nicholas and he felt like for once he had the upper hand with them.

"Hey, Dom," he said with a head nod. He strode past his speechless brother and threw his fist out to the other guys, who bumped it with theirs. "What's goin on, guys?"

"Nothin, man," Jordan said. "You joinin up? I didn't know you worked out."

Nicholas shrugged. "I don't."

Dominick caught up. "What happened to you? Did you dye your hair?"

"Nope." Nicholas didn't offer any info. He leaned on the counter and stared back at his brother.

"And your eyes? Are you wearing contacts or something?"

By way of answering, Nicholas decided to push Dom's buttons a little. He shook his head and looked at Stephanie.

"Steph, do I have contacts in my eyes?"

She blushed and sucked her lips into her mouth in a doomed attempt to keep from smiling. The little personal exchange between Stephanie and Nicholas pushed Dominick a little closer to the edge.

"I'm pretty sure he's not wearing contacts, Dom," she said.

Dominick stepped closer to Nicholas. "What's goin on, Nick? What are you doing here? Are you juicin?"

Stephanie looked at Nicholas in shock. She didn't know Nicholas, so she had no reason to be surprised at the new version. It was the only version she'd seen. The stunned look on the guys' faces made Dominick's question valid.

How does he manage to make me look like a jerk even when the girl likes me and clearly doesn't like him?

"Of course not," Nicholas replied. "I don't even go to the gym, Dom. What would I do with steroids?"

Dominick shook his head. "Nick, you don't wake up one day lookin like this. It takes time and work. And you just said you don't work out."

Nicholas shook his head and put a finger up. "I said I don't go to the gym. You don't need all this crap." He waved a hand at some nearby machines. "I train at home."

Dominick smirked. "Yeah right. It would take hundreds of pushups a day to put on that kind of muscle."

"Yep." Nicholas stared Dominick down with his new lush, violet eyes. "Something like that."

Dominick shook his head. "No way."

Nicholas shrugged. "Like I care what you think. Look, the reason I stopped by was to tell you I won't be working at the

51

shop anymore. I have something else going on that will pretty much be full time."

Dominick's expression darkened. "I don't think so, little brother. You work for me. I expect you to be at the shop by nine."

Nicholas looked him in the eye. A slight smirk crept onto his face. Dominick was playing the tough older brother to impress Stephanie. Time to regain the advantage. He shook his head and turned his attention to Stephanie. He took her hand in his.

Leaning on the counter he said over his shoulder, "Sorry, Bro, no can do. I have a day at the beach all planned out."

Dominick's eyes flashed. He glanced at the smirk on Stephanie's face and tried one more time. "The beach? That's your big plan? What are you, some kind of chick or somethin?"

Nicholas rolled his eyes while still looking at Stephanie. She was on the verge of cracking up, and it was clear she enjoyed watching Dominick get worked into a frenzy. Nicholas grazed his fingertips across Stephanie's palm and winked at her.

"What is this?" Dominick jeered. "Are you two a thing all of a sudden? You guys just met five seconds ago and now she's all into you?"

Nicholas shrugged, still staring into Stephanie's eyes. "What difference does it make, Dom?"

Dominick turned to Stephanie. "Seriously, Steph? You and *him*? You know, he's just my punk little brother. *He* knows who the real deal is in this family."

It was a scumbag thing to say, even for an older brother. As his face tightened into a grimace, Nicholas felt Stephanie's hand grip his. She bit her lip seductively and came around the counter to Nicholas' side.

Putting her hand on his chest and leaning into him with her eyes staring dreamily into his, she said over her shoulder to Dominick, "I don't know, Dom. He felt pretty *real* to me up against the wall a few minutes ago."

Nicholas' eyes widened, his mouth dropped open, and he turned bright red. It took a second for everyone listening to catch their breath. Nicholas shot his older brother a triumphant grin. He raised his eyebrows in a what-was-that-you-were-saying kind of way as Dominick stood, blinking at Stephanie's insinuation.

She didn't stop there. She grabbed Nicholas' phone, swiping and tapping like a pro before handing it back to him.

"There," she said. "Now you can text me if there's a problem later."

"Later?"

"Yeah," she replied with a sly grin. "You were asking me out when your brother interrupted, weren't you?"

Chapter 5

"Wow," Stephanie said. "Look at that moon"

Nicholas followed her gaze out over the Atlantic Ocean and into the night sky. The moon shone like a spotlight over the endless expanse of water, casting shadows that rippled with the ever-shifting sea. Nicholas had never understood the fascination people had with the moon until that moment. He wasn't sure if it had something to do with the changes taking place within his body or the fact that he was standing next to a breathtaking woman. Either way, he joined Stephanie in awed silence at the glorious scene.

She leaned on the boardwalk railing and Nicholas stood directly behind, placing his hands on the railing on either side of her. Dinner had been surprisingly intimate. Stephanie stared into his eyes the whole time and he decided purple was his new favorite color. The conversation was light, mostly about their childhoods, families, and jobs, but Nicholas felt an intense connection and fought to control his urge to touch her. He kept his hands to himself throughout dinner, but on the boardwalk, in the light of the moon, he just wanted his arms around her.

Stephanie didn't complain. When Nicholas leaned into her, she leaned back into his chest and pulled his arms around her— arms Nicholas only recently had any reason to be proud of. She tilted her head to the right and rested it on his shoulder, presenting the left side of her soft, slender neck. Nicholas leaned in and breathed in the scent of her perfume. His heart skipped several beats. He had a fleeting fear that it was a heart attack, but felt no pain. Besides, if he was going to die, he could think of no better way to go than with his arms around blonde-haired, blue-eyed perfection.

He grazed his lips against her delicate skin and she let out a soft whimper. He pulled her in closer, tightening his hold. She caressed his arms and sighed contentedly. Nicholas never felt more out of body. With no prior experience with girls, he suddenly oozed confidence and sexuality, like he automatically knew what to do. He wasn't about to complain.

"I feel so safe right now," Stephanie purred.

Nicholas gently pressed his lips to her neck. "You *are* safe, Stephanie. I'd never let anything hurt you."

He sensed her smile and it made him smile against her neck. He squeezed his arms and nuzzled the top of her head, breathing in the flowery scent of her shampoo. It was like a drug he just couldn't get enough of.

"Do you have any idea how good this feels?" She sighed again.

"I know how good *I* feel," Nicholas replied.

He kissed her neck once again. Stephanie leaned back into him and angled her head towards him, her mouth slightly open. Nicholas loosened his hold on her as his lips found hers and she turned around to face him. She slid her hands up his chest and around his neck as he pulled her in close. She stood on her tip toes and they held their first kiss until they both needed air.

Hours later, after he dropped Stephanie at the door to her Ventnor City apartment, Nicholas found himself unwilling to go home. Thoughts of Stephanie's sweet, soft, lips consumed his mind. He parked on a side street between Atlantic and Pacific Avenues in Atlantic City. Rather than go into a casino, he ventured out onto the boardwalk, which at that late hour, was mostly deserted. He returned to the spot he and Stephanie had kissed, and wandered to the railing overlooking the beach. He let his eyes scan the vast expanse of the ocean.

He felt immediately drawn to the sea. It wasn't pulling him in or calling to him, but Nicholas felt like he understood it in a new and deeper way. There were immense forces at work, hidden beneath its depths, and Nicholas knew he was a part of it all. He felt as though he could harness those forces...draw upon them in some way. He knew it had something to do with the recent changes within his body and mind. He felt the power deep within him all the way to the tips of his fingers. He'd barely scratched the surface and itched to understand his mysterious powers.

A tingling at the base of his skull snapped him out of his thoughts. It was a new sensation, but oddly familiar. Nicholas couldn't put his finger on it; he just knew something was wrong. He spun around, and scanned his immediate vicinity for a threat, but saw nothing. He looked back out over the beach. Nothing. He closed his eyes and tried to shake the feeling. It only intensified. He closed his eyes and focused on the sounds of the night. He detected a distressed voice, off in the distance.

Nicholas stared down the beach. Several blocks away, the pier loomed, stretching out into the ocean. Beneath it, among the pillars, where the sand was damp from the previous high-tide, he could barely discern movement. Instincts he'd never felt before, kicked in, telling him, with precision, where the trouble was. He closed his eyes and within a second he stood under the pier behind a huge piling. Now, much closer to the water, Nicholas breathed in the salty air along with the pungent scent of tar from the piling. The crash of the waves filled his ears but he still heard voices on the other side of the piling.

"I have done nothing."

"You're *breathing*," a harsh voice replied. "That's enough, but don't try to tell me you haven't fed. You can't change what you are."

"Not people," the voice pleaded. "I haven't taken a life in a very long time."

"Sure, you haven't."

Nicholas heard the distinct *shing* of metal. He chanced a peek around the piling and saw a tall, rough-looking man with a beard standing over a shorter, well-built man who knelt with his hands tied behind his back and his feet bound with what looked like green vine. Nicholas was surprised at the detail he could make out in the shadows cast by the bright moon. Apparently, his senses were heightened along with his physical strength and abilities.

He considered his options. He didn't feel right about walking away when someone was in trouble. On the other hand, he didn't have all the facts. It looked like some kind of vigilante justice, but Nicholas couldn't let a murder occur right in front of him. At that moment, his spine tingled and felt wrapped in cold. He lost all sense of fear and the pull of danger consumed him. He had to act.

Stepping out from behind the piling, he said, "What seems to be the trouble?"

The man with the sword spun around, dropping into a defensive position and extending the sword out in front of him. He relaxed somewhat when Nicholas didn't match his threatening posture. That Nicholas was unarmed probably didn't hurt either.

"Who are you?" the guy demanded, holding the sword at the ready.

"Me?" Nicholas replied with a shrug. "I'm nobody. I just saw you guys down here and thought someone was in trouble."

The tied-up guy wriggled against his bindings. "He's going to execute me."

"Shut up!" the swordsman commanded, kicking him in the shoulder and knocking him onto his back. Turning back to Nicholas, he said. "You need to turn around and walk away."

"Really?" Nicholas asked, in the calmest voice he could muster, though his heart raced. "And let you kill a man under the pier?"

The guy squinted at him. "Not exactly, son. Not a man."

"No?" Nicholas looked at him with raised eyebrows and a half-smile. "Then what? He's definitely not a lady."

"Not a *human* at all," the man spat. "Now go away and let me finish my business."

"What do you mean, "not a human"?"

The man lowered his sword. "Look, son, there are things in this world that are best kept under the surface; things that if the masses knew existed, would cause panic and chaos. Guys like me are in the business of eliminating these things whenever we find them."

"Things?" Nicholas asked. "What things?"

"Believe me, young man, you don't want to know. Just turn around and walk away."

"I don't think so," Nicholas replied. His heart picked up pace as adrenaline coursed through his veins. He was in harm's way, yet the cold chill kept the fear at bay. He was more alive than ever before. He felt his eyes flicker and for an instant the whole scene was bathed in a silvery glow. His fingertips tingled and the cold pushed ever farther into his being. Looking down, he saw a greenish glow spreading across his palms. The tall man saw it too and Nicholas detected an abrupt mood shift.

"What was that?" the guy asked.

He brought his sword back up as Nicholas instinctively dropped into a defensive posture. He didn't even know what made him move in such a way, but it was so natural he didn't fight it. His body knew what it was doing and he thought he'd better listen to it when faced off against a guy with a sword.

"Your eyes," the man said. "And your hands. I saw that silver flash and the green glow. That's serious demonic behavior. What are you?"

Nicholas didn't respond other than to look down at his hands and then back up in confusion. How was he supposed to explain the inexplicable? He might as well tell the guy he was an alien from. The guy on the ground chuckled.

"You don't know, do you?"

Nicholas glanced his way. "Know what?"

"You're in transition, aren't you?"

Nicholas frowned. "How do yo…?"

"Is that true?" the swordsman demanded. "Were you turned in some way? I might be able to help you with that."

"Too late," the guy on the ground said. "Whatever got him, got him a while ago. The only help you'll give him is the end of your sword, just like me." He turned to Nicholas. "Help me and I'll help you."

"Shut up," the tall man said.

The bound man ignored him. To Nicholas he said, "Just feel it. Feel your connection to the power within. It's right there at the tips of your fingers. It's waiting for you to unlock your brain. It *wants* to be unleashed."

Nicholas had to agree with him there. Whatever it was inside him wanted out, there was no question about that. Nicholas sensed the raw power he wielded, but had no idea how to unleash it. He didn't know what to do, but he was running out of time. The swordsman held back, his face a mask of confusion.

He raised his sword over the bound man's head. "I said, shut up!" he shouted, bringing the sword down hard.

Nicholas moved, darting forward, ramming a shoulder into the taller man, and sending him sprawling on the hard-packed sand. The swordsman sprang up, the sword still in his grasp. Shoulders tensed and teeth bared, he stalked toward Nicholas, who backed up. His eyes widened and he took in every detail of the advancing menace, but he couldn't process the information into anything meaningful. His thoughts jumbled in his head. He had acted on instinct, his thoughts propelling him to save a life, but now his rational side took over. He could think of no way out of the situation other than to run, but he couldn't bring himself to turn his back on someone in trouble.

As the man slashed the sword at Nicholas' head, Nicholas did the only thing he knew he could do. With only a quick thought, he found himself several paces behind the swordsman, who spun around to face him. His eyes blazed.

"Blinking?" he asked in amazement. "So, you really *are* a demon."

Nicholas stared in confusion. *Blinking?*

59

Before Nicholas could reply, the guy on the ground shook his head. "Not yet, but soon." To Nicholas he urged. "Stop *thinking!* Let go of your need to control."

Nicholas closed his eyes, letting out a long slow breath. As he opened his eyes, the guy aimed a sweeping blow at Nicholas' neck. He only had a split second to react, but it was enough. Time slowed as he released control. Darkness consumed him. He felt ice-cold, and lethal; death was inside him. Everything flashed silver once again as the sword swept through the air toward him. Nicholas saw it and easily ducked as the blade sailed over his head. He stretched out his hand and sent a dark violet ball of energy into the chest of his adversary. It exploded all around the man and hurled him backwards. He tumbled to the ground in a heap.

Nicholas stared in disbelief. He looked down at his hands and then at the guy, fearing the worst. He flung himself across the sand, and knelt, placing a tentative hand over the guy's heart. The steady rise and fall of his chest, along with the steady thump under Nicholas' hand confirmed the guy was alive. Nicholas collapsed back and put his head between his knees, taking several deep breaths.

"Well, I can't say I was expecting *that.*"

Nicholas had forgotten about the guy lying there, tied up. The shock of launching a ball of energy from his hand consumed Nicholas' brain for a few seconds and he had to fight to push the cold darkness back. He turned his attention back to the guy on the ground.

"How did you know?"

The guy grinned. "You simply had the look." He bowed slightly. "My name is Xabier Legartza."

"Nicholas Scarlatti. And what is the look?"

"*Nicholas?*" Xabier snickered. "That won't do." He thought for a moment. "I think…Nico." He nodded with a pleased expression on his face. "Yes. Nico works well, don't you think?" Then he grimaced in pain. "I beg your pardon, Nico, but can you please untie me? Vervain burns something fierce."

Nico?

"Vervain?" Nicholas scrunched his nose. "What is that?"

The guy held up his hands, still bound by the rope made of twisted green vines. For the first time, Nicholas saw the slight mist of steam rising from the guy's blackened skin, where the rope was touching it. It looked painful.

"Whoa," Nicholas said. "Hang on." He grabbed the big guy's sword and moved to cut the ropes, but then hesitated. "Wait a minute. I'm not so sure about this. That guy said…"

"That guy," Xabier said, "was going to kill both of us because we aren't like him."

Nicholas inhaled deeply. "What are you? He said you weren't human."

"No." Xabier shrugged. "Not anymore."

Nicholas stared in silence. He wasn't sure what it was about that answer that made Xabier think it was sufficient. Xabier sighed and shook his head, letting his body sink back into the sand.

"Fine," he said. "Whatever. You're just going to kill me anyway. Might as well get on with it."

Nicholas wrinkled his forehead. "Why would I kill you?"

"Why *wouldn't* you?" Xabier chuckled. "Vampires are the enemies of humans, aren't they?"

"*Vampires?*" Nicholas' mouth dropped open. He alternated between amusement and incredulity, his face shifting from one emotion to the next as his mind fought to process yet another insanity. "You're a vampire?"

"That is correct."

Nicholas stared at him for any sign of deceit.

Xabier's face contorted into a scowl. "Who would pretend to be a vampire to a man with a sword?"

Nicholas had no response to Xabier's logic. He shrugged and sliced through the vervain bonds. Xabier rubbed his blackened wrists and sighed in relief. The burns looked pretty severe to Nicholas.

"Should we get you to a hospital?" Nicholas asked.

Xabier laughed. "You're a funny one, Nico. I think I'm going to like you." He held up his wrists for inspection. "These will heal within a few hours." He looked down at his former captor. "Give me the sword, Nico. I'll handle the messy part."

Nicholas shook his head, though something inside him wanted to see the man flayed open. He ignored the sickening thought and held the sword away from Xabier's grasp. "Absolutely not. We're not killing him. And my name isn't Nico."

"Well, it needs to be something other than Nicholas." Xabier looked at him without humor. "Nicholas is your *old* life. Leave all that behind." He ran his tongue over his teeth. "Listen to me…*Nico*. This man is a *hunter*. Hunters are committed to eliminating *all* supernatural creatures from this world. They never stop and never show mercy. Their sole purpose in life is to kill."

"But why?" Nicholas asked.

"What difference does it make?" Xabier replied. "The point is, either we kill them or they kill us."

"That seems a little extreme," Nicholas pointed out.

"It *is* extreme," Xabier agreed. "And so is the fact that this guy knows you exist; he'll be hunting you too."

Nicholas shrugged. "I handled him okay."

"Yeah, kid, you did. Next time he won't be so unprepared. Trust me; you need to tie up loose ends, otherwise they'll haunt you."

Nicholas shook his head. "I can't kill him in cold blood."

"*I* can," Xabier said with his eyebrows raised. He bared his teeth, giving Nicholas his first glimpse of vampire fangs.

It was an impressive sight, and one that removed Nicholas' doubt as to Xabier's identity, but he shook his head and held firm. "Nobody's killing anybody."

Xabier relented. "Since you saved my life, I shall honor your suicidal request."

Chapter 6

Following the incident under the pier, Nicholas decided it would be best not to be around when the hunter came to. Without any idea how long the guy would be out, he scrambled across the beach and up a set of stairs, leading back onto the boardwalk. He turned and squinted back at the shadowy space under the pier, confirming the hunter was still motionless. Nicholas hurried off the boardwalk and back toward his car.

If Nicholas thought Xabier would disappear quickly from his life, he was sorely mistaken. The...*vampire*... followed along, chattering incessantly about friendship, life-debts, and how the Basque never fail to repay their debts. That led into a monologue on Basque loyalty, commitment, and trustworthiness, which lasted for three boardwalk blocks and two more after Nicholas turned off the boardwalk and hurried to Pacific Avenue. The bright lights of the boardwalk gave way to sporadic street lighting. He could have orbed himself out of there, but thought it might be rude. Xabier never knew how close he came to being abandoned.

"What you don't understand, my newfound friend, is when a Basque man befriends a stranger, who then saves the Basque man's life from a relentless hunter, bent on eliminating his kind from existence, he becomes a loyal friend forever."

Nicholas stopped in his tracks and stared at him, struggling to follow Xabier's stream-of-conscious logic. Nicholas was a man of few words…lots of keystrokes, perhaps, but few words. He was content to say nothing at all and remain in the background of life. Why run the risk of embarrassment? His new body changed all that, but he was finding all the social interaction exhausting.

"So," he said to Xabier. He turned and continued toward his car. "We're friends forever now?"

"Precisely," came the quick response. "And I'll have you know that you can do no better for a friend than Xabier Legartza."

"Is that a fact?"

"It is," Xabier replied, without a hint of humor. "It is indeed. Shall I tell you a story to illustrate?" Nicholas sighed as Xabier continued. "I shall indeed tell you a story. Now then, in the year sixteen sixty-three, Louis XIV was king of Fra…"

"*Sixteen sixty-three?*" Nicholas interrupted. "What are you talking about?"

Xabier shrugged. "Ahh! The age-old question!" He leaned slightly toward Nicholas and grinned. "No pun intended. Things are not so simple in the world in which we exist, is it, Nico? Nothing is the same once you turn. You'll see that soon enough. To answer your query, I was born into the natural world in A.D. fifteen-hundred and four, and turned into my current form in fifteen hundred and thirty-nine…"

As he reached for the driver's-side door handle, Nicholas interrupted again. "You're over five *hundred* years old?"

Xabier leaned on the roof of the car across from Nicholas and nodded. "Indeed. Shall I continue my—"

"Stop acting like you didn't just tell me you're a five-hundred-year-old vampire!" Nicholas exploded.

Xabier's eyes widened. He held up his hands to silence Nicholas, and scanned the area. There was no one near enough to have heard. He turned back and regarded Nicholas.

"Why don't you say it a little louder, Nico?"

"Nicholas!" He slammed a hand on the roof of his Maserati. "My name is Nicholas! Please call me Nicholas!"

Xabier pushed his tongue against the inside of his cheek and raised his eyebrows. "You're not Nicholas anymore. I told you; that was your old life. I'll call you Nicholas when you gain three hundred pounds, put on a red suit, and jump down a chimney."

Nicholas stared at him. "Really? Santa Clause? That's your...never mind. This is insane."

He blew out a long breath and climbed into his car. Xabier situated himself in the passenger seat and Nicholas stared at him for a moment in weary disbelief, but the vampire only smiled back at him. Nicholas shook his head, muttering to himself, as he started the car and pulled away from the curb. They drove in silence for several moments as Nicholas steered through traffic toward the Expressway. After several moments, he took the exit for the Parkway and headed south, still shaking his head and mumbling to himself.

"I can't believe vampires are actually real." He shook his head and muttered, "Vampires, angels, demons, mages..."

"Magi," Xabier corrected in a gentle voice.

"Huh?"

"Magi is the plural of mage...not mages." He kept his eyes forward and rubbed his wrists, which looked a great deal better than they had just fifteen minutes prior.

"Whatever," Nicholas shrugged. He glanced at Xabier with curiosity. "So, can you go out in the daylight?"

"*I* can, yes." Xabier held up his left hand and wiggled his ring finger. He wore an old-looking ring with a large, triangle-shaped, black stone perched on top. "Daylight ring. Without one, vampires must stay out of direct sunlight." He grinned at Nicholas' expression of weary confusion. "It isn't like what you see on TV, my friend. Vampire lore is mostly garbage."

Nicholas nodded, suddenly fascinated. He pulled into the parking lot of his condominium complex and stopped in his assigned space. They got out and Xabier followed Nicholas to his front door, but halted at the threshold. Nicholas turned around. It took only a second, but he grinned at the vampire.

"I know this one." He waved his hand in a magnanimous gesture. "You may enter."

Xabier entered. "Not everything is bogus," he said with a chuckle.

"And that stuff you were tied up with? Ver…what was it?"

"Vervain," Xabier corrected. "Another allergy common to vampires. One of nature's cruel jokes."

"It looked like it burned pretty good." Nicholas led the way to the kitchen and pulled two beers from his refrigerator. "How does it feel now?"

Xabier held up his arms. There was no sign of burnt skin. Nicholas scrunched his brow. A little while ago, the burns looked so severe, he was certain Xabier needed medical attention.

"Vampires are fast healers," Xabier explained with an air of superiority. "It's part of what makes us such spectacular creatures to behold." He took a long sip of his beer, draining half the bottle in a single gulp. He studied the bottle with a satisfied sigh.

Nicholas chuckled as he sipped his own bottle. At least Xabier was fun. Maybe a friend who understood wouldn't be such a bad thing. "I guess I have a lot to learn."

Xabier agreed. "Far more than you ever dreamed, my new friend, but fear not! Xabier Legartza is here to help you sort through it all and guide you on your journey."

"*That*…will not be necessary."

Nicholas jumped at the sound of the voice. He whirled around and stared across the room at Zha'riel, who had appeared out of nowhere. The angel of Heaven cast an ominous glare at Xabier.

$$ ꜩ ᴀ ꝫ ψ ɢ $$

"You have your mission, General."

Abdiel, still weak from Azazel's vicious punishment, responded with a sharp nod. He stood tall and proud before his Supreme Commander, or tried to. He couldn't get the scent of his own burnt flesh out of his nostrils even though he was mostly recovered. Lucifer's gaze bore into him like lasers.

Azazel's eyes terrified, mostly due to a well-deserved reputation of lunacy, but Lucifer's eyes carried a different version of sinister. Other fallen angels had followed on that dreadful day, but Lucifer had led. His eyes conveyed the calm presence of command. He represented all the evil in existence. It could all be traced back to him, and his cool exterior only made him more intimidating.

Standing under the massive arched ceiling in Lucifer's throne room, Abdiel shuddered. A chill washed over him and he felt fortunate to be experiencing even that unpleasant sensation. He had an opportunity to redeem himself and return to the good graces of his lord. Azazel had been restrained from his vengeance, but one more failure and Abdiel knew he would be handed over to the maniacal right hand of the master. It was a fate he was unwilling to suffer.

"Yes, Master."

Lucifer glanced over his shoulder at Azazel, who stood behind him and to the right.

"Anything to add, old friend?"

Azazel glared daggers at Abdiel for several seconds. He slowly shook his head, maintaining his glowing white stare. Abdiel wilted under the stress of Azazel's gaze. He kept his eyes forward and maintained a blank expression. There was no need to express an emotion and aggravate the situation.

Lucifer nodded and turned back to Abdiel. "General, you are dismissed. Do *not* disappoint."

A surge of terror coursed through Abdiel's body and he began to shake all over again. He bowed as formally as he could manage and exited the throne room as fast as his jellied legs could carry him. He was no longer concerned with maintaining his dignity. He just wanted to get out.

As he burst through the doors, he saw the same guards from earlier. They stared in awe. They must have heard what Abdiel went through and were amazed that he'd survived Azazel's wrath. He doubted there *were* many survivors. He gathered himself, straightened up tall, and made his way down the long corridor with a little more gravitas than he'd had in the throne room.

"You should have let me destroy him."

Lucifer turned to face Azazel. "And what would that have accomplished? How many of our own must we lose? It's not as if the Father replenishes our losses."

"And what good is a cowardly failure?"

Lucifer chuckled. "I wouldn't go that far, old friend. He could have sent a lackey to tell you the news of Sansata's demise. Instead he faced you and accepted his punishment."

"You call *that* punishment?" Azazel scoffed. "I barely tickled his belly."

Lucifer pursed his lips. "You must learn to see the bigger picture."

Azazel shifted his stance. "You mean the human who robbed my son's essence? He's going to die a lot more slowly than that pathetic general you released."

Lucifer shook his head. At least Azazel's disdain for the human was undisguised. Duplicity was not Azazel's style. Brute force and terror were, but Lucifer needed his number two to keep those impulses in check when it came to the young human. The Dark Lord paced the massive cavern, stopping along the wall to stare at a massive, and ancient, painting. He clasped his hands behind him and breathed deeply as he contemplated the artist's intent, but he didn't forget his friend standing behind him.

"You will *not* destroy him...not yet."

Azazel's eyes flashed silver and he squinted at Lucifer. "What do you intend for him?"

Lucifer shrugged. "If Abdiel brings him here willingly? I intend to turn him for our purposes."

"You think he will choose evil?"

Lucifer grinned. "Who turns down riches and power?" He raised a finger at Azazel. "All it takes is a bit of selfishness and a little push. Remember Jerusalem?"

Azazel shook his head and gave his old friend a bland half-smile. "Yes, you managed to play right into the hand of the Father."

Lucifer raised his eyebrows. There was no one else in existence that he would allow to speak to him so directly, and certainly no one else from whom Lucifer would accept such criticism. Azazel was the only one Lucifer trusted at all…anywhere.

"It got you out of centuries of bondage, did it not?"

Azazel sighed. Following the collapse of Lucifer's rebellion Michael had taken Azazel captive, and stuck him in the supernatural equivalent of solitary confinement for over two thousand years. When God handpicked His "chosen" people, Michael saw a chance to exact retribution on the angel who encouraged his brother's arrogance and disobedience. He bound Azazel to an ancient Israeli ritual.

On the Day of Atonement, it was customary for the Israeli people to send a goat into the wilderness, burdened by the sins of the people for the year. It was called the "scapegoat." What the Israelis did not know, could not have known, was that in addition to their sins, there was another entity tied to that goat…the fallen angel Azazel. Michael even managed to influence a small historic detail. The sacrificial goat was named the Azazel goat.

For over twelve hundred years Azazel was bound to the Israeli scapegoat. Each year Michael would pull him from his ethereal dungeon and lash him to the goat just as the sins of the people were placed upon it. Then, with the burden of all that sin on his shoulders, Azazel would be taken by the goat into the wilderness. They would wander until the goat died or was killed by another animal, after which, Michael's minions would return him to his dungeon for another year. Azazel tried many times to kill the goat and escape, but as the animal was ordained by God Himself for a specific purpose, he failed every time.

Azazel was alone, and tormented by God's holy wrath, but Lucifer had never forgotten his friend. Azazel managed to escape in what Michael must have considered an ironic twist of fate. In the months following the death and resurrection of Jesus, there was confusion in Israel. The supporters of Christ were persecuted and ridiculed. The Jewish traditions and ceremonies continued as they always had, and on the Day of Atonement, the high priest prepared a goat to be sent out into the wilderness. The angels in charge of Azazel lashed him to the goat, as they always had.

When the high priest performed the ritual, Azazel knew something was different. He felt nothing...no weight on his shoulders. *The sins of the people were not on him!* He didn't fully grasp the meaning of it until he realized that he was tethered to nothing more than a goat! It was not a goat ordained by God. When the goat had wandered far enough, Azazel simply pulled his bonds right through the goat's body, slicing it to pieces. Before he could move, he felt the presence of a legion of angels led by Lucifer himself, and Azazel escaped under guard, moments before Heaven's army appeared.

Azazel had to acknowledge he owed his freedom to Lucifer.

"Perhaps it was a touch over-the-top." Lucifer shrugged. "Anyway, I was happy enough to put that little show-off through some real pain."

"A lot of good it did." Azazel shook his head. "Now, He sits at the Father's right hand, and we're all going to have to deal with Him later."

Lucifer waved a dismissive hand. "Worry about that later. For now, we focus on turning this human to our side. I bet he's already doing part of our job for us without even realizing it."

ᛒ ᴀ ⟨ ᴪ ɢ

Zha'riel's eyes continued their piercing glare at Xabier, who suddenly looked like he wanted to throw up. Nicholas stood next to his new friend and regarded Zha'riel like he had two heads. He alternated glances between his two newest acquaintances.

"Do you two know each other?"

The angel ignored Nicholas' query and kept his electric-blue glow focused on the vampire. "You may leave now, Leech," Zha'riel sneered.

He stood in the center of Nicholas' living room, wearing a crisp white button down and a thin black tie. A black suit and gleaming patent leather shoes completed his attire. Nicholas thought he looked like a lawyer. This was the most animated Zha'riel had been in Nicholas' presence, and Nicholas felt like he needed the angel's help, but he didn't get to dictate who was allowed in Nicholas' home.

"*Excuse* me?" Nicholas said. "This is *my* house."

Zha'riel looked at him. "We need to talk...and not around *this*...bloodsucker." He gestured toward Xabier, who gritted his teeth but said nothing.

Nicholas shook his head. "His name's Xabier. And he's my friend...so he stays."

Xabier grinned at that. He leaned on the kitchen counter. "See that, Your Lordship?"

"Do *not* call me that," Zha'riel shot back, his eyes blazing.

"No problem." Xabier grinned mischievously. "*Almighty...*"

"You *blasphemous abomination!*"

The look on Zha'riel's face bordered on murderous. For a moment, Nicholas wondered if he was going to leap across the room and strangle Xabier with his bare hands, which was strange. In the brief time Nicholas had spent with Zha'riel, he was always controlled and refined in his speech and manners. Until that moment, Nicholas wondered if there were any emotions at all inside him.

"I ask again," Nicholas said. Pointing at each of them, he questioned, "Do you two know each other?"

Zha'riel's gaze remained on Xabier, but he responded with a short shake of his head. "No, but I know *what* he is."

Xabier shook his head in disgust. "Just like an angel of the Lord," he spat, "condemning everything they don't like."

"Abominations," Zha'riel countered, "are to *be* condemned."

Xabier shook his head. "Robots," he muttered. "The Creator created a bunch of robotic puppets for Himself."

Zha'riel pointed at Xabier. "We are *not* robots. Neither are we puppets. Angels can choose."

"Sure, you can," Xabier replied with a sardonic grin.

Before Zha'riel could respond, Nicholas broke in.

"Cut the lovers' quarrel for a sec, and let the new guy catch up!" He pointed at Xabier. "I just found out that vampires are real, so I'm already on edge." He turned to Zha'riel. "Explain how an angel of the Lord justifies hating someone he's never met. Aren't you all supposed to be about love and stuff?"

"Yeah," Xabier chuckled. "Show him your halo."

"Shut up!" Nicholas pointed a finger at him. Xabier "zipped" his lips shut and held out his hands in a gesture of surrender. Nicholas turned to Zha'riel and gestured with his thumb. "Let's talk in my room."

As soon as they got behind a closed door, Zha'riel's blazing eyes focused right on Nicholas. He gestured at the door with a definitive finger.

"You cannot be friends with...*that*," he said. "Or any other beings *like* that."

Nicholas leaned on his dresser and raised his eyebrows. "Who do you think you are? You don't get to pick my friends."

Zha'riel cringed. "I am not trying to choose your friends. I am trying to help you remain on a good path."

"By not letting me be friends with someone you object to? What are you? My father?"

Zha'riel shook his head. "No, Nicholas, I am not your father. I am your friend...the *only* friend you have right now."

Nicholas nodded, ultra-seriously. "And you get to tell me who I can and cannot hang out with?"

Zha'riel shook his head again. "I cannot make you do anything, Nicholas. I am here to ensure you do not stray onto a path of evil. And befriending an abomination like that will not help to keep you away from evil."

Nicholas looked at him in disbelief. "You know, I don't know much about God, but I have a hard time believing He demands this kind of prejudice from His...angels."

"It does not matter what you believe." Zha'riel threw up his hands. "You humans…you all think God cares about your opinions. When will you realize, He does not change to match your views of what He *ought* to be?"

Nicholas shrugged. "To be honest, I really don't care about all that." He moved to his bed and sat on the edge. "I'm not ditching Xabier, so if you want to be around me, you need to get used to hanging out with a vampire."

Zha'riel cringed. "He is an affront to the natural order. Has he yet told you how his kind came to be?"

Nicholas shrugged. "Haven't gotten that far yet, but I really don't care. I don't judge people by their ancestors."

Zha'riel raised a finger. "He is *not* a person."

Nicholas shook his head. "You know what I mean." He grinned. "I like the guy. He's funny. And he kinda owes me one, so, he stays."

"No," Zha'riel insisted.

"*Yes*," Nicholas insisted. "And I'm the only one who gets a vote, so shut up or piss off."

Zha'riel peered at the closet behind Nicholas. He frowned at the door, which was slightly ajar. He opened it. Looking down at the pile of cash, he grimaced. "Already," he muttered, shaking his head in sadness.

"What?" Nicholas asked. "Already what?"

"You are already using your powers for personal selfish gain." Zha'riel closed the closet and looked seriously at Nicholas. "You cannot do this, Nicholas. You are on dangerous ground. You can't even see it, can you? You have been given a gift, but it is a gift that can corrupt your soul."

"What good is a gift like this if I can't use it?"

"That is not what it is for," Zha'riel hissed in a harsh tone. "Your gift is to be used in the service of good."

"Really?" Nicholas asked. "I never signed that agreement, so forgive me if I don't just take every piece of advice you offer."

"Forgiveness is for God alone."

"It's a figure of speech," Nicholas said, rolling his eyes. "Geez! Xabier is right. You're like a robot, saying everything you're supposed to say."

Zha'riel glowered at him. "You mistake my loyalty to my father for a lack of will. You think the Almighty thinks for us and then makes us think what *He* thinks." He gritted his teeth and clenched his jaw in barely controlled anger. "He does not. Angels can rebel just as easily as humans. How do you think evil first became?"

Nicholas held up his hands. "Hey, man. I didn't mean anything by it. I was just kidding with you." He punched Zha'riel lightly on the shoulder. "You need to loosen up, bud. Come on out in the living room with us and have a few drinks. We'll chill for a while and figure it all out later."

Zha'riel sighed. "I suppose I must be civil…for *your* sake."

Nicholas laughed. "That's the spirit!" He hopped off his bed, threw an arm around Zha'riel's shoulders, guiding him out of the room. "So…this is crazy, huh? An angel, a vampire, and a human…Hey, that's sounds like the beginning of a joke…"

Chapter 7

Xabier looked at the pile of cash on the floor of Nicholas' living room. "So, including what you've banked, how much have you gotten so far?"

"A little over ten million."

Nicholas stretched out on his couch while Zha'riel sat at the kitchen table. The open floor plan allowed him to sit on the opposite side of the room from Xabier yet still be in the conversation. It hadn't taken long for the subject of money to come up, and Nicholas revealed to Xabier how he had come into his new fortune. His stomach twisted a little as a tinge of guilt struck. He was a thief. Why was he not *consumed* with guilt? Why was he able to push those thoughts away?

Xabier chuckled, pulling Nicholas from his introspection. "Chicken feed, my friend."

"That's what was there," Nicholas shrugged. "So that's what I got."

Xabier nodded. "Only because you didn't know where to look for *real* money." He tipped another bottle of beer.

"Ten million in cash isn't real money?" Nicholas smirked. He crossed his legs at the ankles and closed his eyes.

"Not compared to *hundreds* of millions." Xabier stood up and went to the fridge for another beer. He tossed the cap in the trash and leaned against the kitchen counter. "I know where…"

"This is ridiculous," Zha'riel interrupted. "Nicholas has already acted selfishly. Why do you push him to even greater selfishness?"

Xabier waved a hand. "Oh, calm down, my angelic *semi-*friend. I'm not talking about stealing anything from good, honest people."

Nicholas' interest was piqued. Why was that? Was ten million not enough? The idea of stealing more money was troubling enough, but even more so was the adrenaline burst the mere *thought* of dong wrong brought him. He couldn't help himself. "What do you have in mind?"

"You consider further treachery, Nicholas?" Zha'riel stared in disbelief. "Do you not realize the danger to your soul?"

"I think I can handle it," Nicholas replied. Turning to Xabier, he said, "So…where do we score hundreds of millions?"

Xabier raised his eyebrows. "In Colombia."

Nicholas scrunched his nose. "What's in Colombia?"

"Drugs," muttered Zha'riel. He turned to Xabier. "You want Nicholas to rob the drug cartels."

Xabier shrugged. "They have the cash, my glorious friend."

"Is it even possible?" Nicholas asked, pulling himself up from his reclined position. The idea of hundreds of millions of dollars appealed to him. The idea of hurting drug dealers appealed to him even more. A cold coil in his gut began to wind its way around his spine.

"Why not?" Xabier spread his hands. "They deal in cash…*lots* of cash. There are piles and piles of it stashed in all their headquarters. I've seen it…even helped myself from time to time."

He looked from Nicholas to Zha'riel, grinning with raised eyebrows and nodding. For a little while nothing was said. They all stood and contemplated Xabier's proposal. The look on Zha'riel's face told him all he needed to know about the angel's opinion. Nicholas wasn't worried about the path of darkness, or whatever Zha'riel fretted about. He *was* interested in taking down a drug cartel. That had to be a worthwhile endeavor.

"So," Xabier shrugged. "What do you think?"

Nicholas tilted his head. "It's interesting."

"Nicholas," Zha'riel sighed.

With a hand extended to shut up Zha'riel, Nicholas said to Xabier, "How dangerous is it?"

"Well," Xabier said. "For most people, it would be a suicide mission, but for a man who can orb, a man with the power to fight off unlimited numbers of men? A guy like that could do it...with a little help from his vampire buddy."

Zha'riel shook his head. "Nicholas, you might have to kill people to get away with this. Think about that."

Xabier pointed. "Yes, angel-eyes, but what *kind* of people? We're talking about the real scum of this world: drug dealers. There can be nothing wrong with killing drug dealers. I say it's a service to humanity."

Nicholas shook his head. "I don't think I can't just run in and start killing guys...even bad guys." But something deep inside him told Nicholas he could...and should.

Xabier shrugged. "It was just a thought." He wrinkled his forehead. "But do you really think you can avoid it at this point?"

"Avoid what?"

"Do you really think you can avoid violence? Those powers aren't invisible to the supernatural world, you know. Using them can draw attention. The authorities may not be able to figure out how your robberies happen, but anyone who knows what to look for could figure it out in no time." He spread his hands. "Violence is your new reality, Nico."

Zha'riel frowned. "Why does he call you 'Nico?'"

Nicholas shrugged. "He thinks I need to..."

"It's because he is a new creature," Xabier announced. "He needs to accept his new reality. He is no longer Nicholas Scarlatti. The sooner he realizes that fact; the sooner he can master his new self." He clapped Zha'riel on the shoulder as he passed by. "Your God always changed His people's names when He chose them, didn't he?" The angel gritted his teeth as Nicholas stifled a laugh.

"As reckless and foolish as your vampire friend is," Zha'riel said, ignoring Xabier's scriptural reference, "he is correct about one thing. You cannot use these powers and remain anonymous to the supernatural world. The chakra draw on this location alone will draw attention. Since your chakra draw is new, you are certain to garner curiosity."

"Chakra..." Nicholas squinted. "Explain that to me. It's like the Force, right?"

"Hahaha!" Xabier howled. "You people and your movies!" He turned to Zha'riel. "They skate so close to the truth sometimes, don't they?"

"Your art often reveals things you innately understand," Zha'riel explained. "Chakra is accurately represented in your Star Wars movies...at least insofar as it is accessed by a variety of beings with a range of powers. It binds the universe, connecting all life, and therefore making everything interdependent."

Nicholas nodded and licked his lips. "So, a 'disturbance in the Force' happens every time I use my powers? And others can feel it?"

"Precisely," replied Zha'riel, rising from his chair. "That is why your use of it must be carefully controlled and minimized until you learn to defend yourself."

He let that sink in for a second or two before continuing. "Nicholas, taking in the essence of good and evil alike means two things: First, you are a target for hunters, just like any supernatural being. That is just something you must deal with. Second, both sides would like to turn you into their ally. Admittedly, I am here to guide you to good, but you need to understand that evil will pursue you, and those beings generally don't care who they hurt or kill to get what they want."

Nicholas was quiet. The weight fell heavily upon his shoulders and he slumped. Xabier stood by him and put a hand on his shoulder.

"Do not worry, my new friend. The powers within you are more than enough to keep you safe. We just need to learn how to access them and control them. Then you'll be unstoppable."

"He does not need to be unstoppable, just safe," Zha'riel interjected.

"Whatever, my white-winged friend." Xabier waved a hand. "The point is we need to get this man in touch with his abilities as soon as possible."

Zha'riel shook his head. "I cannot be involved with the use of demonic powers."

Xabier rolled his eyes. "Of course not, Your Hypocriteness. Why don't you just hang around and complain about everything instead?"

"Silence, peon, before I scatter pieces of your frail corpse all around this planet."

"Both of you shut up," Nicholas said. "We don't have time for this nonsense. Let's get to work. Zha'riel, let's focus on the mage powers..."

$$\text{Ђ}\, A\, \check{\xi}\, \psi\, G$$

Abdiel addressed his audience, a cohort of demon soldiers. "This human is not to be harmed. For the time being, he leads a charmed life until the throne room decides his fate. Our mission is to identify, observe, and then develop a strategy to win him over. Is that understood?"

A cohort was a group of at least one hundred demons, ranging in rank. They all shouted their acknowledgment of the General's instructions. This particular cohort was one hundred fifty-seven strong, overseen by Lord Sarkryal, who served under Captain Ja'roaal. The captain was responsible for Lord Sarkryal along with nine other Lords and cohorts making up an entire legion of over six thousand demon soldiers. Both were present and listened in silence to Abdiel's instructions.

After Abdiel dismissed the cohort, he turned to the two officers. "No mistakes," he said with a menacing glare. "No excuses. I want this man identified, and I want to know everything about him by the end of the week."

Abdiel knew he was asking a lot, but he also knew he was not operating on his own timeline or any other reasonable timeline. He was beholden to Lucifer's timeline, and possibly Azazel's. He needed instant results. That meant his team needed to operate with a sense of urgency.

"General," Captain Ja'roaal asked. "May I ask what is so important about this human? We are allocating vast resources to a simple search and observe operation."

"Yes, Captain," Abdiel said, careful that his even tone not betray his desperation. "We are. The reason is simple. This human is responsible for the death of our prince."

"Sansata?" Ja'roaal lowered his tone in reverence. "We're on a search mission for Prince Sansata's slayer?"

"That is correct, Captain," Abdiel confirmed. "And you would both do well to remember, Sansata happens to be the eldest son of our master's closest confidant."

He didn't need to elaborate. They both understood the implications. Azazel's reputation was legendary. The entire underworld stood in awe of the white-eyed lieutenant of their master. They also trembled in fear of his wrath.

"Needless to say," Abdiel continued, "the throne room has a very...*personal*...interest in this operation. Ensure your team understands, failure will be disastrous for all of us, Lord Sarkryal."

"Of course, General. We will not fail you."

Abdiel nodded. "Excellent. I'll leave you to your mission. Keep me appraised of any developments, no matter how small or insignificant."

Ҍ А Ӟ Ψ Ϛ

"Close your eyes and focus on your heartbeat."

Zha'riel circled Nicholas, his hands clasped behind his back. Nicholas stood in the middle of a clearing, deep in the vast South Jersey pinelands. It was lesson one, and he was already frustrated. Zha'riel's expression never changed as he directed Nicholas. The countless failures didn't seem to faze him as they did Nicholas.

"Feel the life energy pulse through your veins. You need to be in tune with the natural world. That starts with being in tune with your own body and mind."

Nicholas closed his eyes and breathed deeply, searching for the pulsing energy within his body. He continued to breathe in an even tempo. His heartrate slowed and his muscles relaxed. He felt his mind begin to focus and Zha'riel's calm monotone helped him sink into a trance-like state and within moments he zeroed in on a pulsing sensation coursing throughout his body.

"I think I have it," he murmured.

"Good," Zha'riel approved. "Now, follow it all the way from its source to the extremes of your body and all the way back. Feel the energy, the chakras, flow through you."

"So, it's in my blood?" Nicholas questioned in a soft tone.

"Not *just* in your blood," Zha'riel replied. "It's in *everything*. Once you find it in your blood it will be easier to identify it everywhere else."

Nicholas nodded and continued to breathe evenly. He followed the course of pulsating blood all throughout his body and back to his heart. He felt the energy within and imagined he could actually see it.

Xabier, sitting on a fallen tree off to the side, began to get impatient. "This isn't working."

"Silence!" Zha'riel commanded.

Xabier shook his head and paced back and forth, muttering about sneaky, dishonest, no account angels and glaring off and on at Zha'riel, who continued to speak in his soothing monotone, calmly guiding Nicholas through the basics of locating and accessing the chakra within himself.

"Do you feel it, Nicholas?"

Nicholas didn't answer right away. He stood in stunned disbelief. His mind was wide open; at least, that was how it felt. He didn't simply *feel* chakra, he *saw* it. At first, he glimpsed it sporadically, as it flowed through his body. It wasn't long before he could spot it at will and follow its path. He watched it flow outward from his extremities and into every living thing. He was indeed connected to it all. Without thinking about it, he spread his arms. Wind kicked up around him.

Zha'riel smiled. "You have found your center. Mattaeus was a very powerful mage. He had the powers of the *elements* at his disposal."

"The elements," Nicholas repeated.

"Yes, Nicholas," Zha'riel said. "Consider wind, water, fire, earth. You are limited only by your imagination and, of course, by your strength in commanding chakra."

Nicholas gradually felt himself gain some measure of control over his abilities. He could raise and lower the wind force he had called into action. Zha'riel had him direct the wind to a specific target they'd set up ten yards away, swinging from a tree limb. It took several frustrating tries, but Nicholas finally hit it with a strong gust that, had it been a person, would have knocked them clean off their feet.

"Wow!" Nicholas exclaimed. "That was pretty awesome."

He blinked his eyes several times and looked back at Xabier, who grinned his approval.

"Well done, Nico!" he shouted. "Very well done."

Nicholas worked for several hours until he was confident he could call on several powers at will. Toward the end of their session, he conjured one final assault on the target when he felt a sudden surge of a power he didn't quite recognize, but it felt familiar and right. He went with the cold surge and felt the crackling in his fingers. He smelled the ozone fill the air around him. Without warning, he flung both hands out in front of him and toward the target.

Out of his fingers shot dazzling violet bolts of energy which struck the target violently, throwing it backward and setting it aflame within seconds. The rope holding it to the limb burned through and the target dropped to the ground. The flames spread along the fallen leaves and branches. Before Zha'riel or Xabier could react, Nicholas doused the spreading flames with a blast of water summoned from thin air, causing massive sparks at first, but ultimately putting out the fire before it could spread.

For a moment, no one spoke. Zha'riel looked at Xabier, who stood speechless, but he was clearly excited at the unexpected ability. The angel shook his head and sighed.

"Nicholas," he tried. "You must refrain from drawing on your dark powers."

"What?" Xabier was incredulous. "You can't be serious. Did you see how much control he had without even trying?"

Zha'riel took a breath. "Nicholas, you need to understand, the draw toward evil is increased when you succumb to the use of dark powers."

"Rubbish!" exclaimed Xabier. "Powers are just that…powers. They are not inherently evil, any more than words are. It's all how in they are used and applied. You can use your powers for good or evil, Nicholas, just like I can."

Nicholas looked at Zha'riel. "That makes sense, doesn't it?"

Zha'riel nodded in resignation. "Technically…yes. However, those powers are part of an essence…an essence that is purely evil. That evil is within you now. The more you allow it to rear its head, the more susceptible you are to its draw."

Nicholas nodded in understanding. "I think I can handle it. Like Xabi said, it's how I choose to use the powers that will make the difference. I'll just have to be careful not to give in to evil temptations."

Zha'riel sighed. "If only it were that easy."

Chapter 8

"This is going to be superb!"

Xabier slapped his knee and leaned forward on Nicholas' ratty brown couch. He sipped expensive Scotch from a Styrofoam cup. Nicholas didn't have glassware. He always drank water, soda, or beer, straight from the bottle. A disbelieving Xabier had shaken his head and found the Styrofoam tucked way back in an upper cabinet.

Nicholas chucked at Xabier's boyish excitement as he scraped his dinner plate and rinsed it in the sink. In a matter of a couple weeks, Nicholas had mastered the basics of his mage powers. He was able to summon the elements to defend himself. Xabier was convinced Nicholas was prepared to take on any human who stood in their way. Zha'riel was always quick to point out, the human threat was the least of Nicholas' concerns.

In the two weeks since Zha'riel began training Nicholas, everything stayed quiet. There was no indication of a supernatural threat. They were always careful to change up their practice locations and never spent more than an hour or two in one location. Nicholas refrained from using his magic at home. Visions of Sansata's black eyes and the crackling between his fingers haunted him enough to take Zha'riel's dark magic warnings seriously, but the Colombian thing was still on. It was an opportunity to unleash his powers in a far-away place.

"Ready to make a plan?" Nicholas asked as he put the plate in the dishwasher. He was anxious to put his powers to work.

"I say yes," Xabier shook his fist with enthusiasm. "Let's do it."

Nicholas settled into the recliner and held out his hand for a fist bump, which the two had begun doing, mostly because it annoyed Zha'riel. Xabier bumped it and chuckled. He grabbed the TV remote and tapped the power button as he stretched out and found a movie to watch.

"We should think about building a new house," he suggested as he sipped more Scotch. "We need privacy, Nico." He examined his cup. "And real glasses."

Nicholas nodded. "Well, after Colombia, we'll certainly have the cash for it."

"The millions you already stole aren't enough?" Zha'riel broke in. "You still intend to pursue this greed-filled scheme?"

Nicholas chuckled. "Yep. I think we all deserve a little comfort. We'll get this money, find a few hundred acres of woodland, and build the perfect house." He rubbed his hands together in glee. "Plus, I think it's time we joined the War on Drugs."

Xabier laughed so hard he choked on his Scotch.

Zha'riel stared at him for several seconds. "You need to start taking this more seriously, Nicholas. They will be coming for you."

Nicholas shrugged in exasperation. "But why? You keep saying that but you never explain it!"

Zha'riel gave him a look that suggested he couldn't believe Nicholas was so dense. "Do you think Sansata had no friends? No family? Who do you think he served?"

Nicholas sighed. "Do I want to know the answers to those questions?"

Xabier shook his head without taking his eyes off the TV. "Probably not. I've heard the name, Sansata, Nico, and it's never connected with anything pleasant."

Zha'riel nodded. "He is absolutely right, but that is not even the worst of it. Sansata was the eldest son of Azazel."

Xabier gasped. He flicked the TV off and sat up, staring at Zha'riel. Nicholas looked at him and then back at Zha'riel, his eyes widening at Xabier's reaction. His heart began to race.

"W-Who is Azazel?"

Zha'riel shrugged and looked at Xabier. "Why not let your pet answer?"

Xabier ignored the barb and shook his head. It took several attempts before he got words to form in his mouth. "Nico…Azazel is…oh, man…he's Lucifer's right hand."

Zha'riel nodded. "Actually, the two are best friends, since before the fall."

"*Lucifer?*" Nicholas stared at him. "Like…as in, the *Devil?*"

Xabier nodded with his head in his hands. "Satan Himself. Holy sh…"

"You two are telling me I killed the son of the *Devil's best friend?*" Nicholas exploded.

Xabier put his head back against the wall. "Something like that."

"And you're just *now* getting around to this little nugget?" Nicholas stared incredulously at him for several seconds before turning to Zha'riel. "Tell me this is some kind of sicko heavenly joke."

"I'm sorry, Nicholas, but that is not the worst of it."

Nicholas rolled his eyes. "What could possibly be worse than making an enemy of the closest friend of evil personified?"

Xabier pursed his lips. "It would be worse if the friend of the personification of evil also happened to be a homicidal maniac who liked to torture his enemies to death."

Nicholas stared at him with renewed incredulity. "Yeah," he muttered. "I can see how that would be way worse." He stood and looked at Zha'riel. "This lunatic is after me?"

Zha'riel shrugged. "The underworld has been quiet lately. I expect Lucifer knows about you by now. He will seek you out and try to turn you. I believe Azazel is restrained by Lucifer, but I guarantee that will only last as long as he thinks you can be turned."

Nicholas collapsed on the couch next to Xabier. "Wonderful."

Xabier shook his head, but then grinned. "Look, Nico, this is all the more reason to act quickly with these cartel missions. We get ourselves squared away in a great property and we build a fortress. Then we figure out how to fend off a maniac fallen angel."

Before Nicholas could reply, there was a knock at the door and they all fell silent. Nicholas stared at the door and wondered if it was Azazel standing on the other side. Would he knock? Or maybe Lucifer…the Devil himself…was on the other side. Another knock and this time a voice called out.

"Come on, Nick, open up! I can see your fancy new ride out here. I know you're home!"

Nicholas breathed a sigh of relief. "It's my brother, Dom."

He got up and went to the door. "He doesn't know about any of this, so try to act…human."

When Nicholas opened the door, Dominick pushed his way past. "We need to talk, Nick."

Nicholas closed the door. "Won't you come in?" he offered, with a sardonic roll of his eyes.

"Shut up," Dominick shot back. Then he noticed Nicholas' guests. "Who're they?"

"They're my friends," Nicholas replied evenly. "What do you want, Dom?"

Dominick glanced at Zha'riel and Xabier with suspicion before turning back to his brother. "It's time for you to come back to work, Nick."

"No."

Dominick stared at him. "That's it? Just no? You think you can just up and quit on me without any notice at all?"

Nicholas shook his head. "Look, I'm sorry about that, but it is what it is. I have too much going on right now. I'm not coming back."

"Yes," Dominick insisted. "You are."

Xabier grunted and tried to hide his smile. Dominick caught the movement.

"Something funny, pal?"

Xabier chuckled out loud and shook his head. "Not at all, *friend.*"

Nicholas brought Dominick back to the conversation at hand. "Dom, it just isn't going to happen."

"Great, Nick," Dominick complained. "We're getting busy and you just up and bail on me. That's not right. Dad built this up from…"

"From nothing." Nicholas rolled his eyes. "I've heard it all before. I know it sucks, and I know Dad would have wanted the two of us to keep it going, but I just don't want to do it anymore. I'm sorry, Dom, but I can't pass up the money I'm making right now."

Dominick stared at him for a moment. "You know, you're acting weird. First you quit on me. Then you show up at the gym looking all jacked. Then you hook up with Stephanie."

Nicholas waited as Dominick paused his little rant. "Yeaaah?"

Dominick shrugged. "So, what's up with all that?"

Nicholas spread his hands. "Nothing. What difference does it make anyway? You never cared before what I was up to. Why are you so interested now? Is it because of Stephanie?"

Though he had been busy training for the past two weeks, Nicholas had made time to see Stephanie. He didn't know how to explain his situation to her, and Zha'riel was clear that he shouldn't be dragging innocents into his life. The danger was too great, but Nicholas couldn't bring himself to break it off.

"No," Dominick insisted. "It's just you used to be the complete opposite of what you are now. I'm just wondering when all these changes happened."

Xabier chuckled again, drawing glares from both Scarlatti brothers. Dominick looked at Nicholas and jerked his head in Xabier's direction.

"What's with that guy?"

Nicholas shrugged. "He's just a clown. Don't worry about him." He sighed. "Look, Dom, we're kinda in the middle of some things right now."

Dominick looked at him for several seconds before shrugging and nodding. "Yeah, whatever, Nick. I just wanted to make sure you were okay."

"I'm fine," Nicholas insisted walking him to the door. "Give me a call later or something."

After Dominick drove off, Zha'riel looked at Nicholas seriously. "You must keep your distance from your family for a while. They could be in danger."

Nicholas' eyes widened. "Dom's all the family I have. Do you think they'd go after him?"

"I think they're evil, Nicholas," Zha'riel said. "I think they'd do whatever it took to get revenge or to get your attention. It's better not to present an easy target. People you care about are at risk. The closer you are to them, the more likely it is they will be targeted."

As much as he loved his brother, the truth was, Dominick was in danger. Even Nicholas could see that. There was no way he could protect Dom from his enemies. He wondered if he could even protect himself. Visions of Stephanie danced in his mind.

Nicholas closed his eyes. He grabbed his car keys. "I need to get outta here."

ᛒ ᴀ ᖚ ψ ᘓ

Nicholas sat on Stephanie's soft, sectional couch, his arms wrapped around her as they watched whatever chick flick she'd put in an hour ago. Nicholas couldn't have been any happier with his life…sort of. Yes, he was quite possibly being hunted by the most powerful force of evil in the universe. Yes, he was potentially putting his brother at risk. Yes, he was putting Stephanie at risk. No, he didn't know what to do about it. He could back off Stephanie, but what if she was already a target? He would be leaving her defenseless. So, his happiness was hampered by the fact that there was a great deal of uncertainty.

Everything else was going perfectly. He was progressing rapidly in his skills. He and Xabier had a plan to take a big score from the drug cartels. Instead of one score, they decided to hit all five major cartels in one night. It would take careful planning and Nicholas honing his skills. That meant more training. He had plenty of money anyway for the time being. Ten million was more than enough to keep them comfortable while he worked on accessing and controlling his powers.

Perhaps the right thing to do was leave and never look back. That would be the easiest way to ensure Stephanie's safety, but he couldn't bring himself to do it. Cutting her loose would mean leaving her out there without anyone who understood the threat against her. What if the demons already knew who he was and were already watching them? Leaving her alone would serve her up to them on a silver platter. The more he thought about the possibilities, the more he believed staying put was his only option.

Stephanie shifted in his arms. Her soft voice cut through his anxious thoughts. "Nick? What's going on?"

"What?" Nicholas blinked. "Hmm?"

She giggled. "You kinda zoned out. Are you okay?"

He squeezed his arms around her, pulling her tight against his chest. "I'm fine, girlie. Just thinking."

"Not a good idea," she teased. "Try to leave the thinking to those of us who are better equipped for it."

He raised his eyebrows. "Oh really?" He squeezed her tighter. "Did my girlfriend, whom I love with all my heart, just call me stupid?"

He tickled her a little and she squirmed. When he released her, she turned to him, a serious look on her face and tears brimming in her eyes.

"What did you say?"

Nicholas wrinkled his forehead. "*I* didn't say anything. *You* called me stupid."

"No," she whispered, reaching out and touching his cheek. "You said you love me."

Nicholas frowned. "I did?"

Stephanie nodded seriously. "You definitely did. I heard you clearly."

"Hmm." Nicholas pursed his lips and stared at the wall above the couch. The soft green color was comforting. Her place felt like home. "Are you sure? Cause that doesn't sound like me."

She leaned in and planted a firm kiss on the lips. "Does that refresh your memory, wise guy?"

Nicholas thought for a moment before shaking his head. "Not really. Maybe you should try that again."

And she did. And again and again and again. Finally, she broke away and pressed her forehead to his.

"Nicholas," she said, her breath coming in short gasps As soon as his eyes met hers, she continued. "I love you so much. You make me so happy."

Words failed him. His throat tightened and his eyes watered. He could never walk away from her. She was everything to him. Now that their feelings were expressed, he felt like he had to be honest. Zha'riel had warned him against discussing magic with humans, but Nicholas owed Stephanie the truth. She deserved the opportunity to decide for herself based on the facts.

He took her hands before she could say anything further. "Listen," he said. "Before we go any further, you need to know some things about me."

"Okay," she said slowly, clearly fearing the worst. "What is it? Do you have a kid? You're not married, are you? Oh, God! Tell me you're not married!"

"Shhh." Nicholas rubbed her wrists with his thumbs. "Calm down, Steph. It's nothing like that, but it is serious and might change the way you feel about us." He chuckled. "And don't bother trying to guess because you'll never be able to in a million years."

She took a breath. Nicholas could see the doubt in her eyes. He didn't want her to think he was a typical guy, destined to disappoint her.

"Okay, tell me," she said, resignation in her voice.

Nicholas blew out a breath he hadn't realized he'd been holding and tried to determine how he was going to explain everything that had happened to him. He stood and paced the hardwood floor. He ran his fingers over the mantle of the electric fireplace in the corner and examined a picture of Stephanie and her parents in a simple, metal frame. She was smiling in the picture. He wanted her to smile at him now.

"All right, look," he began, replacing the picture. "All the stuff Dom said about me? It was all true."

She looked at him with a scrunched forehead. "Um…okay."

The anxiety in her eyes broke Nicholas' heart "Until right before I met you, I was a computer geek with hardly any friends. I was lousy with girls, and definitely *not* built like this."

Stephanie shook her head and wrinkled her brow. "I don't understand. What are you telling me?"

Nicholas pinched the bridge of his nose, squeezing his eyes shut. How was he going to tell her this and have her believe it?

"Okay," he said, putting his hands firmly on his knees and looking her right in the eyes. "You won't believe any of this, but what I'm about to tell you is one hundred percent true."

Stephanie nodded. "Okay."

"One night, a few days before we met, I was at the granite yard, battening down the slabs. It was the night of the hurricane. It was pouring and really windy. I saw a guy lying face down near the shop…"

He told Stephanie everything he could remember about that night, and to his surprise, she listened without so much as a snicker. It gave him hope. At least she was willing to hear him out before kicking his butt out the door. Maybe she just wanted to see how crazy the story got.

"Now there are a lot of…beings, I guess…trying to find me because I have all these powers and they want me on their side in their stupid supernatural war." He shrugged and shook his head. "Should I leave now?"

Stephanie shook her head. "This is crazy, right?"

"Believe me." Nicholas nodded. "I know *exactly* how crazy it all sounds. But it's true."

"Nicholas," she said. "I don't know what to…"

He grabbed her hand. "Can I show you?"

She nodded, here face a mask of uncertainty. He held her hand and a moment later they were in her kitchen. Stephanie instantly pulled her hands away and backed up several feet until she bumped up against her refrigerator, sending a couple magnets clattering to the ground. Her eyes were wide as saucers and her bottom lip quivered. Nicholas reached out to gently take her hand. She let him pull her close so he could steady her.

"Sorry about that," he said. "I probably should have warned you, but really…would you have believed me?"

She shook her head, her eyes still open wide. Nicholas backed up a few feet and held out his palms. He curled his fingers and a ball of greenish fire appeared in his hand. When he clenched his fist, the flame disappeared. He blew her hair from across the room with his wind ability. He refrained from calling down snow or water considering he was standing in her kitchen. Stephanie stood spellbound, obviously trying to wrap her head around what she was witnessing.

Nicholas could see she was a little shaken, but she hadn't thrown him out yet and didn't seem completely petrified. Although…now that he was watching more closely, he did notice a slight tremble in her hands and the anxiety lining her face. She clenched and unclenched her hands, stopping only when she rubbed them together. He was hoping she'd be a touch more enthralled than she appeared.

"Steph?" he tried. "Are you okay?"

She nodded with vacant eyes. "I-I-I d-d-don't kn-know," she stammered. "This is s-s-so…unbelievable."

Nicholas reached for her, but she jerked back. "D-don't" she squeaked, stepping back and holding her hands out in front of her. "Just give me a minute. I need to think."

Nicholas backed off and leaned against the stove. It hurt his heart to think Stephanie might be afraid of him, but he understood. "That's okay, Steph. Take your time. I can hardly believe it myself half the time."

Stephanie looked at him. "This is…I mean, I don't know how to…" She sighed in exasperation. "How is this supposed to work, Nick?"

Nicholas took a breath. "Well...what has to change? Things were fine a few minutes ago when you didn't know all this. It can be normal. At least, it can *appear* normal."

She shrugged, but said nothing.

"Look, Steph. The real question is how do you feel about me? A little while ago you said you loved me. I know I love you. If you still have those feelings about me..."

"I said that when I didn't really know you."

"Nah." Nicholas waved a hand. "You knew me. You knew who I was. Maybe not *what* I was, but definitely *who* I was. And I'm still that same guy."

He moved closer and glided his fingertips along her jawline. That very moment he felt a major tingling in his spine and a chill spread throughout his body. A sudden fearful thought struck him. He knew what he had to do. "I'm crazy about you, Steph. But maybe it's better...*safer*...if I just leave."

"What?" She stared at him, mouth agape and eyes wide as saucers. "What do you mean, safer?"

Nicholas wrung his hands and gritted his teeth. "Steph, what you just witnessed...there's a whole world out there full of things you would never have believed existed. I've only just gotten a glimpse so far, but what I've seen...what I've heard...terrifies me."

"And now you want to leave me?"

"I think I already have enemies I don't even know about. I think I'm being selfish for being here. I thought I could keep you safe by keeping you close, but now I don't think anything I do could keep you safe."

He went to the window and peered between the venetian blinds. He wasn't even sure what he was looking for, but he felt like something was out there...something not human. He had no reason other than a feeling in his bones, but Zha'riel had made it a point more than once to tell him to trust his feelings. They could be all he had to go on.

Then he saw it. It was little more than a flicker in the night, but his eyes were much sharper than ever before. He stared at the spot in the shadows where he saw the reflected light. A shape began to appear. It was barely discernible, but it was there. It looked to be a man, just standing there and watching the front entrance to Stephanie's apartment.

"Crap," he muttered.

"What?" Stephanie asked. "Is someone out there?"

"Someone," Nicholas confirmed. "Or some*thing*." He looked back at her and his stomach lurched. "I'm sorry, baby. This is my fault."

She smiled at him, but her eyes revealed real fear. "Just don't leave me, okay?"

He nodded, still looking at the spy across the street. Part of him wanted to go out there and confront whoever it was. He could orb himself to a spot right behind the guy and surprise him, but he had no idea what he was up against. The more pressing matter in his mind was getting Stephanie to safety. He could only think of one place.

Turning back to her he said, "Go pack some clothes. I'm taking you to my place."

She nodded without a word and went to her room. Nicholas knew Zha'riel would be angry. He wasn't supposed to be involved with anyone, much less get himself into a romantic relationship. The angel was clear about that, but Nicholas would just have to deal with the impending angelic lecture. Stephanie meant too much to him to risk her life and he was certain her apartment was under surveillance.

When Stephanie returned, Nicholas was still staring out the window, trying to learn something about their stalker. There was little to learn. The guy just stood there, deep in the shadows, staring at the front door. Nicholas saw no discernible features. Finally, he turned back to Stephanie.

"Ready to get out of here?"

She nodded, and to her surprise, Nicholas didn't head for the door, and his car. Instead, he took her hands again and the next thing she knew, they were standing in his living room...

Chapter 9

"Nico!" Xabier exclaimed. "You're back already?" He licked his hand and slicked his hair back. "And just who is *this* lovely creature?"

As Stephanie stood, blushing, in the living room of Nicholas' townhouse, Nicholas pointed a finger at Xabier. "Don't even think about it, Xabs." He turned back to Stephanie. "Steph, meet Xabier. Xabier, this is my girlfriend, Stephanie."

Xabier bowed and took her hand, kissing it like a formal gentleman. He then tucked it under his arm and pulled her along. "Well, well, well. Come with me, my love. There is so much to talk about. Nico...you sly dog! This young lady is perfection!"

Stephanie glanced at Nicholas with a teasing grin. "*Nico?*"

"Don't ask," Nicholas chuckled. "Xabier's a vampire, by the way. Don't let him bite your neck."

She looked at him with a wry grin. "Yeah, okay."

"Show her, Xabs."

Without a word, Xabier bared his teeth, exposing the tell-tale extended canines as well as the rows of needle-sharp teeth sliding out from under his gums. He gave a little hiss for effect, causing Stephanie to hop back a few steps. He chuckled as she recoiled in surprise.

"Do not be afraid, my dear. I do not feed on friends."

As if that would allay her fears, Nicholas thought with a headshake and rueful grin. He mouthed, *I'm sorry.*

Xabier smiled, and patted her arm. She began to relax, casting a nervous glance back at Nicholas, who smiled and waved a hand at her. "He's perfectly harmless, baby. He's like a teddy bear."

"Now *that* is a distortion of the truth," Xabier objected, taking her hand once again. "I am very rugged and manly, and I shall woo you, showing you why you are wasting your time with such a one as the Scarlatti boy. You note I said *boy*, did you not, my dear? That is because he is just that…a boy, while I, on the other hand, am a man. So, you see, the choice is clear."

Nicholas shook his head and went into the kitchen. He grabbed a head of garlic and handed it to Stephanie. "If he gets ornery just hit him with this."

"Won't work," Xabier muttered.

Stephanie held the garlic up. "I thought vampires hated garlic."

"I actually quite enjoy garlic," Xabier retorted. "You shouldn't believe everything you read or see on TV."

"What about crucifixes?"

Xabier opened his shirt, revealing an ornate gold cross dangling from a simple gold chain. "It was my father's. He died when I was sixteen. I have never taken it off."

"Wood and silver?"

"Allergic and *very* allergic, my love, but only if they break the skin. It doesn't hurt if I touch them. Well, silver does a little." He sighed and grinned at her like they were best friends. "Please don't shoot or stab me. It smarts."

Stephanie looked back and forth between Nicholas and Xabier. "This is blowing my mind. Vampires…magic…demons. I swear I'm going to wake up and all of this will be a dream."

"Don't say that, love." Xabier squeezed her arm. "Then you will have never met me. You will have never known true love."

Nicholas groaned. "Where is Zha'riel?"

Xabier wrinkled his forehead. "I believe our angelic friend with the stick up his…" He looked at Stephanie as Nicholas raised his eyebrows. "Ahem. I believe he went…home…for a while. He'll be back, I'm sure." Xabier leaned in toward Nicholas. "Is tonight still a go?"

"As long as Zha'riel is here to watch over Stephanie," Nicholas replied, glancing toward the window and furrowing his brow, "we're good to go."

Xabier frowned. "What happened?"

"Nothing actually happened." Nicholas shrugged his shoulders and grimaced. "I just saw something...well, some*one*...or maybe...some*thing*."

"Okaaaay," Xabier said. When Nicholas didn't continue, he made a rolling motion with his hand. "Care to elaborate?"

Nicholas hesitated. "I don't want to scare Stephanie any more than I already have tonight, so I'd rather talk to Zha'riel and you privately when he gets back."

"Wait a minute," Stephanie shook her head and perched herself on Nicholas' kitchen table. She fixed them both with a defiant glare. "If it involves me, I deserve to know what's going on. No more secrets, *Nico*."

Nicholas tried to withhold a grin, but the way she said *Nico*...he kind of liked it when Stephanie said it. Even amidst what had to be the most traumatic night of her life, Stephanie managed to maintain her sense of humor. She had to be freaking out on the inside though, and he wanted to spare her as much as possible. He knew now that Zha'riel had been right. He should have ended things between them immediately. Now, Stephanie was sucked into a world for which she was ill-equipped...just like him.

She didn't want to be left out of the conversation and Nicholas didn't have the heart to tell her no. Since he was responsible for changing her life, he figured she had a right to know what was going on. He exchanged glances with Xabier, who raised his eyebrows in silent agreement.

"I saw a figure," he began. "It looked like a man, but I couldn't be sure. I thought I saw his eyes in a reflection of light, but now I'm not so sure..."

"What color?"

All eyes turned to the threshold between the living room and the kitchen. Zha'riel stood with arms folded with a concerned look on his face. Stephanie's eyes bulged. She had been looking in his direction when Zha'riel appeared out of thin air, just like Nicholas and she had done earlier.

Xabier laid a hand on hers to reassure her. He leaned in and whispered in her ear, "You get used to it."

She shivered, wrapping her arms around herself, but never took her eyes off the angel, and shook her head. "I hope so."

"Zha'riel, Stephanie," Nicholas said. "Stephanie, Zha'riel." He turned to Stephanie. "Ready for this one? Zha'riel's an…angel."

"The eyes, Nicholas," Zha'riel insisted, ignoring Stephanie's stunned expression. "What color were the eyes?"

"He's not much fun," Xabier said to Stephanie. "In fact…he's rather boring." To Zha'riel, he said, "And his name is Nico."

Zha'riel ignored him as well, focusing on Nicholas and awaiting a reply.

Nicholas frowned, trying to remember. "Assuming it really was the guy's eyes…"

"It was, Nicholas," Zha'riel insisted.

"Nico," Xabier insisted. "Call him Nico."

Zha'riel's eyes glowed brilliant blue. He turned to Xabier and leveled his gaze at the vampire. Xabier shrank back and held up his hands. The glow diminished and Zha'riel's eyes returned to their normal dark brown. He turned back to Nicholas.

"The color?"

"Red," Nicholas replied. "I saw a flash of dark red, barely a glow, then nothing. I never saw it again, but the guy stood there for a while. I decided to bring Stephanie here to be safe."

Zha'riel closed his eyes and his entire posture slumped. "Red," he repeated in a mumble.

"I'm guessing that means something?" Nicholas looked from Zha'riel to Xabier.

"Yeah," Xabier said in a reverent tone. "It means something."

Zha'riel's concern was lost on him. The angel was concerned about everything. His personality was wearing thin. It was Xabier's change of demeanor that unnerved Nicholas more than anything else. The vampire was usually unflappable. Nothing penetrated his larger-than-life persona. Now, all of a sudden, red eyes scared him?

"Demons," Zha'riel said, his eyes boring into Nicholas.' "You saw a demon." He gritted his teeth and shook his head. "This is what I was afraid of. Your out-of-control pull on chakra made it easy. The underworld has identified you."

"The underworld?" Stephanie asked, looking from one to the other. "What is that?"

Nicholas and Zha'riel were caught in a stare down. Zha'riel held Nicholas' stunned gaze, ignoring everyone else. Xabier looked at Stephanie with sympathy.

"Hell," he said. "You know the underworld as Hell."

As her eyes widened. Her lips moved but no sound emerged. Nicholas sighed and leaned against the counter. Stephanie hopped off the table, crossed the kitchen, and rested her head on his chest. He wrapped his arms around her, pulled her close and pressed his face into her hair. He felt a tremble and wondered which one of them shook.

"What you saw, Nicholas, or Nico…" Zha'riel shook his head and continued. "…was a demon. Most demons are low-level. They have black eyes. They are extremely powerful and not to be taken lightly."

Xabier agreed. "Never confuse their low station for weakness. Compared to a human, a black-eyed demon might as well be a god."

Zha'riel cringed at the implication. "They are *not* gods, but humans are quite powerless against them. The next level of demonic rank is yellow-eyed."

"They are some nasty creatures," Xabier said. "I had a run-in with a yellow-eyed demon and I don't want to tangle with another one ever again."

Zha'riel nodded. "The black-eyed demons make up the bulk of the Dark Army. The yellow-eyed demons command them.

Those are Hell's front line warriors. For every forty or fifty demons, there might be one with yellow eyes."

"And the red-eyed demons?" Nicholas asked.

"Red-eyed demons are even rarer."

"And way more dangerous," Xabier added. "They say if you ever see one, it is usually the last thing you see. Red-eyes are like the demon special forces."

"Oh great," Nicholas said. "I'm being stalked by a demonic Navy Seal."

"Something like that," Xabier said with a chuckle.

Zha'riel strode into the kitchen to stand before Nicholas, and spoke in an urgent hiss. "Nicholas, you need to understand that things are moving quickly now. Since he did not attack, it means you are only to be located and watched. It is likely you have been under surveillance for some time. Red-eyed demons do not usually appear until things are ready to progress. You should not have involved this girl."

"Trust me," Nicholas said. "I know, but they know we're together now, so I couldn't leave her there. We need to protect her."

"Fine." Zha'riel nodded. "You need to make a trip to the store, Nicholas. We need to prepare this house for demonic attack."

An hour later, Nicholas orbed back into the living room loaded with bags of rock salt, empty spray bottles, cans of spray paint, and several iron rods. It was a strange list, but he shopped without question. When he dumped it all on the floor, Zha'riel began instructing everyone how to use them.

"First," he said to Stephanie. "Take the salt and pour it in lines on all the window sills, doorways...anywhere there is access to the outside. Demons can aerosolize, but they cannot go through walls. They need some kind of access point. Salt is a preservative. Demons cannot cross a line of salt, but the slightest break in the line will give them instant access, so pour thick lines."

Xabier was sent to fill the kitchen sink with water. When it was full, Zha'riel dropped a rosary into the water and said a prayer. When he was finished, he took a spray bottle and dunked it into the water, filling it. He put the top on it and repeated until all ten bottles were full and lined up on the kitchen table.

"Excellent," Zha'riel said. "Now for something a little more complicated."

He took a can of spray paint and stood on a chair in the kitchen. He painted a large circle with a five-pointed star in the middle of the ceiling. Throughout the picture, he added various images Nicholas thought might be hieroglyphics. When he was done, he stepped back.

"You might want to take a picture of that," he told Nicholas, "so you can do it yourself in the future."

Everyone took out their cell phones and snapped pictures of the design. Xabier stared and shook his head.

"I always thought these things were myths."

"What is it?" Nicholas asked.

"It is called a Devil's Trap," Zha'riel replied. "A demon can walk under it easily enough, but once inside the circle, he is trapped and cut off from his powers. The only way out is to break the circle, which they cannot do from the inside."

Nicholas stared at the image on his ceiling. "What do you do once you have one trapped?"

Zha'riel pursed his lips. "Exorcism."

"But not the kind you see on TV," Xabier said. He turned to Zha'riel. "Right?"

Zha'riel's nod was more of a slight bow. "Humans can perform ritual exorcism, but an angel can expel a demon from a vessel with a single touch."

Xabier nodded. "But that doesn't kill the demon, right?"

"No," Zha'riel agreed. "It does not. Usually an exorcism will expel the demon from its vessel and send it back to the underworld. There are exorcism's that will do other things, but for now, we can just focus on staying alive and getting demons out of their vessels."

"What happens to the...vessels?" Stephanie asked. "They're people, right?"

"Yes," Zha'riel nodded. "They are people. And what happens depends upon a variety of factors. The length of time the demon has possessed them is the most important thing. If it has only been a short time, like a week or two, the vessel stands a good chance of coming out of it with no ill effects. Any longer and damage can happen. That can range from chronic nightmares to madness, to physical injuries and illnesses, all the way to death."

"Death?" Stephanie shrieked. "Really?"

"Absolutely," Zha'riel said. "Demons are not gentle with their vessels. By the time they are expelled, the vessel often endures extreme psychological torment."

"Why?"

"Because demons are evil," Zha'riel explained. "It is in their nature to destroy...to hurt...to cause chaos."

"In other words," Xabier cut in, "They do it because they like it."

Ŧ A Ӡ Ψ Ç

"Just rest, Stephie. I love you."

"I love you too, *Nico*," she smiled. "I think I like that name."

"After the way you handled today, you can call me whatever you like." He leaned in and gave her a soft kiss. "I'm so sorry for putting you through all this."

She put her arms around his neck and pulled him to her. "Don't apologize. Just promise me you'll be careful and that you'll keep me safe."

Nicholas nodded, smiling against her lips. "That's a promise." He stood up straight and flexed his bicep. "No one's touchin my girl."

She giggled. "Ooooh, a tough guy. Show me the electricity again."

Nicholas grinned and held out a hand, calling the greenish bolts out and showing her a brief but ominous crackle at his fingertips. The corners of Stephanie's mouth curled and she bit her lower lip. Nicholas watched as her eyes glazed over.

It was the lustiest look he'd ever seen and would have made him put off Colombia for another night, but he felt an incessant pressure in his head. He couldn't bring himself to ask Zha'riel about it, but the tug toward violence was becoming irresistible. While his heart refused to do anyone harm, his mind strayed toward dark and frightening desires. He pushed the thoughts down and focused on his sexy girlfriend.

"I don't know why," she purred, "but that is sooo sexy."

Nicholas laughed. "Well, there's plenty more where that came from. Now sleep. I have some things to do, but Zha'riel will be here and this room is like Fort Knox to a demon, so you'll be fine. I'll see you in the morning."

"Night."

Downstairs, Xabier and Zha'riel were doing a final walkthrough, making sure every possible point of entry for a demon was secured. Devil's Traps were drawn on the floors and ceilings of every room. Salt covered all perimeter doorways and windows, and everyone carried holy water spray bottles at all times. There was also an iron rod in the corner of every room. Zha'riel explained the significance of iron.

"These are like swords to a demon. If you swing it and hit them, it will cut them down, expel them from the vessel, and send them back to the underworld."

Xabier turned to Nicholas. "So, are we doing this tonight?"

Nicholas nodded with a wry grin. "Let's do it. We're kinda out of time. We need to get moving on a more secure and secluded location. There are too many people around here to keep safe when the bad guys come calling." He turned to Zha'riel. "You're good to watch over Stephanie while we do this?"

Zha'riel sighed. "I will remain here with the girl."

Nicholas put a hand on Xabier's shoulder and they orbed out.

Seconds later, Nicholas and Xabier stood in the jungle, just outside the perimeter of a huge estate with a massive stone mansion in the center, at the end of a long winding driveway. Armed guards patrolled the fence line and were stationed at all entryways. Nicholas' heart thudded in his chest as he surveyed all the security he and Xabier were up against.

"You're sure about this?" he asked.

Xabier chuckled. "These guys cannot kill you, Nico. They can shoot those guns all they want, but they'll be wasting bullets."

"How do you know they can't kill me?" Nicholas asked with a skeptical frown.

Xabier shrugged. "Just a guess."

"That's real reassuring." Nicholas took a deep breath. "Okay, so I orb us into the basement and we take out everything that moves."

"Yep, and the vault is down there." Xabier put his hand on Nicholas' back. "We orb into the vault and take everything we see. You can orb back and forth between the vault and home, hauling the cash and stuff as needed."

Nicholas nodded. "Why not just orb into the vault from here?"

Xabier shrugged. "We can do that." He raised his eyebrows. "Do you know where it is?"

Nicholas considered for a second and nodded. "Good point." He held out an arm for Xabier to hold. "All right, let's go."

Seconds later, they materialized, out of thin air, in a room with eight armed guards sitting around a lot of high-end surveillance gear, and a panel of camera monitors covering one wall. The guards were good. They jerked to their feet, shouting at one another in Spanish. Nicholas incapacitated them all with short energy bursts. A loud zap sounded, and the electronics sparked and sizzled as Nicholas directed bursts at them. Within a few moments, the entire basement command center was cleared, and the surveillance system destroyed, and not a single gunshot had been fired, so no one on the ground level had any idea there was a problem.

Inside the vault, Nicholas and Xabier wasted no time filling their duffels. They loaded stacks and stacks of American currency along with a surprising amount of silver and gold bars and coins. There were even several boxes of German bearer bonds. Nicholas and Xabier took it all. It took a dozen orb trips back home for Nicholas to deliver it all. Zha'riel just shook his head when Nicholas showed up on the last trip, and went to check on Stephanie.

"How is she?" Nicholas asked.

"Sleeping soundly," Zha'riel replied. "It has been quiet. I sense no demon activity around the house. Perhaps they have not found this location yet."

"Good."

Nicholas and Xabier moved on to the next cartel location. It was located in a more mountainous region but was very similar in terms of security and layout. They orbed in and took out the guards in the basement of the compound. They were in and out of the vault within twenty minutes. Three hours, and three cartel compounds later, they had just cleared the basement of the last target of the night.

They were just getting their bearings inside the vault when they heard commotion outside and heard someone operating the digital lock. Nicholas shorted it out with a burst of energy from his fingers and they went to work. As they stuffed the duffels with cash, they heard a confused commotion outside. The door was too thick for them to hear anything clearly. It was only their enhanced hearing that enabled them to hear the sounds at all, but what they could hear sounded more and more frantic by the second as the men on the other side of the door tried to find a way to open the vault manually.

On the inside, Xabier and Nicholas chuckled at how the newest vaults had built in security devices that rendered them virtually inaccessible in the event of a power loss or short. It was supposed to keep thieves out if they got the idea to interrupt the power supply to the lock. That very security measure worked decidedly against them as Nicholas and Xabier calmly emptied out the contents of the vault. Moments after the final gold coin was taken, they were drinking a beer in Nicholas' living room in front of a massive pile treasure.

"I can't believe it was that easy," Nicholas said.

Xabier raised his bottle. "They don't prepare for thieves to orb in and take all their money without even opening the vault. They're more worried about guys with guns shooting their way in."

Nicholas chuckled, clinking his bottle against Xabier's. "They'll regret that strategy."

Chapter 10

Meeting – 1600F

As far as messages went, it was short and simple but said a great deal. There was no location mentioned because the head of every major Colombian cartel knew the rotation of meeting places. There were six, labeled A through F. Time and place was all they needed to know. If a meeting between cartel leaders was necessary, it was unlikely any one of them would require an explanation. The meetings were a conduit for resolving disputes before they escalated to all-out war. They were also a means of banding together to fight a common enemy. Which of those situations they were currently in was anybody's guess.

"What is it, Jefe?" The question came from Alvi's security chief, Ricardo "Rico" Norte.

Alvi Cornega could scarcely hold his temper in check. He breathed long and deep, and squeezed his eyes closed as he fought for control over his emotions. He had been robbed. Millions of dollars in cash, precious metals, and bonds were inexplicably gone…disappeared into thin air from behind the door of a locked vault. The unconscious or dead security guards were the only evidence anyone had been there, but all those guards had been *outside* the vault and none of them had the ability to open it. The security logs showed the vault had not been opened in two days. The whole thing was a giant mystery.

That mystery became even more intriguing when news came that he was not the only victim of a confusing robbery. Within a few early morning hours, it became clear. All the major Colombian cartels had been victimized. That was not good. It meant hundreds of millions of cartel dollars were gone and it seriously weakened their stature. It reduced their ability to fund operations, including the battles they all had to fight against the Colombian government. It was a combination of bribery and violence, both of which required serious cash flow. With their funds depleted, all the cartels were at risk.

Alvi looked up at Rico. "Meeting in a few hours," he said. "Bogata."

Rico nodded He pulled out his phone and spoke to his security team, laying out instructions for the trip. They'd take a plane to a small hidden airstrip twenty miles from the Colombian capital. From there they'd drive to the secret meeting place on the outskirts of the city. Security had to be solid, but minimal for these meetings. Everyone was expected to have bodyguards, but overkill would insult the others. The general rule of thumb was to bring only as many men as can fit into one vehicle.

"Uncle!" Alvi's niece, Rosa, called from the sliding doors. Alvi looked up at her and smiled, though he felt far from pleasant. "Nayra's here."

He nodded. "Bring her out."

The woman who appeared on his patio moments later didn't waste time with pleasantries or idle chit chat. She strode to Alvi's side and touched his cheek. Her dull gray eyes stared into his eyes as if searching for something. Smoothing her long dress, she breathed in and nodded in thought.

"Tell me, my child."

Alvi told her about the robbery and how he had no idea how it happened or who did it. He also told her how the other cartels suffered the same indignation. She listened without expression, her eyes never blinking or leaving his. When he was finished giving her every detail he could recall, she nodded again.

"Take me to the vault."

Standing in the center of the vault, Nayra had Alvi instruct everyone else to leave the room. She needed silence and solitude. Alvi solemnly closed the door behind him, leaving her alone to walk around in the now empty vault as well as the security room just outside. She took deep breaths as she walked around the perimeters of both the vault and the room, gliding her fingertips along the walls. Her eyes remained closed as she walked. Her breathing became more and more relaxed as she settled into deep meditation, ending up in the center of the vault on her knees with her arms spread wide.

A jolt skewered her chest. Her eyes opened and her face contorted in shock. "No," she breathed. "It's…it's…impossible!"

She closed her eyes again and settled her breathing. She seldom had reason to doubt what she saw. After more than five decades of visions, five decades of seeing things most people would never dream of, Nayra saw something even she couldn't quite believe. She needed to be certain. Her godson depended on her to be absolutely accurate. He lived his life in the center of one of the most violent industries in the world. There was zero margin for error.

The events of the previous evening returned to her. Two figures appeared, one of them unleashing a flurry of energy. Ordinarily, she would attribute such behavior to a sorcerer, one who practiced the discipline of bending energy to his will, but that didn't feel right. There was something different about his essence…and something familiar as well. The second figure was easy: Vampire.

"A sorcerer with a vampire accomplice," she muttered, her eyes still closed. She wrinkled her forehead. What was that? She moved through the vision, looking for the anomaly. And then…there it was. It just couldn't be. It was like seeing double. It made her unsteady, as if she were drunk, but she was stone sober. Then, she recognized the essence.

"Mattaeus?" she whispered. "But what is the other…?"

110

It was like nothing she had ever come across. Dueling essences? How was it possible? One individual…one essence. That was the way of the natural world and the supernatural realm alike. Some things just didn't—*couldn't*—happen. This one had obviously taken in the essence of Mattaeus, but he also seemed to possess a second and far darker…essence.

It was possible to take in the essence of one you kill, but then their essence merges with yours and a new essence is formed. Seers like Nayra could distinguish to an extent the various parts of one's essence, but in this case, the two essences were distinct, and in her lifetime of experience, Nayra had never felt nor heard of anything like it.

She focused on the inexplicable essence, trying to see it more clearly. It was definitely dark, definitely evil. That made it even more confusing. Mattaeus was not evil. He spent his life battling *against* the forces of evil. How could his essence share the same space as such darkness? She vaguely recalled something Mattaeus mentioned a long time ago. He was toying with an idea, something to do with combining powerful dark and powerful light powers. It wasn't something she believed could happen, and at the time, even he was unsure about it.

Had he done it? Had the crazy old man actually found a way to combine powerful essences from both good and evil? And had he given up his *own* essence in pursuit of this accomplishment? News of his death at the hands of a Dark Prince had spread through the supernatural world like wildfire. There were rumors about the death of a Dark Prince as well though that was unconfirmed. The Underworld kept a tight lid on information like that.

But if it *had* happened, this unidentified human was clearly involved. Now, he was using those powers for his own enrichment. Interesting. The extraordinarily powerful evil essence must be asserting itself. The pursuit of self-enrichment was evil no matter who you stole from. Doing evil to evil people—and Nayra had no illusions about her godson—was still evil. It was difficult to leave that path once one started down it.

"Nayra?"

The voice of her godson, Alvi, pierced her thoughts. She snapped out of her trance-like state and looked up at him. She was silent, staring at him with a quizzical expression as if to ask, *why are you disturbing me?*

Alvi wasn't one to apologize...not to anyone. He was the boss of his organization and no one expected him to be polite or gentle, but when it came to Nayra, he was always respectful, soft spoken, and deferential. She had been in his life since birth and had always treated him like her own son. Now that his parents were gone, she was the guiding force in his life, and he relied on her particularly for her spiritual guidance.

He lowered his eyes. "Divina," he said, calling her by title. It was also a term of endearment for him. "We must go. We will be late for the meeting."

After a quick flight, Alvi, Ricardo, Nayra, and three security personnel made their way to Site F in a large white SUV. Located just outside the Colombian capital of Bogata, the cartel leadership met in an old hotel, which boasted an upscale clientele of moneyed tourists and government officials. For the cartels, it was like hiding in plain sight, and it was rather risky meeting so close to the capital, but it was the most central location to all of them. The other five locations were specific to each cartel.

As they pulled into the parking area, Alvi could tell he was the last to arrive. He was just a few minutes late, but he hurried to get in as he knew tensions were high and he wasn't interested in petty squabbles. The hotel manager led Alvi, Nayra, and Rico to a large meeting room where the other four cartel leaders waited with their security chiefs.

Alvi entered the room. It was a dimly lit meeting room, filled with the sweet pungency of cigar smoke. Two eight-foot tables sat side-by-side in the center of the room with simple white linen covering them to make a conference table. Pitchers of water sat, untouched, in the middle of the table, while two bottles of tequila were already half-empty. Alvi sniffed and smiled grimly at the others.

"Apologies for my tardiness," he said, nodding to each of his colleagues, "but I have information I believe will prove useful."

"Already?" asked Lupe Rojas, head of the Tumaco cartel, from the Southwestern region of Colombia. Operating from the port city after which they were named, the Tumaco cartel was involved, not only in drugs, but also a thriving weapons business. Lupe Rojas was called "El Gato" because he was rumored to have fought and killed a mountain lion with just a knife when he was sixteen years old. "Did they leave evidence at your place?"

Alvi shook his head. "Not the kind of evidence you're thinking of, Lupe."

Guillermo Diaz rolled his eyes impatiently. "Don't tell us your witch knows who did it. I don't have time for this."

"Well," Alvi replied, leveling his gaze at the hot-headed leader of the Los Llanos cartel. "You need to make the time, Guillo. Because unless you have a lead of your own to discuss, this is all we've got to go on."

"I'd rather not waste any time listening to some old lady ramble on about visions."

Alvi slammed his hand down on the table. "Then leave!"

Guillermo leapt to his feet and lunged across the table. He was grabbed by Isidro Lopez, leader of the Caqueta Cartel, and Lupe Rojas, before he could get his hands on Alvi, who stood with his arms spread as if to say, *"Come and get me."* It took several seconds to return Guillermo to his chair. He sat, glaring daggers at Alvi who glared right back.

"Are you two going to get over it and act like adults so we can figure out what is going on here?"

The question came from Ernesto Gonzalez, who had been quiet until then. He was the one in the group most suited to the business side of things. He was always level-headed, yet willing to go to war if necessary. But war was expensive, so he preferred to find less costly ways to solve problems and get results.

Alvi was the first to look away. He felt like an idiot for allowing Guillermo to suck him into a stupid fight. He should have ignored the hot-headed lunatic. He needed to manage his anger better. Nonetheless, he had information that he felt was important so he had to get it together and at least try to convince the group to unite and act on it.

"Okay," he said. "This is my madrina, Nayra." He gestured with an open palm at his godmother. "Some of you may have heard her called La Divina."

Lupe Rojas narrowed his eyes as he looked the older woman over. She met his gaze easily and he turned away. Nayra had that effect on many people. Her icy gray stare carried with it the ability to convey her true capabilities. It made people uncomfortable.

Sid Lopez's eyes widened. "La Divina," he said with respect in his voice.

Alvi knew all of them had heard of Nayra. Legend had it that she had correctly predicted the precise attack plans of the Medellin cartel, giving Alvi plenty of time to plot a massive series of ambushes, decimating Medellin and ultimately triggering its demise. Word about her divination had spread, resulting in her rise as a local legend. To most people, that's all she was...a legend. She kept herself out of sight as much as possible, adding to her mystique.

"Yes," Alvi smiled. "And she has taken a preliminary look at our situation. After several hours of meditation in my vault and in the surrounding security rooms where the intruders were, she discovered some information I believe will lead to us finding them and perhaps getting back what was ours."

Ernesto cast a sidelong glance at Guillermo, who steamed quietly in his chair and continue to glare at Alvi. He shook his head.

"I think," he said, "that we would all be interested in a result such as you have mentioned. What information has the lady gleaned?"

"I'll let her explain," Alvi replied, gesturing to Nayra and taking his seat.

Nayra stood and moved to the center of the table where she could meet the gazes of everyone present. She had no qualms about being in a room full of the most powerful and violent men in the country…possibly the world. She had seen violence in her day on a scale far more frightening than any these men were capable of causing.

"I saw two men," she began. "The first was a vampire."

Guillermo Dias exploded. "Vampire!" he shouted. "Are you serious?"

"I am," Nayra said. She set her ice-gray gaze on Dias in an unblinking stare. "He moved with extraordinary speed and had unusual strength. There is little doubt."

"This is insane," Dias shook his head. "We don't have time for this."

"I'm inclined to agree," Ernesto Gonzalez nodded.

Nayra gestured to Alvi, who shook his head. "I should have known this would be a waste of time."

Ernesto narrowed his eyes. "Did you honestly expect us to listen to a story about mythological creatures robbing us?"

"Mythological?" Nayra countered. "What a fool statement that is!"

"I beg your pardon," Ernesto said with a smile, "but I am not interested in wasting my time on a conversation about vampires."

"Good," Nayra replied in a grim tone. "Because the vampire is the least of your worries. You need to be thinking about how to deal with a demon mage."

The room fell silent as the men all stared at her. That was news even to Alvi. Nayra had told him about the second man, but at the time, she hadn't been sure what exactly he was. Now, she seemed more certain. After several moments of silence, Lupe burst out laughing. Ernesto broke into a tired smile while the other two stifled their grins. Nayra shook her head and leaned down to whisper in Alvi's ear.

"Let's leave, my son. These men are unbelievers and fools. They are of no use to us."

Alvi nodded and stood. "Gentlemen, thank you for your time. I will take my leave now and follow this up on my own. I will inform you all of any findings."

"You cannot just leave, Alvi," Ernesto objected. "We have much to discuss."

"I can," Alvi replied, "and I will. You don't want to listen, fine. You all have nothing to go on. These thieves left no trace other than their auras and you aren't interested in discussing that. As I said, if I find anything further, I will inform you."

Chapter 11

"This is kind of annoying having to do this, ya know?"

Nicholas and Xabier put the finishing touches on Stephanie's apartment. They painted multiple Devil's Traps and lined all the entry points with salt. Xabier had the idea of adding a second element to their system. Instead of simply pouring the salt on the window sills or on the ground in front of the doors, they first painted on a thick coat of adhesive, and poured the salt on top. Once the glue dried, the salt was stuck in place. It would take more than a light breeze to break the salt line.

"Well, my friend," Xabier replied, "we must do whatever it takes to keep our loved ones safe."

"We haven't gone over to Dom's place," Nicholas pointed out.

"Only because we have no reason to believe they know about him. It would seem they only know about *this* location. We haven't even seen any demonic activity around *your* place, so for now we'll count our blessings...if you believe in that sort of thing."

"What sort of thing?" Nicholas asked as he continued his work with a spray can. "Blessings? What do you have against blessings?"

"Nothing, I suppose," said Xabier with an off-hand shrug.

Nicholas stopped spraying symbols on the floor of Stephanie's living room and squinted at him. "You don't believe in blessings?"

Xabier shook his head. "Not in the sense that God grants them."

"Then who does?"

"I believe what you refer to as blessings is really little more than good preparation combined with the ability to make the most out of an opportunity. When things go right, it usually can be explained by good planning and proper execution."

"Makes sense." Nicholas nodded. "But what about when things don't go right and you still come out on top?"

Xabier grinned. "I never said I didn't believe in luck, Nico." He let out a loud hearty laugh. "Now then, where does that pretty lady of yours keep the wine?"

Before he could reply, Nicholas felt the tell-tale tingle on the back of his neck. It rippled down his spine, tickling the small of his back. He knew what it meant. While he was still skeptical of his own abilities, he was certain his—call it a sixth sense—was an evil presence radar. He went to the window and peered out through the blinds.

"What?" Xabier crouched and made his way to Nicholas' side. "Something out there?"

"I'm not sure," Nicholas whispered. "I'm just getting a serious tingling in my spine. Last time I felt it, I saw that red-eyed demon across the street."

"Is he there now?"

Nicholas scanned the street. "I don't see him, but I know something's out there." He looked at Xabier. "I think it's time we deal with this a little more...*aggressively*."

Xabier raised his eyebrows. "Uhhh, Nico. Normally I'd be the first to suggest a more direct approach, but in this case...do you really want to try taking on a demon today?"

Nicholas tasted bile rising from his stomach, along with a desire for action. He was tired of waiting for the demons to make their move. At least by confronting them, maybe he could get some answers and deal with the situation head-on instead of sitting around waiting. And if things went badly…well, at least Stephanie was out of harm's way. There was much to be said for controlling the when and where.

He nodded. "I think I do."

Xabier sighed. "Well, then, my friend. I am with you. How do you want to play it?"

Nicholas thought for a moment. "We need to get this somewhere private. My car's still outside. Let's get in and drive it to a more secluded location. I'll orb out before we get there and when he follows, I'll come in from behind and surprise him with a bucket of holy water."

"Sounds dangerous for the guy driving the car," Xabier said nervously. "You better be on your game today, Nico."

"We'll be fine," Nicholas assured him.

Forty-five minutes later, Xabier pulled Nicholas' Maserati down a wooded path into a clearing used by deer hunters to stage overnight expeditions. Pulling to the far end of the clearing, Xabier put the car in park, took a breath, and opened the door. As he got out, he saw a blue Nissan Sentra creep into the clearing. Xabier hastened to the trunk and opened it as the Sentra came to a stop.

The door opened and a man with spiky dark hair got out. He had dark eyes, but Xabier was certain they would glow red if the demon chose to reveal himself. He felt his heart rate triple instantly as the air around him chilled. The man approached him and smiled like he was just another fella out for a drive on a summer day.

"Nice weather," he said to Xabier with a pleasant smile.

Xabier almost rolled his eyes but thought better of it. "Yeah," he replied with his own smile. "Sure is."

The guy gestured toward the car. "Nice ride you got there. Yours?"

Xabier shook his head. "Nah. My friend's. I'm just taking it out for a ride since it's such a nice day and all."

The guy wrinkled his forehead. "I could have sworn I saw two of you in there." He peered through the rear window. "Where'd the other guy go?"

Xabier shrugged. "Not really sure what you're talking about, chief. I'm the only one here."

"I see."

The guy raised his hand and Xabier felt his throat tighten, as if a hand gripped it. The trunk suddenly slammed shut and the next thing he knew he was sprawled across it, unable to move. The man closed the distance, his eyes now glowing red, confirming his identity.

"See now," he said with a cheerful, yet sadistic, grin. "We got off on the wrong foot. I was asking about the owner of this vehicle…and you were saying?"

He relented in his grip just enough for Xabier to choke out two words. "Not…here…"

The red-eyed demon stood over him and shook his head, his eyes downcast. "You're not going to last much longer, *Fang*. If you don't have a better answer than that, I'm going to rip your head from your body. You might want to think really hard about my question. I just want to talk with your friend. I'm not here to hurt him."

"That's good to know." Nicholas appeared behind the demon.

Xabier felt grip around his throat slacken and he gasped for breath. A second later the demon was lifted off his feet and sent sprawling onto the ground ten feet away.

Nicholas' eyes burned with rage and whatever it was inside him, yearned for release. He used the full bucket in his hands to douse the red-eyed demon with holy water and was rewarded by instant screams of agony as the liquid boiled his skin like acid.

"Arrrrggg!"

With all the control he could muster, Nicholas struck with a multitude of attacks. He sent thousands of bolts of energy from his fingertips into the demonic figure and was rewarded with more screams of pain. As his wrathful energy rained down on the demon, Nicholas felt the power surge through him as if he grew stronger the more he used it. Though he was causing tremendous pain on another, Nicholas felt all semblance of remorse fade away as the scene before him bathed in brilliant silver.

Within seconds, the demon was subdued and spent, lying sprawled on the ground. Nicholas stretched out his hand and the demon was lifted up and slammed against a tree with a grunt. Nicholas was able to hold him there in much the same manner as the demon had done with Xabier, who had finally recovered from the encounter.

Nicholas approached the barely conscious demon, pulled out a little spray bottle, and spritzed a shot of holy water onto his face. The demon screamed in pain and the sizzling sound of burning flesh filled the air. Nicholas recoiled at the acrid odor, yet felt an unpleasant sense of satisfaction. The steam rose off the demon's body as he struggled against Nicholas' iron chakra grip.

"Who are you?" Nicholas asked, keeping his voice even and sinister to mask the fear raging inside. The conflict of emotions he felt was beginning to tear him apart.

The demon responded by spitting in his face. Nicholas instantly put his forefinger right between the demon's eyes and without a second thought, unleashed a torrent of electrical bolts. As he energy left his fingers, Nicholas felt pressure drain along with it. It was a light, airy sensation, while also dark and sinister, and he wanted more of it. The demon convulsed as the bolts surged through his body and shot out of his every extremity. After a few seconds, Nicholas pulled his finger away and wiped the spit from his face. The demon hissed something in a language Nicholas couldn't identify.

"I'm sorry," Nicholas said in a bland monotone. "I didn't get that. French, was it? You were about to tell me your name."

"Screw you!" The demon spat again.

Nicholas put his finger under the demon's chin and repeated his brutal torture. The demon screamed in agony and writhed around, trying to break Nicholas' grip, but he was powerless and growing weaker by the second. Nicholas wasn't sure what would happen if he continued in his current course of action. He wasn't sure the demon could be killed, and he was more interested in information than killing.

He had a brief flicker of sorrow for the demon's vessel, though, Zha'riel had made it clear there was little chance the vessel was even still alive after prolonged demon possession. Still, deep in his gut, Nicholas knew he ought to feel something more. He just didn't.

"Feel like giving me your name yet?" he asked.

He was rewarded by a garbled series of unintelligible words.

"What?" he said, smacking the demon on the forehead. "Speak English, chief. What is your name?"

The demon laughed in his face. "You think you can make me talk, *mage?*"

He said mage like it was an insult. Nicholas hadn't really thought of himself as having a title, but it made sense. Mattaeus was a mage, and, according to Zha'riel, a powerful one. It shouldn't come as much of a surprise that his successor would be given the same title. But how did the demon know to call him that? Was it something that could be seen by other supernatural creatures?

"How do you know me?" Nicholas demanded.

"Everyone knows about you," the demon sneered. "You killed Mattaeus and took his powers." He looked into Nicholas' eyes, his red glowing pupils piercing through Nicholas' veil of bravery. "Are you scared, boy?" He chuckled. "Well you should be, because I'm through playing games."

Before Nicholas could respond, a strong force pushed back against his grip on the demon. It was like a supernatural arm wrestling match and he could feel himself losing...*fast*. He felt an impact in his chest as if he'd gotten punched. The next thing he knew, he staggered backward, landing hard twenty feet away and tumbling to a stop against a tree.

He was on his feet in an instant, and the demon charged him. Nicholas sent a fierce burst of wind, sending the red-eyed monster backward. It bought him a few seconds and he moved forward, eager to press his advantage. It was a wasted effort because the demon had already conjured a ball of fire in his hand and hurled it right at Nicholas' chest. Nicholas dove for cover as flames flew at him from every direction.

From behind his car, Nicholas watched Xabier sneak up behind the demon. Before the vampire could make a move, the demon rained fire in his direction igniting his clothing instantly. Nicholas popped up and called down a torrent of water, dousing Xabier before real damage was done. He immediately turned his fury back on the demon, sending the crackling energy at him, but before the bolt could reach him, the demon disappeared.

Nicholas crouched behind his car, waiting for its return. He peered out from behind the rear bumper and realized, too late, there was a presence behind him. He felt an iron grip on his head and, before he could react, he was hurled into a tree trunk, head first. Just from hearing and feeling the splat, he knew the damage was severe. He sat in a stunned, bloody silence and looked up through a blurry haze at the red-glow staring down at him. He wondered if that would be the last thing he saw in the world. The demon spoke in the same unintelligible tongue as before.

Nicholas felt hands reach down and pull him to his feet, but he had no strength to stand, nothing left with which to resist. The demon shoved him against the tree.

"I was going to take you to my master in one piece," the demon hissed. "Now, I think just your head will be enough." As Nicholas drifted in and out of consciousness, the demon also said something about the great reward awaiting him in the underworld...

"Perhaps," a familiar voice said from behind the demon. "But not today."

An earsplitting tone sounded. The demon whirled around, releasing Nicholas at the sound of the dreadful noise. Nicholas dropped to his knees. He tried to cover his ears to block it out, but it didn't help. His head felt like a speaker. The wind kicked up all around them and Nicholas had the vague feeling they had all been sucked up into a tornado though he still felt the ground beneath him.

Nicholas could only watch as the demon recoiled in fear as Zha'riel stepped forward. The surprise Nicholas felt was surpassed only by the effect the noise had on him physically. It was like his body was being shaken to death. He actually felt like he might come apart. Through it all, Nicholas felt the demon attempting to access his power to flee, but somehow, he was unable to do it. Zha'riel must have the ability to inhibit a demon from accessing chakra.

"Hello, Seir," Zha'riel said, pronouncing it "sah-year." "It has been a long time."

Seir didn't respond. He stood there, his face betraying his resignation. Zha'riel continued to stare him down, fully in control. He looked as though he had all the time in the world. The demon finally managed to find words.

"Zha'riel," he said. "What are you doing here?"

Zha'riel responded with a thin smile. "I would ask you the same question, Seir. Why has Azazel's pet been unleashed on this young man?"

Seir's lips pressed together. Nicholas watched his eyes flick from side to side. Seir knew he was dead. Nicholas wondered if he would fight or try to make a break for it.

"Why should I say anything to you? You're just going to send me back to the Underworld without my vessel."

Zha'riel raised his eyebrows. "We both know I can do far worse to you than that, don't we, Seir?"

Seir gritted his teeth. Even Nicholas could sense his desperation. Zha'riel was either unaware or didn't bother to address it. He was in complete control.

"So," Zha'riel prodded. "Is this mission retaliation? Are you the avenger of the son of Azazel?"

The demon's glowing red eyes flashed at the mention of the powerful and feared fallen angel. "You know?"

Zha'riel narrowed his eyes. "Of course we know, Seir, but I wouldn't have expected your king to permit even Azazel to destroy such a valuable asset." He stood closer and breathed in deeply as if in thought. "Which means…you were either here to gather information for the prince…or Azazel has gone rogue."

He looked closely at Seir. "Which is it, demon? Is Hell divided over this little incident?"

Seir shook his head and looked at his feet. "I don't know what you're talking about, angel."

Zha'riel sighed and drew a gleaming sword from within the folds of his robes and stepped closer to Seir, whose eyes widened in terror and his lips began moving more and more rapidly. Nicholas heard the same, unintelligible language as before. Suddenly, the small clearing swarmed with black-eyed demons, all aiming their powers at Zha'riel, who spun around to confront them. That was all Seir needed to make his escape.

Too late, Zha'riel realized the demons were not there to fight him. They were just a distraction. Seir hadn't been trying to overpower Zha'riel and escape. He was merely sending a distress signal. His demon squadron responded with just enough of a display to give their boss time to fade into the ether before they followed. Zha'riel, too late to stop Seir, shook his head and turned his frustrated expression onto Nicholas.

"Foolish boy," he scolded. "What did you hope to accomplish?"

Nicholas closed his eyes. "I was trying to take the fight to them rather than wait for them to come for me."

Zha'riel shook his head again. "Take the fight to a red-eyed demon. You're lucky he didn't kill you."

"I thought my powers were from a fallen angel and a world-class mage," Nicholas protested.

Zha'riel nodded.

"Yes. And the two who had those powers before you knew how to use them. They knew how to stack spells and attacks to maximize effect. You are still learning. You have miles to go before you can battle demons. You must be less impulsive, Nicholas, or you are going to get yourself and everyone around you killed.

Chapter 12

"I get it, okay?"

Nicholas banged his head against the kitchen table. It shook enough to rattle the empty plates and silverware. He needed new furniture, sturdy furniture. Of course, if he continued to butt heads against demons, he might not survive long enough to enjoy the fruits of his "labors."

"No!" Zha'riel shouted. "You most certainly do *NOT* get it, Nicholas! You almost got you and your foolish, bloodsucking friend over there killed because you *think* you get it."

Nicholas endured a twenty-minute lecture from Zha'riel on the stupidity of his decision to confront a red-eyed demon, or *any* demon. He understood, but he could only take so much of the angel's condescension before it made him want to hit something. For the moment, he stifled the urge to lash out at Zha'riel, but he was beginning to boil over. He wondered what Zha'riel would do if Nicholas cracked him one.

"Think that through," Zha'riel threatened. He must have caught the look in Nicholas' eyes. "You failed to handle a lone demon. Now you think to challenge an angel of the Lord?"

Nicholas shrugged. "Whatever. I don't care. Maybe if you would teach me this crap, I wouldn't make stupid decisions. Either help or get out."

Zha'riel raised his eyebrows. "You think I have not been helping you? How many days and hours have we spent on your skills? Who was that helping you out in the woods?"

"Yeah, sure," Nicholas scoffed. "You helped me with the weaker…softer skills, but you know I have a lot more power inside me. I know it because I can feel it gripping me."

"What you *feel*…is evil!" snapped Zha'riel. "I refuse to…"

"No!" Nicholas shot back. "It's *real* power…more power than you're admitting to. Why won't you help me?"

Zha'riel stared at him for a long time. Nicholas tried to match his gaze but it wasn't worth it. The angel had the market cornered on cold-blooded staring. Instead, he stood, opened the fridge, and grabbed a beer. He leaned against the counter and waited for the angel to speak.

Zha'riel pressed his lips together. Nicholas had the distinct impression the angel was holding out on him again. He sipped his beer and controlled his flaring temper with several deep breaths. His angel friend needed to come clean.

Zha'riel sighed. "You do not understand what you are asking."

Nicholas drained the last of his beer. He tossed the bottle in a recycling container and took a seat at the kitchen table. "All I want is for you to tell me everything. Stop holding out on me and help me use my powers so I'm not defenseless the next time I come across a demon."

"There are some powers you cannot wield," Zha'riel replied in a soft tone. He shuffled behind the table so he stood across from Nicholas. He placed his hands on the table and leaned over Nicholas "There are some you *should* not wield. Some are not meant for humans to possess. Mattaeus was insane to think your body could contain the darkness you took in."

Nicholas shook his head. "That's not it. You're afraid of something, but it isn't darkness. This power is…" His eyes grew wide. *Could it be that simple?* His voice dropped into a reverent whisper. "Oh, my God. It's *angelic* power."

"Angelic," sniffed Zha'riel. "You are deluded…and foolish. The power inside you is demonic and it will destroy you."

"No," Nicholas said. "It may be dark. After all, Sansata was evil, but…" He thought for a minute, tapping a finger on the table. Pieces of information floated in his mind. He tried connecting a few dots "Sansata wasn't a demon, was he? You said it before. He was a—a "prince of darkness? Something like that?" He looked at Zha'riel, who frowned. "Tell me about Sansata."

Zha'riel sighed and shook his head. He pulled a chair out and sat with both palms laid flat on the table. "Sansata was an officer in Lucifer's army. He was not a demon. Demons are soldiers."

Nicholas let out a long breath and dropped his chin to his chest. "I knew it. So how high was his rank in Lucifer's army?"

Zha'riel pursed his lips. "He was a prince."

Xabier had been silent until then. He hadn't engaged the angry angel the way he normally did. Nicholas figured he wanted to stay out of angelic line of fire. He broke his silence by letting out a whistle.

"Whoa!" he exclaimed.

Nicholas turned to him with raised eyebrows and then shifted his attention back to Zha'riel. "What does that mean? What is a prince?"

Xabier answered. "Think of him as a four-star general." He shook his head in admiration. "You really hit the motherlode, Nico. Son of Lucifer's closest friend *and* a top-level officer? You, my friend, are carrying some serious juice." He looked up at Zha'riel. "Way to be up front with the info, you white-winged flake."

Zha'riel answered in his typical deep, calm monotone. "There was no need to burden Nicholas with everything all at once."

"Yeah," Nicholas retorted. "Or maybe I could have been honing my skills with the *real* power inside me instead of playing around with a weaker set of skills."

Zha'riel shook his head. "Nicholas, when will you realize that the powers are not so different? It is the ability of the individual that determines their effectiveness. Remember, it was the dark powers you were trying to use against Seir, not the powers we worked on."

"Yeah, because I felt how much more powerful they were."

"No," Zha'riel objected. "You felt the path of least resistance. That is the tug of evil. It is powerful, but you must resist or it will lead you straight into the arms of Lucifer himself. And *he* will turn you into a demonic force for evil."

Nicholas shook his head and glanced at Xabier who shrugged uncertainly. "I don't know. It seems like you only tell me enough to get me to do what it is you want me to do. You leave me to figure out the rest and then get mad when I do something you don't like."

"You mean, like almost get yourself killed?"

"Yeah," Nicholas said. "Some friend. I thought angels were supposed to be nice…helpful."

Zha'riel snorted and stood so abruptly, his chair skidded back and slammed into the wall behind him. "Nicholas, I am not a fluffy-feathered, white-robed, little man sitting on your shoulder, telling you what you should and should not do. Angels are warriors…soldiers of the Lord. We have been fighting this war for eons, before time itself. Your world is less than ten thousand years old. That is but a moment to us. So, when I come here to "help" you, rest assured, I am not here to be your best friend. I have come to prepare you for war."

Nicholas stared at him. "Is that right? Well, I'm not fighting in your stupid war."

"If that is what you think."

"That's what I *know*," Nicholas spat.

"Of course you do."

Nicholas sighed in frustration. "You know what? I'm really starting not to like you."

Zha'riel shook his head. "Nicholas, I am not here to be liked. This is not a friendship. My mission is to keep you alive and help you avoid making the fatal mistake of choosing darkness over light, which, in my opinion, you are in serious jeopardy of doing."

ᚦ A ᛆ ψ ᏻ

"So," Azazel said, his face an unreadable mask. He stood at the edge of the one thousand-foot cliff, overlooking the Barents Sea at Nordkapp, Norway. "You were lucky to make it out of there alive?"

Seir nodded. He stood at rigid attention as his master scanned the horizon in the dim glow of Nordkapp's midnight sun. It was their standard meeting place, mostly due to the nominal population. The prying eyes of the underworld were often more intrusive than Heaven, but no one cared about such remote lands. It was a quiet place, perfect for secret meetings, but so were a lot of other, even more remote places. Seir secretly believed his master preferred the view from the Cape. Ordinarily, Seir could enjoy the view as well, but not this night.

"Yes," he replied. "Another few seconds and I'd be talking to you from Purgatory right now, if that's even possible."

Azazel leveled his fierce white eyes on him for several silent seconds before turning back to the seascape. "It isn't." Then, his face broke into a wry grin. "So, you went up against one of my little cousins and almost met your demise." He guffawed as his eyes roved across the still sea. "You did well to escape."

Seir didn't know which was scarier, Azazel when he was angry, or Azazel when he wasn't. His temper was legendary, but legend also had it that he did his most terrifying work in complete and utter calm. Seir had witnessed both and hated the mere thought of being on the wrong end of either. As he sat listening to Azazel's sinister pleasure at his expense, Seir wondered if he would end up feeling Azazel's wrath. He had never failed his master before.

"Almost," Seir repeated.

Azazel clasped his hands behind his back and breathed in the cool sea air. "You let the human surprise you."

It wasn't a question. Seir could sense the disdain in his master's voice. He was already humiliated. If word spread around the underworld that a human got the drop on him, Seir might have trouble down the road. That kind of news made a demon appear weak to his peers and sometimes it brought out challengers. One's status in Lucifer's army was often in flux, with demons willing to kill allies for the opportunity to grow stronger and advance their ranking. And why not? With new demons constantly arriving, as fresh souls poured into Hell, there was no shortage of new soldiers with nothing to live for and a great deal of tormented anger to unleash.

It was no secret that Lucifer, and to a greater extent, Azazel, encouraged a cutthroat attitude at the demon level. It only erupted in the demon ranks, particularly at the lower levels. The red-eyes were so highly trained and professional they were seldom challenged. Then again, red-eyed demons didn't get beaten up by humans, even a special human.

"Yeah," Seir admitted. "He surprised me…for a minute."

Azazel tilted his head and squinted. "And you're certain he unleashed dark energy?"

"No question about it. It was nasty stuff, like I've seen *you* dish out."

Azazel held up his hand, palm up, and brought crackling energy to his fingertips. He stared at the violet energy, sizzling as it arced from finger to finger. He knew the power to harness energy was not the stuff of beginners.

"He couldn't have been very strong," Azazel stated with conviction.

"Not really," agreed Seir. "The power was definitely the real deal, but I've seen you vaporize a demon in seconds. He didn't have that kind of control. He didn't really know what to do with it. I'm not sure how that's possible though."

Azazel narrowed his eyes. "It's possible," he said, disdain still dripping from his every word. "It's possible if the powers aren't really his."

Seir frowned, considering this possibility. "But how would he…?" Then his eyes grew wide as the reality sank in. He stared at Azazel, mouth agape. "Sansata?" He whispered the name with reverence.

Azazel's white-hot eyes flashed silver with controlled rage. He nodded once, maintaining his cool demeanor. The cool exterior wasn't much of a disguise. Azazel was a masterful tactician and warrior. He was feared throughout the ranks of the underworld and even throughout Heaven's army. Just the mention of his name was enough to send waves of panicked fear washing over legions of angels and demons alike, but he was unpredictable, even to his allies.

"How do we proceed?" Seir asked. It was the best way to handle the situation. Maybe if he still wanted the case, Azazel would give him further orders rather than tear him apart.

Azazel studied him for a few moments, and Seir got the distinct impression his mind was being read. Azazel was on to his little mental game, he was sure of it, but if that were true, Azazel didn't let on. His eyes flicked to some passers-by, tourists probably, out to see the midnight sun for the first time. He said nothing while they gazed in awe at the phenomenon. Azazel was suspicious of everyone, constantly on the alert for an attack from the other side. That's what twelve hundred years of torment at the hands of Heaven's most powerful and terrifying archangel would do to you. Azazel never stayed put, never let his guard down.

Azazel considered for several moments as he scanned his surroundings. He had to be careful. Going against Lucifer's commands was a dangerous game to play, even for one as powerful as Azazel. There was crazy and then there was stupid. Azazel was not stupid, but his need for vengeance outweighed his loyalty to the Dark Lord. Lucifer should never have denied him vengeance for his son.

But he had to proceed with caution. Lucifer would have to react when he found out his closest advisor was undermining his efforts at seducing the human to his cause. Since Lucifer was maintaining secrecy, keeping his operation closely guarded, it was easy for Azazel to find high-level demons willing to work for him personally. Seir had no idea he was involved in a plot that went directly against the wishes of the Dark Master. Had he known, he would have refused. Seir was loyal, but there was a limit. No matter what reputation Azazel had garnered in his eons of war alongside Lucifer, he could never compete with the one who had defied the Father to His face and survived.

Azazel remembered that day. Lucifer had already done the unthinkable and refused to follow the command of the Father. His brothers, Michael and Gabriel, pleaded with him to reverse course, but Lucifer was stubborn. Azazel supported his friend. They both knew there was no way the Father was going to allow him his rebellion. There would be dire consequences. The only solution was to take the throne.

Michael had gotten wind of their intentions and rallied the Heavenly Host to an unprecedented war footing. Never before had Heaven seen such crisis, but a civil war loomed. Azazel remembered the surprise when he and Lucifer, backed by roughly one third of Heaven's angels, made their move and were confronted by Heaven's massive army, led by Michael. The brothers faced off, prepared to battle to the death, when the Father intervened. Heaven shook as His presence filled the ether. His anger froze the entire assembly in place as his fist crashed between the two sides, forever separating those who defended Heaven from those who sought to destroy it.

Azazel would never forget the look on Lucifer's face as they fell away from Heaven. For the briefest of moments, he thought he saw regret, but even if that were true, it quickly changed to a look of utter defiance and rage. And it was contagious. Azazel thought he would take the blame and Lucifer's wrath because of his encouragement and the role he played in the disastrous plot, but he didn't. Lucifer became more and more convinced of his power and authority and ultimately came to consider Azazel his closest confidant, his true brother. The power Lucifer exercised from that moment on was unlike anything Azazel had ever imagined.

Now, for the first time in their long relationship, Azazel considered an act of defiance. The last thing he wanted was to have Lucifer turn on him, but he also wasn't about to work with the human peon who killed his son. No, that young man wasn't going to make it that far. He would be dead soon, preferably long before Lucifer got his hooks into him. Everyone thought

Azazel was insane, and they were right, but defying Lucifer might be the craziest thing he'd ever considered...*since* advising his best friend to challenge God Himself.

He turned to Seir. "We need to end this kid...soon."

"He's got an angel guarding him," Seir replied. "Now that they know we're after him, I doubt we'll get another chance to get close."

Azazel's eyes flashed silver again. "Well then," he said in an even tone. "I suppose, since you allowed yourself to be discovered and then failed to complete your mission, you are eager to redeem yourself."

Seir nodded and sighed softly. It was a suicide mission, but Azazel care. He was sending his best man in irrespective of the likely outcome. One the one hand, it was what he had been trained for. On the other, it seemed like a waste. A demon against an angel wasn't close to fair, and Zha'riel was an ancient warrior, one of Rafael's special soldiers. Seir would have to figure out a way around Zha'riel if he had any hope for success.

Chapter 13

"If you want me to get on board with whatever it is you've got in mind, then you need to teach me what I need to know."

Nicholas took a brand-new rocks glass from Xabier. It was heavier than he expected. He gulped the brown liquid and swished it around his mouth before swallowing. He liked the taste…a lot. And Xabier was right, it did taste better in a nice glass. He slid the glass down the counter to Xabier who grinned and refilled it before sliding it back.

"I knew you'd like Scotch." Xabier sipped from his own glass and savored the smoky flavor. "It's a true gentleman's drink."

The vampire tilted his head and raised his eyebrows at Zha'riel, who stood in impatient silence. The angel declined Xabier's offer to pour him a glass. He turned his attention back to Nicholas.

"I cannot teach you to use the powers of darkness," Zha'riel stated.

Nicholas' stomach churned with icy rage. "Then get out."

"Nicholas," Stephanie said. "Don't do this."

Nicholas shrugged. "Trust is important, isn't it? I don't know if I trust this guy."

"But I *can* help you," Zha'riel insisted.

"How can you help me if you won't *help* me?"

Nicholas finished his drink and pulled a beer from the fridge. He didn't want to get wasted, and he would if he kept drinking the Scotch. His tolerance was way up, but he feared he liked the taste way too much for his own good. Beer was the better option for an argument with an angel anyway.

"The evil you now face," Zha'riel said, "is an evil we have spent eons fighting. We know them better than anyone."

Zha'riel pressed his lips together. Nicholas could see the wheels spin in the angel's mind. He knew he had to lay out a lot of information if he had any hope of remaining in Nicholas' life. Nicholas understood Zha'riel had orders and was limited in what he was allowed to divulge, but enough was enough. He needed to tell Nicholas the truth.

"In the beginning," he said, taking a breath. "There was God, the Father, His Spirit, and His Son, all together as a single entity, yet with three distinct personas. And there were legions upon legions of angels...the Heavenly Host. The Father announced a plan. It was a strange and fascinating plan, until the Father demanded the Heavenly Host bow to the Son."

Zha'riel's eyes softened as he recalled a time in the far distant past. "You have to understand...we were created to worship the Father and no one else. It was a major shift, but a command from the Father was not to be questioned, just obeyed. Most obeyed without question."

"Most?" asked Nicholas sitting down on the couch in the living room and pulling Stephanie to curl up with him on his lap. She rested her head on his chest, but kept her eyes fixed on Zha'riel. "But not all?"

"Not all," repeated Zha'riel, his eyes misting over. "Lucifer refused to bow. He accused his brother, Michael, the eldest of the angels, of thoughtless obedience, and Gabriel the youngest of the three, of being blindly led around by Michael."

Xabier shook his head. "Oldest? Youngest? Angels have ages?"

"Of course," Zha'riel said, as if it were obvious. "Michael was the first created being, followed by Lucifer, and then Gabriel.

There were many created after those three, but they are the eldest of all the angels and considered the Father's direct descendants."

Nicholas nodded as though he recognized the names. Stephanie straightened up on the couch and stared at Zha'riel. He could see she was trying to work through something in her head.

"So, the angels Michael and Gabriel are actually *real?*" she asked. "All these stories the church tells are true history? Even the angel stuff?"

Zha'riel nodded. "Even the angel stuff. Angels are the messengers of God, the warriors of Heaven, the defenders of God's people. Your Bible doesn't focus on angels. That is not the purpose of those stories, so you're understanding is skewed. You must realize, what you know of the supernatural world is shrouded in religion, myth, art, and lore. As man has digressed, since his own fall, he has gradually lost touch with the supernatural until only a select few have managed to maintain their connection, and *that* connection is often tenuous at best."

Nicholas bit his lip. "But Mattaeus was very powerful, right? You told me he was one of the most powerful mages who ever lived."

"And he certainly was, for modern times. In the beginning of time, men like Mattaeus were the norm. Now, there are few who ever approach that level of achievement. Mattaeus was quite special."

Nicholas nodded. He wrapped his arms around Stephanie like she was a life preserver, or perhaps his only real link to a normal life. "So, what happened with Lucifer and Michael? You said they were brothers?"

"Correct," Zha'riel said. "Lucifer, with urging from Azazel, his closest friend, openly defied the Father's command. Have you ever wondered *how* evil came into existence?" He held up a finger and shook it. "That was the moment. You see, there can be no such thing as evil if there does not first exist a rule or a command to be defied. When the Father issued His command, Lucifer became the first being to ever act on his impulse for autonomy."

Nicholas nodded and looked over at Xabier, who sat in rapt attention. Zha'riel followed his gaze. In the short time Nicholas had known him, he could never remember anything holding his interest for so long. The vampire was never this fixated and somber.

"You're awfully quiet," Nicholas said, pulling Xabier from his trance. "Are you buying all this?"

"You're not?" Xabier raised his eyebrows and dropping his jaw. "This is fascinating stuff, Nico. How often do you get to hear the history of history from someone who was actually *there*? He's talking about things that happened *before time existed*...before this universe was born. How can you *not* be amazed?"

Nicholas grinned and nodded. He leaned back and looked at Zha'riel. "Go on."

The angel continued. "Lucifer openly defied the Father. To make matters worse, he decided his only course of action was to try to take the throne. He actually sought to take the life of the Son. How he intended to accomplish that goal is still a mystery to all of us, but one day, he, along with one third of the Heavenly Host, marched on the throne. Of course, standing in front of the entrance was Michael and a massive army of angels. It was going to be a civil war, but the Father intervened, casting out Lucifer and all of his followers. That is why we refer to them as 'fallen' angels."

Nicholas, Xabier, and Stephanie stared in awe as he Zha'riel presented the condensed version. Zha'riel didn't totally understand their fascination. As he paced the worn carpet of Nicholas' living room, he struggled to remain in control of his emotions. For him, the story was the saddest story ever told. It was the beginning of an ongoing war, one that would continue in perpetuity until the Father ended it. It meant the deaths of countless of his brethren, to say nothing of the loss of one third of the original angelic host. Lucifer's rebellion changed history...for everyone.

Zha'riel continued. "Heaven had to quickly reorganize. Angelic duties were divided. Michael took charge of building Heaven's army while Gabriel led the Heavenly Host. Meanwhile, in the ether outside of Heaven, the fallen angels quickly descended into civil war. Many rejected Lucifer's leadership and blamed him for their loss of grace. Others just wanted to be the leader. It was fierce and ugly. We watched from Heaven as they destroyed one another, thankful they kept the war to themselves. Ultimately it came down to Lucifer's Dark Army versus everyone else. The others dubbed themselves Titans."

"Wow," Stephanie breathed. "I'm trying to imagine a war between the most powerful beings in existence."

"Your imagination could not even come close," Zha'riel replied. "It was horrifying. But then, the Father put the next part of His plan into place. He created the natural world, or rather, the Son did, at the Father's bidding."

Xabier's mouth dropped open. "So, He created the world in the middle of a supernatural war?"

Zha'riel nodded. "In retrospect, I suppose it was a strange decision, but He does what He does for His own reasons and those reasons are perfect. We know that, so the war must have been foreseen, as was the resultant failure of mankind on Earth."

"God knew what would happen and created the world anyway?" Nicholas asked, bewildered. "That makes no sense at all."

Zha'riel felt the corners of his mouth curl. He'd had the same conversation a thousand times before, even with his angel brethren. "Well, your opinion is biased, right? God's reasons are probably not in line with what you *think* His reasons were for creating the world. Remember, it is never about the creation. It is about the Creator…about *His* glory."

"Sounds kinda self-centered to me," Nicholas replied.

"Perhaps," Zha'riel said, raising a shoulder and pursing his lips. "But when is the creation more important than the creator? And once the creation rebels, why would the creator ever concern himself with it again?"

Nicholas shrugged. "Fair enough. So, that's what happened?"

"It is," Zha'riel said. "Everyone has heard of the Garden of Eden, right? Lucifer found a way into the natural world."

"Why would the Father do something like that?" Stephanie asked with a frown. "Allow evil into His creation?"

Zha'riel nodded. "Another very good question, Stephanie. And one that only the Father knows the answer to. Perhaps because it was the only way to truly *test* His creation. You see, He created this beautiful paradise and then placed man at the center of it all with only one rule. But it was not enough to simply set a rule. He needed a temptation…a differing perspective, if you will. And the only differing perspective in existence at the time was Lucifer."

"So Lucifer and God got together to test man?" Nicholas asked, perplexed. "Why would they ever work together?"

"I think," Zha'riel replied, "the more likely scenario is that God was aware of Lucifer's desire to enter the creation and destroy it. Lucifer can do nothing the Father does not allow, but He tries and tries. I believe the Father allowed a small opening for Lucifer to exploit and then events just unfolded."

Nicholas shook his head. "So, God just let it happen…*made* it happen."

"No," Zha'riel shook his head. "He *allowed* it to happen."

"Like that makes a difference," Nicholas retorted. "If I see something bad about to happen and I'm in a position to stop it, I should stop it."

"Yet you continue down a path of selfish gain even though you are well aware that selfishness is a bad thing and that stealing, no matter from whom, is also a bad thing."

"Because," Nicholas pointed out, "I can do good things with the money, and crippling drug cartels has to be better than letting them run rampant."

Zha'riel nodded. "If you say so, but then how can you condemn the Father? He gave His creation the chance for immortality and perfection, and it chose destruction, but He continues to show mercy even as the world descends into chaos."

"It's pretty twisted," Nicholas said with a wry smile. "But I guess it is what it is. What happened next?"

Zha'riel continued the story. "After man fell, the Father cursed the Earth. Lucifer then was able to bring his minions into the natural world. The Titans soon followed and the war spilled over into the natural world. On top of all that death and destruction, the fallen angels began seducing and then impregnating human women,"

"How?" Xabier asked, leaning forward. "I was under the impression that angels were...you know..."

Stephanie giggled and buried her face in Nicholas' chest as everyone looked at her. "Sorry," she said in a muffled voice.

"Angels were not created as male and female," Zha'riel said. "However, once the natural world came into being and we were allowed to enter it, we all assumed a human form, even the fallen angels. It was better than the alternative, I suppose. Having angels in their true form would kill humans on sight, but with a human form came human characteristics, including the ability to engage in sexual relations."

Nicholas blinked. "Sooo...angels having sex with humans..."

"*Fallen* angels," Zha'riel pointed out. "An angel of the Lord is prohibited."

Nicholas shook his head. "So, *fallen* angels were seducing human women...why?"

"Demons," Xabier breathed. "That was how the demon army was created."

"High-level demons," Zha'riel added. "You see, there are two ways a demon is created. The first is when a soul is sent to Hell. Lucifer's minions who rule the Underworld torture human souls until they are stripped of their humanity. At that point, they become purely evil and assume the form of a demon, which is basically a kind of black steam or smoke. That is their true form. From there, they can possess a human vessel, making that vessel superhuman and able to travel between the natural realm and the supernatural realm. They have jet-black eyes and are the lowest form of demon."

"So," Nicholas said, "Seir was a red-eyed demon. That means he wasn't a tortured human soul?"

"Probably not," replied Zha'riel. "The higher-level demons came into being in a little more complicated manner. First, a fallen angel would mate with a human. The resultant offspring would generally be a lesser version of the fallen angel, but still powerful enough to be considered angelic. That generation would mate with another human, and so on, until the resultant offspring would not rise to the level of an angelic being, though they would still be far more powerful than a tortured human soul."

"So," Stephanie mused, "it's kinda like diluting their gene pool by reproducing with weaker mates."

Zha'riel nodded. "Exactly. Just like humans mating with someone who has a genetic condition. It passes along through the generations, especially if the offspring finds another human with the same genetic disposition. Each generation is weaker than the last. So, there are many, many levels of supernatural evil beings. In fact, when lower-level demons mated with human women, there was often offspring that was more human than demon. You've heard of giants, for example?"

Nicholas' head snapped up. "You mean like David and Goliath?"

"Precisely," Zha'riel gestured with an open hand. "Goliath was a direct descendant of a black-eyed demon named Coraeu. So, you can see how even the lowest level demon can produce something far more powerful than the average human."

Silence hung over them as Zha'riel paused. Xabier sat in stunned amazement. Nicholas' eyes revealed his confused state. Zha'riel watched as Stephanie followed Nicholas with her eyes. Her deep concern was obvious to Zha'riel. He wished she could be sent away to a safe place until the situation could stabilize, but she would never allow herself to be apart from Nicholas even though the circumstances were becoming increasingly more frightening.

"Demons are also responsible for the dark chakra that is in the world today. Remember, man was created to be in harmony with nature, so what we generally refer to as light, or good chakra has always been a part of the natural world. That is what Mattaeus gave to you, Nicholas. But the demons, in addition to producing physically mutated offspring, also produced mentally mutated offspring. This meant that there were now humans with dark chakra inside them and the ability to bend or access nature to their will. Now we have witches and warlocks on both sides, sorcerers and magi, all manner of psychic, and countless other variations of these things."

Nicholas sighed. "And now I'm right in the middle of all that."

The young human was despondent. Zha'riel could see that much, and he felt for the kid. It was so much bigger than he ever imagined. His mind wasn't ready to wrap itself around so much ancient and ageless history, but he didn't have a choice, and Zha'riel had little time to coddle the boy.

"Yes," Zha'riel nodded. "It is finally coming clear."

"I..." Nicholas felt his throat tightening. He got up and paced for several seconds, trying to get control of his emotions. Finally, he kissed Stephanie on the top of her head and said, "I have to get out of here."

And with that, he was gone.

Chapter 14

He started out on the boardwalk. It was late, but there were still tourists enjoying the cool breeze, vendor food, and shopping. The salt air washed over him and filled his lungs. His heart began to settle as he approached the spot where he was when he first saw Xabier and the hunter. Nicholas chuckled to himself as he realized how close he had come to witnessing a murder, and it hadn't even been the strangest thing that happened to him that day. In fact, so much had happened since then that Nicholas hadn't given those events a second thought.

That hunter had to be out there looking for Nicholas as well as Xabier. He wondered where the guy was right then. He wondered if the guy would accept the fact that Nicholas had no intention of hurting people, or would he try to hunt him anyway? Surely the hunter had to know that at least *some* of the supernatural creatures in the world were good. Did he just not care about that? You'd think hunters, if they were really trying to protect humans, would make allies when and where they could.

His thoughts drifted to Stephanie. She was never far from the front of his mind. He pictured her soft blonde hair as it fell just below her shoulders, which were perfectly toned, like every other muscle in her body. What Nicholas really admired was her mental toughness. He imagined most girls would have run away immediately upon hearing his insane story. Even when faced with the reality that vampires and angels were real, and she was actually talking to them, Stephanie managed to maintain her composure and keep a level head about everything.

And she loved him. He couldn't forget that little nugget of information. Nicholas never had a girlfriend. Now, he was with a beautiful blonde-haired, blue-eyed, sweetheart of a girl who was in love with him even after hearing his secrets. It swelled his heart to think of her soft blue eyes staring into his and her telling him she wasn't afraid of him…that she wanted to be with him no matter what…that he couldn't get rid of her if he tried. He was so sorry he'd ever brought her into his world. Now she was in real danger and it was all because of him.

Had he been successful against Seir, Nicholas would have felt better about the future, but Seir handled him with such ease, it rattled him beyond belief. For the first time in his life, Nicholas knew what death's presence felt like. It was only Zha'riel's intervention that saved him. It was only Zha'riel's presence that kept Stephanie safe. Nicholas was painfully aware of his own weakness. It was amusing, sort of…not really. Before the supernatural transformation, Nicholas had always been the scrawny kid who played video games and tapped out code on his laptop. He didn't get girls and did his best to stay out of the spotlight. Now he was strong, had the body and looks to get the girls, and felt even weaker than before.

Sure, he had Stephanie. What was he to do about her now though? He couldn't just leave her on her own. The underworld was aware of her connection to him. Nicholas had no choice but to try to protect her. That meant he had to learn fast; he had to *use* his powers. Despite what Zha'riel claimed, Nicholas knew the dark powers were his best option and he wanted to hasten the learning curve. Those powers pulled at him, the need for release greater than ever. He felt more and more powerful every time he unleashed them.

"What the…!"

The shout snapped him out of his thoughts. Nicholas raised his eyes and he saw three men, in their twenties, all dressed in sagging shorts, with tank-tops and open button-down shirts.

Glancing around, Nicholas realized, in his aimless wandering, he had ventured into a rundown part of Atlantic City known for violence, drugs, and other criminal activity.

Cold washed over him and Nicholas felt himself fade into the background. He should have been terrified. He should have run away. He should have pulled out his phone and called the police. He should have at least *wanted* to do those things, but something took over his thought process. He knew what was about to happen, yet, he could do nothing to stop it. It was different than before, when he was in control. Now, he felt possessed, out of body.

"Can I help you?" he asked in a pleasant tone as they approached with menacing snarls on their faces.

They laughed.

"Can I help you?" one of them mimicked before bursting into another fit of laughter.

"Yeah, you can help us," another said, licking his lips and punching a fist into his palm. He was obviously the leader. "You can empty them pockets."

Nicholas nodded. "Yeah, sure, that's easy." He turned his pockets inside out. He had nothing at all on him. Even his cell phone had been left at home.

The three guys exchanged puzzled looks. "You ain't got nuthin?"

Nicholas shrugged. "Nope. Sorry, dudes." He turned, and continued on his way.

One of the guys grabbed him by his shirt and yanked him back. "Where you think you goin?"

"Just walking around," Nicholas replied. He fought against his own amusement. He didn't want to do what he was about to do. He had to find some way to gain control. On the other hand, these guys were the ones looking for trouble. Why couldn't they leave people alone?

"Yeah, well, you wanna walk round this town, you gotta pay."

Nicholas yawned. "I'm broke. I guess I'll just go home."

"Nah," the guy replied. "You ain goin nowhere."

Nicholas nodded and pursed his lips as the cold coil around his core tightened and thoughts of mercy faded. He had to leave if he wanted to spare the bloodshed, but he couldn't make himself orb out. "Tell you what. I'm going to give you one chance to walk away from me, and then I'm going to make you wish you were never born."

They all laughed until the leader pulled out a black pistol and put it to Nicholas' head. "You think this is a game?"

Nicholas had never seen a gun before, and certainly never had one to his head. He would have thought the experience would frighten him, but it didn't. Instead, he felt an eerie calm wash over him as he stared past the weapon and right into the eyes of the guy holding it. Righteous anger coursed through him as some part of him labeled the gun-wielding guy a danger. Nicholas fought the homicidal urge, but he was fighting from a place deep within himself, and felt as though he was falling. Nicholas felt his eyes flicker and saw the scene in front of him through his silver filter, and he knew something bad was about to happen.

The guy with the gun saw the silver flash in Nicholas' eyes and his own eyes widened in shock.

"What the…?"

Before he could form the words, he was sent reeling back as Nicholas sent a burst of wind into his chest. The gun flew out of his hand as he tumbled to the ground. His friends stood there in disbelief because Nicholas hadn't even moved. Nicholas nonchalantly stepped away and strode down the block as though nothing had happened.

The guys recovered from their surprise and reached out to grab him. Nicholas spun at the last second and threw out his hands in a twisting motion. He unleashed a wave of super-cooled air that lifted them off their feet and slammed them to the ground several feet down the block. When they landed, with dull thuds, Nicholas saw they were immobilized. They twitched and struggled, but it was as though their bodies were frozen stiff.

Nicholas had no idea what he'd just done to them, but it had felt so natural, flowing from deep within. He turned as the first guy found his gun and leveled it at Nicholas.

"Don't," Nicholas warned.

The guy hesitated, just for a second, looking like he was going to drop the gun. Then Nicholas saw the flash of hatred in his eyes and knew a peaceful solution wasn't happening. Nicholas' perception was such that everything moved in super-slow-motion. In reality, the guy aimed and fired in less than a second at point-blank range. Nicholas should have taken a bullet to his chest or stomach.

It didn't happen because Nicholas twisted away and the bullet sailed wide. He flicked his hand and the gun flew into the street. Another flick of his fingers sent the guy flying onto the hood of the black BMW the crew had been leaning when he'd approached. He slid off and fell to the asphalt. Nicholas strolled up as the guy picked himself off the ground. As soon as he was up, Nicholas grabbed him with a chakra grip and slammed him face first into the hood of the car, denting the hood and breaking the guy's nose. Blood gushed down, around the guy's mouth and dripped off his chin.

In most cases, the sight of so much blood would sicken Nicholas, and he was horrified to find that it didn't. As he fought for control, something clicked in his mind. He wasn't responsible for these thugs. *They* were the ones out looking for trouble. *They* were the ones who wanted to do *him* harm. This was self-defense. They deserved to have their own violence shoved back at them, didn't they? Perhaps his horror was unfounded. Perhaps, everything happened for a reason. Perhaps, Nicholas was in a position to clean up some of the evil in the world.

Nicholas was about to finish the guy off, but another thought floated across his mind. "Say, who do you work for?"

"Screw you!"

CRASH! The guy slammed, headfirst, through the passenger side window of the BMW. Nicholas' hands-free grip pulled him right back out, covered in broken glass and bleeding from a deep gash on his forehead. Blood continued to pour from his nose.

"What was that you said?" Nicholas asked cheerfully. "I didn't quite catch that name."

"I ain tellin you n…!"

CRASH! The passenger side rear window went next and the guy emerged, still locked in Nicholas' chakra grip. He could barely stand on his own, but Nicholas held him up. He stood in front of the guy and pressed his lips together.

"I don't know how much it costs to replace these windows, but compared to the damage we're doing to your face, I'm guessing it's pretty cheap, huh?" He glanced over at the two other guys who showed signs of life. Whatever he'd done to them, it wore off quickly and didn't seem to leave ill-effects.

Looking back at the bloody mess in front of him, he asked, "Do you feel like telling me the name and address of the guy you're working for now?"

"I-I can't. He'll kill me." The guy's voice trembled and Nicholas finally saw stone-cold fear in his eyes.

Nicholas didn't hesitate. Seconds later, the guy's face smashed the entire back window out of his seventy-thousand-dollar car. It took three blows to complete the task. Nicholas then held him up again and gave him the same basic choice.

"Now," he said. "There are two more windows that I know I can break with your head. But if we get to the windshield, I don't know how many times I'll have to smash you into it to get it to break out of there, so think before you answer. Who do you work for, and where can I find him?"

"O-o-o-ok-okay," the guy surrendered. "His name's Jamal." He gestured at a small, two-story cottage across the street on the corner. Nicholas looked at the house the guy indicated.

"The yellow one?" he asked.

"Y-y-yeah."

Nicholas looked at him. "You know, if you're lying to me, I'll have to bash your skull in."

"I ain't lyin, man! Come on! Lemme go!"

Nicholas released him and the guy dropped to the ground. The other two began to move their arms and legs. He thought about hitting them all again, but figured they'd been punished enough for ruining his walk. He strolled toward the yellow house on the corner, propelled by a force he still could not control, let alone fight.

He orbed right into the living room of the house, where two guys with small machine guns sat on chairs near the door. The looks on their faces when Nicholas appeared in front of them was priceless. They recovered quickly, raising their guns. Nicholas unleashed a vicious burst of wind aimed at their heads and snapping their necks. Despite the terrifying reality of killing two men, Nicholas couldn't stop himself from moving. On autopilot, he stalked from room to room, taking out two other armed men before going up the stairs.

In the bedroom, Nicholas found a well-built shirtless guy in his mid-thirties sleeping in the master bedroom. The girl he was with awoke first, and Nicholas would have told her to get out, but her first course of action was to yell, and her second was to go for the gun she had under her pillow. Nicholas rolled his eyes and sent a slap of air at her hands, knocking the weapon to the ground. He then sent a violent burst of energy that slammed her back against the headboard. Before she could drop to the floor, Nicholas flung her across the room with a flick of his wrist. She shattered the window before she fell out, hanging by only her fingertips as she tried to climb back in.

By now, Jamal was wide awake but unable to do anything to help because Nicholas had him by the neck. He threw the bigger guy across the room like a rag doll, obliterating the wall. The drywall was knocked out and two of the studs cracked in half. Jamal wasn't too badly injured because he jumped to his feet and lunged at Nicholas, who easily sidestepped and, with a massive burst of chakra energy, sent Jamal headlong through the door and tumbling out into the hallway.

As Jamal staggered to his feet Nicholas' chakra grip slammed him into the wall.

"One question," Nicholas said. "And one chance to answer correctly. Who do you work for and where do I find them?" He tilted his head and wrinkled his forehead. "I guess that was two questions, wasn't it?"

"You a dead man, you know th...?"

"Wrong answer!" Nicholas shouted, slamming the guy repeatedly into the wall until the drywall was completely gone and the studs obliterated. He flung the barely conscious Jamal down the flight of stairs.

When he got to the bottom of the staircase, Nicholas grabbed the guy and pulled him to his feet. He was standing on very wobbly legs.

"Who and where?" Nicholas asked again.

"Kiss my a—"

Nicholas hurled him across the room, taking out a small table and chair set before smashing through another wall. Without waiting for the dust to settle, Nicholas blinked his eyes and he was at Jamal's side, grabbing him and flinging him across the room back toward the staircase, right into the ornate wooden handrail. He smashed through that like it was made of toothpicks and wound up sprawled upside down on the stairs. Nicholas grabbed him by the shoulders and stood him up.

"So," he said matter-of-factly, "how many more walls am I going to have to smash up before you tell me what I need to know?"

"I don't give a f—"

Nicholas smashed his head backwards into the wall and threw Jamal to the ground.

"All right, you scumbag," he said, blind rage welling up inside his heart. "I'm through being patient with you."

With that, he unleashed a wave of crackling green energy from his fingertips. It was a vicious attack he thought would get out of control. He fought with all of his being to rein it in. The rage came within a hair's breadth of consuming him, but it yielded a positive result. Jamal held out his hands and pleaded with him.

"Don't do that no more," he whimpered. "I'll tell you."

"Excellent," Nicholas replied, leaning down to hear the information.

Moments later, as he was preparing to leave, Nicholas whirled around as two of the guys from earlier came crashing through the back door with guns blazing. He held out his hands and flicked his fingers. He had no idea what he was doing, but he felt something against his hands even though he was pushing at the air. Whatever it was, it gave and the next thing he knew, the two guys' heads snapped back like they'd run into a wall. They went limp and collapsed on the floor. Nicholas almost dropped to his knees in grief, but leaned against a wall for support.

With a snarl, Jamal staggered into the room with another gun. He leaned against the wall, but was strong enough to take aim at Nicholas and fire. Nicholas was surprised when the bullet struck his shoulder and didn't really hurt, but he didn't wait for another shot. He unleashed a fiery blast from his hands which consumed Jamal in seconds. Nicholas stuck around long enough to bathe the house in flames from every direction, setting each interior wall ablaze.

The sounds of police sirens approaching made him smile. Nicholas wondered what the police would think of the scene. They'd probably chalk it up to just another drug deal gone bad. Not that he cared. Nicholas had bigger fish to fry that night. He took one last look around and orbed out.

Chapter 15

Lord Sarkryal slammed a hand on the table. He was sick of search detail. They'd been tracking Sansata's essence for two weeks. Whenever they came close to pinpointing a location, it vanished. This was the fourth time in as many days. The screens displaying maps of the region along with the chakra-tracking overlays indicated nothing. The blip was gone. The mood in the Residence Inn suite went from excited anticipation to dread.

Abdiel appeared as the team was in full scramble mode. He frowned as Lord Sarkryal approached.

"It's like he just disappeared."

"Really." Abdiel's response came not as a question, but as the skeptical reply of an impatient leader wondering what his subordinates were doing with their time.

"General, we are working around the clock," Lord Sarkryal insisted, running a hand through his long, dark-brown hair. He usually pulled it into a tight ponytail, but now it fell between his shoulder blades as he worked. It felt like it freed his mind...not that it was helped in their search for the human. "We *had* him." He let out a long breath. "I don't know what to say."

"How can this be?" Abdiel replied, his piercing dark eyes flashing in frustration. "He's got two powerful essences trapped inside him. The conflict alone should be visible to us. Power like that in the untrained psyche of human would drive him insane if he tried to hold it in. The power has to spill out at some point."

Lord Sarkryal shrugged. "If it is, we haven't seen it."

"Well, that's stating the obvious, isn't it, Lord Sarkryal?"

Sarkryal didn't respond. It would only serve to further annoy his superior. He understood the general's impatience; he shared it. There was no reason for their failure to track down a lone human. Like the general stated, there should be some trace of this young man in the ether, but so far there was nothing. It didn't make sense. Unless…

"Angels," he muttered.

Abdiel frowned and turned to face him. "Did you say *angels?*"

"Yes," Sarkryal nodded, feeling his confidence rise as he considered the new possibility. "Think about it. There is no way this human could control his effect on chakra. Like you said, his essence will strain to be unleashed. So, he's either using the powers, or expending a great deal of energy trying to remain in control. Either way, he should be visible to us."

Abdiel put a knuckle to his pursed lips and raised his eyebrows. "So, something must be obscuring our view into the ether."

"Perhaps we should…" Sarkryal cut himself off and shook his head. "Never mind."

Abdiel frowned. "You had a thought, Lord Sarkryal. What was it?"

"It's stupid."

"Tell me anyway."

Lord Sarkryal sighed. "I was thinking maybe instead of looking for something new and unexpected to spike in the ether, maybe we should try looking for what *isn't* there."

Abdiel narrowed his eyes. "What *isn't* there," he repeated, his eyes narrowing. "So, what would indicate something that isn't there?"

Sarkryal shrugged. "That's why it's stupid. I feel like there's a good idea there, but I don't know how to use it."

Abdiel leaned against the back of a chair, appearing deep in thought, while Lord Sarkryal continued to focus on what they knew. It wasn't much, but they needed to bring in some results soon or risk angering the throne room and potentially having them all banished to some soul-retrieval detail in a far corner of the underworld. He hoped Abdiel would hold off telling Lucifer they'd lost the trail again. His personal rule was never volunteer bad information.

Abdiel was the first to speak. "Working on the theory that Heaven is somehow involved…*and* that they are somehow shielding the human's chakra pull, perhaps we can look for the *angels'* pull on chakra…something new over the past few weeks. Then we look for a human-sized gap close by."

Sarkryal wrinkled his forehead in thought. "A human-sized gap? We would have to know what was new and what was old in terms of chakra usage…"

"Which is why you have specialists assigned to you, Lord Sarkryal."

"I know who to call," Sarkryal nodded, opening the door and calling out.

Seconds later, a short-haired, platinum-blonde yellow-eyed demon entered the room. She bowed her head to Abdiel and turned her attention to Lord Sarkryal.

"My Lord, I believe we have something."

Sarkryal held up a hand. "First, Ruta, tell me, is it possible for you to focus on only *new* chakra use in a particular region?"

She pursed her lips together. "*New* use, Lord?"

"Yes," he replied. "New and consistent. Like the kind of pull you might see if angels are shielding something night and day."

"Ahhh." A glimmer of understanding crossed her face and she breathed in, long and slow, as she considered the possibility. "That makes sense," she nodded, her eyes glazing a bit as she thought about it. After a moment, she straightened up and looked Lord Sarkryal in the eyes. "Yes, I believe I can do that."

"And then," continued Sarkryal. "Find a gap where a human should be."

Her eyes widened. "Whoa. I'll need help."

"Whatever you need, Ruta. Make this happen quickly."

"Yes, My Lord."

"Now," he said. "You mentioned you had something?"

"Yes." Ruta nodded. "While we're not finding much locally, we did find a huge pull recently in the South American country of Colombia."

"Colombia?" Sarkryal frowned. "What could that possibly have to do with us?"

Ruta shrugged. "It was an unusual amount of chakra activity and it centered on five major cartel compounds. I believe they were all attacked supernaturally and relieved of hundreds of millions of dollars in cash and valuables."

Abdiel raised his eyebrows. "Like the banks in this country."

Ruta nodded. "We had the same thought, General." She shrugged. "Maybe it's not our guy, but…" She shrugged.

Abdiel glanced at Sarkryal, who spread his arms slightly and said, "It *could* be something…"

Abdiel was about to reply when he heard a knock on the door. "General?"

They all turned to see a young-looking demon with straight, slicked, jet-black hair, fierce green eyes that glowed red when he revealed his true presence, and a tattoo covering almost the entire right side of his face and neck, disappearing beneath his black shirt. He was an imposing presence, confident, and all business despite his thuggish appearance.

"Marmut," Abdiel said, waving him in. "You have something?"

Marmut entered and closed the door. "I think our guy just popped up." He handed Abdiel a file. "In this file, you'll find pictures of a crime scene in Atlantic City, New Jersey, less than ten miles from here. As you will see, the scene is a complete disaster. The house was burned to the ground. The police have no leads or suspects." He gestured to the file. "But look at the photos in the back of the stack. I took those myself."

Abdiel looked at the photos. He squinted his eyes and turned the images in his hand as he scrutinized each one. The blackened walls and charred ceilings clearly indicated a raging inferno that had to have multiple points of origin. Abdiel frowned.

"An odd way for fire to burn…" He glanced up at Marmut. "This is him?"

Marmut handed him a second file. It contained a similar scene. "This happened moments later, on the other side of town." He handed a third file over. "And this happened shortly after that." He produced a fourth file. "And this happened after *that*. Same kind of skipping fire, and more importantly, the same condition of the bodies."

Abdiel scanned the coroner's reports for all four crime scenes. "All the bodies had multiple broken bones and severe damage to the face and head," he said aloud as he read. Looking up, he said, "As if they were severely beaten before death."

"And," Marmut continued, "the condition of the house was unusual. Walls were smashed in and windows broken from the inside out." He pointed to the first file. "This house had an entire staircase railing splintered. A fire wouldn't do that."

"But a supernaturally strong and angry human might," Abdiel finished with a smile. "It would appear this human is going to do some of our work for us."

"How is that, General?" asked Lord Sarkryal.

"Well, if our goal is to seduce him to darkness, his willing pursuit of wrathful vengeance is a good sign."

Marmut peered at the photos. "I wonder what made him go after *these* people, though. They're just small-time criminals, especially the street dealers."

"But connected," stated Abdiel, scanning deeper into the file. "Our friend worked up the ladder, extracting information from the lower rungs, leading him to the higher ones." Abdiel closed the files and looked at Lord Sarkryal. "I think we have two leads we need to work on." He gestured to the files. "I'll handle this angle." Looking at Marmut and Ruta, he said, "I want you two to go to Colombia and take a look at those cartel robberies you found."

Marmut frowned. "Colombia? Robberies?"

Abdiel gestured to Ruta, who stood in silence as her superiors discussed the matter.

"Ruta here will fill you in on Colombia."

ᚦ ᚪ ᛄ ᚹ ᚸ

"You must stop this course of action, Nicholas." Zha'riel had changed tactics, no longer making demands, but he continued to implore Nicholas to change his path. "It will destroy you."

He cringed as they watched the morning news. All over the television, news crews reported from the various scenes of Nicholas' drug dealer rampage from the previous night. Xabier and Stephanie were riveted at the descriptions of each scene while Zha'riel's stoic monotone façade frayed at the seams. Regret seeped into his outward presence and he didn't like it. Angels were not permitted to engage in human emotions. They certainly felt them, to some extent, but acting on them and engaging with human beings based upon them was a mistake.

Zha'riel knew his superiors in Heaven were nearing the end of their patience with Nicholas. It was the second time Nicholas' antics had made the news. His bank thefts had been reported nationwide, but authorities had nothing to go on. The local news outlets seemed just as perplexed by the fires and murders of criminals. The best guess anyone was making was that a rival crew was responsible.

Nicholas shrugged in nonchalance...on the outside. On the inside, he cringed at the callous words about to spill from his lips. "What is the problem exactly, Zha'riel? Every single one of those people was evil. Every one of them was responsible for pouring filth into our communities, destroying neighborhoods, killing children, threatening and terrorizing everyone forced to live near them. They all deserved what they got."

Zha'riel returned Nicholas' petulant attitude with an incredulous look. "Just like the banks you robbed? Remember? They stole from the poor and powerless, right? And now you walk through a poor neighborhood and, instead of orbing out when you run into trouble, you choose to stay and annihilate powerless human beings." He shrugged and spread his hands. "Whose side are you on, exactly, Nicholas?"

Nicholas snorted. "Human beings? If you're going to stick up for someone, how about the people those "human beings" terrorize every day?"

"That," Zha'riel countered, "is not the point, Nicholas. You do not decide, on your own, who deserves what. That job is God's and God's alone."

"Well then, maybe I'm just God's…"

"Don't." Zha'riel pointed a finger at him. "You are *not* God's instrument. You are putting yourself at risk from powers that you have not even begun to consider."

Nicholas laughed. "You mean worse than Lucifer and Azazel? Tell me, Zha'riel, who is worse than Lucifer and Azazel?"

Zha'riel lowered his eyes and shook his head. Xabier and Stephanie stared, wide-eyed, at the exchange. Xabier frowned as he watched Zha'riel. He shook his head and let out a long, slow breath. Nicholas gave him a look.

"Just say it, Xabs."

"Heaven," Xabier breathed. He stood and put a hand on Nicholas' shoulder, looking him in the eye. "He's saying the angels are going to turn on you." He spun around to face Zha'riel and asked, "Am I right?"

Zha'riel nodded. As reluctant as he was to impart such terrible truths, Nicholas had pushed Heaven to its limit. "I am sorry, Nicholas, but if you continue on your present course, you will force the angels to destroy you before you can be fully consumed by darkness."

"But I'm *fighting* evil!" Nicholas slammed a hand on the counter. "What is it with you people? I took out drug dealing scum and you're telling me the angels are *pissed* about it?"

Zha'riel nodded. "Yes. Murder, no matter how you justify it, is not the way we handle evil. There is a process, and we do not act on our own. Killing human beings is strictly monitored and limited to necessary and authorized action only."

Nicholas rolled his eyes. "And you guys wonder why you never seem to get ahead in this war."

Zha'riel shrugged and clasped his hands in front of his belt. "It may not be efficient, but it keeps us from straying into the sin of wrath, which, as you have discovered, is very seductive."

"It's not seductive," Nicholas insisted, though Zha'riel could see his fingers fidget. "It's necessary…and it works. You should think about how many evil people we could rid the world of in a single day if we took some initiative and went to work."

"That is not something I would advise you to even consider." Zha'riel was beginning to feel like a broken record. The job of keeping Nicholas Scarlatti off the path of evil was proving futile. The kid seemed bent on destroying himself. "Understand, Nicholas, you are treading in dangerous waters. Think carefully about the next decisions you make because they will no doubt determine the direction of your life. And if you choose to follow a course of evil, make no mistake, you will be hunted down and destroyed."

Just then all the lights and windows shattered into dust and an excruciating, high-pitched squeal filled the room along with a blinding white light. Xabier and Stephanie cried out in pain and did their best to cover their ears. Nicholas dove for Stephanie and shielded her. Zha'riel stood his ground. He knew what was happening. In fact, he was a little surprised it had taken Rafael so long to make an appearance.

After several terrifying seconds, the searing light died down and the noise subsided. Nicholas had Stephanie wrapped in his arms, her face buried in his chest. He had his back to the light, so as he opened his eyes, all he saw was Xabier peeking out from between his fingers.

Nicholas staggered to his feet, pulling Stephanie up with him. When he turned, the first thing to catch his eye was a huge shadow filling one entire wall in the shape of a wing. Before he could blink, the shadow disappeared and Nicholas was left to wonder if he was hallucinating. Stephanie clutched the front of his shirt. He felt her tremble as he ran his hands over her back.

"It's okay, Sweetie," he whispered into her ear. "You're okay. I'm right here."

Zha'riel was the first to speak. "Nicholas Scarlatti, allow me to introduce the archangel Rafael."

Nicholas watched Xabier's eyes widen in terror. He squinted and faced the newcomer. If he had never heard of the supernatural world, Nicholas would swear Rafael was a professional football player. About six-foot-six with a broad chest, near-black skin, and massive arms, even his crisp, expensive suit couldn't disguise, he looked to Nicholas like he belonged on a big, green field, pushing through offensive lines and sacking quarterbacks. His golden-brown eyes revealed no emotion. He stood, towering over everyone. He was big and tall, but his presence made him appear three times his actual size.

Nicholas had no idea what an archangel was, but when he realized they weren't under attack, he grew angrier by the second. His home was a mess. Something inside him refused to back down and his eyes blazed.

"Do archangels clean up after themselves or do they just go around wrecking people's houses for the fun of it?"

Rafael didn't smile, didn't frown. He didn't react at all. He just leveled his steady gaze at Nicholas, his fierce eyes boring into him. Nicholas shrank a little, but tried to stand tall. His attempt at combining humor with sarcasm seemed lost on Rafael. He should have known.

"So," Rafael's deep voice filled the room. "This is the insolent human who chooses evil over good?"

He set his face at Nicholas while directing his query to Zha'riel.

"I believe he will ultimately choose good," replied Zha'riel.

Rafael flicked his eyes from Nicholas over to Zha'riel. "Is that so? Is he not fresh off a rampage which left fourteen people dead and three buildings destroyed?"

"Don't forget all the drugs that were destroyed along with the scum drug dealers," Nicholas shot back.

Xabier shot him a warning glance. His wide-eyed disbelief made Nicholas briefly second-guess his attitude, but that was soon replaced with indignation. He was tired of the angels and their high-and-mighty condescension. Who did they think they were?

Rafael's eyes darkened and his glare bored into Nicholas. "You would do well to watch your tone, human." His voice somehow deepened and grew even more monotone. It made the threat seem that much more sinister and imminent. "Your arrogance will bring you nothing but pain."

Nicholas tried to match his gaze, the anger inside him propping up his bold front. He knew he was fighting a losing battle, but the cold darkness had a stranglehold on him and wouldn't let him back down. It was odd, feeling one thing while expressing the exact opposite. He also felt like he was being bullied by the big kids on the playground, and the only way to get respect was to stand up to them.

And *that* had nothing to do with cold darkness.

"Yeah?" He raised his eyebrows. "Well maybe if the good guys stopped threatening me all the time, I might have a little more respect for them."

"We don't issue threats," Rafael answered. "If you listened to what the...*good guys*...said, impositions such as this would be unnecessary."

Nicholas shook his head. "You call it what you want. To me, you're just as bad as the demons. Just say what you came to say and leave, so I can clean up your mess, you big phony."

"Phony?" Zha'riel interjected.

Nicholas smirked. "Phony good guys. You two are just the flip-side of the demons who are after me. Both sides are after me, and whichever side I choose, the other side will kill me." He shrugged. "So maybe I'll simply choose *no* side."

"Nicholas," Xabier warned. "Don't."

"Maybe you ought to listen to your unsavory friend," Rafael suggested. "Though he is an example of everything that is wrong with you."

"At least he's a *real* friend," Nicholas shot back. "You guys are a couple of bullies with big giant sticks up your—"

"Understand *this*," Rafael replied, his voice rising with every syllable. "We are not here to be your friends, human. Make no mistake, you arrogant fool. You will not be permitted to continue as you are. I am here to put you on notice, Nicholas Scarlatti. Turn from your dark powers and allow Zha'riel to guide you. It is the only way you will be allowed to live."

Chapter 16

"Carlos! The boss wants to see you!"

Marmut was deep in thought, standing in the center of the security room, trying to get a sense of what had happened and if it could somehow be connected to their search for Sansata's killer. So much activity had gone on in the room since the robbery, they were having a hard time getting anything into focus. Ruta nudged him.

Marmut...or rather, his current vessel...was being summoned. They had set aside their regular vessels so they could possess the Los Llanos security team. It was the only way they would be able to freely roam the grounds and investigate without drawing attention to themselves.

"Answer," she hissed, "before they get suspicious and we have to kill them all."

Marmut grinned. He knew she wouldn't have a problem with that, but she was trying to be professional. Before leaving for Colombia, she had reviewed her entire theory with him and he hadn't rejected it. Instead, he filed every detail in his mind before. His peers thought Marmut was hot-tempered and unreasonable. He was nothing of the sort. He was quiet, calculating, and ruthless.

Marmut looked up and nodded at the guy, who nodded back before exiting the room. Marmut glanced at Ruta.

"Try not to kill anyone while I go see what this cockroach wants."

She almost burst out laughing. "Yes, sir," she said with a mock-salute

When Marmut entered the office of Guillermo Diaz, he immediately didn't like the guy. Guillermo was a short, well-built lunatic who looked like he was itching for a fight. Everyone around him was petrified of him, which Marmut knew was a fairly common leadership style for the drug industry...and for the demon industry as well for that matter.

"What do you have for me, Carlos?"

As he crossed the ugliest carpet he'd ever seen, Marmut shook his head, pulling the information from his new vessel's mind. Possessing a human body didn't just mean taking over an empty shell. The person was still in there. Even in death, a person's mind retained the information it had accumulated over its lifetime. Demons could usually pull off impersonating their vessel, at least in the short term.

"Nothing, sir." Marmut almost forgot to speak in Spanish, but at the last moment he managed to get the right words out.

Diaz narrowed his eyes, squinting at his security chief. "You'd better give me something soon or you'll find yourself floating down the Meta."

"I'm sorry, Jefe, there just isn't anyone talking about it. We've been spreading money around, trying to entice someone to come forward, but so far there's nothing."

Guillermo slammed his palm down on a handmade card table. "That's not good enough!"

Marmut, resisting the urge to tear the human's throat out, put his head down in submission and closed his eyes. "I'm sorry, sir."

"Shut up!" Diaz yelled, working himself up into a lather.

Marmot could see Guillermo Diaz called him up just to vent his frustration. He was looking for an excuse to take his frustration out on someone. His security chief was the obvious choice, especially since they were coming up empty on their search for the culprit who had the audacity to steal from a cartel boss. Diaz was the kind of boss who couldn't control his temper and needed someone to blame and punish.

"Now tell me," Diaz hissed. "What am I paying you for? What am I keeping you *alive* for?"

Marmut didn't want to get involved in that kind of nonsense, but he also didn't want to just kill the cartel boss. For one thing, guys like Guillermo Diaz were useful at times. More importantly, killing the cartel boss would just cause a lot of confusion at a time when he needed things calm. The last thing he needed while posing as the security chief was to have the entire cartel looking at him, wondering what he was going to do to find their dear leader's murderer.

Diaz came around the table toward him. Marmot knew Diaz would lash out and beat the security chief half to death. When Diaz reached out to grab Marmut by the throat, the demon flashed his glowing red eyes and with a flick of his wrist sent the cartel boss careening backwards against the wall. Diaz slid to the ground unconscious. Marmut kneeled at his side, touched the palm of his hand to Diaz's chest, and hit him with a surge of power.

He placed the cartel leader on the couch over by the large window and positioned him comfortably, as if he was lying down for a nap. No one rushed in to investigate the crashing and slamming sounds. Marmot figured it was fairly normal for those noises to come from Diaz's office, and no one bothered to worry about it anymore. He was on limited time. The jolt he gave Diaz bought him a few extra minutes, but he and Ruta would have to hustle to complete their investigation and disappear.

"We need to hurry," he said to Ruta when he returned.

"What happened?"

Marmut shrugged. "He wanted someone to take his anger out on. I had to put him out for a while."

She rolled her eyes. "Why are humans so out of control?"

Marmut chuckled. "weren't you human, Ruta? You don't feel the tug of human emotion?"

"I remember," she muttered.

Marmut watched her for several seconds, curious. He finally went back about his task. Working in silence, they scanned the entire security room and the vault, but came away with very little.

"Okay," Marmut announced when they were back in their own vessels and standing deep in the woods, a half mile from the Los Llanos compound. "What's next?"

"Cartegena," Ruta replied, scanning her list of cartels.

ᛒ ᚪ ᚼ ᚹ ᚷ

"Got him."

Abdiel turned to see the excited face of one of Ruta's demon underlings who had been searching the area's recent chakra pull, looking for anything that would indicate angel activity and the masking of an individual's chakra pull.

He raised his eyebrows, fighting back the excitement he felt at finally getting a break in their search. "Tell me."

The black-eyed demon, who, for the life of him, Abdiel could not remember his name, handed him a slip of paper. Abdiel looked at it for a few seconds before slipping it into his pocket. He looked the demon over, nodding as he did so.

"You're sure?"

The demon nodded with all eagerness of a recruit trying to impress his master. "Yes, General. We found one specific location where the chakra pull is especially large and definitely angelic. If we weren't specifically looking for something like that, we would have ignored it, assuming angel activity, but when we looked more closely, we noticed the amount of pull was strangely consistent...like, no variation at all. So, we looked closer and noticed that the chakra pull moved around slightly, just within the local area, and every time it moved, there was another pull, emanating from very close by."

"And that was our guy?" Abdiel asked, fascinated at the intricacy of sifting through the past and finding a needle in a haystack.

The demon nodded. "We think so. The angel tried to adjust his pull to match that expended by the second guy. It's impossible to do that perfectly, but he got pretty close. No way we'd have found it unless we were specifically looking for it."

Abdiel nodded. "Well done."

He strode to the room he had commandeered as his personal office. Pulling out a cell phone, he tapped the screen and waited for a response. The Dark Army was perfectly capable of telepathic communication, but with angels directly involved, they took no chances and used human technology to mask everything.

"Yes."

One single syllable carried with it such power and terrifying menace, even over the impersonal electronic device in Abdiel's hand, he still shook when he heard it.

Abdiel cleared his throat. "Master," he said with as much confidence as he could muster. "We believe we have found him. I would like to initiate contact."

"Are you certain?"

Abdiel bit his lip with indecision. He felt certain, but he knew better than to raise expectations. They'd be high in any case, but he didn't want his own words tossed back in his face should the lead not pan out.

"This is our best lead, Master, but I would like to make contact to be sure. He appears to be under the care of an angel."

The silence on the other end of the line was palpable. Abdiel's breath caught in his throat. He wondered if he would pay the price for an angel beating him to the human. He'd seen his peers punished for less reason than that, and at his level, the punishments were often vicious, as he'd already experienced.

"Do you have a plan to lure him away from the angel?"

Abdiel squeezed his eyes shut. He hadn't thought that far ahead. In his haste to bring positive news to Lucifer, he hadn't thought through the situation. How *would* he make contact with an angel present? It was nearly impossible for a dark presence to get past an angel of the Lord.

Abdiel thought quickly. "My team is assessing the situation right now. I wanted to be certain you were informed the instant we had a solid lead. We're checking his background for potential opportunities."

"Good. Family. Friends. Coworkers. Any of these may provide the necessary leverage, Abdiel; leave no stone unturned."

"Yes, Master."

"No mistakes, Abdiel."

"Yes, Master."

After the call, Abdiel took a moment to let out a breath he hadn't realized he'd been holding. After calming himself, he considered his options. He didn't want to get too close too soon. If the angel got wind of his presence, it would result in a fight Abdiel didn't want. Under normal circumstances, he might orchestrate a battle under the same conditions, but his task was to infiltrate the human's life as under the radar as possible.

When he walked back out into the main room, the black-eyed demon who had presented him with the information was there.

"General," he said, standing at stiff attention. "I would like to accompany you when you go after the human."

Abdiel frowned at him. "This is not a kill mission. We are not here to destroy this young man, but to seduce him to our side."

"Our side?" The demon wrinkled his forehead. "But...he's with an angel."

"Yes," Abdiel replied. "Which means we must be very careful, doesn't it?" He studied the reaction of the young demon. "Still want to come along?"

Peering through the window of the town house across the parking lot from Nicholas Scarlatti's place, Abdiel and his new demon conscript, whose name turned out to be Tomas, considered their options. Abdiel definitely felt the angelic presence of one of his former brethren. The constant pull of chakra made it easy to distinguish. Typically, chakra was pulled in bursts, not often with any long-term consistency. In most instances, one pulled exactly what one needed to execute a given task such as spell-casting or orbing. Humans pulled chakra in minimal bursts. To supernatural beings, the pull of humans on chakra barely registered. Now and then, a superhuman feat might be accomplished where a human would exercise unexpected strength. In those rare cases, one might see a quick spike in his chakra pull, but it would quickly return to normal levels.

With supernatural beings, the bursts were more sporadic, sometimes extending for longer periods of time, but always fluctuating, much like a person's heart rate or adrenaline levels. The more effort he exerted, or the more fatigued he became, the more his chakra pull increased and he pulled more. For an angel, that fatigue wasn't often experienced. Simply shielding another being's chakra pull would not be very taxing on the angel. That explained why the demons saw no fluctuations.

Abdiel had another thought. Angels knew they were the superior beings in both the natural and supernatural realms. It made sense they would get complacent and secure in their power. That kind of superior attitude made them vulnerable to the right kind of attack. For a few brief seconds, Abdiel allowed his mind to wander to thoughts of luring out and killing the angel inside Nicholas Scarlatti's home. What a coup *that* would be!

It was far too risky. If he failed, his current mission would be impossible to salvage. Who knew what lies the angel was telling in there? If Abdiel was the aggressor, he'd never get the trust of the Scarlatti guy. Abdiel would have to be patient and bide his time. He stared at the closed door across the parking lot and let his mind wander at all the possibilities. He needed an in.

Suddenly, Abdiel felt a presence. He narrowed his eyes as he focused in on the newcomer. It was familiar, yet it wasn't anyone from his team. He looked through the window and scanned the parking lot, searching for anything or any*one* familiar. He closed the blind and strode to the rear door. He didn't want to telegraph his own presence, so he kept his movements slow and humanlike. Abdiel stepped out onto the rear patio and continued to scan his surroundings. Though he saw no one, he was certain of a dark presence somewhere very close.

As he proceeded around to the front of the building, Abdiel, staying deep in the shadows of the large oak tree, saw the door to Scarlatti's house open and a figure exit. He peered into the darkness and knew, in an instant, it wasn't their target; it wasn't even a human.

"Vampire," Abdiel muttered. "He's got an angel *and* a vampire with him?"

He wondered how the human could have already come into contact with a vampire and even more interestingly, how come the angel inside hadn't already destroyed the vampire. Angels were notoriously intolerant of "abominations" in the Father's creation. Vampires were at the top of that list, especially considering their origin.

A pretty blonde girl appeared at the doorway and shouted to the vampire. "Not just red, okay? Get a bottle or two of white! And don't crash Nico's car!"

Nico?

The vampire waved, made his way to a Maserati which looked conspicuously out of place for the neighborhood, and peeled out of the parking space in front of Scarlatti's townhouse. Just as the vehicle turned to leave the parking lot, Abdiel caught a glimmer of movement in the trees across from him. He saw a flash of red and then the tell-tale trace of an orb trail. He had a split-second in which to make an identification. It was enough.

"Seir," he muttered. He was confused and concerned. "Tomas!" he called out as soon as he reentered the building.

"Yes, General."

"Do you know who Seir is?"

The demon's eyes widened in recognition and admiration. "Of course, General. He's a legend...Azazel's personal assassin."

Abdiel nodded. "Well, he's here." He told Tomas what he had just witnessed.

Tomas' eyes grew even wider. "But...he...*why?*"

Abdiel shook his head and collapsed into a recliner. "I don't know...yet. Seir is seldom deployed unless there is a hard kill target."

"Could he be trying to kill Scarlatti?"

Abdiel pressed his palms together and brought the tips of his forefingers to his lips in thought. "It doesn't make sense. Lucifer personally instructed me in this operation. Azazel stood right behind him when I was given the orders."

"And you're certain it was Seir?"

Abdiel ignored the insubordinate nature of the question. Seir's presence was too disconcerting. He had a sinking feeling in his gut and had no idea what to do about it.

He closed his eyes. "It was definitely Seir."

"Okay," Tomas said. "And he blinked into the car with...who?"

"A vampire."

"What would he be doing with a vampire?"

Abdiel shrugged. "The vampire was driving Scarlatti's car, so think through a friend scenario."

Tomas puffed his cheeks and let out a long, slow breath. "Okay. He's either going to kill the friend or..." Tomas looked at Abdiel. "...or possess him."

"Okay," Abdiel said. He had an idea form in his mind. "That's a possibility. What does he gain by killing the vampire?"

Tomas shrugged. "Nothing, really. I guess it might make Scarlatti mad enough to come out and fight him."

Abdiel shook his head. "It would likely bring out the angel too."

"Okay," said Tomas. "So he possesses the vampire and just walks right in the front door. He can kill Scarlatti at will."

Abdiel tilted his head and raised his eyebrows. "He still has the angel to worry about. It's a suicide mission, and Seir isn't a demon you'd want to throw away on purpose. You can send a black-eye for that."

He met Tomas' stunned gaze and chuckled. "You don't agree?"

"No...I mean, I do...I was just..."

"Surprised I'd come right out and say such an insensitive thing?"

Tomas was speechless. "I don't know..."

"Understand, Tomas," Abdiel declared. "Resources are resources. They are to be used to accomplish tasks. Some resources are more valued than others. A red-eyed demon like Seir is just too useful alive to risk on a suicide mission."

"But black-eyed demons aren't."

"Black-eyed demons are more plentiful and less skilled. They are fairly interchangeable." He surveyed Tomas' disappointed expression. "But some manage to work their way into an indispensable position. It's all about the skill set, Tomas."

Tomas nodded. "So Seir is unlikely to try to enter the house with the angel in there."

They sat in silence for several moments. Tomas shook his head. "Maybe he'll try to lure the angel out somehow?"

Abdiel's eyes widened. "Not the angel!" He looked at Tomas in a near panic. "Quickly, Tomas! Find the locations of nearby liquor stores and bars!"

"Yes, General," Tomas replied without hesitation. He sprang into action, pulling out a tablet and finding the information.

"I have it, General."

"Excellent," Abdiel replied. "Let's go."

"Are you sure?" Tomas asked.

"Definitely," Abdiel said. "Seir is going to kill Scarlatti *right now*!"

Chapter 17

"Everything okay?"

Stephanie tilted her head as she watched Nicholas' face. Her stomach churned with the weight of the things she knew. Her boyfriend was a murderer. What was she supposed to do with that? Was she supposed to stand by him? Call the police? And tell them...what? That her boyfriend was a supernatural creature who could kill people with the power of his mind, with the flick of his hand?

She could never do it. She loved Nicholas. Despite the horrible things he had done in recent weeks, she felt no fear being close to him. He was clearly a dangerous man, mixed up in dangerous things, but he was still sweet to her, and every person he'd hurt deserved it. They were all bad people, who hurt others. While the violence certainly scared her, she somehow still trusted Nicholas.

He looked at the screen of his phone with a wrinkled forehead. The text came in only seconds before, but she sensed his change in mood. She waved a hand in front of his eyes. He didn't respond, but instead tapped on his phone for several seconds as she waited. He looked up and showed her the screen.

I have to sneak out for a few minutes. Zha'riel can't know about it.

She said nothing, but looked at him with a dozen questions in her eyes. Nicholas erased what he had just written and swiped to a different screen. He held the phone out to her again. This time, she read a text from Xabier.

Nico, slip out and meet me at our favorite pub. I'll be around back. DO NOT tell our treasonous angelic friend.

Stephanie slumped her shoulders. Treasonous? Zha'riel was a stiff; there was no doubt about that, but she trusted him to protect her. What had Xabier found out? Nicholas tapped away at the screen again. He held it out for her.

Not sure what that means, but if Xabier wants to talk away from Zha'riel I should go talk to him.

Stephanie nodded and took a deep nervous breath. "Okay."

Nicholas tapped on the screen again.

We need to make out a little bit and then go to my room like we're gonna...you know ;) Then we'll turn on the TV and you can hang out in there while I go see what this knucklehead wants.

She nodded with a smile. Stephanie could play her part; she could barely keep her hands off him as it was, so there wasn't whole lot of acting necessary. Within minutes, they had escalated their little make-out scene and Nicholas stood and pulled her to her feet.

"Let's take this upstairs," he said loud enough for Zha'riel to hear in the kitchen.

Stephanie giggled and wrapped her arms around his neck. "Carry me."

Moments later, they were kissing in Nicholas' room. They went on for several minutes before Nicholas pulled away and looked at her with a mischievous grin.

"Ya know," he said, with a sly grin. "I don't really care anymore what Xab wants."

Stephanie giggled and touched her palm to his cheek. She loved looking up at him and staring into those mesmerizing, violet eyes. She didn't want to distract him with potential trouble right under their roof.

"That message seemed pretty urgent," she said.

Nicholas sighed and stood. "He better not be playing me. If he lured me away from you for nothing, I think I'm going to strangle him with a vervain vine." He kissed her one more time and said, "Okay. Depending on how long I take, Zha'riel might figure it out. Just tell him I snuck out to meet Xabier and you have no idea where."

Seconds later, he was gone. Stephanie laid back against the pillows and tried not to worry. She clicked on the TV, found a show she didn't really care about and did her best to let her mind wander so she wouldn't dwell on the fact that the guy she was falling in love with was out on his own with demons and God knew what else looking for him.

Nicholas orbed into the wooded area behind a pub on Rt. 50. It was a local bar and not all that busy on the weekdays even in the summer months when tourists flocked to the Jersey Shore. It was far enough off shore, and dingy enough, that only the regulars really came out. Plus, it wasn't the most inviting establishment. Driving by, one might get the impression that it was a biker bar or some other kind of hick dive where trouble was a nightly routine. In reality, the bar was mostly frequented by blue collar workers, truckers, and a lot of hunters. Nicholas and Xabier liked it because it was quiet.

He saw his car parked on the side of the building as he strode out of the woods. He halted and scanned the immediate area. He noticed movement at the back of the building. Xabier leaned against a cement post and pushed off when he saw Nicholas coming.

"You made it," he said. "I was beginning to wonder if you'd be able to sneak away."

"I got away," Nicholas assured him. "Now what's this all about?"

"What's it all about?" Xabier repeated as he stretched out a hand. Nicholas felt something grip him and send him hurling backwards against a big green dumpster.

"Ooomph!" Nicholas gasped as the breath rushed from his lungs and he raised himself to his hands and knees. "What the…?"

Xabier was on him in a flash. Nicholas took three vicious kicks to his ribs before Xabier let up for a moment. As he lifted his eyes to face his friend, Xabier's fist connected with his right cheek. Nicholas felt the bone under his left eye shatter. The pain was a lot more tolerable than he would have expected. In fact, what he was feeling most of all was rage.

After taking several more blows to his head and more kicks to his torso, Nicholas finally gathered his wits and blinked his eyes. A split second later he was several yards away, on his feet and launching a vicious counter attack consisting of crackling energy and hurling balls of fire which Xabier attempted to fend off. After several moments of them exchanging attacks, Nicholas felt like he was holding his own. At the same time, they both stopped and caught their breath, circling one another.

Nicholas was drained. He wondered how much longer he could hold out against the vicious chakra attacks. More than that, he wondered how his so-called friend could turn on him so easily. He took a few deep breaths, touching his fingers to his broken eye socket. Amazingly, it still didn't hurt all that much. He was grateful for that and assumed it to be another benefit of his new body. He looked at Xabier, who appeared equally exhausted, though not too exhausted to glare daggers at him.

"So," he said, standing up straight. He wasn't going to show any more weakness to this traitor. "Are you going to explain what this is all about?"

Xabier straightened. His eyes were weary, but then a serene smile came over his face. His eyes sparkled with humor. He chuckled and shook his head. "Did you think you'd worn me down, *Nico*? Ha, ha! No such luck. We are just getting started, my friend."

"But why?" Nicholas asked, feeling dread wash over him. Something wasn't right. Xabier wasn't acting like Xabier. Granted, Nicholas had only known the guy for a couple months, but it didn't make any sense at all.

"You haven't figured it out?"

Nicholas racked his brain, trying to buy time. The fight or flight instinct was leaning heavily toward flight, but he couldn't bring himself to run just yet. His curiosity overpowered his instinct for self-preservation.

"All I figured out so far is that my friend suddenly wants to kill me."

"Ahh, inexperience rears its head." Xabier laughed. "I forget your powers are stolen, not earned."

Nicholas shrugged. "And?"

Xabier continued to smile at him, but it didn't feel like Xabier. It was like something was wearing Xabier. The eyes looked just a little bit glazed over and the way he stood was not Xabier's normal posture. Everything was off.

"Are you starting to figure things out?" Xabier asked. "Need a little hint?" Suddenly the pupils of Xabier's eyes glowed a deep crimson red.

Nicholas' eyes widened in stunned disbelief. "B-but how? What's happening?"

"Not what's happening," replied Xabier. "What's *happened*." He smiled in a less-than-reassuring way. "Don't worry; your little fanged friend is fine. At least he will be as long as you and I settle our business tonight."

"I don't understand," Nicholas said.

"Then let me make it clear." Xabier stood within a foot of Nicholas and peered directly into his eyes. Nicholas held his ground and steeled himself for another attack. "My name is Seir. I am here on behalf of my master. I took the liberty of borrowing your friend's body. I am here to close the account you opened with my master when you killed his son."

"Xabier...?"

"He will be fine," Seir replied, "as long as you stay right here and fight for your life, but if you run like a coward, I will ravage this pathetic meat suit and scatter him all over the city. I will make him chop off every one of his own fingers and toes. Then I'll make him chew off his limbs, until the only thing left is his head."

So, Xabier hadn't betrayed him. He was possessed by a powerful demon. Everything had been the red-eyed demon's way of isolating Nicholas from Zha'riel, the only one who could protect him.

"All this effort just to kill me?" Nicholas asked.

Seir's eyes burned from Xabier's face. "My master would like to meet you. He will be here shortly, but before then, I have been instructed to…warm you up."

His eyes glowed an even deeper crimson. Nicholas assumed it was how he expressed his delight. Seir was looking forward to tearing him apart piece by piece. Nicholas racked his brain for a way out, but he had nothing. He couldn't run because even if he managed to get away and get Zha'riel, Seir would simply disappear and Nicholas didn't doubt Seir would do everything he'd promised.

"Seir smiled as Nicholas' mind raced. "You know, someone once said the *anticipation* of death is worse than death itself." He shrugged. "I think that the *means* of death is what people really fear. What do you think, *Nico*? Are you more afraid of dying, or are you more afraid of what you will go through on the way to death?"

Nicholas didn't answer. Instead, he braced himself for the inevitable. He couldn't fight back. Not really. If he dealt a fatal blow, wouldn't it kill Xabier too? He knew nothing about possession. He knew nothing about what happened to possessed people. He couldn't risk his only real friend's life.

Before his thoughts were even completed in his mind, Nicholas felt the pressure as he was flung high into the air and across the darkened rear parking lot, skidding to a stop near the woods. He picked himself up and prepared for more.

Seir stood before him, a wicked grin on his…Xabier's…face. "This is going to be more fun than I thought."

He raised his arm to deliver a blow to Nicholas' face, but the blow never came. Nicholas had closed his eyes in anticipation of the strike. When he opened them, a third figure had joined them. He was holding Seir back in what appeared to be a chakra grip. He didn't seem to be struggling as Seir fought to regain control.

The newcomer finally released him and he spun around. "Abdiel!" he said gasped, the surprise registering on his face.

"I beg your pardon, *demon*?" The authority in the voice of the newcomer was unmistakable.

"I mean, General," Seir said, bowing his head slightly. "My apologies, General. I was not expecting you."

"I should think not," the General agreed. "In fact, I wonder what you are doing here at all."

Seir didn't respond.

"Seir," the general said pointedly. "I know who you are and I know who you work for. My question is, are you here on direct orders from him?"

Seir lowered his eyes. "General, I cannot speak about my orders."

The general pursed his lips. "I am here on specific and direct orders from the Grand Emperor himself. If you have been sent to harm or kill this man, then you are acting in direct conflict with the throne."

Seir's eyes widened. Nicholas watched in rapt attention. Who were they talking about? Nicholas knew Seir worked directly for Azazel, but who would be more fearsome than he?

"Oh my God," Nicholas murmured.

All eyes turned to him. The general patted him on the shoulder.

"Do not worry, Nicholas," he said in a gentle voice. "You are safe."

Turning to Seir, he said, "Leave the vampire one hundred percent intact when you remove yourself."

Xabier's head tilted skyward, his mouth opened and a steady stream of black soot-like smoke poured out, angling over the trees and out of sight as Xabier collapsed on the ground.

The general helped him to his feet. "Are you okay?"

Xabier shook his head to clear it. "That vile creature!"

Nicholas breathed a sigh of relief. "I thought you were trying to kill me."

Xabier closed his eyes and shook his head. Despair registered on his face. "My sincerest apologies, Nico. I was in there, fighting him, but I wasn't strong enough. I thought I was going to have to watch you die at my own hand. He taunted me the entire time."

The general nodded. "Yes, that sounds like Seir. He works for someone very powerful, whom I *thought* was on our side." He licked his lips. "Apparently, I was wrong."

"Who are you?" Nicholas asked. "I mean, thank you for your help and all that, but…how did you know…?"

The general nodded with a kind smile. "I apologize. My name is Abdiel. And Nicholas, before you return to the protection of your angel friend, I think we should talk."

From a shadowy, wooded area several yards away, Azazel watched and considered his best course of action. Now that his plan had completely backfired a second time due to unexpected interference, he was exposed. There was no way Abdiel wouldn't report the suspicious situation to Lucifer. Azazel had hoped to make Nicholas disappear after dying a slow and agonizing death, and then simply wait for things to die down and go back to normal without some silly human at the center of everything. Abdiel would certainly mention his skirmish with Seir, and that could lead nowhere but back to Azazel.

Lucifer would demand an explanation, and would no doubt be skeptical of anything he was told, even by his closest friend. Everyone knew Seir loyally served him and was not some loose cannon. He would never have attempted to harm Nicholas if Azazel had not ordered it.

He could just go over and take all of them out, but who knew how many demons Abdiel had in the area? He'd never be able to explain attacking a Dark Army general on a mission from Lucifer himself. Watching as they all orbed out, Azazel came to one conclusion.

"Perhaps it is time I strike out on my own."

Chapter 18

"I must admit, Guillermo, this is most unexpected."

Alvi reclined on an outdoor couch next to a huge rectangular in-ground pool. The patio behind his home boasted a breathtaking vista. He loved living high up in the mountains of Colombia. The air was clean, the temperature cool, and he didn't have to deal with bugs and rodents. It wasn't beachfront property, but at least he didn't have to deal with tourists all year round. He put his feet up on an ottoman and gestured to the chair to his left.

"Of all the men at the table, you were the last one I thought would come around."

Guillermo Diaz sat down and lit a long, thin, cigarette. He took a deep drag and blew out the smoke in a huff. "Yeah, well, I'm having a hard time believing it myself."

When the request for a face-to-face meeting came from the head of Los Llanos, Alvi almost laughed out loud, thinking it had to be a joke. The two had almost come to blows and now Diaz wanted a meeting alone. The next text message was even more shocking.

I'll come to you and I'll come with only one guard. This is important. GD

There could be no safer meeting place for Alvi than his own compound, surrounded by his own trusted guards. If Diaz wanted to wander in with only one of his men, he was clearly not going to be trying anything stupid. It would be suicide. Alvi agreed to the meeting.

"Something to drink?"

Without waiting for an answer, Alvi poured several fingers of tequila in a tumbler with a few ice cubes. He knew Diaz's favorite drink and was determined to be a good host even though the two were almost never friendly toward one another. He set the glass on the end table between them and poured a second for himself. They raised their glasses and nodded to one another.

"Salud." Diaz swallowed half his drink in one gulp. He swirled the glass and stared at the clear liquid. "I believe you."

Alvi frowned. "You believe what, exactly?"

"I believe your suspicions about the robberies." Guillermo drained his glass and stood up. He walked to the iron fence and stared down at the sheer two-thousand-foot drop. "I know I said I didn't, but I do now."

"Why the sudden change of heart?"

Diaz lowered his voice as if he was afraid someone might be listening. "Something happened."

Alvi said nothing. He sat back and studied his colleague's expression. Diaz wasn't playing him. He wasn't the type to play the con. He was more of a brute force type. He wasn't afraid to be the guy on the front lines, cracking skulls and pulling triggers. Alvi couldn't be sure, but he could swear he saw fear in Diaz's eyes.

"I was talking to my security chief, ready to smash his face because he had made no progress."

"Naturally." Alvi shook his head.

"Yeah, well, all of a sudden, his eyes changed."

"Changed how?"

Nayra's voice pierced through their hushed tones. She made her way across the patio and around the pool to the lounge area. She was present at Guillermo's request...another in his long chain of surprises.

Diaz looked at her. "They flashed or something and then all of a sudden they glowed blood-red. Then he struck me cold. When I woke up I contacted you."

Nayra inhaled sharply. "They glowed, you say?"

"Yeah, why? You know what it was?"

"Demonio," she hissed and shook her head. Her eyes went from disapproving to fearful.

"Demonio?" Diaz frowned. "Are you serious?"

"Si," Nayra said. "And a very powerful one. The red-eyed ones are the most powerful."

"Demons? Here?" Alvi wondered. "Why?"

"I don't know why." Nayra turned and retraced her steps back toward the house. "But I must prepare."

ᚦ ᚨ ᛥ ᛉ ᚷ

Darkness fell over the region. Marmut and Ruta stood in a wooded area deep in the mountains outside the Manizales Cartel compound. The place was on complete lockdown so they hadn't managed to get to any of the security personnel. They had seen several guards patrolling the fence line and could have possessed one of them, but it would have created other problems in terms of gaining access to the rooms they needed to enter. They were in their own vessels, waiting for the early morning hours when they would attempt to slip in and out undetected. At least, if there were guards standing watch they would be unlikely to be as alert and would be more easily subdued.

They orbed themselves to a point just outside the mansion and crept along the outer wall until they found a door leading to the basement level, where they assumed the security team was stationed. They held hands and orbed in together. It was dark and quiet. Marmut immediately felt uneasy, but he saw no immediate danger. He and Ruta moved to opposite walls and crept along them, scanning every room in the lower level and coming up empty. No one was present. They found the security room empty as well with the vault door closed securely.

"I don't like this," Marmut grumbled.

"You'd rather we had to fight our way through a dozen guards?"

He shrugged. "I don't like surprises. There ought to be a room full of sleepy guards in here."

Ruta thought for a moment. "Nothing really to guard until they replenish, right?"

Marmut didn't answer. He continued to sweep his gaze around the empty space. He looked up at the ceiling and down at the floor. Everything seemed as it should be, but the unsettled feeling continued.

"I don't like this."

"Let's scan the room and get out of here," Ruta suggested.

"Fine," he replied.

They orbed into the vault and instantly knew they made a mistake.

"What the...?" Marmut exclaimed, feeling the chakra disconnect.

"You've got to be kidding me," Ruta said, looking at the ground. Then she looked up and saw what she knew would be there. She pointed at the vault ceiling.

Marmut followed her gaze. "Son of a..."

They were staring at two Devil's Traps. One would have been enough, but with one above and one below, it made an accidental failure almost impossible. Demons could get into a Devil's Trap, but could not escape unless the circle was somehow broken from the outside.

"Welcome."

The lights came on and the vault door slowly swung open to reveal a woman in her fifties, barefoot, wearing dark robes, and carrying a large basket filled with a wide assortment of items. Ruta and Marmut glared at the woman as she set the basket down and began to remove the items. First were several large black pillar candles. She spaced them around the outside of the circular perimeter and lit each one. Next, she turned off the lights.

"Much better," she replied, turning a pair of dead-gray eyes on them. "Don't you agree?"

"Let us out," demanded Marmut.

"Oh, no," the woman replied with a chuckle. "I don't even know who you are." She looked at them her eyes darkening in the shadows as the humor drained from her face. "Or why you're trespassing on our property." She cast them a grim smile. "But I will find out."

The trapped demons could do nothing but grit their teeth and watch as the woman prepared a small altar on the floor, just outside the vault door. She lit more candles, pulled out a large chalk, and drew a smaller pentagram with symbols at every point. Marmut and Ruta recognized the symbols and realized what they had wandered into.

"Witch," Marmut muttered.

The woman looked up and smiled at them again. "I've been waiting for your arrival. When I heard one of my godson's colleagues was attacked by a red-eyed man, I thought, it couldn't be…but just to be on the safe side…" She tilted her head. "And here you are."

"What do you want with us, witch?" Ruta glared at her.

"You say *witch* like it was a bad thing." The woman laughed. "But in the interest of being a proper host, I suppose I should introduce myself. My name is Nayra. And your names are…?"

The demons remained silent and Nayra shrugged.

"No matter. In due time, I will know all."

She continued setting up her altar, pulling a short, ancient-looking, ornate dagger and placing it beside a large chalice that looked just as old and ornate as the dagger. It was like they belonged together. She placed several items which Marmut and Ruta couldn't quite see into the chalice and then pulled up her sleeve, took the dagger, and without hesitation, cut a short line across her wrist. The demons watched as the blood dripped into the chalice as Nayra squeezed her hand into a fist and released repeatedly to get the blood flowing faster. She then wrapped a bandage around her wrist and knelt in front of the chalice.

"*Ooma ka si nefli garamas,*" she chanted. "*Ooma ka si nefli garamas.*"

After several moments, repeatedly chanting the same words, Nayra opened her eyes.

"Hello, Marmut," she smiled. "Pleased to meet you, Ruta."

"Cute trick," Ruta sneered. She had an extreme desire to rip the woman into pieces and feed the bloody parts to lions.

Nayra ignored her. "Now…whatever could you be doing here?"

She closed her eyes again and resumed her chants, this time adding some new lines to the original. She continued for nearly an hour as Marmut and Ruta tried from time to time to break her concentration. She never once wavered at their catcalls. When she opened her eyes again, she said only two words.

"Nicholas Scarlatti."

Ruta's eyes widened, as did Marmut's.

"Who is he?" Nayra demanded. When the demons didn't answer, she shrugged and returned to her trance-like state, chanting and breathing. By daybreak, she knew it all.

ƀ ʌ ⁊ ψ ɢ

"I'm sure you have a million questions, and I will be happy to answer all of them."

Nicholas glanced at Xabier who shrugged. Abdiel saved him from Seir, but that didn't necessarily mean anything. He was called "General," which meant he was in a supernatural army. The only armies Nicholas was aware of were Heaven's and Lucifer's. Since he didn't want to meet Zha'riel, Nicholas had to assume that Abdiel worked for Lucifer, which was terrifying.

"You're a general, right?" Nicholas began. "In what army?"

Abdiel leaned on a railing. In the interest of safety and privacy, they'd orbed to a small park, hundreds of miles away from Nicholas' Southern New Jersey home. Xabier knew of the place and suggested it so no one they knew would be able to find them. Abdiel began his story.

"I am a general in Lucifer's army. By the look in your eyes, I can tell you have some ideas of what that means." He smiled with a gentle chuckle. "Let me assure you, much of that is lies…simple propaganda from one side of a war against another."

Nicholas raised his eyebrows. "So, you're saying you guys aren't evil and the other guys aren't good?"

Abdiel guffawed. "*Everyone* considers their side the good guys. Nicholas, we are just a group of…beings, for lack of a better word? Some more evil than others." He spread his hands and made a face. "What does evil even mean anyway? Don't we all have our own definition of what is evil and what is good? Of what is right and what is wrong?"

Nicholas shrugged and glanced at Xabier, who was still suffering from what Nicholas assumed was some sort of PTSD resulting from being possessed by a demon. He was pale and shaking, and wouldn't be much help. He turned back to Abdiel.

"I guess."

"Exactly," continued Abdiel. "One side manages to get their story into the hearts and minds of human beings and the other side…us…well, we have to play catch-up."

Nicholas ran a hand through his hair. "You're saying God *didn't* throw you guys out of Heaven?"

"Oh yes." Abdiel shook his head and cast a wistful stare out over the landscape. "He certainly did. That was one miserable day." His eyes misted over at the recollection. "But I think you have a misconception of the reasons involved."

Nicholas shrugged and spread his hands. "All I know is Lucifer tried to take over or something. He and Michael had some kind of standoff and God stepped in."

He could scarcely believe he was having *another* conversation about the day God threw angels out of Heaven…this time *with* one of the angels God threw out of Heaven.

Abdiel shook his head. "That is a distortion of the truth, Nicholas. Indeed, there was a standoff and God did intervene before the conflict could escalate, but no one tried to take over Heaven. It was quite the opposite in fact. We were trying to *protect* Heaven."

Xabier snapped out of his funk at that point. "Really?" he asked with a skeptical frown. "That's seems a little pretentious, don't you think?"

"Not at all," Abdiel objected. "We were being asked to do something that for eternity past was unthinkable."

"And what was that?"

Abdiel looked from Nicholas to Xabier and back, his eyes conveying just how serious he considered the point he was about to make would be.

"We were asked to bow down to someone other than the Father."

Xabier and Nicholas exchanged a look. It jibed with what Zha'riel had told them.

"And Lucifer didn't want to." Nicholas stated it as a fact. He already heard the story.

"I don't think *anyone* wanted to," Abdiel said with raised eyebrows. "But it was Lucifer who acted. About a third of Heaven stood with him. You see, Lucifer reasoned something so preposterous could only be a test of our devotion. There was simply no way He would require us to bow down to another. Lucifer refused, stating His love and devotion to his Father as his reasons for doing so. The Father insisted he reconsider his position and Michael tried to strong-arm him into compliance, but Lucifer stood firm, becoming more and more adamant the more his brother pushed. Ultimately, it led to a confrontation, which then led to the standoff you mentioned."

Xabier was dumbfounded. "So," he said. "You're telling us this whole war between the Devil and God...all that bloodshed throughout the ages, just in human history, to say nothing of the supernatural, all the misery, suffering, pain, violence...all of that is really the result of one, big, cosmic misunderstanding?"

Abdiel chuckled. "When you put it like that it does seem rather silly, but at the time, it was deadly serious. I would caution you though, about whom you refer to as 'the Devil.' It is rather insulting, especially considering you've never met him. And the war isn't with God. It is with Michael and his angel army."

"So where does God stand in all of this?" Nicholas asked.

"You mean," Abdiel smiled. "Whose side is He on?"

"I guess."

"Well," Abdiel replied, "since the dawn of this created world, all He really concerns Himself with is humanity. As far as this vendetta Michael carries towards Lucifer, He really hasn't intervened since removing us from Heaven."

"This is insane." Xabier shook his head in disbelief.

"Is it?" asked Abdiel. "Is it so hard to believe that there might be another side to the story you have been taught? Is my angel cousin so convincing? Am I really so terrifying?"

Nicholas pursed his lips as he considered those words. "You know Zha'riel?"

Abdiel tilted his head and smiled. "Zha'riel is the one charged with your protection? Well, you *are* in good hands then. And yes, I know him very well, though I haven't seen him for many thousands of your years. Once demons moved to the front lines and the battle moved to the natural realm, I don't get to face my former brethren all that often."

"So, what do you want with me?" Nicholas asked. "I'm not fighting in your little war. I told Zha'riel the same thing."

Abdiel shrugged. "And, why should you? It's not *your* war. I'll be very honest with you, Nicholas. I was sent here to bring you on board if possible, but the main reason I am here is because what you truly need right now, is friends."

Nicholas frowned. "Friends?"

"Of course," Abdiel insisted. "You have entered a world that is so much grander than the one in which you previously existed. It's a world where powers like the ones you possess attract creatures of varying degrees of ethics. You need not only to learn how to navigate the supernatural realm, but most importantly, how to *use* your strange new powers."

Nicholas instantly reacted to those last words. Those were *his* thoughts precisely. Zha'riel insisted the use of those dark powers would result in evil taking control of his heart. He explained that to Abdiel, who let out such a hearty laugh and went on for so long, Nicholas thought he was going to have a heart attack...if angels could have heart attacks.

"I'm quite certain Zha'riel told you exactly that," Abdiel finally managed in between chuckles. "And as frightening as that sounds, allow me to assure you, it is quite preposterous. After all, powers are just powers. They are things...tool, if you will. Isn't evil or good found within the heart of the individual? Sure, powers like the ones we have can corrupt, in the same way money or fame can corrupt, but they can also be used for good things too. Didn't you recently relieve the world of some unsavory individuals, Nicholas?"

"I did," Nicholas admitted. "Then Zha'riel flipped out on me and Rafael threatened to kill me."

Abdiel's eyes widened. "You met Rafael?"

"Yeah." Nicholas rolled his eyes. "He's kind of a jerk."

Abdiel chuckled. "Did he tell you to turn from your wicked ways and get onto the good path?"

Nicholas cracked a smile despite himself. "Yeah, kinda."

"Well," Abdiel said. "You need to take him very seriously. He's an archangel, just like Lucifer and Michael. In fact, Raphael is one of the original twelve...very powerful angels."

"Original twelve?"

"Yes," Abdiel tilted his head to one side. "First there was Michael, Lucifer, and Gabriel. The Father then created nine more. The rest of us came in various numbers. Those original twelve are all archangels. There are more archangels now, but the first twelve are the most powerful by far."

Nicholas pursed his lips, his mind absorbing all that Abdiel had revealed to him.

"You want to know something funny?"

Abdiel shrugged. "Sure."

Nicholas chuckled. "I've learned more in this conversation than I have since I first got these powers."

Abdiel closed his eyes and smiled in understanding. "You must understand that the powers are fearsome and Zha'riel only wants to protect your soul. You are still human, Nicholas, in that you still possess humanity, the part of you that feels human emotion. We angels don't possess that. The Father never saw fit to give us that gift."

Nicholas wrinkled his forehead. "I can believe that about Zha'riel and Rafael, but you seem to be the exact opposite. You seem pretty normal to me. We could be sitting around drinking a beer together and talking about the upcoming football season."

Abdiel chuckled. "I do enjoy a good ale," he said. "And a good game."

Chapter 19

"Things are progressing on schedule, Master."

Abdiel stood at rigid attention as he presented Lucifer with the details of his budding relationship with the Scarlatti kid. Lucifer couldn't have been more pleased. With Heaven closely guarding the human, Abdiel had done well to take advantage of the opportunity presented by Azazel and Seir.

"Excellent," he said. "You have done well, General."

"Thank you, Master."

Lucifer regarded Abdiel's straight posture and his quick, sharp responses. He'd regained a measure of confidence since the last time he stood in the throne room. Lucifer had been skeptical of Abdiel that day, but the general proved himself. He came through in finding Nicholas Scarlatti, and then he had done a fantastic job, winning the young man's trust, or at least enough to begin a cordial relationship.

Abdiel found an easy in when he offered to help young Nicholas understand dark magic. Over the course of several days, he explained the various techniques for accessing chakra and how to maintain a consistently alert mind, aware of potential threats around him at all times. Abdiel walked him through the many levels of attacks and defenses, explaining that those who use magic need to understand how to stack their spells and casts to achieve maximum effect. It looked like Abdiel was on his way to gaining the human's trust. Of course, it didn't hurt to have the vampire around to concur with anything negative said about the angels of Heaven.

"And no sign of Seir?"

Lucifer was pleasantly surprised the general chose to inform him of the exact circumstances of his initial encounter with Scarlatti. Seir's involvement was troubling, especially since Azazel was incommunicado at the moment. The general exercised impressive tact when reporting the events of that night. Abdiel accused no one and left the chore of determining what the information meant to Lucifer himself.

"No sign, Master. I haven't seen or heard from him since that night."

"That night," replied Lucifer, looking off into the distance as if he were staring at a sunset. The dim torch-lighting of the Throne Room flickered shadows across his face. He turned back to Abdiel. "Tell me, General, what do you make of Seir's presence that night?"

Abdiel hesitated. It was a moment of truth for Lucifer. Would the general shrink from insulting Azazel? If so, how could the ruler of Hell trust him with more responsibility?

Abdiel pressed his lips together and wrinkled his forehead. "I'm not sure what to make of it, Master. Seir doesn't act on his own. On the other hand, Azazel was standing right behind you when you ordered Scarlatti was not to be harmed."

"Yes," Lucifer agreed. "He was." He sighed and turned to face Abdiel. "So, why does my oldest and closest friend betray me?"

He had no expectation Abdiel would answer; it was probably better if he didn't. Abdiel was a professional. His opinion had never been asked on anything other than mission specifics. Lucifer's question came from a personal place; one he hadn't realized still existed.

Abdiel shook his head. "I do not know, Master. Azazel has always been…unpredictable? Perhaps his loss pushed him over the edge. Perhaps his need for revenge consumed him."

Lucifer turned away, his eyes again gazing off into the distance. "Yes," he said, letting his thoughts drift. "Yes, I'm sure you're right, Abdiel."

Abdiel's eyes flickered. Lucifer just called him by name. He had never called Abdiel anything other than his official title. Was it a momentary slip or did it mean something deeper? It certainly felt as though his master was pulling Abdiel closer. Perhaps he was preparing to groom him to replace his old friend. Abdiel wondered if that was something about which he should be pleased or terrified.

ℏ A ⸼ ψ ς

"His name is Nicholas Scarlatti."

Alvi looked up and saw Nayra standing at the entrance to his study. A bandage wrapped her wrist and her hands were covered in what had to be blood. Her eyes were glassy, almost as if she had been partaking in some of the cartel's products, though Alvi knew that was not the case. Her tone was the only indication she was in control of her faculties. She was as sharp as ever.

"The man who took your money," she urged.

Alvi's eyes widened. "They told you?"

"Not exactly."

Alvi could stomach a lot, but the supernatural made his skin crawl. He knew all about their visitors and was less than thrilled that Nayra trapped a couple of demons in his vault. It was impressive though, that she was able to do it. He was skeptical when she first explained her plan, but he let her clear the security room and vault, and even allowed her to paint her crazy symbols on the vault floor and ceiling.

Now, after witnessing the scene downstairs, his godmother was far more intimidating than he had ever dreamed. She was always the strange mystic who seemed to know everything. He'd learned over the years to trust her judgment and rely on her to see the road ahead. He never thought it went any further than that. Now, he had two demons stuck in his vault and Nayra extracted information from their minds without their consent. Things were getting just a little bit strange.

Information was information, though, no matter how it came about. He would make use of it and see about getting his…and the rest of the cartels,' money back. He lifted the phone as Nayra stepped further into the room. She held up a hand and shook her head.

"What are you doing?"

Alvi frowned at her. "I'm getting a team ready to go get this pendejo."

Nayra shook her head. "Don't be rash, my son. Your team could walk into a dangerous situation."

Alvi chuckled. "They're used to that."

"Just wait." Nayra sat in the leather chair across from Alvi. "I am working on a spell."

"What kind of spell?" he asked. He narrowed his eyes in suspicion. He didn't like the idea of Nayra casting spells. It was disturbing enough that she was able to capture demons.

"One that will compel the demons to do our bidding."

Alvi dropped the phone on his desk and leaned back in his chair. "You can do that?"

"I believe so."

"But you don't know."

Nayra shook her head. "Give me a few days to work it all out."

Alvi sighed. "Fine. Go work on your spell."

After she left, Alvi shook his head and lifted the phone. A voice on the other end answered almost immediately.

"It's me," Alvi said, looking at the paper Nayra had handed him. "I have a name and a location. Feel like putting a joint team together? Two of yours and two of mine…I say we keep this between us for the time being…Exactly. It will keep everything simple… I'll text you the travel details."

ᛒ ᚨ ᛝ ᚢ ᚷ

Nicholas stood in the center of a huge, empty warehouse. He had been coming to the massive structure with Abdiel for over two weeks as he learned to access the powers flowing through his body. At firs,t he'd been nervous about the angels finding out he was even *talking* to the other side, much less training on the use of his dark powers, but on their first day, Abdiel pointed out a series of symbols etched into the building's siding and roof.

"They're Enochian sigils," he said.

"Enochian?" Nicholas repeated as he squinted at the images.

Abdiel smiled. "It's the language of the angels, Nicholas. Created by the Father himself."

"What do they mean?" Nicholas had asked.

"Those are used for cloaking…specifically, to cloak the interior of this building from angels' eyes." He grinned. "We could cover the building in Enochian warding sigils, but then *I* wouldn't be able to enter it myself, so blinding them will have to do."

Nicholas was still concerned. "What if they track me to this location?"

Abdiel smiled. "Think about it, Nicholas. If you orb in and out, how could they possibly know where you are?" He put a hand on Nicholas' shoulder. "Remember, angels are extremely powerful, and archangels even more so, but no being, save the Father, is omniscient. They can't see everything all the time. And one thing that they can*not* do is track an orb trail that disappears. Meaning, if you orb into a cloaked location, that orb trail will disappear into the ether as soon as you enter. The only way you could be tracked is if they were tethered to you."

"Tethered?" Nicholas asked.

Abdiel smiled. "Don't worry, Nicholas. If you know what to look out for, you would feel it. We will cover all that in due time."

Now, more than two weeks later, Nicholas was a different person. He was learning just how powerful he had become. Under Abdiel's instruction he grew in understanding of how chakra actually worked. Abdiel's teaching fell in line with what Zha'riel had taught him, but went far deeper and he wondered more than once why Zha'riel withheld such a wealth of knowledge from him.

"It's almost like he really didn't want me to learn," Nicholas complained aloud one day.

He stretched out his hand and unleashed a volley of energy, striking a series of paper targets set up fifty feet away. Each target vaporized instantly. The only remaining trace was a puff of smoke. He grinned for a second but remembered his question and turned to Abdiel expectantly.

Abdiel shrugged. "Try not to be too hard on him, Nico."

Nicholas stared at him. "You too, with the Nico nonsense?"

The fallen angel chuckled. He gestured for a demon, named Tomas, to set up a new set of targets. When he turned back to Nicholas, he pursed his lips as though he wasn't sure he ought to say what was on his mind. A skeptical look from Nicholas served to push the issue enough. Abdiel nodded and gestured to Xabier, who sat quietly and tried not to grin in triumph.

"Your friend makes an interesting point. You are no longer the being you once were. You are having trouble accepting your new reality. I can see the struggle in your eyes. The inner conflict is tearing you up inside. You still think you're human." He shrugged. "Maybe a slight change to your name will help you move on from your former life."

"Maybe I need to deal with it *my* way." Nicholas shook his head and glared at Xabier. He sat down on a set of steps leading to some second-floor offices. With no power to the building, and few windows, the only significant source of light came from a bunch of torches the demons scattered throughout the area. Nicholas wondered how such powerful creatures could still be stuck in the Stone Age. He sighed. "Anyway, if you know all this, I assume Zha'riel does too."

"He does," Abdiel affirmed. "But it is more complicated for him. Angels of Heaven have different rules…more stringent guidelines than we do."

"But *you're* an angel," Nicholas pointed out. "And you're nothing like Zha'riel."

"True," Abdiel conceded. He leaned on the railing next to Nicholas. "But I'm not an angel of *Heaven*...at least, not anymore, and thus, not encumbered by their rules. You see, I *like* the idea of having a powerful friend, and as much as you may want to be left alone, it is not a realistic expectation. *That* is why I train you. I want you to be able to defend yourself against whoever comes against you, but I also believe that one day you will be forced into the war on one side or the other."

"And why would that happen?"

Abdiel pursed his lips. "Life," was his simple reply. "Things happen. We get pushed and pulled as the tides ebb and flow, until one day, something drastic changes us forever."

"I can't imagine something making me want to fight a war."

"Six months ago, did you imagine having the powers you have now?" Xabier chuckled. "Did you ever imagine you would meet angels and vampires and demons?"

Abdiel gave him and broad smile and patted Nicholas on the shoulder as he responded. "Touché."

Tomas had the targets prepared and Nicholas spent some more time on his casting accuracy. After that, Abdiel had Nicholas work on combinations of attacks and defenses.

"Think of it like a boxer," Abdiel said. "He'll use rights and lefts, jabs, uppercuts, and so on. Each should lead to the next. A good combination of punches is designed to set the other fighter up for the final blow. It's the same here. If you are far more powerful than your opponent, combinations might be overkill, but against a demon like Seir, the sequence of spells and casts matter."

"Shouldn't I be a lot more powerful than Seir?" Nicholas asked. "I thought Sansata was high-ranking."

Abdiel nodded. "Oh, yes. You have the power inside you to rival archangels, Nico. You have dual streams of chakra to draw from and that is very rare. You will get there, but right now, your mind and body are not able to handle what is inside you."

The first round struck Nicholas dead-center in his chest, a split-second before the loud crack shattered the silence. The slug exited his back, just to the left of his spine. He stood there for a second eyes wide and mouth agape, before looking down at the hole in his bare chest and the blood flowing down to his waistline Two rounds later and Xabier went down in a heap. Nicholas felt two more slugs tear through his torso. His eyes dimmed and the ground rushed up to meet him.

He hit the ground and was suddenly wide awake. The gunfire came in bursts as Abdiel stood and glared at the large windows. Bullets ripped into him and he looked down and shook his head. He stood over Nicholas as Xabier stirred.

"What the hell was that?" Xabier muttered. He rolled to his knees and crept behind a stack of huge tires. He surveyed the room.

"It would appear," Abdiel replied, "that we are under attack."

Xabier stayed low and crept over to the window. The gunfire ceased. He peeked out and scanned the area.

"I see two...no, four guys with rifles...automatics considering how many rounds they just fired at us."

"Nicholas, get up." Abdiel pulled Nicholas to his feet and laughed. "First time getting attacked by fools with guns?"

Nicholas nodded as he inspected his body. The wounds were already closing. He couldn't believe his eyes. His first thought was to be glad the bullets blew out his back. At least he wouldn't have to worry about loose lead floating around his chest. He ran his hands over his torso and shook his head.

"Itches a little, doesn't it?" he said with a cocky grin.

Abdiel smiled. "Are you ready to handle these fools?"

Nicholas took a breath and nodded. "Absolutely."

"Good," said Xabier with a ruthless grin. "Because they're coming."

As the men approached the building, they switched to smaller automatic weapons. They moved in unison. Two moved from behind an outbuilding to a closer position while the others covered them. They continued until they reached the building. Nicholas strode to the center of the large, open warehouse while Abdiel and Xabier stood in the shadows to watch. It was an unexpected opportunity for Nicholas to demonstrate his progress. The men had no chance to defeat him, but Nicholas would get to practice under fire, on live, moving targets.

Nicholas was calm. He controlled his breathing. He kept his eyes clear and alert. He hadn't taken a life since his little drug dealer rampage. That was a few weeks back, and he was aware of an intense desire, deep inside, to take down more murderous thugs. It was only the threat of annihilation by the angels that had kept him from acting on his desires. Now, he was presented with a nice opportunity for release, but he wanted to know *why* these men were attacking. He didn't have much time to think about it.

The men breached the door hard and fast, like a trained SWAT team. They kicked it in and came through, one behind the other, each focusing on a different area of the room. Nicholas stood in the center of the massive space with his arms spread and nothing in his hands. It threw the killers off for a moment. The first guy through leveled his weapon at him, shouting in Spanish as he approached Nicholas with caution. The other three men swept through the room quickly, ensuring there were no other threats. They missed Xabier and Abdiel, hidden deep in the shadows on the second floor.

Finally, they all came to stand around Nicholas, who despite being pushed and shoved and threatened in Spanish, continued to stand with a lazy grin on his face and his arms still spread slightly. The leader finally got frustrated with him and went to crack Nicholas on the head with the butt of the weapon, but Nicholas sidestepped, and using the man's momentum, coupled with his newly discovered powers, hurled him thirty feet across the room.

The other men reacted in an instant and leveled their weapons at Nicholas. The Spanish chatter flew fast and furious. Nicholas didn't give an inch as they tried to shove him to the ground. One guy pressed the muzzle of his gun right to Nicholas' temple, and Nicholas reacted by hitting the guy with a small jolt of electricity to his abdomen, dropping the guy instantly.

"What do you want?" Nicholas demanded as the other two tried to figure out what in the world was going on.

The first guy had gotten up and was shaking his head and looking on with a dazed expression on his face. As soon as he gathered his wits enough to stand, he went for his weapon and leveled it at Nicholas with a vengeful scowl. Nicholas stretched out his hand and made a grabbing and pulling motion. The gun flew from the cartel hit man's hand and landed at Nicholas' feet.

Nicholas flicked his wrist, and the other two guys flew across the room and landed, sprawled out, on the floor. He pushed his hand out to the side as the electricity wore off and the second guy came at him. With another flick, Nicholas unleashed a ball of fire and the guy was consumed in flames.

As the unfortunate gunman screamed in agony, Nicholas took down the first guy with a chakra grip on his throat, crushing his windpipe. The other two were scrambling to their feet when he sent bolts of green energy at one of them. The other leaped out of the way as the mini electrical storm consumed his friend. He stared, wide-eyed, at Nicholas and held his hands out, pleading with him in Spanish to spare his life.

"Who are you and why are you here?" Nicholas demanded, his eyes flashing silver, causing the guy to panic even more.

The terror in the man's eyes was surpassed only by the violent trembling of his body. Nicholas understood. He was expecting to walk into a gunfight, but found himself in the middle of something he could never wrap his mind around

"I-I-we were sent," he stuttered. "By Alvi Cornega and Guillermo Diaz."

Xabier and Abdiel stepped out from the shadows. Xabier frowned.

"Those names sound familiar."

The man looked at him. "You stole their money."

"Ah, yes," Xabier nodded and looked at his fingernails. "The cartels."

"They *found* us?" Nicholas exclaimed. "How?"

"I don't know," the man replied. "But they gave us your name and we tracked your cell phone with GPS. Senor Cornega wants his money back."

Abdiel frowned. "Why didn't Marmut call me?" he muttered. Looking at Nicholas, he said, "I must leave now. I have to track down a couple of missing demons. Are you okay to finish up here?"

Looking at the last cartel hit man standing, Nicholas laughed. "I think we can handle it from here."

The hit man looked at Nicholas, pleading with his eyes and mouth. "Please don't kill me."

"Why shouldn't I?" Nicholas demanded. "You were going to kill *me*."

The man fell to his knees and begged. Finally, Nicholas relented. "Okay," he said. "Stand up. I'm not going to kill you." He began to walk away and the guy breathed a sigh of relief.

"He's all yours, Xab." Nicholas sat back down on the steps as Xabier launched himself.

Chapter 20

"A toast!" Xabier raised his glass. "To sticking it to the angels!"

"Here, here!"

Nicholas laughed at Xabier's continued disdain for Heaven's citizens. He clinked his glass with Xabier and Abdiel before knocking back the pricey Scotch and setting it down along with the rest of the empty shot glasses that went before. It was Dominick's birthday, and he'd left countless voicemails and texts, threatening everything from bodily harm to excommunication if Nicholas wasn't at the bar to help celebrate. Nicholas, in turn, invited Xabier and Abdiel. It was a pleasant surprise when Abdiel accepted his invitation.

After everyone was introduced...as humans, of course...the gathering split up into the usual cliques. Dom and his gym-rat friends; the girls they'd brought along. The supernatural crew— Nicholas, Xabier, and Abdiel—wound up at the end of the bar. Stephanie, who seemed to know everyone there, flitted effortlessly between the groups. Nicholas enjoyed watching her interact with the others. It made him feel like her life hadn't been completely destroyed for meeting him, though he knew, in reality, it had.

"Interesting choice of company."

Nicholas' thoughts snapped back to the present, and he whirled around to find Zha'riel staring at him with a look Nicholas hadn't seen on his face before. Sadness? Defeat? The angel's eyes went dark and his nostrils flared with every breath as he shifted his gaze over Nicholas' shoulder.

"Hello…brother," Abdiel said.

Nicholas would have sworn the fallen angel was actually glad to see Zha'riel.

Nodding to the bartender, Abdiel twirled a finger. "Another round, Jimmy. And bring one for my long-lost brother."

Within seconds, the bartender produced fresh glasses and poured generous portions of Scotch. Everyone except Zha'riel picked up a glass. Nicholas and Xabier shifted their glances from Abdiel to Zha'riel, wondering if sparks were about to fly. Nicholas tried to imagine what it would look like to see two angels go head-to-head. It must be pretty spectacular.

Abdiel's eyes never left Zha'riel's as he waited, holding his glass in front of his chest, for Zha'riel to pick his up. Nicholas and Xabier each held theirs at the ready, and Nicholas imagined neither had ever wanted a drink more than at that very moment. Finally, Abdiel placed his glass down and folded his hands in front of his navel.

"What's the matter, brother?" he asked. "Unwilling to share a drink with your enemy on such a joyous occasion? Lighten up! It *is* a party."

Zha'riel glared daggers. "I do not consort with those who betray the Father."

"Why not?" Abdiel needled. "The Hero did the whole time he was on Earth."

Zha'riel made a move as if to confront him, but Abdiel's eyes shifted to those standing all around the bar and Zha'riel hesitated. Abdiel calmly returned his gaze back to Zha'riel and raised his eyebrows.

"How many?" he asked. "How many innocent people in this bar will die tonight if we decide to clash in *their* world?"

Zha'riel's face twitched. Nicholas had never seen him lose control. The angel clenched his jaw and his fists as he fought to reign in his temper. The stand-off lasted several agonizing seconds. Nicholas glanced from one side of the bar to the other, wondering if anyone else was picking up on the tension on their side of the room.

Abdiel chuckled, picking up his glass again. "How many years has it been, Brother?" He shook his head in amusement. "All this time and still you follow the rules."

"I suppose that would be funny to such a one as you, who knows no loyalty save to himself."

Abdiel nodded. "And to my friends," he said, picking up his glass and clinking it with Nicholas' and Xabier's. "Now, brother," he said, his tone far more ominous. "Pick up your glass and have a drink like a gentleman."

"Absolutely not," replied Zha'riel.

Abdiel turned to look at all the people. "Pick it up," he said, his tone even and steady. He turned his hand over showing the crackle of energy in his palm. "Or I will *make* you defend yourself, and everyone in this bar will suffer."

Zha'riel gritted his teeth, and flicked his eyes around the room. He reluctantly picked up his glass and stepped closer until he stood right in front of Abdiel. Clinking their glasses together, he slugged it back in one gulp, as did Abdiel.

"Ahhh!" exclaimed Abdiel, slamming the empty glass down. "That's much better. See that, brother? It's fun, right?" He clapped Zha'riel on the shoulder and turned to Nicholas and Xabier. "Zha'riel's a bit more partial to wine though, aren't you, brother? Ever since the Hero did the trick with the water, the Heavenly Host drinks nothing but vino!"

He let out a loud laugh as Zha'riel's face turned beet red.

"Stop calling Him that," he hissed.

"What?" Abdiel asked, signaling for another round. "Hero?" He waved a dismissive hand. "What shall I call him? He's just a showoff. Water to wine. Hmmph. Casting out demons? Please. Restoring eyesight? It was all just a show for the biggest egomaniac of all time."

Zha'riel chuckled, humor finally making its way to his face. "Egomaniac? And what would you call a bunch of angels who refuse to follow the commands of their Creator?"

Abdiel stuck out his bottom lip as if in deep thought. "Ummmm, I don't know…free thinkers?"

"And look where your freedom has gotten you," Zha'riel scoffed. "You are all on a path to destruction."

"Perhaps," Abdiel conceded. "At least, that's what you all keep telling us." He chuckled. "Look at you, Zha'riel. You're bursting at the seams with pent up anger. You're ready to battle to the death, aren't you? Is that what the Father has done to you?"

"You know *nothing* about us." Zha'riel's voice came through as a barely controlled hiss.

Abdiel smiled in empathy. "Oh, my poor brother. You are wrong about that and you know it. Tell me…is Michael still the life of the party? Are there even parties in Heaven anymore?"

Zha'riel's face flushed with rage or embarrassment. Nicholas couldn't tell which, but he couldn't believe how unhinged the angel was getting over Abdiel's barbs. His stoic, unemotional persona was turned inside out. Nicholas supposed what was true on Earth was also true in Heaven. Dysfunctional families notwithstanding, those who knew you best could push your buttons easiest.

"Heaven is utter perfection," Zha'riel chastised.

Abdiel laughed. "Yes, I can see your joy and contentment are overflowing. Nico, can't you see the joy oozing out of Zha'riel?"

Xabier came to Nicholas' rescue as he was about to stutter out something incoherent, trying to wriggle out of the loaded lose-lose question. He threw an arm around Nicholas' shoulders and grinned at the two angels.

"I don't think it's a good idea for the two of us to get in the middle of what is clearly a family squabble."

"Hahaha!" Abdiel raised his glass and downed yet another shot of Scotch. "Very tactful, Xabier, but it was rhetorical. Zha'riel knows I'm right. He was always a rule follower, even when the rules were confusing and cumbersome."

Zha'riel replied, "You speak as though that is a bad thing, Abdiel. After all, *you* broke the rules…you and the scoundrel…"

"Be careful whom you mock, brother." It was Abdiel's turn to threaten to lose his cool. His voice dropped to a threatening deep tone and his eyes darkened several shades. "You may not be willing to destroy these people, but I think you know I will scorch every one of them in defense of my master's honor."

Zha'riel chuckled. "Well, well, well. The irredeemable has found redemption in the embrace of his deceiver. Good for you, *brother.*"

He sneered the last word. Nicholas noted that when Abdiel used the term, it was as affectionate as it was mocking. Zha'riel, on the other hand, did not seem to recognize Abdiel as his equal. Angels were more confusing the more he learned about them. There was obviously a serious deep-seated issue between the two. He supposed being on opposite sides of an eons old war could do that. He let Xabier pull him away from the angelic stand-off.

Abdiel managed to calm his anger and replaced his scowling glare with a more comfortable and relaxed smile. "Deceiver?" He smirked. "You think I didn't know what I was doing when I refused to bow to a lesser entity?"

Zha'riel shook his head. "No, I think you were perfectly aware of what you were doing, but I also believe you have been deceived into believing you were doing it out of love for the Father."

"You question my motives."

Zha'riel shook his head. "Not yours."

Abdiel gulped his drink and stood. "Well," he said, turning to Nicholas and Xabier. "I think I'd better leave before I do something all of us would regret." He turned back to Zha'riel. "Well…all except me." He gave Zha'riel an affectionate cuff on the cheek, causing the angel to jerk back in disgust. "Brother…it has been too long." His eyes softened as he looked at Zha'riel. "Shall I send the master your regards?"

"You can give your master the tip of my sword," Zha'riel countered.

Abdiel chuckled. "Clever," he replied. "You are a clever one, Zha'riel." He nodded. "Until we meet again, brother."

"*If* we meet again," replied Zha'riel, "one of us will die."

Abdiel smiled sympathetically. "Don't be so angry, brother…and don't be so quick to draw your sword. You never know…we could end up fighting side by side again."

"That could never happen."

Abdiel chuckled with a knowing smile.

"One more thing," Zha'riel said, walking a few steps away, out of earshot of Nicholas and Xabier. "Stay away from him." He gestured to Nicholas.

Abdiel wrinkled his forehead. "Is Heaven choosing the young man's friends for him?"

Zha'riel glared. "We are trying to keep him from destroying himself."

"Ahh." Abdiel nodded. "But what have you done to *help* him?"

"I have been protecting him since the day he was turned."

"Yes," replied Abdiel. "But what have you done to *prepare* him?"

"I've taught him how to access the good powers within him."

Abdiel smirked and gave Zha'riel a thumbs-up. "Of course, you did…all the while denying him his more powerful essence."

Zha'riel glanced at Nicholas, who stared back at him with invigorated interest. It was touch and go for Nicholas now that he trusted Abdiel. If Abdiel was going to unleash Nicholas' dark essence, Heaven would have no choice but to act preemptively. The whole thing was about to blow up in all their faces. With Abdiel now firmly in the picture, Zha'riel no longer knew how to protect Nicholas.

"You will ensure his destruction," Zha'riel whispered.

"If it comes to that," Abdiel replied. "But we weren't going to simply let you have him. After all, it is the essence of one of our own inside him. At least we're not threatening his life, as you and Rafael are." He chuckled. "You make it so easy, Zha'riel. The boy needed a friend, not a parent. Why does Heaven insist on dictating? It is always rules, warnings, threats…doom and gloom…always your way. You never take the time to listen, because you really don't care about others."

"And you do?"

Abdiel shrugged. "I can at least fake it. He trusts me, and I withheld nothing from him. Can you say the same?"

He stared at Zha'riel's eyes for several seconds before nodding in condescension and shaking his head. "Sooo predictable, Zha'riel. Go ahead…take him out." Then he saw something in Zha'riel's eyes that made his eyes widen in disbelief. He grabbed him by the elbow and moved him even further away from Nicholas. "You don't want to, do you, brother?"

Zha'riel said nothing and kept his eyes focused away from Abdiel. He tried to reject his emotions, to no avail. He could easily hide them from humans, but from another angel, even one as fallen as Abdiel, he was an open book.

Abdiel shook his head in pleasant disbelief. "This is a surprise," he said. "I think you and I might be comrades even more quickly than I thought."

Zha'riel shook his head. "Just because I have doubts and might not be pleased with my current mission doesn't mean I would switch sides."

"No," Abdiel agreed. "Of course not. Though I suspect you will soon be put to a decision that will cost you either your conscience or your grace." He shook his head. "I remember making my choice. Having my grace ripped out was agony, but I have also seen what guilt can do to an angel. Just ask Azazel."

ℨ A ⅔ ψ ϛ

"Stupid boy." Nayra slammed her hand on the desk. "You should have waited."

Alvi sighed. "I didn't think there was any reason to wait."

Nayra shook her head and looked at her godson with disappointment. "The idea that you were robbed by someone who could pass through the walls of your home and vault, incapacitating your entire security force, didn't make you stop and think that perhaps your silly little four-man team wasn't enough?"

Alvi slumped in his burgundy, leather seat. He hated it when Nayra looked at him like a smacked ass. She was worse than his mother had been when she was still alive. For some reason, she had the ability to make him feel like he was two inches tall.

"I'm sorry." He groaned. "I should have spoken to you first."

"You *did* speak to me!" Nayra exploded. "And I told you to wait. I told you I was working on something that might be able to help us, but you decide to go off and get four of your men killed."

"Two," Alvi corrected. "The other two were from Los Llanos."

Word had come in over an hour ago from his contacts in the States. The entire team had been killed and it was not pretty. It was only a matter of time before the team was identified as cartel personnel as no effort had been made to hide the bodies.

"Whoever got them was creative."

That was the only real clue his contacts were able to provide, but Nayra knew. She didn't even bother to ask questions.

"Oh wonderful, you *fool*," she spat. "Getting friendly with the craziest of all the cartel leaders will do wonders for you, won't it?"

Alvi shrugged. "We joined up to get our money back. That's all. It's just business."

"Of course, it is," Nayra replied, her skeptical gray eyes boring into him with disgust. "And what did you two manage to accomplish together? You got four men killed."

Alvi was silent. He was well-aware of his mistake and what it had cost him and Diaz. Nayra was absolutely right; four good men were dead. Men like that were not easy to replace. What it really meant to him was that Nicholas Scarlatti's debt was growing and when Alvi got a hold of him, he was going to suffer mightily.

"Now," Nayra said, her tone still patronizing and condescending. "Are you ready to listen? Are you ready to fight the supernatural *with* the supernatural? Or are you going to continue to pour gasoline on the fire and watch it spread?"

Alvi sighed. "I'm ready to listen, Madrina."

Nayra nodded. "You understand bullets and bombs will not work?"

"Yes."

"So, we need a weapon that neutralizes the advantages his supernatural essence gives him."

"Okay." Alvi understood neutralizing the enemy by taking away their advantage. It usually meant eliminating their advantage or obtaining an equivalent advantage yourself. "So how do we get him?"

"*We* don't," she said with a smug grin. "We have our demon friends get him for us."

She let it sit there for several moments as Alvi stared at her. He hated it when he didn't understand something. These days, it seemed like Nayra was constantly a step or two ahead of him, and with the supernatural, she was light years ahead.

"And how do we do that?" he asked. He gave up trying to comprehend her words.

She looked pleased. "I have cast a very complex spell which compels the demons to do my bidding as long as I am within close proximity."

Alvi squinted his eyes. "Are you sure they'll do whatever you want?"

"Absolutely," Nayra replied. "I have already tested the spell. In fact, our demon friends are right outside." Turning in her chair, she called out. "You may enter!"

Alvi watched in stunned amazement as the two demons, previously trapped in his vault due to a bunch of symbols painted on the floor and ceiling, entered the room. Their demeanors were very different than it had been when he had first seen them. Then they had been defiant, threatening. Now they were tame and docile, like trained wild animals, but he could still see the blazing rage in their eyes. It made him nervous.

Nayra nodded to them. "As you can see, my son, they are under my command."

212

Alvi stood and approached the demons. "Very impressive, Madrina. But is this dangerous? It seems like we're playing with fire."

"As long as the spell is unbroken, they are under my control," Nayra assured him.

"How do you break the spell?" Alvi asked.

Nayra smiled. "Only I or another witch can do that, but they'd have to overpower *my* magic, which few can do." She raised a finger. "Or they could get exorcised. At that point, they would be freed because my spell will not work on them in their supernatural state."

Alvi nodded. "So, they have to be in these human bodies."

"Precisely," Nayra replied. "A witch can only affect the natural world. We can affect supernatural beings, too, but only through their human connections to the world. Once that is severed, the spell is broken."

Alvi pressed his lips together in a thin smile. "So, Madrina, it appears you have solved our problem."

The corners of her mouth turned up and she bowed her head to him. "Now, my son, are you ready to reclaim what is yours?"

Chapter 21

"You must make a decision."

"Why?" Nicholas argued. "I've done nothing since you and that Rafael stiff threatened to execute me."

The doorbell rang and Nicholas checked through the peephole before opening. The delivery guy was outside with two large pies. Nicholas paid for them and closed the door. He brushed past Zha'riel and tossed the boxes on the table. He grabbed some paper plates and pulled two slices of pepperoni from the top box. Without a word, he sprinkled garlic powder and a liberal amount of crushed red peppers on both slices. He bit into one slice and stared at Zha'riel.

The angel crossed his arms and raised his eyebrows. "*Nothing*, Nicholas? You think befriending a Dark Angel and training under his supervision is *nothing*?"

Nicholas shrugged and chewed. "I don't think you get to decide who I hang out with or what I do. I understand you don't want me going around killing criminals and all that, and I haven't. I don't see why I have to report to you and run my friends through you."

"No one said you have to run your friends—"

"Good," Nicholas shot back. He gestured toward the pizza boxes. "Then grab a slice and shut up about it."

Zha'riel sighed. "Nicholas, do you think taking a petulant attitude, such as you are right now, is going to stop Rafael from annihilating you?"

Nicholas finished the first slice and started on the second. He thought for a moment as he swallowed a bite and washed it down with a swig of beer. "Honestly, I really don't care. Abdiel explained your rules. I don't think they can touch me if I don't actually *do* anything."

"And you trust Abdiel to tell you how Heaven operates?"

"I think he hasn't lied to me so far, unlike you." Nicholas sipped his beer and held up a hand. "Don't get me wrong; I know he wants me to join their side and all that, but he's not pushy about it. So far, he seems to be content to help me understand the powers I have inside me, which *you* refused to do."

Zha'riel shook his head. "You just do not understand how dangerous this is, Nicholas. And I would point out that it has not been Abdiel protecting you and your friends twenty-four hours a day, has it? Has he even *offered* his hedge of protection?"

Nicholas sighed. "No, he hasn't."

Zha'riel shrugged. "You may be right, Nicholas. Perhaps my superiors will not strike you down. However, I suspect that when I report in, they will require me to withdraw my protection."

Nicholas nodded. "I guess it is what it is." He looked at Zha'riel with disgust. "It's interesting, isn't it?"

"What is interesting?"

"You claim all this righteousness and goodness, but really you angels are just a bunch of bullies and selfish jerks as far as I can see."

"And how exactly is that?" Zha'riel frowned. "We have been incredibly generous in our efforts to keep you safe."

"Yeah," Nicholas said, spreading his hands. "As long as I do what you say. Your generosity comes with strings and threats. Abdiel has made no such threats and has asked for nothing from me."

"And you believe that will continue? You really believe Lucifer has no ulterior motives? You can't be that naïve, Nicholas."

Nicholas sat down at the kitchen table and tapped the bottom of his beer bottle on the table as he considered the angel's words. Of course Lucifer had ulterior motives. Abdiel was clear they wanted Nicholas on their side. That wasn't the point. At least Abdiel offered help even after Nicholas made it clear he wouldn't join them.

"Ulterior motives or not, I'm learning a lot. The powers I have in me are not demonic, as you accused. They are angelic, just like yours. Coupled with Mattaeus' mage powers, Abdiel thinks I might be able to rival one of your archangels someday." He shrugged. "So, you see, I really don't care what they think."

Zha'riel shook his head. "You play a very dangerous game, Nicholas. It is insane to suggest you can successfully defeat an archangel. They are the most fearsome beings in existence. Their powers are unrivaled."

"That may be," said Nicholas, unfolding his arms.

He quickly extended his right arm and suddenly there appeared, in his grasp, a gleaming sword. Zha'riel stood, mouth agape. Nicholas saw the recognition in his eyes.

"Where did you get that?" the angel demanded breathlessly.

Nicholas moved the sword through the air, allowing Zha'riel to get a good look. "Mattaeus gave it to me. This is how I killed Sansata and Mattaeus that night." Nicholas wrinkled his forehead. "I thought you knew. You were there that night, right?"

"Not until after," Zha'riel replied. "I did not see the sword." The angel fell silent for several seconds. Then he nodded. "Did Mattaeus speak any unfamiliar words when he gave the sword over to you?"

"Yeah, he did," replied Nicholas. "How did you know that?"

Zha'riel nodded knowingly. "The old mage bound it to you." He chuckled and shook his head. "Very clever, Mattaeus."

Nicholas had no idea what he was saying. "Abdiel said something like that, but I forgot to ask about it. What does that mean?"

Zha'riel took a breath. "Mattaeus knew you would likely be incapacitated in the early stages of your transition. The chant bound that sword to your soul, like a supernatural sheath. It stayed with you even when I moved you."

Nicholas nodded. "Wow. That was quick thinking. Mattaeus was pretty good, wasn't he?"

"Indeed, he was," agreed Zha'riel. "And what do you plan to do with that sword?"

Nicholas shrugged. "Since angels are going to try to kill me, I figured it would be a good idea to keep it handy."

Zha'riel nodded with a sigh. "So, you know what it is."

Nicholas chuckled. "Yes. Abdiel filled me in. It's an angel sword, right? It is the only thing that can kill...*truly* kill...an angel." He looked at the sword in appreciation. "Abdiel reacted when he saw this. I mean, I'm sure it's a big deal that anyone other than an angel has one, but he was staring at it like it meant even more than that." He shrugged. "And I couldn't give it to him to inspect. I mean, he couldn't take it. It was like his hands and the sword were magnets pushing each other away."

Zha'riel crinkled his forehead. "May I see?"

Nicholas placed the sword on the table and Zha'riel tried to pick it up. The sword slid away from his fingers, just like a magnet would repel another magnet. He pulled his hands away and leaned over to inspect the sword. It was familiar, somehow, though not quite the same as the blade he carried. It was a little longer and thicker. As his eyes roved over the surface of the blade and then the hilt and handle, he saw the etchings. His eyes widened and his mouth dropped open. He felt his heartbeat quicken and his hands trembled.

"It cannot be!" he exclaimed under his breath. "It's *impossible*."

Nicholas gave him a confused look. "What is it? What's the big deal?"

Zha'riel looked at him with eyes that appeared tired and glazed over. "Abdiel knows about this?"

"Of course," Nicholas replied. "How do you think I learned the angel draw?"

He was referring to the way the sword was carried supernaturally with him and how he could make it appear with a mere thought. It was a technique specific to angels. Abdiel had explained that if a sword was soul-bound, it could be carried supernaturally.

Zha'riel was lost in thought. After a few silent moments, he looked up. "I must return to Heaven to report in." His face grew serious. "That sword is special, Nicholas. I don't think it would be good if Heaven learned that you had it."

"Why?" Nicholas asked. "What's so special about it?"

"You mean other than being an angel sword?" Zha'riel asked with raised eyebrows.

Nicholas peered at the elegant weapon. "You didn't seem to think much of it until you saw it up close." He held the sword up and inspected the markings. "What's so special about *this* sword?"

Zha'riel looked uncomfortable, which was unusual. He averted his eyes and fidgeted. Nicholas rolled his eyes and turned away.

"Fine," he said. "Don't tell me. I'll just ask Abdiel later."

"No!" Zha'riel replied. "Do *not* show Abdiel that sword ever again unless you intend to kill him with it."

ᛒ ᴀ ⳩ ψ ɢ

"It is impossible."

Alvi frowned. He looked at Nayra. "Aren't they supposed to do what you say?"

Nayra nodded. "But they still have their minds. If they cannot accomplish a task, they will tell me." She turned to Ruta. "Why is it impossible?"

"He is protected by an angel. There is no way we can approach that house undetected. We would never get close enough to grab him."

Nayra nodded. "We need a different way in."

Alvi gritted his teeth. He was used to calling the shots. He was used to swift and painful retribution, the kind of retribution that conveyed a message to everyone around that crossing the Manizales Cartel was suicide. Recovering his money was vital; he couldn't operate without it. But the idea of *not* making Scarlatti suffer for the indignities he caused was unthinkable. He wanted to go in strong, but swore he would let Nayra take the lead.

"After we recover the money, I will send a message."

Nayra looked at him with a smirk. "I never said Mr. Scarlatti wouldn't suffer, my son, only that we must take things step by step."

He nodded. Turning to Ruta and Marmut, he asked, "Does he have family? Friends?"

Marmut spoke. "He has a girlfriend, but she is under the protection of the angel inside that house. He also has an older brother who does not live there."

Alvi nodded and glanced at Nayra. "Let's go get the brother."

ᛒ ᚨ ᛉ ᚦ ᚲ

Nicholas' phone vibrated for the third time. He glanced at it and saw it was another text from Dominick.

Nick, get over here. I need your help.

Nicholas shook his head and replied.

Sorry. No can do. I'm tied up all day.

The next text was an image. Nicholas almost dropped his phone as he recoiled in terror. The image on his screen was his worst nightmare. The message accompanying the image was even less encouraging.

You stole from us. We are at Scarlatti Stoneworks. You have until midnight to bring everything you stole. Come alone, or we'll kill your brother, disappear, and deal with you later.

Nicholas couldn't breathe. He was glad Stephanie was at work. Since Nicholas hadn't seen any sign of Sier in weeks, she decided to return to her life…at least her job. Nicholas was against it, but Zha'riel had given her an angel relic, which she wore around her neck. It would serve as a beacon and alert Zha'riel of the presence of any supernatural being in close proximity to her.

Dominick wasn't given anything like that. Even if he had, Nicholas was certain he was dealing with the Colombian cartels and not any supernatural creatures. As he considered that likely scenario, he began to breathe easier. A human threat he could handle. He would have to ensure the element of surprise, but he was certain he would be able to orb in undetected, and as long as guns weren't trained on Dom, he ought to be able to incapacitate everyone within seconds.

"What's wrong?"

Nicholas looked up. Xabier stood over him with a concerned expression on his face. His posture indicated he was ready for bad news. Nicholas had gotten to know a lot of Xabier's mannerisms over the past couple of months. Their friendship had grown by leaps and bounds and it was getting so they could read one another's thoughts.

"Don't act like everything's fine," Xabier said before Nicholas could do just that. "I can tell by the way you reacted to that last text that something big is up. So talk to me and let's work through it."

Nicholas showed him the image of Dominick being held at gunpoint. His lower lip was bleeding and there was a developing bruise around his left eye. He appeared to be alert, but petrified. Xabier gritted his teeth in anger.

"Cowards," he said, his voice shaking with rage. "Pitiful little cowards."

Nicholas shook his head. "Why go after Dom, though? Why not just come after me?"

Xabier shrugged. "They kinda tried that already and it didn't work out all that well, did it?"

Nicholas nodded. "I guess." He looked at the photo. "Something's wrong. I just can't put my finger on it."

"Well," Xabier said. "I'd say trust your instincts. What are you thinking?"

Nicholas shook his head in uncertainty. "I'm not sure." He looked at the time. "It doesn't matter anyway. There's no way we can get everything here by midnight. They have to know that."

"Makes sense. So what do we do?"

Nicholas bit his bottom lip. "Feel like human blood tonight?"

Xabier returned his look with a fierce grin. "I believe my arm could be twisted, my friend."

Ƀ ᴀ ǯ ψ ç

They orbed in, ready for war, but upon appearing in the middle of one of the wide-open bay areas of the granite shop, Nicholas sensed something was wrong. The room was cold and there was a faint scent of sulfur. Over the past several weeks he had become acutely aware of the presence of living beings in close proximity to him. He had even begun to discern between the various types of beings. Angels had a far different presence than humans and Xabier's vampire presence also had a distinct feel to it.

So, when he appeared and scanned the room, reaching out mentally to scan even those places where his eyes couldn't see, he was struck by an eerie sense of emptiness. He could detect no one present save himself and Xabier, who had used his lightning speed to sweep through room after room and ensure that they were indeed alone. It still didn't feel right.

"There's no one here, Nico," he said finally, stepping out from the front office area.

"Okay," Nicholas replied. "No lights. These cartel guys...I don't know if they'd use a bomb, but let's not turn anything on just to be safe."

They stood in the center of the room and thought about what to do next. Had they walked into a trap? It didn't make sense that the cartel would simply disappear without their money, though the demand to get it all back in just a few hours was pretty unrealistic in the first place. As his eyes adjusted to the darkness, his heightened sight suddenly made out a shape crumpled on the floor in the center of the next bay over.

At first, Nicholas had assumed it to be a pile of debris or a tarp or something left on the floor. He rushed over and dropped to his knees, praying he was wrong, but knowing he wasn't.

"No, no, no!" he cried in panic as his fears were confirmed. It was indeed a body...a lifeless body. "Please God, no."

He tugged on the shoulder of the corpse and fell back as he saw the battered face of his brother staring back at him, his lifeless eyes still open and conveying his final thoughts...fear and pain. The weight of his own guilt fell heavily upon his shoulders. His eyes filled with tears and he fell face down on the floor, crying out in grief. Nicholas felt the jolt deep down in his soul and let out a tormented cry of despair and sorrow.

Xabier put a hand on Nicholas' shoulder. He bent down and found a piece of paper tacked to Dominick's chest with a dagger. He removed the dagger and read the paper.

"You stole from us. Consider this a token of our appreciation. You will suffer this scene again and again until you return what is ours."

Nicholas' eyes blazed, but before he could react to those words, a new presence joined them.

"Nicholas." Zha'riel appeared before them.

Nicholas looked up, his tears flowing and his eyes burning with a mixture of rage and anguish. He lunged and grabbed Zha'riel by the lapels. He shook the angel and pleaded.

"Bring him back," he begged. "I'll do anything. Just bring him back."

Zha'riel looked at the lifeless corpse and shook his head sadly. "I am sorry. I can do a great deal of things to help a living person, even heal a fatal wound, but bringing the dead back to life? I do not have that power. I am so sorry, Nicholas."

Nicholas shoved him away and dropped to his knees, his breath coming in short gasps. "Then why are you here?"

Zha'riel looked at him with compassion. "I heard you cry out. So here I am."

Xabier scoffed. "A lot of good that does us."

Zha'riel ignored the comment and scanned the scene. "Who did this?"

Xabier sighed as Nicholas' cell phone vibrated. "The cartel probably," Nicholas said. He pulled out his phone and looked at the screen. "Thing is, they didn't even try to get their money back…" He tapped the screen. "Hello?"

"Nico?" Abdiel's voice came through. "Are you okay?"

Nicholas got to his feet and walked away from Xabier and Zha'riel. "No, actually I'm not." He described what happened, pausing several times to collect himself and push back the tears that wanted to fall endlessly.

"Nicholas, I'm so sorry, my friend. I felt your anguish. I would have come but I knew Zha'riel must have felt it too. Is he there?"

"Yeah," Nicholas said.

"And?"

"And what? He can't raise the dead."

"No," agreed Abdiel. "But he knows those who can."

Nicholas was silent as he gathered his thoughts. "Are you talking about God?"

"Well," Abdiel replied. "Sure, the Father can resurrect the dead, but I was thinking more along the lines of a bit lower power."

"Like who?"

"Like perhaps an archangel?"

Nicholas shook his head. "Oh great. They all hate me."

"They're not allowed to hate you, Nicholas."

"Well, whatever. They are not going to help me."

"You could at least ask. Maybe you'll find a sympathetic one up there somewhere."

Nicholas shook his head. "Doubt it." A thought then struck him. "Abdiel…how many of the angels that were cast out of heaven were archangels?"

Abdiel sucked in a breath. "There were many. Thousands actually. Many have since died. They were the first ones that Michael sought to destroy in the wars. But many still exist."

"Lucifer?"

"Yes," Abdiel said slowly. "But Nicholas, do not be rash. Think carefully about what you would be willing to give up, because bringing a man back to life will cost a hefty premium and even if it seems like the right thing now, it is almost always better to let the dead stay dead."

"He's my *brother*," replied Nicholas.

"I understand that," said Abdiel. "If you insist, I will help you, but you will have to give yourself to Lucifer. A life for a life is the least of what he will demand."

"So, you don't think I ought to do it?" Nicholas asked incredulously. "I thought you'd jump at the chance to bring me on board."

"I will," Abdiel said with a chuckle. "Of course, I want you on our side, but I want you to make that decision with a clear head and an understanding of the commitment. Think about it and we'll talk later."

"Okay," Nicholas sighed.

Zha'riel spoke when he hung up. "Abdiel?"

When Nicholas nodded, the angel said, "He felt the same thing I felt." He took a breath. "Did he make you an offer?"

Nicholas shook his head. "He suggested I ask you to talk to an archangel."

Zha'riel sniffed. "Of course, he did."

"Thanks for telling me about that option," Nicholas snapped derisively. "I appreciate your willingness to help."

Zha'riel pressed his lips together, restraining the frustration he was feeling. "I did not mention the archangels because they will not help you, Nicholas. Your brother is dead because of your actions. I warned you about the consequences of greed and selfish gain. You chose to ignore me."

Xabier jumped to his feet. "What kind of friend are you?"

"I am not here to be a friend," countered Zha'riel. "I am here to guide Nicholas onto the right path, but he insists on befriending an abomination. He insists on befriending a fallen angel. He insists on using his powers for selfishness and greed. There are consequences to those choices."

Xabier was about to say something else, but Nicholas shook his head. "No, he's right," he said. "Zha'riel's absolutely right. This is all my fault and if I want to bring Dom back to life, I'll have to go to Lucifer, won't I?"

Zha'riel's eyes widened. "You wouldn't…"

Nicholas shrugged. "I don't know. I don't want to be owned by Lucifer, but if he's the only option…"

Zha'riel shook his head emphatically. "You must remember; your life will go on a great many years longer than your brother's will. He might have another sixty or seventy years left if he is fortunate. Your life will go on for centuries or even millennia after he is long gone. How many innocent people will suffer at your hands if Lucifer is pulling your strings?"

Nicholas was silent for a long time after Zha'riel disappeared. He sat on a stack of pallets with his head in his hands, eyes closed, just trying to breathe. Xabier came over and laid a hand on his shoulder. He held up the note left by the Colombians.

"What do you want to do?" he asked gently.

Nicholas looked up. "I want to kill them all."

Chapter 22

"Why not go straight to Manizales? We know it was them, right?"

Nicholas strode down the mile-long stretch of road leading to the Cartagena Cartel compound. He was dressed in a simple, classic, Japanese style, with loose cotton pants and what he referred to as "Bruce Lee shoes:" black, slip-on moccasins worn by the martial arts master. His upper-body was covered in a tunic-style garment that was tied at the waist and left open in the front exposing his chest.

Xabier had asked why he was going with a martial arts style outfit instead of something a little more befitting a powerful mage, but Nicholas hadn't bothered to respond. In fact, Nicholas hadn't said much of anything since leaving his dead brother's side. Xabier let him be silent, but he stayed close by. Whatever Nicholas decided to do, he would have Xabier at his right hand.

At first, Nicholas planned to orb out when Xabier wasn't looking. He didn't need Xabier with him to annihilate the cartels, but Xabier was his friend and he didn't deserve to be iced out, especially since he had shown such fierce loyalty in the face of some terrifying situations. Nicholas knew Xabier wasn't with him because he felt he owed it to the guy who saved his life. He really *wanted* to be there. He *wanted* to help Nicholas exact vengeance.

"I want Manizales to know I'm coming," Nicholas replied. He kept his eyes straight ahead. "I want them to know *I'm* bringing Hell to their doorstep."

Xabier shook his head. "My guess is they'll all clear out."

Nicholas disagreed. "Nope. They killed Dom because they *wanted* me to come here. They're *expecting* me to come."

"Which means," Xabier said, his voice slow and even, "we're walking into a trap."

Nicholas nodded. "Yep."

Xabier breathed in, slow and deep, and let it out in a long, slow hiss. He shook his head with a slight chuckle and looked at the perfect blue sky. He grinned at Nicholas. "Okay then. This should be fun."

Nicholas gave him a solemn and thoughtful shake of his head. Then, he threw his arm around his friend's neck. Pulling Xabier in tight, he kissed him on the cheek with a loud, "Muuuah!" causing Xabier to recoil in disgust and shove Nicholas aside.

"What was *that?*" he exclaimed in fury, wiping his cheek as though it had a toxic chemical on it.

"That was 'cause I love you, buddy," Nicholas said. "Now get ready. There's the fence."

"What are you gonna say to them?"

"Nothing."

With that, Nicholas increased his pace as he approached the gate. Several well-armed men spilled out of the guard house on the side of the road. They spread out along the fence. Nicholas raised his arms in the air and the men relaxed their postures somewhat. They still remained ready for anything…

…anything, that is, except for an attack from above.

Without warning, fire rained from the sky like something out of an apocalyptic nightmare. The men scurried about in circles, trying to dodge the molten droplets. When Nicholas dropped his arms, it got even worse. It rained fire and the men were caught out in the open. There was nowhere to run. The guards dropped their weapons and tried, though, but who could outrun rain? Where could they run? A couple of the guards made it to the guard house, but that only bought them a few moments. The structure soon succumbed to the flames. They had no time to warn anyone over their radios, but it would have done no good anyway.

The gates exploded open with the flick of a hand as Nicholas exercised powers he had only recently mastered. His right hand went up one more time as he and Xabier entered the compound. Immediately, Xabier saw something surround the two of them, like a dome that blocked the shower of fire all around them. It was just shy of transparent and he could see the little droplets of fire extinguish right above his head as they walked.

"Stay within a five-foot radius of me," Nicholas directed.

Xabier got closer. "When did you learn the force field thing?"

Nicholas shrugged. "Not sure. I just kinda knew to do it."

"Oh," Xabier said with a sidelong glance at him. "That's...comforting."

The guards at the main house were scrambling to respond to the chaos outside. The gates being blown off their hinges was second only to fire raining down from the sky. As they poured out of the house with their guns drawn, Nicholas turned up the intensity.

The winds kicked up and the fiery droplets came down in blazing torrents. The men quickly realized they were about to be overtaken by the fire storm and turned on their heels to get under cover. Some of them tried firing their weapons at Nicholas and Xabier but the shield was more than enough to repel the bullets.

Xabier tilted his head at Nicholas. "How long will this shield last, Nico?"

"No idea." Nicholas chuckled.

"I feel kinda useless," Xabier complained. "You have the fire thing going and the wind and I don't really get to do anything."

"You get to watch." Nicholas smiled. "*And* keep me company."

Xabier grumbled under his breath about showoff mages with evil angel powers, but he stayed by Nicholas' side as they approached the house. Nicholas bombarded the mansion with larger bursts of fire, crashing through the roof, windows, and the sides of the house. Within moments the entire structure was engulfed in flames and there was no way out. Nicholas heard the screams from within as men realized there was no escape.

Nicholas and Xabier walked the property and ensured there was no one left. Nicholas ceased the fire storm but kept the shield up just in case. He wasn't in the mood to get shot again. They remained long enough to see the entire mansion collapse in on itself and go up in a gigantic ball of white-hot flame. It burned fast and hot. It took only minutes to leave the mansion a charred pile of ashes. As the fire trucks began to make their way through the gate, Nicholas and Xabier moved on, orbing to the next cartel location.

Alvi came into his study, wide-eyed in terror. Nayra was reclining on the couch while Marmut and Ruta each sat in chairs nearby.

"Cartagena has been destroyed!" he cried. "And so has Caqueta!" He flicked on the television. "Both completely obliterated."

"How?" asked Nayra, lifting herself up to look at the screen.

"Fire!" replied Alvi. "Look!"

The screen filled with the images of two equally leveled structures surrounded by blackened earth that seemed to go on forever. Usually, fires would leave *something* recognizable. The images showed nothing, just soot-colored ashes as far as the eye could see.

"What could have done that?" Alvi asked. "It's like a bomb went off!"

"An angel could do that," Marmut spoke up.

All eyes turned to him, but he said nothing further.

"Speak!" Nayra screeched. "What do you mean…angels?"

Marmut shrugged. "Those images look like fire poured out of the sky and consumed it all." He looked at Alvi directly. "You might want to think about getting yourself out of here."

Nayra slammed her hand down on the table. "No!" She pointed her finger at Marmut and Ruta. "You two will destroy him the moment he sets foot on this property!"

Marmut glanced at Ruta, then back to Nayra. "If you send us out there, we will go and fight, but if this is an angel of the Lord…then we will have no chance of defeating him."

Nayra shook her head and laughed. "You think we're stupid. You just want us to leave so you can be free of the spell."

Marmut looked back at the scenes of devastation on the television screen. "I suspect we will be free of the spell soon enough, one way or another."

ℬ 𝐴 ⱬ 𝜓 𝒢

They approached all the compounds in the same manner. By the time Alvi and Nayra had watched reports of the first two cartel compounds to fall victim to Nicholas' wrath, two more had been decimated in the same manner. Now, the Manizales compound was the only one left of the five major Colombian cartels, and Nicholas strode up the mountain road toward the front entrance.

Within minutes, Nicholas dispatched virtually everyone on the grounds. Those who stayed to fight were dead. The rest fled the carnage and saved their own lives. As Nicholas turned his attention to the mansion, he saw two figures emerge. Considering the panicked exodus that had just preceded, it was an interesting development, especially considering the fire was still raining down. The two newcomers didn't appear at all affected.

Without warning, a man and a woman blinked to a position less than ten feet away from Nicholas and Xabier. The man's eyes glowed crimson-red, while the woman's glowed brilliant yellow. Nicholas ceased the rain of fire and faced his demon adversaries. He glanced at Xabier who grinned.

"I knew it," he muttered.

"I know," Nicholas replied under his breath.

"Knew what?" Yellow-eyes sneered. She clenched and unclenched her fists. Her black eyes revealed nothing but hate and rage.

Xabier looked at her, matching her wrathful gaze. "I knew Dominick's killer was supernatural. His head was twisted nearly all the way back. No human could have done that, and a cartel hit would have been a gun to the head or something more creative."

She continued to glare at them, though, the longer Xabier watched, the more confused he became. Xabier could tell her confidence wasn't all that high. She seemed on edge. It was as if she didn't really want to be there.

"Why are you protecting this peon?" he asked. "You must have better things you could be doing."

Red-eyes shrugged, almost in resignation. "Does it matter?"

Nicholas shook his head. His eyes flashed silver, then returned to a steady violet glow. "Not to me. I'll tell you what. One of you killed my brother. Step forward and the other can leave. Otherwise, I'm going to send you both back to Hell."

The man glanced at his partner. At that moment, Nicholas knew who the killer was. A second later, he also knew Red-eyes would not give up Yellow-eyes without a fight.

Red-eyes sprang forward but the simple flick of Nicholas' hand repelled him, and he sprawled across the lawn. Nicholas turned to the woman, who stared in stunned disbelief. She regained her senses in time to feel the energy engulf her body, lifting her up into the air at Nicholas' direction. The red-eyed demon picked himself up and, seeing his partner screaming and writhing overhead in agony, he let loose on Nicholas with the full force of his power. It was enough to break Nicholas' hold for the moment, but then the energy burst was turned on Red-eyes.

Nicholas, holding the demon in a stream of crackling violet energy, suddenly yanked him forward. Powerless to stop himself, the demon hurtled toward Nicholas and, more importantly, the tip of his gleaming angel sword extended out in front of him. As the sword plunged into the demon's abdomen and buried itself all the way to the hilt, he came within inches of Nicholas' face.

"Don't worry," Nicholas said to him, staring into the dying demon's eyes. "She'll join you soon…after I rip her to pieces."

With a violent torque of his wrist, he twisted the blade and Marmut grunted and groaned as the life poured out of him. Suddenly a black soot-like smoke or steam…Nicholas couldn't tell which…rushed out of the rigid body. It swirled around as if in anger before falling to the ground, incinerating upon contact. Within a few seconds, it was all over and Nicholas pulled the sword from the lifeless body, letting it drop to the ground in a crumpled heap. Seconds later, it too disintegrated in flames, leaving nothing but charred earth where it once was.

Yellow-eyes finally regained her senses enough to stand. She screamed in despair and attacked with everything she had. Nicholas, his strength now so much greater than when he had faced Seir, took her initial attacks easily and with a flick of his wrist flung the female demon through a knee-high stone wall surrounding the front of the mansion. He followed that up by grabbing her in a strong chakra grip and pulling her to her feet. He approached, and pulled a spray bottle from an inner pocket.

"I've been carrying this stuff around everywhere I go," he told her as he doused her with holy water.

She screamed as the water burned her like acid. Smoke rose from her skin the moment it made contact and Nicholas heard the sickening sound of sizzling flesh. Bubbles rose and burst on her face as the water burrowed into sinew and cartilage. He knew it wouldn't kill her, but holy water was acid to a demon and he was intent on making it last as long as possible. She was the demon who killed his brother with her bare hands. The least Nicholas felt he could do was make her suffer a little before removing her from the world.

He grabbed her by the back of her head, his fingers tangling in her short, bleach-blond hair and he forced her head back. Pulling a second bottle out of his pocket, he flicked the top off and poured a little holy water into her mouth. As soon as it hit, it sizzled and scorched. She screamed and then shut her mouth as tightly as she could. Nicholas responded by sending a jolt of electric energy into the back of her head, causing her to scream out. When her mouth opened, he emptied the contents into her throat, and then jammed his hand under her chin so she couldn't spit it out.

As the holy water seared through her intestines, she screamed out in sheer agony and writhed around on the ground, unable to do anything to ease the pain. Holy water on skin was agony for a demon, according to Zha'riel, but went away as it steamed off. Holy water inside a demon-possessed body lasted a long time.

"P-please," she begged. "Just k-k-kill me."

Nicholas scoffed. "Is that what my brother said just before you snapped his neck?"

She shook her head. "H-he was dead before…me."

"You beat him and then you killed him!" Nicholas screamed, sending a burst of violet energy into her, causing her to convulse for several seconds before being able to speak again.

"Th-th-th-that…w-w-was…n-n-not us," she managed. "H-he did that. He b-beat him. He l-lost control."

Nicholas knelt next to her. "You're talking about Alvi Cornega?"

She nodded, still grimacing in pain and unable to move. "And his witch made us help."

"His witch?" Nicholas asked in surprise. "What are you talking about?"

Yellow-eyes gasped as she coughed and blood spewed from her mouth. "How do you think they made us do all this?"

Nicholas stared at her. "A witch can *make* you do things?"

"If she is powerful enough," she croaked. "And if she can get us to stay still long enough."

Nicholas thought for a minute. "Devil's Trap."

"Score one for the new guy," she said, collapsing onto her back in exhaustion. "Now will you please just get on with it?"

Nicholas nodded and drew his sword.

Chapter 23

When he entered the burning house, Nicholas found only dead bodies from one room to the next. He hadn't noticed when Xabier disappeared from his side during his confrontation with the demons, but now he saw the dead bodies all bore the tell-tale signs of a vampire's rampage. Many had deep chunks ripped out of their throats. Others had their necks snapped, leaving their heads twisted in an unnatural position. Xabier had torn through the cartel security in a violent hurry. There was one or two with the simple bite marks that suggested Xabier took time to feed and recharge his energy, but the rest were ripped apart and discarded.

"Xabs!" Nicholas shouted from the bottom of the staircase leading to the second floor. "You up there?"

He heard a muffled grunt and then watched as a body fell from the second floor and landed not ten feet away. Xabier came into view at the top of the staircase with a devilish grin, the lower half of which was covered in blood. The front of his shirt was drenched in blood. He quickly came down the steps.

"Whew!" he said, licking his lips like a ravenous wolf. "That was fun, Nico. Much better than watching you do all the work." He jerked his head in the direction of the second floor. "Upstairs is clear. No sign of the boss."

Nicholas nodded. "Must be down-stairs. Where it all began."

"Let's go," replied Xabier, leading the way to the basement entrance.

When they reached the bottom of the stairs, Xabier suddenly leaned heavily on the railing. "Whoa!" he said, reaching for his head. He pinched the bridge of his nose and grimaced.

"What is it?" asked Nicholas.

"I don't know," Xabier said, trying to clear his thoughts. "Feels like a needle pushing into my brain." He shrugged it off as best he could. "Never mind. Let's go."

They moved through the basement and made it to the security center, where the vault was located. Xabier was still feeling the pain in his head. As far as Nicholas could tell, it was getting worse by the minute.

"Why don't you go get some air?" he said. "I can handle this."

Xabier shook his head. "No way. I want to see these people and look them in the eye."

Nicholas pushed open the door and instantly saw Alvi Cornega with a submachine gun aimed right at him. On the one hand, it was the most ridiculous thing Nicholas had ever seen. Alvi had to know the gun was useless. On the other hand, what else could he do? Alvi had no defense against the supernatural, so he'd obviously decided to go out with a gun in his hand. Nicholas was only too happy to oblige.

Before Alvi could pull the trigger, Nicholas had him slammed through the wall behind him and into the adjoining room. The gun was on the floor and not a shot had been fired. Just as Nicholas prepared to launch a painful barrage of energy into Alvi, Xabier fell to the floor in agony, clutching his head. Alvi quickly scampered to his feet and Nicholas grasped him in a chakra grip. He slammed Alvi up against another wall, lifting him several inches off the ground and holding him there.

"Xabs!" Nicholas shouted. "What's wrong?"

He heard a cackling kind of laughter coming from behind the vault door, which he had noticed was slightly ajar. A moment later, a woman stepped out. She was maybe in her fifties, with long black hair tinged with streaks of gray. Her piercing gray eyes betrayed nothing. She made little squeezing motions with her outstretched hand as Xabier groaned in misery.

"You must be the witch," Nicholas said. "What are you doing to him?"

"I'm Nayra, *Nicholas Scarlatti.*" She glared at him. "You didn't bring the money."

Nicholas glared right back. "You killed my brother."

"Because," Nayra said, "you didn't bring the money."

"He was dead long before midnight," Nicholas said. "You gave me until midnight. You and your drug-dealing godson murdered an innocent man."

Nayra stared at him like a mother looking at her four-year-old son who'd just told her the chocolate cake on his face wasn't really there. She glanced over at Alvi, still hanging suspended in Nicholas' grip. "Let my godson go, or I will crush your friend's head like an orange," she said. "Ask him what that would do to a vampire."

Nicholas shook his head. "You do that and you'll watch your godson die screaming in agony and then you'll follow."

"You would let your best friend die just for vengeance?" she asked.

"You killed my brother," replied Nicholas. "Xabier would never forgive me if I gave you two up to save him. Anyway...two for one seems pretty fair to me. And then I can go back to dealing with the rest of my life."

"Alone," Nayra said. "That's how you choose to live?"

Nicholas shrugged. "Seems like that's how it's going to end up anyway."

Nayra nodded. "So sad," she said, pressing her lips together in thought. "What if we *both* walked away?"

"What do you mean?"

Nayra shrugged. "I don't really want to die today, and I don't think you want to lose your friend. What if we both just...walked away?"

Nicholas frowned and squinted his eyes at the witch. "You expect me to trust you?"

Nayra shrugged again. "Perhaps there is still honor in this world."

Nicholas shook his head. "Not that I've seen lately."

She chuckled. "No, you're probably right." She sighed. "So how do you propose we end this nonsense?"

Nicholas thought for a moment. He really wanted to crush every bone in Alvi's body and tear him limb from limb, but he was not willing to give up Xabier to get his revenge. He could always catch up with Alvi Cornega later.

"I'm going to release this piece of trash, and take my friend out of here. Then I'm going to give you two sixty seconds to get out of here before I burn it to the ground. I want one thing perfectly clear though. If you don't release him…If anything goes wrong like he dies…I'm going to make you suffer like nothing you have ever imagined."

Nayra nodded. "Very well. I agree to your terms."

"And if you come for me again, nothing will save you." Nicholas' eyes flashed silver and returned to a violet glow. "You gave up any chance of me returning your money the moment you laid a hand on my brother."

Nayra gritted her teeth and nodded. Nicholas released Alvi and he dropped to the floor gasping for breath, but otherwise unharmed. Nayra let Xabier go as well and Nicholas saw the relief on his friend's face. Part of him wanted to renege on the deal. After all, they did kill Dominick. At least for now, they would get away with it, but Nicholas had killed most of his crew and burned down much of his operation. That would have to do for now. He took Xabier by the arm.

"You ready?"

"Let's get out of here, Nico."

Nicholas turned to Nayra. "Remember…sixty seconds. Then this place turns to ashes."

After he and Xabier orbed out, Nayra and Alvi quickly ran to the door. After peeking out to see that it was safe, they exited and made their way to a garage located a hundred yards to the rear of the mansion. Alvi kept several beautiful and expensive cars in the large structure. As they pulled out in a late model H2, they saw the fire completely consume the mansion and bring it down in on itself, just as Nicholas had promised.

Alvi stared at the flames, the anger burning inside him. "I'm going to kill that man," he promised.

"Later, my son." Nayra laid a hand on his and squeezed. "There will be time for that later."

After Nayra and Alvi had exited the mansion, two figures stepped out from the shadows. As flames engulfed the mansion, they stood and contemplated the scene.

"He is certainly getting stronger."

"That he is, Abdiel," Lucifer replied with a satisfied nod. "You have done well instructing him in the use of his powers."

"It wasn't more than a few weeks ago that Seir handled him without any trouble at all. Today, Marmut never had a chance."

Lucifer was pleased. "He is close, is he not?"

Abdiel nodded. "He is very close." He grinned. "Perhaps the slightest push would finish it?"

Lucifer nodded with a slight smirk of his own. "Perhaps," he said thoughtfully, nodding in satisfaction. Breathing in the burning wood, plastic, and concrete, he smiled. "And now..." His expression darkened. "...what to do about a traitor...?"

"You've carved out a nice little home for yourself, Brother."

Azazel scanned the rugged terrain of Northern Europe. Over the years, he'd admired the scenery and took time to enjoy the peace and quiet. There were few places on Earth that appealed to his sense of beauty. Most were infested with scores of humans. The Arctic climate of Nordkapp kept those numbers to a minimum.

"Yes," came the careful reply. "It's perfect...beautiful in a broken and desolate kind of way. But it's peaceful. After eons of war, peace is my only pursuit." He grinned. "And a little fun."

Azazel chuckled. Loki had always been about fun. Prior to the Fall, Loki was something of a court jester among the highest-ranking angels of Heaven. He was renowned for a particular practical joke that caused Michael such embarrassment their relationship had never been the same. After the fall, Michael had sworn specific vengeance upon three angels by name: Lucifer, Azazel, and Loki.

Loki, crafty and highly intelligent, turned into a superior military tactician. When war between the fallen angel factions had broken out, his services as a general and battle planner were highly sought after. He was a master of deceit, misdirection, and what the Russians call maskirovka. Fierce fighter though he was, he hated it, and when the opportunity came to rest, he took it and claimed for himself a small piece of undesirable land in modern-day Northern Europe.

Azazel cast him a sidelong glance. "You could have had so much more. I never understood why you settled for such a desolate and boring area. No one cares about this place."

"Precisely," agreed Loki. "That, my good friend, is *why* I chose it." He stared out over the Barents Sea. As always, the view was breathtaking. Loki never got tired of the sunsets in his little corner of the world. Still looking out over the sea, he asked, "So, what brings you to a place no one cares about, my friend?"

Azazel sighed. "I fear I have made an error in judgment that will cost me my status in the eyes of the Morning Star."

Loki's eyes flashed in surprise. "I can't imagine that. The two of you were always inseparable."

Azazel nodded. "That we were, but events have conspired to drive a wedge between us. Now I fear I cannot return to his presence."

Loki shook his head with a sigh. The last thing he needed was to be in the middle of a Luciferian vendetta. The Dark Prince was notorious for his punishment of those who aided his enemies. If something was about to erupt between Azazel and Lucifer, the best thing Loki could do was stay out of it. But he couldn't turn away a friend. He was, if nothing else, loyal.

"There must be quite a story."

Azazel nodded. "Indeed. You heard about Sansata?"

"I did," replied Loki with a nod. "I was sorry to hear of his demise." He squinted. "Didn't I hear something else about that? Something about his essence passing on to a human? Or a mage? I forget which."

Azazel's eyes flashed silver and glowed pearl white. "Mattaeus had a human standing ready to deal the final blow and take in his essence after Sansata fatally wounded him. But before that, he must have directed the human to take Sansata first."

Loki raised his eyebrows. "Sooo, you are saying that this…this *human,* has within him the essences of an angel *and* a supreme mage?"

Azazel shrugged. "I would not have thought it possible, but yes."

Loki pressed his fingers to his lips in wonderment. "Interesting. I wonder what that will look like."

Azazel's anger burned within him. "He will look very *dead* shortly."

Loki's eyes met Azazel's and he nodded in understanding. "Ahh. So Lucifer forbade you from exacting your revenge?"

"Yes."

"And you ignored his orders?"

"Yes."

"But you failed…or rather, your demon failed."

Azazel's hands shook with rage. He had been on the verge of tearing Seir apart molecule by molecule when the realization had hit him that Lucifer might find out his secret at any moment. With time to calm down, he was glad he hadn't destroyed his best and most trusted servant. It wouldn't have been the first time he'd lost a good servant to his temper.

"That is correct, Loki. And Lucifer is bound to find out, if he hasn't already."

Loki nodded and then shook his head. "Direct disobedience. Lucifer will have to take action, especially if others are aware of what you have done."

Azazel shrugged. "And that is why I am here. Could I impose upon you, old friend, for quiet refuge, until I can figure out the next move?"

Loki sighed. "I don't want war with Lucifer. But I won't turn you away, my friend. Please keep your head down while you're here."

Seir sat on the stool beside Azazel as they downed several pints of the favorite local brew. Loki had them set up in an apartment across the street from the old pub. Azazel was deep in thought, trying to plot his future. Seir was happy he was still alive and determined not to fail his master again.

"The human is under angelic protection," Azazel said. "We can't get to him directly, so we need to bring him to us."

"It seems as though the cartels tried that," Seir said, holding out a tablet and showing Azazel the images of destroyed mansions and land, "using his brother as bait, and he destroyed them all."

Azazel nodded as he scanned the images. "Impressive enough," he said. "Which is why this will be so much fun. He will be brazen and overconfident." He pointed to Seir's screen. "He appears to be growing stronger. This is interesting and creative work."

Seir looked again at the tablet and nodded. "So what do we do?"

Azazel finished his pint and stood up. "*We*...don't do anything. I'll handle young Nicholas myself."

"Please, Master," Seir said, his head bowed in submission. "Allow me to help. I failed you one time. I won't fail again."

"I know you won't." Azazel breathed in deeply. "Come, my friend. I think it's time we met Scarlatti's pretty young lady, don't you?"

Chapter 24

"I told you about interfering, Zha'riel."

Rafael was furious. Zha'riel couldn't tell what it was that angered the archangel more, that Zha'riel was personally involved in Nicholas' situation, or that Nicholas had just taken a plunge toward darkness with his vengeful actions in Colombia. It seemed like Zha'riel would take the brunt of Rafael's anger over both.

Standing in the center of Rafael's immaculate penthouse living room, Zha'riel had the fleeting thought that Rafael might splatter him all over the pearl-while marble floor. In his anger, the archangel somehow seemed even larger than his usual massive frame. There was little that could intimidate or frighten an angel of the Lord, but the sight of a furious archangel was more than adequate.

"I apologize for my interference," Zha'riel replied. "It just seemed like the right thing to do. There was an innocent involved."

"It is irrelevant," snapped Rafael. "Your instructions were to observe and report. To do nothing other than to guide the boy to the light, not affect the consequences of his decisions."

"Should I have let him die, Rafael? Because that is what Seir would have done."

"That is not a decision for you to make!" Rafael stepped close to Zha'riel. He towered over the smaller angel and his golden-brown eyes blazed in anger. He pointed a finger in Zha'riel's face. "Nicholas Scarlatti chose to enter our world. He does not get to make that choice, reject our grace, and still enjoy the benefits of our friendship. That kind of relationship requires something from him as well."

"He is just a kid," Zha'riel pleaded. "Can we not give him a break?"

"A break?" repeated Rafael, with unmasked disdain. "You have spent too much time with your earthly friends, Zha'riel? We do not "give breaks" in Heaven…certainly not to violent ingrates like young Scarlatti…*who*, by the way, just *murdered* hundreds of people and destroyed acres of property."

Zha'riel could hardly argue. Nicholas had taken revenge to the nth degree and the violence of it all was not lost on him. He could have taken revenge far more surgically. With the specialized powers he possessed, he could have limited the fallout to only those specifically involved in the murder of his brother. But he chose to make a statement…to unleash his darkest powers.

It might be good strategy in the long term—*if* he were able to handle the consequences—but Zha'riel doubted Nicholas had even considered the consequences. If he had, his choice reflected a poor understanding of his circumstances. The angels were not likely to let such violence slide.

"Please, Rafael," he begged. "Consider everything the boy has gone through…*is* going through. He had not taken a life since we last spoke to him about it. This was entirely due to the murder of his brother. The cartels attempted to kill *him* first."

Rafael raised his eyebrows. "And those lives? What about the lives of his would-be killers?"

Zha'riel frowned. "What about them? That cannot count against him. He was defending himself."

Rafael shrugged. "Was he? How do you know? The building was covered in Enochian cloaking sigils. Did his demon friend tell you that?"

Zha'riel gulped. Rafael knew far more than he had hoped and it looked bad because Zha'riel had obviously kept some facts to himself. He'd tried to give Nicholas space to figure out who his real friends were and now it looked like Zha'riel was hiding things from his superior.

Rafael folded his arms over his massive chest and stared down at Zha'riel. "So...tell me, Zha'riel...how is our exiled brother, Abdiel?"

Zha'riel could barely breathe. He even knew the who! Rafael was far from stupid. Zha'riel had no idea what made him think he could keep so much from the archangel. He could come up with nothing in response to Rafael's words. He just stared back at him, his eyes surely conveying his grief.

Rafael chuckled. "You really thought I wouldn't find out?" He shook his head. "How sad that you have lost your faith in the Father's highest order."

Zha'riel hung his head. "I have not lost faith."

"Then what?" asked Rafael.

Zha'riel pressed his lips together in thought. "Perhaps I have placed a bit too much faith in humanity. I thought he would make the right choice."

"Of course, you did. And that is the problem, Zha'riel." Rafael nodded in understanding. "You are too...*involved*...with them. They are petty, insolent, murderous little creatures who treat one another with callous disregard for the fact that the Father created them in *His own image*!" He paced the floor, working himself up into a frenzy. "You must realize these little maggots are *not* angels. They will *never*...*can* never...make the right decision. They are corrupt and evil and sinful. They are unholy rejects, like the Fallen Ones, and deserve the same fate. Why the Father is so longsuffering with them is beyond me, but He is, so we continue to put up with them."

Zha'riel nodded. He could remember a time when he felt the same way. It was not long before he met Nicholas Scarlatti. Human beings had always been arrogant, egotistical fools who thought their ignorant rejection of a Creator somehow made them more enlightened. Watching from their perches in Heaven, the angels had always gazed in wonder at the Father's adoration for such pathetic and weak creatures, yet He never seemed to look upon the angels with such love and tenderness.

When the Father sent the Son to take on the nature of a human being, the uproar in Heaven was unprecedented. They stood and watched the earthly drama play out—saw the Son, in the form of a human, nailed to a filthy tree, humiliated before the Father, the angels in Heaven, and the entire human race, and then his lifeless vessel placed in a tomb while He paid the debt for all humanity in the Unspeakable Place.

The angels continued to gaze in wonder at the Father's response to the murder of His Son. He was *pleased* at the turn of events. Was there no end to what He would put up with concerning these human monsters? Why should He be so longsuffering? Why should He allow his Spirit to be constantly grieved? Was not the murder of the Son of the Living God enough for Him to take action? He had all but wiped humanity out once before for far less cause than the murder of his Son. When the Son was raised from the dead, a collective gasp had escaped the lips of the entire Heavenly Host. Had they all been holding their breaths?

Many of the angels' questions were put to the Father directly, but His response was always a knowing smile. The angels were only given glimpses and only at certain specific times for specific reasons. No one knew the whens, the wheres, or even, and most importantly, the whys. It was all shrouded in the mystery of the Father's divine plan. Sitting on the outside of that frustrated Rafael.

"So *no more*, Zha'riel!" he continued. "You are forbidden from contacting him, helping him, protecting him *or* his friends and family. There will be no more heavenly presence in this boy's life until he learns something about consequences." He pointed a finger. "I don't believe he will ever learn that lesson, by the way. I believe we must prepare ourselves to put an end to his violence. To that end, I have requested permission to terminate him."

Zha'riel's eyes widened. "W-w-what? You cannot be serious."

Rafael turned away from Zha'riel and clasped his hands behind his back and sighed. He stood before the wall of windows facing the northern skyline of New York City. In the blackness of the night, the bright lights of the city proved there was at least one place in the world that never slept.

"I am deadly serious, Zha'riel. I just wanted you to hear it from me. He is a threat to the balance of chakra. He cannot be allowed to turn to evil. And I fear he has already strayed too far to be turned back."

ɮ ᴀ ꒱ ψ ɢ

"Come on," Nicholas said. "One more." He signaled the bartender for another round. "It's a celebration."

"Seriously? Your answer to all this is to get screaming drunk?"

Nicholas lost track of the amount of alcohol he and Xabier had consumed so far and Stephanie was long since annoyed at the whole scene. She was doing her best to support Nicholas through his grief, but he was becoming a bit insufferable. The images she saw on the television the previous night kept her awake and she trembled throughout the day. She wasn't sure if it was fear, sadness, or disappointment.

Xabier and Nicholas returned, inconsolably frustrated, having left their mission largely incomplete, at least in their minds. Alvi Cornega was alive and at large. He and his witch/godmother Nayra orchestrated the death of Dominick Scarlatti. The fact that he still had breath in his lungs caused Nicholas no small amount of heartache. Xabier shared in his frustration but tried to keep the peace between all of them.

"Why don't we slow down, Nico?" he suggested, lifting his glass. "Let's head home after this one."

"My name," Nicholas slurred, as the bartender set another double Scotch in front of him, "is Nicholas."

Xabier shook his head. "My friend, you need to *face* reality and not try to drown it."

Nicholas gulped his whiskey down and signaled for another, causing Stephanie to roll her eyes. She'd had enough for the night.

"You know what?" she asked. "I'm leaving. I'll get a cab."

"Wait!" Xabier said, nudging Nicholas. "I'll drive you." Turning to Nicholas, he said, "Keys, Nico. Unless you'd prefer to take her yourself, like a gentleman."

Nicholas tossed the keys to the Maserati onto the bar and turned back to his drink. Stephanie shook her head. Xabier scooped the keys up and turned to Stephanie.

"I'll be right out, love."

After Stephanie made her way to the door, Xabier smacked Nicholas on the back of his neck.

"Oww! What the...?"

"Shut up," snapped Xabier, showing his anger for the first time that night. "Are you deliberately trying to ruin things with that girl?"

"What?" Nicholas frowned. "What are you talking about?"

Xabier put a hand on his shoulder and gripped it firmly. "Listen to me, Nico. I was there. I get it. And that girl out there? She gets it, too, but you're hurting her and she doesn't know why. She's leaving pissed at you and it almost seems like you want her to."

Nicholas slumped his shoulders. "Look, it's not..."

Xabier shrugged and held up his hands. "Tell *her*, not me."

Outside, Nicholas found Stephanie leaning on the passenger side door of his Maserati. He watched her for a moment before approaching. He couldn't believe he was such a jerk. What was happening to him? Sure, he had gone through some incredible changes, but that should have been a good thing, especially since he had gotten Stephanie as a direct result of his transformation.

"Hey," he said, leaning next to her and bumping her shoulder with his.

"Hey," she mumbled.

After a few quiet seconds, he leaned gently into her shoulder again. "I'm a jerk," he said.

She giggled despite herself. "Yes," she agreed. "You are."

He put an arm around her shoulders and pulled her into a hug. She hesitated for a second, but then came to him and wrapped her arms around his waist, laying her head on his chest. He buried his face in her hair and breathed in. "Mmmm." He sighed. "Still my favorite smell in the world."

She squeezed him tighter as he ran his fingers through her thick locks.

"I'm so sorry," he said. "I've been a prick lately…taking you for granted. You deserve better from your boyfriend."

"It's okay," she said. "I know this is really hard." She pulled back and looked him in the eyes. "Just…don't shut me out, okay? I want to be there for you." She lowered her eyes.

Nicholas tilted her head back up and pushed some stray hairs out of her face. He kissed her lightly on the lips, and then rested his forehead against hers.

"I couldn't imagine having to go through life without you, Stephanie."

She smiled through the tears filling her eyes. "I'm going to work tomorrow morning so I have to sleep at my place tonight. Will you stay with me?"

Stephanie's car had been at her place the entire time she'd stayed with Nicholas. Since she had to be in early to open the gym, she just wanted to go home and sleep. Zha'riel had been escorting her to and from work, but he was nowhere to be found. She didn't want to be late the next morning so Nicholas orbed home so she could get some rest.

Stephanie had grown used to sleeping in Nicholas' arms. She claimed she couldn't sleep without him. Nicholas, with a knowing smile on his face, pulled back the covers and lay down, pulling her close to his bare chest. She lay on her side and pushed herself back into him, pulling his arm under her own and smiling contentedly as she drifted off.

"I'm so glad you're here," she murmured. "I love you so much."

He took in a sharp breath. Her words, though welcome and amazing, kind of made him feel even worse. He treated his girl like a jerk and she still found it in her heart to love him. He buried his face in her hair and breathed her in.

"I love you, too, Stephanie Ambrose. I always will."

Ђ А З̌ Ψ Ϲ

After kissing a sleeping Nicholas on the forehead and locking her front door, Stephanie slid into her car and headed off to the gym. It was still dark at four-thirty in the morning. It was her favorite time to drive. There was scant traffic on the road at that hour, and everything was peaceful. After the events of the past few weeks she felt glad to get back to her normal routine.

It amazed her that she and Nicholas were still together after all the stress and uncertainty surrounding him. Their new relationship had been through a great deal in such a short time, yet they hadn't been torn apart. In fact, after last night, she felt they were stronger than ever. Their declarations of love made her smile throughout her early morning drive.

"He loves me." She smiled. Then louder, "HE LOVES ME!" She laughed as she pulled up to a red light.

"How wonderful for you."

The monotone voice came so matter-of-factly from the back seat, she almost thought she'd imagined it. Then, she looked in the rearview mirror, saw the glowing white corneas staring back at her, and she let out a short scream. She would have jumped out the door, but she couldn't get it open. She pulled frantically on the handle, but the door wouldn't budge. Tears fell from her eyes as she struggled to escape. The whole time, Azazel watched in mild indifference.

"The light is green, my dear."

Stephanie sat frozen in fear. Azazel leaned forward. "Drive, Stephanie."

Tentatively, she pushed the gas pedal and the car lurched forward. Her hands shook even though she gripped the steering wheel. Azazel gave directions as they drove. His voice never rose more than a notch above a whisper.

"What are you going to do to me?" she asked, resigning herself to the likely answer.

Azazel tilted his head. "*Do* to you?" He sighed. "I think you're missing the bigger picture here, Stephanie. This has nothing to do with you, though like the rest of us, you have a role to play. So while it isn't *about* you, it doesn't make you any less important."

"I don't know what that means."

"Of course you don't."

Stephanie looked in the rearview mirror at Azazel. "Are you...Lucifer?" she asked in a hushed whisper.

Azazel stared back in disbelief before breaking out into a hearty laugh. "No, I am not Lucifer. Though, I am his closest friend...at least, I was...until...well, until your coward friend murdered my son. Now it seems I am at odds with my old friend." He stared wistfully out the window. "Alas."

Stephanie looked at him in the mirror, her insides quivering in fear, her hands slick with sweat. Her brain ran through every possible scenario it could come up with. She ran back every conversation she'd ever had or overheard since meeting Nicholas Scarlatti. Through it all, one name floated across her mind.

"Azazel," she whispered, all hope vanishing as a whole new paradigm of terror enveloped her.

His tight smile told her she guessed correctly. "I see my reputation precedes me." He sighed. "You seem intelligent, Stephanie. I'm sorry we met under such...*distasteful* circumstances."

"So, what are you going to do to me?" she asked again.

Azazel looked her in the eye as she stared back through the mirror. "Do you really want to know?"

She gasped as she realized that she wasn't simply going to die. It was going to be slow. It was going to hurt...a lot. She was going to live a nightmare before dying in agony, and something told her Nicholas would be made to watch. Without thinking, she stomped on the gas pedal, speeding the car up to over eighty miles per hour. Then, she lurched the wheel to the right as they approached a large building.

But nothing happened. The car slowed to a normal speed and continued in a straight line down the road. Stephanie looked around in confusion.

Azazel shook his head, making a tsk tsk sound with his tongue. "That won't do. It wouldn't matter anyway, sweetheart. You see, I'd just bring you back to life and continue on with our day." He leaned forward and rested his forearms on the back of her seat. "If it makes any difference, I'm sorry. He shouldn't have brought such a lovely thing as you into his life. His brother should be here instead."

"Nicholas already lost his brother," she pleaded. "What more do you want from him?"

"*I* didn't take his brother," Azazel snapped. "Those idiots from Colombia did that, and they did it poorly. There was no...art. They just beat him up a little and had the demons snap his neck. It was pathetic." He stroked a loose strand of her hair. "Real vengeance must be considered...thoughtful...purposeful. Losing you will break him. Watching you suffer for *his* sins." He smiled grimly. "That will *end* him."

Chapter 25

"Sorry, I haven't seen her since she left early this morning…Okay…I will…Bye."

Nicholas hung up the phone and immediately pulled out his cell. He tapped and swiped until he found Stephanie's contact information. He hit "call" and listened to her phone go straight to voicemail. It was off or she had no cell reception. Either way, she was somewhere other than at work and unreachable. It was eight in the morning and he began to panic.

"Zha'riel!"

He threw off Stephanie's thick, pink comforter and swung his legs out of bed. He rushed through the apartment. He scanned every room before looking out the window. Her car wasn't at the curb.

"Zha'riel!" he shouted again, swiping at his phone again and tapping on Xabier's icon.

"Nico!" His friend's exuberant voice filled his ears. "How are you this fine…"

"Xabs!" he interrupted. "Have you seen Steph?"

"Stephanie? Today? No. I thought she was with you. Wait! Isn't she supposed to be at work?"

"Yeah," Nicholas said. "She left this morning around four-thirty and never made it to the gym. No one knows where the hell she is."

Xabier was silent. "Okay, let's not panic. Get home and we'll figure it out."

Nicholas thought for a moment. "Okay. First, I'm going to check along her route and see if she had an accident. Maybe it's that simple."

Twenty minutes later, he was standing in his own living room. He paced the room and punched one fist into the other. Xabier slumped in the recliner with a finger over his mouth.

"Nothing!" Nicholas said. "No trace of her or her car anywhere along the route to the gym. I even checked out other possible routes. Not a *single* trace! She just friggin' vanished off the face of the earth." He shook his head in frustration. "And where is Zha'riel? What a jerk! Wasn't he supposed to be looking out for her? What good is he if he never answers?"

"Try to remain calm, Nico."

"*Calm?*" Nicholas shouted. "That's your advice? My brother is dead and my girlfriend, who put all her trust in me to keep her safe, is missing. There are angels and demons after me, to say nothing of the lunatic cartel head and a witch who knows how to capture and control demons, and your best advice is to calm down?"

Xabier nodded. "I understand. Just—"

"Just what?" asked Nicholas with his eyebrows raised. "Just calm down?"

He stalked off into the kitchen and returned with a bottle of water, which he drank in a single gulp. He crumpled the bottle and threw it across the room.

"So how do we find her?" he asked. "Zha'riel won't answer, the prick."

Xabier raised his eyebrows. "How about your...*other* friends?"

Nicholas looked at him. "Abdiel?"

"Why not?" Xabier shrugged. "We have supernatural problems. The 'good guys' aren't taking our calls. I bet you Abdiel answers."

"Do *not* call him."

Xabier and Nicholas turned to face the kitchen. Zha'riel stood in the space between the kitchen and the living room. He looked tired. Nicholas was the first to speak.

"Oh, look who finally showed up," he said in disgust. "You're a great friend, you know that?"

"I am sorry," Zha'riel replied. "I was forbidden. I should not be here now."

"Oh, well, don't get in trouble on our account," Nicholas sneered. "It's only an innocent girl who was kidnapped. But let's make sure Rafael doesn't get annoyed."

Zha'riel shook his head sadly. "Look, Nicholas, I am truly sorry, but I am forbidden from interfering in any more of your affairs, even to do good. You have to face the consequences of your actions. That was always going to be the end result. I should not have gotten so involved in the first place."

Nicholas stared at him. "So that's it? You just walk away now?"

Zha'riel winced and offered a grim shake of his head. "I cannot get involved. Remember, I tried to warn you abou—"

"Oh, shut up," Xabier interrupted. "Stop talking like a bureaucrat, Zha'riel. Just say you're bailing on us and leave, so we can get on with it."

Zha'riel looked at Nicholas with an apologetic expression, gritted his teeth, and bowed his head. "I am truly sorry, Nicholas. Good luck." And he was gone.

Xabier shook his head. "What a maroon!" he exclaimed. "Can you believe that guy?"

Nicholas shrugged. "It doesn't matter. We need to—"

His vibrating cell phone interrupted his thought. He pulled it out of his pocket and glanced at the screen. Holding it up for Xabier to look at, he shrugged and swiped to receive the call.

"Nico," Abdiel's voice came through. "We have a problem."

"No kidding," Nicholas replied evenly. He didn't know who to trust. Abdiel had been his friend so far, but Nicholas wasn't oblivious to the agendas all around him.

Abdiel didn't seem to catch Nicholas' tone. "Is my angel brother still there?" he asked.

"No," Nicholas said, his voice dripping with disdain. "He just left. I doubt he'll be back any time soon."

"What happened?"

"No idea. I guess he got in trouble for helping me and now he's off the case…or something like that."

Abdiel was silent for a second. "That sounds about right," he finally said.

"Yeah?" Nicholas replied. "Well maybe for you, but I really need help right now. Stephanie is missing."

"What? When?" Abdiel's surprised sounded genuine enough, but Nicholas knew these angels, fallen or not, were born liars.

"I guess on her way to work…about three or four hours."

Abdiel shouted something unintelligible. "Nicholas, I have an idea of what's going on. Let me get some answers. Stand by and don't do anything until I get there."

It took less than twenty minutes for Abdiel to show up, but it felt like days to Nicholas, who continued to pace the room, fear gripping him like a vise, paralyzing his mind. All he could see in his mind's eye was his beautiful Stephanie being tormented by a lunatic angel who took pleasure in inflicting pain. When Abdiel appeared, Nicholas was on him immediately.

"Tell me this isn't you guys," he demanded.

"Nicholas," Abdiel said, "I think I know—"

"Just tell me where she is!" Nicholas screamed.

Abdiel folded his arms across his chest. "Calm down, Nicholas. In this kind of situation, you must stay calm and keep a clear head."

"I don't care about training right now, Abdiel. What I want to know is where Stephanie is. I swear to God, if you guys have her—"

"What?" Abdiel asked, pointing a finger in Nicholas' face. "Tell me, Nicholas. What exactly will you do if we have Stephanie?"

Nicholas stepped right up in Abdiel's face until they were standing chest to chest. He stared straight into the pale green of Abdiel's eyes. He saw what years and years of hate and war did to the soul. He wondered if Abdiel could even remember what it was like to be happy.

"Do you really want to find out?" Nicholas threatened.

"Please. You have no idea what you are saying." Abdiel rolled his eyes and turned his back on Nicholas as he walked away shaking his head. Turning back, he pointed a finger right in Nicholas' face. "Do you *really* think we took your Stephanie? You think it's all some big elaborate kidnapping plot to get you on our side?" He stepped closer. "I've got news for you, you arrogant, narcissistic egomaniac. Not everyone cares about what you do."

He shoved Nicholas backwards. "I've been a friend to you." Abdiel shoved him again. "I've taught you when the other guys...the *good* guys...have done nothing but hang you out to dry." Another shove. "*I'm* the reason you were able to go on your little Colombian rampage." An even harder shove" *I'm* the reason you feel like you can stand up and defy the angels." One more shove was enough to slam Nicholas into the front door. Abdiel closed the distance and stuck a finger in Nicholas' face. "So maybe you should shut your mouth, recognize that some people are on *your* side, and *SHOW ME SOME DAMN RESPECT!*"

He shoved Nicholas one last time before stepping back and shaking his head. "What do I have to do to convince you?"

Nicholas licked his lips in uncertainty. "I don't know. I'm sorry. But...if it's not the angels and it's not you...who could it be? It's not the cartel. It's way too soon for them to regroup and get back here."

Abdiel shook his head. "You are not going to like my answer, Nicholas."

Nicholas shrugged. "Tell me. What am I dealing with?"

Before Abdiel could reply, Nicholas' phone rang. "It's from Stephanie's phone," he said, wrinkling his forehead.

"Uh oh," Xabier frowned.

"Hello?" Nicholas said into the phone. "Steph?"

"Mmmmmm," came a terrifying monotone voice. "I'm sorry, but your little Stephanie is, shall we saaaay…incapacitated…at this time. That would be the gentle way to put it, I suppose."

Nicholas' heart ached at the words. His breath caught in his throat and he couldn't respond.

"Are you there, young Nicholas?" the voice taunted.

"I…" Nicholas choked and took a deep breath, trying to force back the emotions flooding his mind. "I'm here."

"Good. My name is Azazel. It's time we met."

ᚠ ᚪ ᚴ ᚹ ᚷ

They sat in silence. Abdiel was deep in thought, while Xabier stared at the ceiling and shook his head every few seconds. Zha'riel had been unreachable since he left and Nicholas' repeated calls went unanswered. Nicholas slumped down in a chair. He glared straight ahead as if in a trance.

He said nothing. Azazel had given him no hope. It was an unusual demand. In the movies, the kidnapper would dangle the life of the victim in front of the family and friends as bait. Something like that from Azazel would have prompted instant action from Nicholas. It would have made his thought process so much clearer.

But Azazel made no such demand. He made no promises at all, except to promise what would happen if Nicholas did *not* show up at the time and place appointed. Stephanie would continue to suffer until Azazel saw fit to end her. And then, like the Colombians threatened, he would come for everyone Nicholas loved. If he didn't love anyone, Azazel would watch until he made a friend, and he would destroy that person as well. Nicholas would live out his days completely alone and isolated. He could never have love. He could never have friendship. And one day, Azazel would come for Nicholas.

"I have to go," Nicholas said absently.

"She's already dead," Xabier replied. "It won't save her."

"He said she was alive," Nicholas pointed out. "Why lie about that? If he was going to lie, he would have told me everything would be okay."

"He's right," Abdiel added. "Azazel doesn't need to lie. I'd bet he's going to do exactly as he says. If Nicholas doesn't show, he will torture Stephanie every day for the rest of her life, which, I might add, he can extend indefinitely. And he will make sure you hear every scream and see every drop of blood."

Nicholas closed his eyes, trying not to imagine his beautiful Stephanie terrified and in pain, waiting for him to rescue her. He could practically hear her screaming his name, praying he would get there before it was too late.

"I know," he said.

"But if you do go, Nico," Abdiel continued, "you must also be prepared for whatever show Azazel has planned for you."

"Show?" Xabier frowned.

Abdiel ran a hand over his mouth and pursed his lips. "Azazel is a master of elaborate demonstrations. He is an expert in the art of torment. He is legendary for his ability to cause pain, whether it be physically, emotionally, or spiritually." He looked at Nicholas. "Understand that she is going to be tortured and killed before your eyes and there will be nothing you can do to stop it."

"Why nothing?" Nicholas asked in desperation.

"Because Azazel is an archangel," Abdiel replied. "One of the most fearsome creatures in existence. He was Lucifer's closest confidant and friend for eons. He has had millennia after millennia to perfect his craft. He will have thought of everything. You must be prepared for what you will see."

"Can he be killed?" Nicholas asked.

"*Azazel?*" Abdiel replied. His mouth dropped open and he wagged his head back and forth, searching for words. "He...well...technically, yes. He is an angel. He was created and therefore can be killed, but...Nicholas...he is an archangel, one of the original twelve...created by the hand of God Himself. Even killing a *regular* archangel would be a staggeringly impossible—"

"But technically, I already did something like that, didn't I?" Nicholas asked.

"Sansata?" Abdiel asked. "Yes, he was very powerful, but Nicholas…do not think one leads to the other. Your arrogance will get you killed along with your girl."

Nicholas nodded. He closed his eyes and drew in a deep breath before opening them again. Then he looked Abdiel in the eyes. "I'm going to kill Azazel."

ᚦ ᚪ ᛜ ᛦ ᚷ

"Nordkapp? What the heck is Nordkapp?"

Azazel made contact late the next morning. He even apologized for losing track of time.

"I've been spending some quality time with your lady friend, Nicholas." He smiled, holding a short silver dagger in front of the screen. It was dripping with what appeared to be fresh blood. Nicholas felt sick to his stomach, but he also felt rage building within his soul. He was determined to hold onto that rage and hoped it continued to build.

Azazel demanded Nicholas meet him at Nordkapp in fifteen minutes. "Don't be late, Nicholas. At fifteen minutes and one second, I will disappear with your little blonde-haired princess and you will spend the next fifty years receiving bits and pieces of her in the mail *EVERY SINGLE DAY!*"

"I'll be there."

Nicholas looked at a map on his phone. "It's at the northern tip of Norway." He frowned and looked at the ceiling, losing himself in thought. "Why would he want to meet there of all places?"

"Loki." Abdiel chuckled, snapping Nicholas back to the present. He looked at Nicholas and Xabier with an amused expression. "Of course."

"Loki?" Nicholas scowled. "What's a Loki?"

"It's not a what," replied Xabier. "It's a who." He looked at Abdiel. "What would Loki have to do with this?"

"Loki," Abdiel explained, "is another archangel who settled in what you know as Northern Europe. We hardly ever hear from him anymore, but he was once great friends with Lucifer and of course, Azazel. It makes complete sense Azazel would turn to him for assistance, though I doubt Loki is thrilled about having to cover for him. Things could get sticky if Lucifer decided to take offense."

Nicholas sighed. "So now I have two of them to worry about?"

Abdiel shook his head. "Unlikely. Loki and Azazel are friends, but my guess is Loki will stay out of the fight. He'd give Azazel asylum, but it is doubtful Loki would participate in anything that goes against Lucifer."

"Well." Nicholas shrugged. "I guess I might as well get this over with. At least I can end Stephanie's suffering by showing up early."

Xabier came closer, making sure his arm was around Nicholas. He didn't want Nicholas orbing out without him. "I'm coming too."

Nicholas was about to reply when Xabier held up his hand. "Azazel never said anything about coming alone."

Abdiel nodded. "I have to inform Lucifer. I'll try to bring help. Just hold out and stall as long as you can, Nicholas. Remember your training."

Nicholas nodded and orbed out along with Xabier.

Ҍ ᴀ ᴣ̌ ѱ ɢ

Abdiel pushed past the guards at the throne room entrance. "This is an emergency!" he shouted, throwing open the doors. "Master!" he cried as the guards grabbed him and held him up. "Master, please! You must hear me now!"

"Release him!" came the calm response.

The guards holding Abdiel immediately softened their grip. He wriggled free and hurried into the main room. Lucifer rose from the table where he sat with his viceroys. He came around the table and met Abdiel in the center of the room.

"What is it, Abdiel?" he asked, putting his hand on Abdiel's shoulder. "This is not how we communicate."

"I know, Master, and I am sorry." Abdiel bowed his head. "This is most urgent. Nicholas Scarlatti has gone to face Azazel."

"*WHAT*?" Lucifer's eyes widened in shock. It was by far the most emotion Abdiel had ever seen in the eyes of his master. "Is he crazy?"

"He's in love," Abdiel replied. "Azazel took his woman."

Lucifer closed his eyes, regaining control as Abdiel stood before him, petrified, regretting his proximity to such power. He took a deep breath and thought for a moment. Abdiel could imagine the thoughts running through his mind. Did he really want to go to war against his best friend? He was already at war with his older brother, Michael. Azazel had already betrayed him, and now, he was attempting to finish the job in a most cowardly fashion. Lucifer looked at Abdiel, his eyes flashing like golden galaxies.

"I want you to tell me where…"

Chapter 26

Xabier looked around. "What a gloomy place."

"I don't know," replied Nicholas. "There's a kind of rugged beauty to it." He scanned the scene in all directions. "I could think of worse places to die."

Xabier shook his head. "Don't talk like that, Nico. No one's dying here today…except maybe a lunatic angel."

Nicholas chuckled and shook his head. He had chosen a good friend in Xabier. He was sorry that this would be the final stand of their short-lived friendship. Xabier didn't deserve to go out like this, and Nicholas hated that there was nothing he could do to get him to leave.

"I know what you're thinking," Xabier said without looking at him. "And don't. We will be friends in this life *and* the next."

"What a wonderful sentiment."

The voice, in its epic monotone, was even more terrifying in person. Nicholas whirled around to face a well-built man with long, thick, black hair and glowing white eyes. It was such a pure white, Nicholas could scarcely tear his own eyes away. The man's overly calm demeanor left no doubt as to his identity.

"Azazel," Nicholas said, finding strength he didn't know he had inside him. "I was expecting thunder and lightning and earthquakes."

Azazel glanced at his fingernails, as if inspecting a manicure, and shook his head. "Not today, young Nicholas...not today." He looked up. "No, today is not about fanfare and attention."

"Right," Xabier said. "Too loud and Lucifer might hear."

Azazel never took his eyes off Nicholas. In fact, Nicholas never saw him move. Azazel's forehead twitched and Xabier crumpled to his knees screaming in agony and clutching his chest. Azazel's eyes flicked down at him.

"Mind your tone, my little fanged friend."

"Let him go," Nicholas said. "I'm the one you're here for, right?"

Azazel looked at him like he was nothing but a bug to be squashed. Then he nodded his head to the right and Xabier soared through the air, crashing onto a pile of rocks nearly a hundred yards away. Nicholas watched him tumble down the pile to the ground, and lie still.

"Now then..." Azazel returned his attention to Nicholas. "Where were we?"

"Where is Stephanie?" Nicholas demanded. "What have you done to her?"

Azazel suppressed a smile. "I would think you'd be more concerned about what I am going to do to *you*?"

"Where is she?" Nicholas demanded again, meeting Azazel's terrifying gaze.

Azazel gave Nicholas a lazy shrug and held a hand out to one side. Stephanie appeared, and Azazel instantly took hold of her arm. She was barely conscious...and barely recognizable. Nicholas had never seen a body so disfigured. He couldn't tell where the burns ended and the bruises began. Her skin was scorched and blackened; patches of unburnt skin appeared here and there, but she was mostly covered in severe burns. Her hair, or what was left of it, hung in clumps. She was so swollen Nicholas could see where the skin had stretched and split in places. She was naked, her clothes long ago burnt to ash. Some of the pieces, Nicholas observed, had actually melted and fused to her skin. She was stripped of any semblance of dignity.

Nicholas was heartsick and guilty, but he focused that energy on his rage and hatred.

Azazel watched him with a bored expression. "Get a good look, Nicholas Scarlatti. I want this memory seared in your mind so that you can take it into the next life, and the next, and the next. But before we get to that." He held out his free hand. "Let's close the chapter on this pretty young thing, shall we?"

With that, he sent a massive jolt of crackling violet energy into Stephanie's body, waking her up from her agonized slumber and drawing screams of absolute horror and pain from deep within her tortured soul. Azazel sent even more through her and Nicholas moved to come to her aid, but was frozen in place as Azazel stretched his free hand toward him.

"No, no, Nicholas!" Azazel had to shout to be heard over her screams. "Stand and enjoy the fruits of your impudence! The girl you love will die in agony right before your eyes, you insolent young *fool!*"

Azazel's glowing white eyes took on a maniacal glare as he sent a final burst of energy into Stephanie's weary and battered body, rocketing her hundreds of feet skyward. Nicholas watched helplessly as she slowed in mid-air and began her terminal descent back to the earth. She landed with a dull thud, shattering her bones and what was left of her organs. It was violent, but her pain was over.

Nicholas, finally able to move again, fell to his knees in shock. Stephanie was gone. His love was no longer. As he knelt, feeling wave after wave of emotion wash over him, the anger coursed through his veins. He had felt the rage building from the moment Stephanie's broken form had appeared. Nicholas knew Azazel would never allow her to survive. Stephanie was dead the moment he had gotten his hands on her.

There was only one thing left to do. He slowly got to his feet, pushing back the tears he felt behind his eyes. It was time to let the monster inside him loose. The cold fury twisted in his core, winding itself up through his being. When he reached his full height, he turned his furious gaze on Azazel who was standing there with an amused smirk. His hands were clasped in front of his belly.

"Nicholas?" he said. "There is one more thing I wanted you to witness before I avenge the death of my son."

He gestured over to where Xabier was getting to his feet. Nicholas' eyes widened as he saw Seir standing behind him with his glowing red eyes and a sadistic grin on his face.

"I thought I'd let Seir have the honors with your friend," Azazel said. "He was humiliated a couple of times trying to get to you." He shrugged. "It seemed fair."

Nicholas closed his eyes. He felt as filled to capacity as he'd ever been with rage and seething hatred. In an instant he lunged forward, his angel sword flashing into his palm just as he struck at Azazel's abdomen. It was a surprise attack, and he was almost successful. Azazel saw it in time to twist away, though Nicholas' blade did manage to slash through his robes and slice him on his side.

"Arghh!" he yelled, looking down at the bleeding wound.

Nicholas wondered if Azazel had ever been wounded in battle. Azazel struck him as the type who didn't give many opportunities. His eyes flashed in surprise and fury as he stared down at the bloody mess that was his side. Azazel gritted his teeth and grunted as he touched the wounded flesh through the slice in his robe. He glared at Nicholas who stood at the ready with a satisfied expression on his face.

"That must hurt," Nicholas said. "Does it hurt? It looks like it hurts."

ᛒ ᴀ ⌇ ᴪ Ꮯ

Xabier came to his senses just in time to curse his enhanced hearing. Though he was suddenly alert, his body was slower to recover and he had to listen helplessly to Stephanie's agonized screams. As he dragged himself to his feet, he saw Azazel lift his hand skyward and Stephanie soared straight up and came back down to the ground with an unceremonious thump. He fell back to his knees as he watched Nicholas' stunned and distressed expression. Though the two of them had known things were likely to end badly, neither was truly prepared for the reality of it.

Xabier was beyond the pain now. He was beyond the feelings and the humanity of it all. It was just too painful, so he shut that down quickly. All he could feel now was hatred and rage. Now he just wanted to kill something.

He felt the presence behind him before he heard the voice.

"Hello, *Fang*."

Without bothering to stand, he glanced back at the figure standing behind him. He immediately saw glowing red eyes and knew who it was.

"Ahh," he said. "Azazel's red-eyed pet. I thought I smelled you."

Seir suppressed his reaction to the insult. "Are those your last words, *Fang*? Or do you have something more profound to say before I tear you apart?"

Xabier shrugged and turned back to the scene developing before Azazel and Nicholas. Seir followed his gaze.

"It won't last long, Fang. Your little friend will be dust soon enough."

Xabier nodded. "I suppose the big guy had to come and do it himself since you disappointed him..." He sniffed in derision and turned his eyes on Seir. "...twice."

Seir's eyes flashed and he took a step forward. "I'm truly going to enjoy this, Fang. I was told to do with you whatever I want as long as you ended up dead."

"Oh," Xabier retorted. "How wonderful for you."

Without warning, he launched himself at the red-eyed demon.

ℬ ᴀ ⵣ ѱ ɢ

Azazel barely had time to react as Nicholas, completely out of control, struck again and again, raining down vicious blows, slashing at his head and torso. Azazel's own blade finally appeared and they clashed over and over again as Nicholas focused every ounce of rage and hate he had on the fallen archangel. Try as he might, he could not penetrate Azazel's defense.

"You are quite skilled, young Nicholas," Azazel said as they circled one another, breathless from the fast-paced battle. He grinned. "I must tell you, in fairness though—it's not nearly enough and I haven't even begun to fight you."

Just as Nicholas began to lunge at him again, Azazel jabbed out with his left hand and Nicholas felt the blow right over his heart. It felt as though he was being stabbed, and he slammed backwards onto the ground, dropping his sword. Azazel threw his sword straight down into the ground so it was sticking up and then stretched out his hands toward Nicholas, sending the same violet electrical storm into his body as he had done to Stephanie.

Nicholas' body instantly stiffened and arched as the energy coursed through him. Rather than fight the pain, he fought *through* the pain and slowly raised his own hands. Fighting through muscle spasms and screaming bones, he willed himself to pull chakra. He felt the release as he sent his own burst of fiery energy at his assailant. Azazel, caught off-guard, took the full brunt of the fiery burst in his chest and it broke his flow of energy. He staggered backwards in stunned amazement.

Nicholas scrambled to his feet and the two faced off again. He could see the surprise in Azazel's eyes as they glared at one another. He knew the fallen archangel had not been expecting a real fight. The expression on his face wasn't one of concern— just surprise.

"Who taught you that?" he demanded.

Nicholas just grinned at him. "You weren't expecting to feel pain today, were you?"

Azazel's eyes burned with rage. He nodded. "Very well."

Suddenly, the attacks came from everywhere. Nicholas was pummeled from all directions while Azazel scarcely moved. It was a hurricane meeting a tornado meeting a cyclone. Throw in fire, electricity, and debris coming at him from all directions and Nicholas' strength drained in moments.

Azazel then stepped in close and beat him with his hands. Blow after blow rained down on him with lightning speed and effectiveness. He knew what was happening. Azazel was in a position to kill him whenever he chose. Instead of going for the kill shot, he was making it last, breaking him apart piece by piece, just like he promised. He felt every bone break in his chest and back. His arms and legs were jelly and his head was cracked open. Blood poured from the wound, along with his eyes, nose, ears, and mouth. He felt consciousness begin to slip away.

Ђ ᴀ ᶎ ᴪ ɢ

Seir chuckled as he tossed Xabier down for a third time. He was just toying with the vampire, beating him up a little before he began the real pain. Azazel wanted Nicholas and Xabier to suffer, and Seir was not going to disappoint him again. As Xabier picked himself up, Seir was all over him. He landed several punches to his torso, doubling Xabier over. Next, he pounded on his back and ribs, driving him back to his knees. Finally, he landed a series of vicious kicks to Xabier's sides and stomach before a final, nasty kick to Xabier's face. The force of it lifted Xabier up and flipped him onto his back, broken and bleeding.

"Are you feeling okay, *Fang*?" the demon sneered. "You don't look well."

Xabier choked on a mouthful of blood. "Don't worry about me, *lapdog*. You hit like a woman."

Seir chuckled. "Still with the jokes. Unbelievable." He grabbed Xabier by the neck and hoisted him to his feet. "But I like that. It makes me want to try even harder."

He quickly jabbed several lightning fast blows right over Xabier's heart, making him gasp for breath as his ribs cracked under the weight of the strikes. The demon then threw him time and time again into the outcropping of rocks, shattering bones and slashing skin with every effort until Xabier was unrecognizable.

"And now," Seir said, leaning down to hiss his words into Xabier's ear, "I am going to put you out of your misery."

ƀ ᴀ ᶎ ψ ᏻ

Nicholas felt death's warm embrace and was inclined to surrender, to seek refuge in forever's slumber. In the fog of his subconscious, he saw someone approach in the distance. The stranger was dressed all in black, his face neither smiling nor frowning, his demeanor neither aggressive nor passive. He approached, hand outstretched, beckoning Nicholas. Nicholas stretched out his hand…

Suddenly…everything stopped.

First came the high-pitched drone. To Nicholas it was just noise, though he thought it sounded vaguely familiar. Azazel ceased his attack and spun around. The sound intensified until Nicholas could hear nothing else. Though his arms were limp noodles, he did his best to cover his ears. Then the brightest light he had ever seen filled the sky and everything around them. Nicholas buried his face in the crook of his elbow as a scorching light soaked him through. The sky seemed to crack open and suck all the energy from the area before plunging it back into twilight.

There was utter silence. Nicholas lay on his side, against a rock, his blood pooling all around him. Through blood-blurred eyes, he saw only vague images of figures standing nearby. His brain was unable to force his eyes to focus properly, but he could hear their voices.

"Lucifer," Azazel said.

"Old friend. What are you doing?"

Nicholas heard the crunch of gravel underfoot as Lucifer approached. Even in his severely diminished state, Nicholas felt the tension between the two powerful beings. As fascinating as the showdown promised to be, Nicholas had no desire to be around for it.

"Something," Azazel replied, "you should have allowed in the first place."

Lucifer glanced back at Nicholas. "Is it so necessary that you exact vengeance on him beyond what you have already done?"

"Every breath he takes insults my honor."

Lucifer shook his head. "How many eons, Azazel? How long have we lived? Was our friendship so meaningless to you?"

"That question could be turned on *you*, old friend."

Lucifer nodded and took a breath. "Fair enough."

He glanced over at Nicholas, lying still on the ground twenty yards away. "Am I too late?"

Azazel replied. "He yet lives."

Lucifer stepped over to where Nicholas lay in his semiconscious state. He knelt and examined his broken body. He was moments away from death.

"I cannot let him die, Azazel. He is too unique. He could be another archangel. Don't you understand that? Imagine it. A *human* archangel! What an affront to Heaven's honor!"

"I do not care," Azazel replied. "About any of it. One day I shall deal with Michael myself and settle our account, but today, I only care about closing *this* particular account."

Lucifer shook his head. He reached down, his fingers about to touch Nicholas' forehead. Nicholas had no idea what was happening but couldn't do anything about it even if he did.

"Don't do it," Azazel warned.

Lucifer looked up at him with a quizzical expression and tilted his head. "My friend...since you *are* my friend, I am going to allow you to walk away right now."

Azazel shook with anger. He stared at Lucifer with a defiance borne of betrayal. Though he was at a severe disadvantage in a battle against Lucifer, he wasn't helpless, and Lucifer clearly didn't want to fight him. It was time for his old friend to learn that there were some things more important than the next big weapon in his cosmic temper tantrum. He stood his ground.

Lucifer stood up and faced Azazel. "Was it worth it, old friend?"

Azazel raised his eyebrows in question.

"This little vendetta...was it worth giving up your place at my side? Was it worth throwing away our friendship?" Lucifer asked.

Azazel considered for a moment and then shook his head. "I don't know, though one-sided friendships are not really friendships, are they?" He gestured toward Nicholas. "I imagine he'll learn that soon enough as well."

Chapter 27

Seir stood poised to deliver the final death blow. Vampires could only be killed in specific ways; Seir was well-aware of all of them. The most common method used by human hunters was to chop off the head. Seir rejected that method, as it was virtually painless. He wanted to inflict maximum pain even with his killing blow. He pulled out a silver dagger and thrust it into Xabier's abdomen, causing the battered vampire to scream out. The silver caused severe pain, but was not fatal unless it pierced the heart. Once the silver entered the heart, it would be pumped quickly throughout the body, into every organ, causing extraordinary agony until it completely contaminated the blood. Ultimately the vampire would suffer intense agony as every one of his organs shut down and his heart exploded in his chest.

Seir grinned sadistically as he pierced Xabier's body time and time again. The pain seared throughout every body part and Xabier could do nothing but suffer through it. He refused to give Seir the satisfaction of hearing him plead for death, though he wanted nothing more than to sink into its warm embrace.

"Say it," demanded Seir. "Beg me for death, *Fang*."

Xabier choked as silver-laced blood filled his throat. The blade hadn't pierced his heart, yet Seir had stabbed him so many times he would likely die of silver poisoning anyway. But he wouldn't ask for death. Instead he steeled his resolve and did his best to clear his throat for one final remark.

"I-I-I'll b-b-beg you for n-n-nothing…p-p-p-*pet.*"

Seir laughed as he jabbed him again and again. "Good for you, Fang, but it looks as though you are close to your end as it is and I really want to carve your heart up, soooo…it's been fun—"

And Xabier felt the dagger slide ever so slowly between his ribs under his right arm. Seir even took his time with the final blow. It seemed to happen in slow-motion and was excruciating in its application. Azazel taught his demon well the art of inflicting pain. Finally, he felt the tip of the blade pierce his heart and knew he was mere seconds away from the end. He felt the searing silver begin to flow through his arteries, flooding organ after organ with poison. He closed his eyes and rode out the pain, screaming in agony the whole time.

Finally, he felt it all shut down. One piece at a time, he lost feeling as his body sank into its death spiral. His eyes rolled back in his head and the images in his mind faded to black. He felt the warmth of nothingness as he slipped away…

$$Ƀ \, ʌ \, \check{Ʒ} \, ψ \, ς$$

Nicholas, unable to move, could only lay against the rocks and watch. His vision was still a mere haze. He looked through a fog of blood and pain. Though death was nearby, and he could feel the life draining out of him, his fascination with the events playing out before him remained. He recalled wondering what a battle between supernatural beings would look like. His clashes with Seir, Nayra, and her demons, had all been more or less what he had expected. The same had been true of watching Zha'riel and Seir battle all those days ago.

His battle with Azazel had been a lesson—a clinic really—in how unevenly matched things could get in the supernatural world. He had known his chances for success had been close to zero, but he thought he'd put up more of a fight. Now Azazel faced off against Lucifer. Nicholas had experienced the ferocity of Azazel's attacks, and that had been frighteningly awful, but an all-out chakra war between two masters? He couldn't fathom what was about to take place.

"This is a mistake, old friend," Lucifer warned as he and Azazel circled one another. "I do not want this."

Azazel glowered at his former master. "This is what you *chose*, Lucifer."

"No!" Lucifer shouted. "This is what *you* chose. You are still my friend."

"Ha!" Azazel retorted. "I thought so, too. Now I realize, I was *never* your friend. All I ever was," he sneered, "was your *lackey*."

Lucifer shook his head. "That kind of mindless foolishness will be your undoing, old friend." He stopped circling and held out his hand. His sword appeared from the sleeve of his robe. His eyes glowed a fierce golden hue. "Last chance."

Azazel's hand stretched out and his sword, stuck in the ground several yards behind him, flew into his palm. He held it out before him, its tip angled slightly downward. Lucifer's sword dangled lazily at his side, though his stance widened slightly in preparation for a clash.

Azazel wasted no time. He attacked with a flurry of strikes and Lucifer handled each with ease. They went at it like that for several clashes and Lucifer never struck back at Azazel, who became increasingly frustrated. Finally, he feigned another sword attack, but at the very last second, he pulled back and unleashed a massive burst of energy from his hands, catching Lucifer off-guard as the violet-hued energy engulfed him. Nicholas could hear the grunts of pain as Lucifer wilted under Azazel's attack.

Lucifer called out of the glow of violet all around him. "Do not make me do this, my friend."

Azazel shook his head and leveled more and more energy at Lucifer's struggling body.

For the rest of his life, which at the moment didn't seem like it would be all that long, Nicholas swore he would remember the moment when Lucifer...*Had*...*Enough*. Azazel's extra effort seemed to jolt Lucifer even more than the blasts of purple energy swarming all around him. Nicholas watched the golden hue of his irises flash to black as he reared his head back and snarled something incomprehensible to Azazel. The next thing he knew, bolts of energy exploded outward as Lucifer broke free from Azazel's chakra hold.

Lucifer then went on his own attack. Azazel met him, and they stood toe to toe, trading shots like two heavy weight boxers slugging away on each other. It had to be the most epic battle the universe had seen since the fallen angels declared war amongst themselves. The chakra draw alone caused havoc on the local conditions. The sky tore open and wind swirled in every direction. Rain pelted down, accompanied by sleet and hail. Thunder boomed from the heavens. Nicholas looked up and saw lightning crackling in the sky, which had gone from day to night in a seeming instant. It was unlike anything he had ever seen.

$$ Ђ \wedge \check{\xi} \psi \varsigma $$

"Xabier! Xabier! Open your eyes, Xabier!"

The pain receded. He heard the voice, but could not open his eyes. Death had come and he had welcomed it with open arms. But where was he? He assumed he would end up in some version of Hell...Purgatory, probably. He'd heard of the place and hoped he hadn't landed there, but anything had to be better than an excruciating death by silver poisoning.

"Xabier! Wake up! Open your eyes!"

Why? I just died. Can't I rest for a minute?

"Xabier! Open your eyes!"

After several seconds of struggle, he began to slowly open his eyes. All he could see at first was a blurry image amid a blinding white light. He tried to focus but couldn't. Was it possible he ended in Heaven? Could a vampire even make it up there? He doubted it, but where else does a dead person see a blinding white light?

"Come, Xabier! Try to focus."

The voice sounded familiar. Xabier knew he'd heard that voice somewhere before. He tried to focus on clearing his vision. The blurry image began to take shape and after several seconds he recognized the face leaning over him. He also realized the light was coming from his forehead and chest, where Zha'riel had placed his hands.

"Z-Z-Zha'riel?" he croaked, his voice ragged and dry. "Whaaa? How?"

"Just rest for a minute," the angel said.

"Am I in...? I mean...Did you bring me up here?"

Zha'riel looked a little confused. "Up where?" Then his eyes widened. "Oh!" He leaned closer. "Xabier, you're not dead."

"What?" Xabier's voice grew stronger and his surprise was evident. "How can that be?"

Zha'riel removed his hands. "You will be fine." He looked at Xabier's confused expression. "I arrived as Seir was finishing you off."

"But I felt it go into my heart. I felt the silver everywhere."

"Yes," replied Zha'riel. "I drew the poison out. It was very close, Xabier. Five or ten more seconds at most."

"Is Seir...? I mean...did you—?"

"Seir got away," Zha'riel interrupted. "I didn't have time to exorcise him. We'll have to deal with him later."

Xabier nodded. "And what about Nicholas?"

Zha'riel looked back over his shoulder. "He doesn't look good."

ꝏ ꓥ ⟨ ψ ꓛ

Lucifer versus Azazel. It was as horrifying as it was fascinating. Nicholas felt the end of his life fast approaching, and as the two archangels faced off, the sky turned even blacker and the weather grew even more violent. It felt like the end of the world to Nicholas, who was still lying there, unable to move his battered body.

The attacks came with dizzying speed, one after the other as two of the most powerful beings in existence clashed in a one-on-one supernatural death match. The angels took blow after blow from one another in a full-on chakra battle. Before long, it became clear that Lucifer would emerge victorious. To Nicholas, it seemed as though he was only striking Azazel in response to Azazel's attacks. He was not taking advantage of his own superior power.

Azazel, it seemed, had decided it would be his last stand. Though Lucifer pummeled him into submission, he wouldn't let up. He sent burst after weakened burst of energy, fire, and whatever else he could muster. Lucifer swatted away each burst, sending his own jolts in response, but clearly holding back. He wasn't trying to kill his traitorous friend.

Azazel was barely able to stand and could no longer lift his arms, yet he was defiant. His mind still functioned, weary as it was. He continued to attack his former friend using whatever his mind was able to conjure, but Lucifer, remained in control, his restraint evident to all who witnessed the contest. The fight was long since over. Why was Azazel continuing to make these pathetic efforts?

"Stop," Lucifer commanded. "You are no longer effective, Azazel. Leave now and we can continue this discussion at a later date."

"*Discussion?*" Azazel spat. "You continue to insult."

Lucifer shrugged. "You leave me no choice, old friend. Shall I simply stand here while you pester me with these futile attacks? You cannot even lift your sword, Azazel. Take your leave while my mercy yet holds."

Azazel laughed. "Your *mercy?* Is that what you call this? Humiliating me in life by allowing this insolent young thief to live? Or defeating me and then refusing to end me on the battlefield like a warrior deserves?"

Lucifer wrinkled his forehead. "Is that what you want, old friend? Death on this forsaken ground?"

"What I want," Azazel hissed, staggering forward, "is *justice* for my son. Failing that...yes...death would be preferable to existing alongside his murderer."

"Interesting," Lucifer replied. He thought for a few moments and glanced back at Nicholas. "I need to return to young Nicholas." He bowed slightly. "It's been...eye-opening...old friend. Now go."

Azazel stepped forward, trying to raise his arms and renew his attack. "You deny me a proper death as well, Lucifer?"

Lucifer spun around and grabbed Azazel by the front of his shirt. "*Proper death?* You betray me, act behind my back *and* against my wishes, try to kill me, and you want *me* to provide you with a warrior's death? Believe me, old friend, the only death I would give you today is an excruciating and humiliating death, and not one befitting a great warrior such as yourself." He shoved the exhausted archangel back. "Now...take your leave," he said again, "before my patience runs out once and for all."

Azazel staggered back and stared at his former friend. Finally, he nodded. "Very well, *Morning Star.* As the humans are so fond of saying...to be continued..."

When he was gone, Lucifer turned back to Nicholas. Kneeling, he inspected his battered body. He shook his head with a sigh.

"Young Nicholas," he muttered. "What did he do to you?" He knelt in closer. "Do not worry, my son. I will guide you back. You will be stronger than you ever imagined."

Nicholas lay there, on the verge of death, feeling more terrified than ever before, yet strangely at peace. His heartrate faded and he could barely keep his eyes open. Lucifer gently cradled his head in the crook of his elbow. He drew a short, jeweled dagger from within the folds of his robes. He held the dagger over his wrist, but hesitated and cocked his head to one side.

"If your intent is to attack," he said, without even so much as a glance behind him. "You need to come up with a better plan than this." After several quiet seconds, he shifted his position so he could see who was behind him. His eyes widened at the sight. "Zha'riel?" he said, a tinge of delight in his voice. "Is that you?"

Zha'riel froze in place, his sword falling to the ground. "Lucifer," he said softly. He hadn't seen the archangel in eons. Even after all this time, Lucifer was still a riveting presence. In more glorious times, Lucifer's beauty had been unmatched anywhere in the Heavenly Host; being near him had always been a surreal experience. Eons later, nothing had changed. Zha'riel could still barely breathe in his presence.

Lucifer smiled sadly as he looked at the sword lying at Zha'riel's feet. "I guess this is what it all ultimately comes down to, doesn't it?"

Zha'riel closed his eyes with a soft sigh. "I suppose it does."

Lucifer nodded. "And your friend? Would that be Xabier?" He nodded at a ragged-looking vampire, standing beside Zha'riel. When Zha'riel nodded, he said, "It's a pleasure to make your acquaintance. Abdiel has told me about you." He looked down at Nicholas, who was now fully unconscious. "I would shake your hand, but I'm afraid if I do not act quickly, we will lose our young friend here."

He quickly cut deeply into his wrist and clenched his hand over and over again to get the blood flowing. Zha'riel's eyes widened. He took an inadvertent step forward, but hesitated when Lucifer cast a glance his way.

"What are you going to do?"

Lucifer raised his eyebrows. "I'm going to save his life."

"With your blood?"

"Do you know another way, Zha'riel?" Lucifer asked. "Azazel fried everything that makes a human body work. Either one of us could fix that, but what will you do with his scorched soul? He is alive solely because he has an amazingly intense chakra connection. There are some injuries even an angel's grace cannot overcome."

"You could allow him to die," Zha'riel replied. "And then…"

"Raise him from the dead?" Lucifer asked. "You're right, I could." He smiled up at Zha'riel. "But that wouldn't accomplish anything, would it?"

Holding his wrist over Nicholas' face, he dripped blood all over his lips. Nicholas responded slowly. As the drops touched his tongue, his lips moved and he began licking them slowly. Lucifer moved his wrist closer so that Nicholas could drink from it directly. He chanted.

"Ko ma talio. Rasch mana ka. Toma fi dera manamas!"

Zha'riel wanted to act. He wanted to throw himself at Lucifer and make him stop, but it was hopeless and he knew it. Lucifer would get exactly what he wanted. Zha'riel couldn't help but wonder if he had orchestrated events from the very beginning.

Lucifer looked up at Zha'riel. "Don't fret, Brother. This was always going to be." He nodded towards the heavens. "Up there, the angels have the advantage. Down here, *I* am all powerful." He watched for a moment as Nicholas drank greedily. "And this one...is mine."

Epilogue
One month later...

Nothing matched the solitude of a mountaintop. At such high altitude, there was no chance of being disturbed.

Over the past several weeks, Nicholas had come to love the time he had spent in solitude. Covered in a thick, blinding, white layer of snow seldom disturbed on the North Summit, Mount McKinley provided him exactly what he needed...peace and quiet.

He was recovered from his encounter with Azazel. It had taken only a few days. As soon as he felt well enough to leave his bed, he left a note for his friends and orbed away without a second thought. He needed time to think without the distractions surrounding his life. Friends were the furthest things from his mind...at least, he wished they were. He hated the memories that followed him when all he wanted to do was forget.

One decision...That was all it took. He wasn't unique in that regard. Each day, people make decisions that have lifelong ramifications and widespread consequences; but how many people made decisions that thrust them into entirely new worlds? Nicholas, with a single decision, and one in which he placed almost no thought at all, now found himself in the middle of a war that had been raging, in perpetuity, for untold millennia. He found himself in the middle of a world in which he was sought after by exceedingly powerful beings who wanted to use him for their own purposes…or destroy him.

He could almost live with all that. In fact, at first, he had almost reveled in it. But he soon found he wasn't able to think far enough ahead to keep his loved ones safe. He couldn't see the bigger picture for what it was. Even when his friends tried to show him, he had still been unable to make the right choices. Now, his brother was dead, killed out of spiteful vengeance by Nicholas' enemies. The girl he loved was dead, tortured mercilessly, killed, and tossed aside like a sack of filthy rags by a being so powerful and insane that it had taken evil personified…*Satan himself*…to defeat him.

Nicholas was forced to continue on in the knowledge that he had gotten two people he loved killed while he survived. He was spared because of his ability to hurt and kill others, and while he had taken great pleasure in hurting evil people, he certainly had no desire to fight on any side of a war he had nothing to do with, and he certainly didn't want to spend his eternity hurting people on someone else's orders.

He had no idea who he could trust anymore. Aside from Xabier, who was lucky to be alive, Nicholas had no one. Zha'riel had abandoned him when Nicholas needed him the most. He had proven to be less than trustworthy, though he did show up just in time to rescue Xabier. Abdiel had never let Nicholas down, but could he seriously trust a fallen angel…a *dark* angel…who fought under the direct orders of Lucifer himself?

Lucifer.

Nicholas shuddered to even think the name. It was horrifying to consider the fact that the founder of evil had rescued him from the edge of death. For what reason, Nicholas couldn't even begin to imagine. Lucifer placed himself between his age-old friend and Nicholas, and refused to allow Azazel to end him. And then…he had given Nicholas his blood.

Nicholas still didn't quite understand what that meant. It couldn't be good, though he did recall the rush of power that surged through his body the moment Lucifer's blood entered his system. He remembered his body filling with chakra energy, his mind opening and comprehending things he had never thought to consider. It was like a trillion revelations all at once, as though he could see endlessly in all directions through space and time. He remembered the blinding light that filled the sky and how his eyes flashed so many colors he thought he was looking through a kaleidoscope, before finally settling on a soft golden hue.

He didn't know what that blood had done to him other than the fact that he felt more powerful than ever. He felt more in control of his power than ever before. He felt clear of all restraints. Had Lucifer's blood augmented his powers? Was Nicholas now somehow connected to Lucifer's power...to *Satan himself?* Until then, Nicholas had been convinced that the individual controlled whether the powers were evil or good. Good people used powers for good while evil people used them for evil and selfish reasons.

But when the Devil takes the time to feed a dying person his own blood, there must be some significance. He never had the chance to ask. Just like the night of his initial transformation, Nicholas had felt the initial surge of power and energy course through every fiber of his being but then he'd fallen unconscious. He awoke two days later, fully healed of all his physical injuries and wounds, yet emptier inside than ever before.

He couldn't bring himself to face Xabier. He didn't want to think about how close his best friend had come to being lost forever. And now, Zha'riel had disappeared again, leaving behind far more questions than answers. Nicholas suspected that he had done something terribly wrong by intervening and would pay a heavy price, but he was grateful. At least Xabier was safe...for now.

And that brought him to an inevitable conclusion. Nicholas' eyes were now opened to the truth. He saw his life for what it was, and he knew no one he loved would ever be safe. No one he cared about could be protected. Every person, supernatural or otherwise, would be a target for those who wanted to harm Nicholas or bend him to their wishes. He would never be free of their war. He would never be free to live his own life. As he stared out over the vast white-topped mountains, he realized he was left with a simple choice…

"Ahhhh, the magnificence!" bellowed a familiar voice. "And you sought to keep it all to yourself! You are a selfish bastard, Nico…Selfish indeed."

Despite the interruption of his serene surroundings, Nicholas felt a smile tug at the corners of his mouth. As guilt-ridden as he felt about nearly getting his friend killed, and as much as he didn't want to have to face him, Nicholas still loved his company, even when he was being an obnoxious clown. Xabier perfectly complimented Nicholas' new quiet, thoughtful demeanor.

"How did you find me?" Nicholas asked without turning around. "And how did you get all the way up here?"

"Ha! Wouldn't *you* like to know!" Xabier slapped him on the back, handed him one of three opened bottles of Txakoli red wine, and took a sip from one of the others. "Nico, when will you realize there is nothing a Basque on a mission cannot do?"

Xabier sat beside him, looking out over the stunning scene and taking a deep breath and another pull off his bottle. "Beautiful," he commented, taking a moment to enjoy the view. "Not quite as beautiful as the Basque Pyrenees, mind you, but for an American landscape, it is quite acceptable."

"Glad you approve," Nicholas said dryly. He took a small sip of wine.

"Mmmm," replied Xabier. "Now then…back to your original question. How did I manage to find you hidden among the many peaks and valleys of this great mountain? How did I ever manage to make my way up to the very spot where you were perched, enjoying this magnificent scene…selfishly, as I mentioned…in peaceful serenity?"

"I assume Zha'riel brought you up."

Xabier stared at him for several seconds. "No one likes a smart-alec, Nico."

"So, he really saved you from Seir, huh?"

Xabier tilted his head. "Well…*he'd* like to think so." He leaned closer to Nicholas and whispered in a conspiratorial tone.

"Truth be told, I was just about to relieve that red-eyed serpent of his life when angel-eyes stepped in and saved the day. In fact, I would even go so far as to say that our fine feathered friend saved the life of that demon swine."

Nicholas nodded solemnly. "I'm sure."

Xabier chewed his bottom lip and then took another long swig off his bottle.

Nicholas looked around. "So, where is he?"

Xabier chuckled. "I think he's feeling a little embarrassed right now."

"Why is that?"

Xabier shook his head. "It would appear, Nico, that the punishment for helping a vampire survive a demon attack is to be exiled from Heaven."

Nicholas stared at him wide-eyed. "Are you kidding me?"

"No, he is not."

Zha'riel appeared next to Nicholas. His face was tired and his expression downcast. Nicholas thought he almost looked sad. He had dark circles under his eyes, as if he hadn't gotten enough sleep, or…as if he'd been crying. Did angels sleep…or cry?

"You got kicked out of Heaven?" Nicholas asked.

Zha'riel shook his head. "Not forever."

"But you've been exiled?"

"*Temporarily*," Zha'riel insisted. "It is punishment for rebelling. I consider myself fortunate. After all, Lucifer can *never* return."

Xabier shook his head. "So, in other words, he feels lucky that he received a lesser punishment than the angel who flipped God off to His face." He laughed and handed the third bottle to Zha'riel. "I'll never understand the halo crowd. It's like Heaven doesn't care about anything but its own stupid rules."

Zha'riel shrugged and looked down at the bottle of red wine in his hands. "Those 'stupid rules' are what keeps the universe from collapsing in upon itself, Xabier. Breaking them can have catastrophic consequences. You should understand that by now."

Nicholas nodded sullenly. "That much I can attest to."

Zha'riel looked at him in sympathy. "What are your plans, Nicholas?"

He shrugged. "Trying to figure that out now." He looked at his fingers, thinking about how much lethal power he could release from them at any moment, for any reason. "I don't think I can hide, and I doubt they'll ever let me live in peace."

Zha'riel nodded. "You're probably right…unfortunately."

Nicholas nodded. "So, the only thing left to do is try my best to honor the memories of those who died because of me."

Xabier wrinkled his forehead. "And how do we do that?"

Nicholas stood and stretched. "By defending good and destroying evil wherever we find it."

"Like superheroes," Xabier joked. Then he saw Nicholas' expression. "Only better."

Zha'riel sighed. "You realize Heaven will object."

"And by object," Xabier said wryly, "he means they'll come after you."

"Yes," Nicholas said. "I have some ideas about that."

Zha'riel squinted at him. "Ideas? What ideas?"

Nicholas shook his head. "I think the less you know, the better. I might have to make some unlikely allies."

Xabier grabbed Nicholas by the shoulder. "When you say *I*, I assume you mean *we*," he said evenly. "Because I know you don't intend to leave your friends behind to wonder what's going on with you."

Nicholas dropped his gaze to the ground. "Look, Xabs…I love you. You know that. I just can't stand the thought of you suffering again because of me. I just can't go through that again. I *won't* go through it again. I can't ask anyone else to sacrifice their lives for me."

Xabier shoved him. "You don't get to make that choice now any more than you got to make it for me before. I was on that hill with you by *my* choice…*mine*, you selfish, egotistical nitwit! Not yours! So, don't lay your guilty, stoic, narcissistic martyr trip on me. You're my friend. I stand with you." He glared into Nicholas' eyes. "No matter what."

Zha'riel stood and placed his hand on Nicholas' shoulder. "Me too, Nicholas."

Nicholas stepped close to the edge of the plateau and looked out over the expanse of snow-white peaks and valleys. He pursed his lips and nodded, almost to himself. He turned back and clapped Zha'riel on his shoulder.

"Call me Nico."

Xabier's eyebrows shot up, but he recovered and frowned at Zha'riel. "Drink, already!" he insisted. "What? Do they really expect you to get exiled from paradise and not come down here and drink up?"

Zha'riel thought for a moment and then shrugged. "Interesting point." He took a long swig. He looked up and saw Xabier and Nico staring at him in surprise. "What?" he said, frowning. Then he smiled and shrugged. "Screw 'em," he said, and drank again.

Nico shook his head as Xabier roared with laughter.

Excerpt
(Present Day)

The old man beckoned them to follow. He didn't wait for them to move before he scampered over the fence and around the abandoned metal shacks. He had already led them through the Wadi Rum, past the Visitors' Center, through the tourist areas, and into the restricted sector. The army had all but deserted their guard duties, decades ago, when war broke out in neighboring countries. They never returned to their round-the-clock posts, choosing the merits of mobile patrols over committing manpower to the useless task of guarding the restricted mountains. They did erect fences to keep the general public out, and the signage threatened severe consequences for trespassing.

The three foreigners exchanged glances before following the old man over the fence and behind the metal shacks. He was waiting for them at the mouth of a small cave. Had he not pointed it out, they would never have thought to explore it on their own. The opening was so tiny the old man had to slide in feet first. As soon as his head disappeared, the three foreigners exchanged skeptical glances.

"This guy better be for real," one said, pulling his wavy, shoulder-length brown hair back and securing it with an elastic band. He was dressed in well-worn jeans and a black concert T-shirt, which left a number of tattoos exposed on both arms. His amber-tinted eyes glared at the opening as he considered the punishment he would inflict on the old guy if he was indeed putting them on.

"Relax, Gamut," another replied. He was the more refined of the group, dressed in pressed slacks and a button-down light blue shirt. His black hair was slicked straight back with expensive product. He exuded the kind of confidence that comes from breeding and wealth. "We're here to follow every lead, no matter where it takes us."

"Is that right, Yared? Well it better take us somewhere worthwhile soon. I'm tired of spending day after day with a blood-sucking parasite."

Yared turned his ice-blue gaze on Gamut, his nostrils flaring at the insult. "Be careful, Gamut. Your canine slobber would barely make my skin itch and anyway, I'd snap your neck before you ever opened your mouth."

"Oh, bloody hell! Will you lot stuff it? It's too bloody hot in this God-forsaken place for this nonsense!" Garland MacElroy shook his head and ran a hand over the back of his neck. Feeling the warmth, he cringed, wishing he'd remembered sunscreen. Scotts weren't built for the desert. He shook his head. "Bloody vampires and werewolves. Two abominations fighting a centuries-old war like a couple of galoots! C'mon! Heid doon arse up!" He brushed between the other two and strode toward the opening.

Gamut frowned. "What did he just say?"

"Scottish slang," Yared said. "It means 'get on with it.'"

Once they all dropped through the opening, they found themselves at the beginning of a tunnel large enough for a man to walk through without bending over. The old man sat on a rock outcropping. He gestured down the passage and babbled something incomprehensible. Yared gestured for the man to lead the way but the guy didn't move. He shook his head emphatically and repeated his previous statement.

Yared frowned and exchanged a glance with Garland. They both turned to Gamut, who sighed and gritted his teeth. "He won't go any farther. He says the passage is evil."

Yared stared at the old man for a moment. The fear in his eyes was real. The old man really didn't want to go any further. He focused his gaze on the man's eyes for a second and applied a slight mental twist before gesturing down the passage. The old man got up and led the way into the passage.

Garland grunted. "Hmph! You don't even need to say anything?"

"I don't speak Arabic," Yared replied. He shot a grim smile at Garland. "It worked, didn't it?"

They followed the old man through the long passage. Darkness enveloped them after a few steps. That was no problem for the werewolf, Gamut, and the vampire, Yared, but Garland was a warlock. He was human, and therefore, without the kind of night-vision the others possessed. He made due with a small flashlight. A series of caves dotted either side of the passage, some small, the size of child's room, others much larger. They inspected each cavern in turn. They came to the end of the passage and found themselves in the center of a massive cavern, big enough to contain a house.

"How could this be?" Gamut frowned.

Yared shrugged, scanning the giant cavern. "We've been walking gradually downward for close to two miles I'd estimate." He gestured. "Spread out. If it's here, we'll find it."

They split up and scoured every nook and cranny of the jagged room. Garland felt a shimmer. He stood tall and narrowed his eyes trying to figure out what was different. It was a similar feeling as the one he got when summoning chakra for his spellcasting. Only now, it ran through him without any effort on his part. There was something magical nearby.

"It's here," he declared, his brow furrowed in concentration. "I can feel it."

Gamut laughed. "Good for you." Turning to Yared. he smirked, "Here that, Yared? The mage can feel it."

"I am NOT a mage!" Garland glared at him. "You would do well to remember that."

Gamut frowned. He tugged at his collar in discomfort. He looked at Garland apprehensively.

"Feeling warm, werewolf?" Garland's eyes were shades darker as his glare intensified. "You see, my canine friend, mages draw their power from the light. Warlocks…" His intense eyes glared daggers. "Well…let's just say a warlock's power is a bit…darker."

Gamut scratched at his chest. His bones suddenly felt heavy. As the seconds passed, he felt his blood boil in his veins and his heart felt as though it would explode at any moment. The itching intensified, causing his mind to overload. His eyes bulged in their sockets as fear overcame him. He collapsed on the ground, writhing in pain. It all took less than thirty seconds.

Yared rolled his eyes. "Knock it off! Garland, we don't have time for this."

Garland chuckled and waved a hand. Gamut sank to the ground, his breathing gradually returning to normal. When he regained his strength, he sprang up from the floor, darting behind the smirking warlock, prepared to bite down on his neck.

"Careful," Garland warned with another chuckle. He didn't fight the werewolf at all, tilting his head to one side and offering a clear shot at his neck. "You should know I consume copious amounts of wolfsbane, just as I do vervaine."

Gamut snarled in his ear. "Maybe, but I can still snap your neck like a twig."

"Enough!" Yared shook his head. "Gamut, let him go."

Gamut paused for a couple beats before shoving Garland aside. "I don't know why we ever thought this could work. We don't mix well. We should stick with our own kind."

"That kind of short-sighted thinking," Yared replied in a condescending tone, "is why we find ourselves on the precipice of extinction. Perhaps we should complete our task. We can worry about killing one another later."

He turned to Garland, who grinned at Gamut and stifled a laugh. "You said you felt something?" Garland didn't respond, his eyes still locked on Gamut's. Yared rolled his eyes. "I'm dealing with children," he mumbled. "Garland!"

The warlock blinked and turned slowly to face Yared, who raised his eyebrows. "What do you *feel*, Garland?"

The warlock snapped out of it. "Right. I feel something here…in this room." He looked around the room. "Something powerful."

Yared nodded. "Let's find it."

"Yeah," Garland agreed. He pointed at the other two. "Just stay here. Your chakra pull might interfere. Let me stand in the middle of the room and see if I can pinpoint it."

He made his way through the dark cavern. Standing in the middle, he closed his eyes and turned in slow circles, focusing all his senses on the magic emitting from somewhere in the underground cavern. It took less than two minutes before he pointed and walked deeper into the cavern and to the right. He stood before a wall and felt around, mumbling under his breath. He finally grinned and looked back at his companions. He grasped a little ledge and pulled hard. A large rock slid out from the wall, falling at his feet.

Yared and Gamut stood spellbound as Garland grinned and peered into the hole with his flashlight. He glanced back with a smile.

"Something's in there."

Yared and Gamut hurried to join him. Garland reached into the hole and pulled out what looked to be a clay box. It was about the size of a shoebox and not very heavy, indicating it was also hollow. It was covered in symbols and glyphs.

"This is it," Yared said, taking it from Garland and inspecting it. "The key is in here." He turned it over in his hands and marveled at the intricate artwork. He looked up at the others and frowned. "I know some of these but the rest are foreign to me."

"Who cares about the glyphs?" Gamut said. "Open it and get the key."

Garland shook the box but heard nothing. He spun the object in his hands again and frowned. "I can't see a way to open the bloody thing. Could *this* be the key?"

Yared shook his head. "My understanding is that the key was hidden in a box." He pointed to the clay container. "That has to be the box. It's just as described."

"Well, there's no lid," Garland shined his flash on it, peering over every inch. "I don't see any lines. There's nothing to move or push. I see no levers or buttons. What the bloody hell?"

Yared shook his head. "It's not supposed to be easy to get to. Remember what this key is for."

Gamut grabbed the box. "I say we crack it open and get outta here."

He was poised to smash it against the wall but hesitated and glanced at the other two. He raised his eyebrows. Yared and

Garland shrugged before nodding. Gamut threw the box into the wall.

It hit and dropped to the ground, unscathed. They exchanged amazed glances and Gamut picked it up. He threw it to the ground as hard as he could. Pieces of rock exploded from the ground as the impact shook the room. The box was undamaged.

"This is maddening."

Yared shrugged. "It's cloaked by a magic spell." He turned to Garland. "Is this something you can work on?"

"I can try, but I'm guessing a witch cast this spell."

Yared picked up the box and turned toward the passage. "We've done our job. Let's get out if here. We'll figure it out later."

They made their way out of the underground passage. Having no further use for the old man, they left his corpse in one of the smaller caves off the main passage. His neck was snapped in one fast, efficient motion and they left him without a second thought.

When they emerged into dwindling daylight, Yared pulled out his phone and sat on a small rock. He tapped and swiped before holding the phone to his ear.

"Yes?"

Yared smiled. "We have it."

"I swear, Yared, if you jest…"

"Fear not, brother." Yared smiled and patted the artifact at his side. "The key has been uncovered. Or I should say…the box has been uncovered."

"Was the key inside?"

Yared sighed. "It would appear, dear brother, that the box is spelled. We cannot open it."

"Of course." His brother swore under his breath. "Bring it home. You have done well."

"How will we open it?"

"The same way it was locked. We need a witch." Yared heard his brother sighed, letting out a long slow breath. "We need a very powerful witch."

ᛒ ᚨ ᛃ ᚹ ᚷ

"That's gotta be them."

Alvi Cornega peered through the high-powered binoculars handed to him by his new number two, Isidro Vargas. He searched the approaching vessel for any sign that it might be naval or police. He saw nothing suspicious, but that didn't mean much. The authorities weren't totally stupid. They knew how to disguise their vehicles. He only bothered to look out of sheer habit.

Alvi hated these kinds of deals. He hadn't made a field exchange in years, long before he took over the Manizales Cartel. It was dangerous work. Drug trafficking was a violent business, and those at the top needed layers of protection, not just from the authorities, but also from their rivals, and even from their friends…sometimes even more so from friends. One could never be too sure who was in bed with who and what deals were being struck. A friend today could just as easily shoot you in the throat tomorrow.

Since his operation was recently burned down, literally, and his cash flow was crippled, Alvi had to make ends meet. The five cartels were decimated but not completely destroyed. There was a huge power vacuum in the Colombian drug trade, and the tattered remains of each cartel was scrambling to protect its own interests. It wouldn't be long before they were at each other's throats. They were fortunate enough that Nicholas Scarlatti hadn't gone after their underground labs and warehouses. There was still product being harvested, processed, and packaged. There just wasn't money for the kind of security he was used to, and even fewer trustworthy individuals left to make things work without his direct supervision.

On top of all that, the Mexican Montenegro cartel demanded a face-to-face at the exchange. They were concerned about the situation in Colombia and nervous about dealing with unfamiliar faces. They also told him they wanted to make sure Alvi was in a position to rebuild. In reality, they just wanted to make sure Alvi was on site in the event things went south in the wake of the Scarlatti disaster.

Without taking the binoculars off the approaching ship, he turned to his Lieutenant. "Get everyone ready. If they don't stop at a half-mile out, we're unloading on them."

Isidro turned and spoke into the black microphone clipped to his lapel. Moments later, Alvi heard boots scrambling across the deck and clambering up the stairs to the upper level. He watched three of his guys on the lower deck spread themselves out across the port side of the 220 foot Heesen yacht. Each carried military-grade RPGs, supplied by his contacts in the Colombian army.

As agreed, the incoming craft slowed and maintained a distance of one-half-mile. Alvi waited until he saw the signal repeated several times through his binoculars. He squinted as he raised his hand, signaling his own guy to signal back to the other craft.

"Okay, Sid," Alvi called. "Bring us in." He raised his voice for everyone to hear. "Okay, men! We're moving in. Be alert! This shouldn't take long."

The two yachts pulled up alongside one another and men on either side lashed them together. Tensions were high but it was a common method of transacting their business, so everyone knew the drill. Eyes darted back and forth but no one really expected the other side to start trouble.

Alvi greeted the Montenegro representative and they discussed the transaction for a moment before shaking hands. Alvi waved to Sid, who ordered some of his guys to bring the product up, twelve crates of pure Colombian heroine. Each crate contained 60 kilos. It represented Alvi's entire stock and the funding to rebuild his operation.

The Mexicans carried box after box of their own over to Alvi's vessel. Alvi took a huge risk putting everything into one transaction, but it netted him a hundred million American dollars for an afternoon of work. He was nervous about popping up out of hiding, but things had been calm for the past few weeks and he desperately needed funds. He could feel the vultures circling. His only comfort was the knowledge that the vultures were just as crippled as he was.

The exchange was fast and efficient, with each box checked and stowed below decks. When both leaders were satisfied, the transaction was complete. They signaled their men to untie the boats. As the vessels drifted apart, Alvi nodded to his Mexican counterpart and waited as the motors revved and they backed away under power. As they sped away from the meeting place, Alvi and Sid exchanged pleased glances.

Alvi descended the stairs and relaxed into a soft chair in his private cabin. He closed his eyes and let the anxiety of the day fade away. He breathed deeply as his heart rate returned to normal. His eyelids grew heavy and he dozed off. It lasted until a chill washed over him and a presence of pure evil loomed over him.

Alvi's eyes snapped open and he sprang up from his seat, bringing his pistol up in one fluid, practiced motion. His eyes found the shadowy figure and he took aim. He felt a sharp jerk, and the gun flew from his hand, skittering across the vinyl floor. Something struck him in the center of his chest. It was as if the wind had formed a fist and lashed out at him. He slammed backward into the seat again. When he caught his breath, he looked up and saw two ghostly white eyes staring back at him.

They flashed silver and then back to pearl-white just as quickly as Alvi focused on the figure standing before him. He was dressed in flowing black robes, trimmed in gold. The look on his face was serene, as though he hadn't a care in the world, as though he wasn't on a yacht full of men with automatic rifles ready to kill anyone Alvi commanded.

When Alvi opened his mouth to scream for help, the man held up a finger and Alvi saw the crackle of purple electricity surrounding it. His mouth snapped shut in stunned disbelief. The man smiled and the electricity disappeared from his finger.

"No need to involve your crew," he said. "I am not here to harm you."

"Whaaa…Who…Who are y-y-you?"

The man gave him an amused look. "Oh…I'm terribly sorry. How rude of me. Though you must admit, *you* were the one who pulled the gun." He bowed. "You may call me Azazel."

"Azazel?" Alvi repeated. "What…I mean…who…?"

"What…would have been the better question," Azazel said. He waved a hand. "Shall we dispense with the small talk?" Without waiting for a reply, he continued. "Believe it or not, you have something I require."

"Just take whatever you want and go," Alvi said.

Azazel chuckled. "Did I say some*thing*? I meant some*one*. I require the services of a powerful witch." He leaned forward. "I understand you are acquainted with such an individual."

Alvi frowned. "Nayra? What do you want with her?"

"Nothing too difficult." Azazel raised his eyebrows. "I merely require her special skills to open a door."

Alvi frowned. He sat up a little straighter, interested despite himself. "What door?"

Azazel smiled. "A very special door." He looked at Alvi for a moment. "Shall we discuss a fair price for her services?"

Alvi knew a dodge when he saw one. Even with a frightening presence in the room, he knew when he held an advantage. Since the…whatever he was…was on *his* yacht asking for *his* help, it meant Nayra's cloaking spell worked, and their new home was undetectable by the supernatural. Azazel must have staked out his yacht and waited for him to show up.

"Actually," Alvi said, crossing his legs and pulling a cigar out of his shirt pocket. He held an expensive lighter to it and eyed Azazel as he puffed. "I'd like to know more about this door you want opened."

If Azazel was surprised or annoyed, he didn't let on. He smiled at Alvi and nodded.

"Of course, you would." Azazel thought for a minute. "It's the impudence of youth. I once knew another with such impudence. He thought to question a power higher than himself. When those in a position to see things more…clearly…warned him to abandon his foolishness, do you know what he did?" His pearl white eyes flashed silver once again before returning to their pearl-white hue.

Alvi suddenly felt like his advantage might be all in his mind after all. He couldn't remember why he had thought he was in a position to exert any pressure on Azazel. He did his best to remain calm but felt like his emotions lay bare before Azazel.

Azazel continued. "Self-destructive though it was, he continued with resolute determination. He even convinced many of his detractors that he knew what he was doing, that he knew something the rest of them didn't." Azazel shook his head and let out a sad breath. "In the end, he led them all to their destruction."

Alvi frowned and nodded. He couldn't keep his hands from shaking.

Azazel shook his head and sighed. "The point, my impudent young friend, is that you might think you are making wise choices; you might think you are doing what is best." He wagged a finger at Alvi. "But you are playing in a realm for which you are woefully ill-equipped."

Alvi continued to frown. He rubbed his palms together to stop them from shaking "What does all this mean?"

"It means you should avoid questions, the answers of which are a burden to you once you get them."

The words sounded so sinister in Alvi's ears, perhaps because of their strange eloquence as they tumbled off Azazel's tongue. He spoke with the confidence of one as ruthless as he was powerful. He could back up his words and he knew it. Azazel was not a man to be trifled with.

"What is Nayra's help worth to you?"

Azazel smiled and spread his hands with a slight bow of his head. "Ahhhh. *Now* you are asking the right questions."

Other Books by Christopher Merlino

A Quiver of Cobras Series
Follow a group of Kendall High School students as they navigate their high school social scene, experience new relationships, and test the bonds of friendship and love.

> **Beginnings**
> **HEAT**
> **Broken**
> **Desire**
> **Limbo – Coming Soon**

The Zak Fischer Chronicles
Zak Fischer is a teen age musical prodigy who is on the verge of fame and fortune. He is also a strong Christian kid with beliefs that are contrary to the pop culture world he wants so badly to be a part of. As he and his band rise to national prominence, Zak must deal with all the temptations that come with it.

> **Viral – Coming Soon**

Nico Scarlatti Novels
Follow Nico Scarlatti as he struggles to navigate a world few ever get to see. With enemies on all sides, and a darkness inside him he can barely control, Nico.

> **Essence –**
> **The Alphas – Coming Soon**
> **Mother of All – Coming Soon**

The Collide Series
The story of Harper and Riley. She is the number one female artist in the world and he is a nobody who writes a little and plays music with his buddies. She hangs out with the most talented and recognizable people in the world. He has a close

circle of friends, none of which have ever graced the cover of Vanity Fair. A chance meeting brought them together. They both knew it could never work. But the attraction was too much for either of them to resist. The only question left is, what will happen when two vastly different worlds collide?

Worlds Collide – Coming Soon
We Collide – Coming Soon

About the Author

Christopher Merlino is married to Charmine Merlino, and the father of three beautiful girls, Alexis, Cecilia, and Isabella. He makes his living selling cars and insurance. He has a Master's degree in English and Creative Writing. In addition to writing, Chris spends his time in his woodshop, making things like pens, bowls, and other knick-knacks out of domestic and exotic woods.

Chris is a fan of most genres of books from non-fiction historical and theological to fiction drama, action, fantasy, and comedy. He enjoys music and golf...well...who really *enjoys* golf? He *plays* golf from time to time and generally refers to the game as "The Refiner's Oven." He was born and raised near Atlantic City, New Jersey, and currently makes his home in Egg Harbor Township, New Jersey.

www.ingramcontent.com/pod-product-compliance
Lightning Source LLC
Chambersburg PA
CBHW051522260626
47170CB00003B/734